FLIGHT
OF THE
FALLEN

ALSO BY HANA LEE

The Magebike Courier Duology

Road to Ruin

FLIGHT OF THE FALLEN

The Second Magebike Courier Novel

HANA LEE

SAGA PRESS

LONDON **NEW YORK** TORONTO
AMSTERDAM/ANTWERP NEW DELHI SYDNEY/MELBOURNE

1230 AVENUE OF THE AMERICAS, NEW YORK, NEW YORK 10020

For more than 100 years, Simon & Schuster has championed authors and the stories they create. By respecting the copyright of an author's intellectual property, you enable Simon & Schuster and the author to continue publishing exceptional books for years to come. We thank you for supporting the author's copyright by purchasing an authorized edition of this book.

No amount of this book may be reproduced or stored in any format, nor may it be uploaded to any website, database, language-learning model, or other repository, retrieval, or artificial intelligence system without express permission. All rights reserved. Inquiries may be directed to Simon & Schuster, 1230 Avenue of the Americas, New York, NY 10020 or permissions@simonandschuster.com.

This book is a work of fiction. Any references to historical events, real people, or real places are used fictitiously. Other names, characters, places, and events are products of the author's imagination, and any resemblance to actual events or places or persons, living or dead, is entirely coincidental.

Copyright © 2025 by Kristin Hana Lee

All rights reserved, including the right to reproduce this book or portions thereof in any form whatsoever. For information, address Saga Press Subsidiary Rights Department, 1230 Avenue of the Americas, New York, NY 10020.

First Saga Press trade paperback edition June 2025

SAGA PRESS and colophon are trademarks of Simon & Schuster, LLC

Simon & Schuster strongly believes in freedom of expression and stands against censorship in all its forms. For more information, visit BooksBelong.com.

For information about special discounts for bulk purchases, please contact Simon & Schuster Special Sales at 1-866-506-1949 or business@simonandschuster.com.

The Simon & Schuster Speakers Bureau can bring authors to your live event. For more information or to book an event, contact the Simon & Schuster Speakers Bureau at 1-866-248-3049 or visit our website at www.simonspeakers.com.

Manufactured in the United States of America

1 3 5 7 9 10 8 6 4 2

Library of Congress Cataloging-in-Publication Data has been applied for.

ISBN 978-1-6680-3570-2
ISBN 978-1-6680-3571-9 (ebook)

*For anyone who still reaches for love
in a world divided by hatred*

PART ONE

CHAPTER ONE

FIRST HOUR OF THE STORM

Observation #520: Storm prediction is a frustrating, imprecise science. Nature always follows a pattern, but this one evades me. Hypothesis: No true randomness in nature. Storms artificial? —O

Third Age of Storms, 1st Summer, Day 63
Kerina Sol – House of Steel Heavens

Deep in a dream, Yi-Nereen floated through the streets of Kerina Rut in a palanquin. Her city hummed around her; temple bells rang out, deep and sonorous. It was worship day. She was on her way to light bowls of fragrant oil and make her sacrifices to Rasvel, the Giver of Blessings.

The crowd outside her palanquin was unruly. She glimpsed faces contorted with anger, heard voices rising in a muted roar. What were they saying? It was like they were speaking a different language. Her people needed something from her, but she couldn't understand what it was.

The low, musical sound of the bells climbed higher, frantic, stirring panic in Yi-Nereen's blood. Her palanquin bearers struggled to make headway through the crowd. The platform jerked and tipped—Yi-Nereen tried to scream, but her voice was gone.

The bells! They were tearing through her head.

Now her people were swarming her fallen palanquin, shouting and reaching for her. They were going to tear her apart.

And she still didn't know why.

Yi-Nereen opened her eyes, a gasp caught in her throat. Moonlight bled through a crack in the drawn curtains of her bedchamber, painting the furniture in shades of soft gray. It came back to her in a dizzying rush: she was lying abed in the House of Steel Heavens. In Kadrin's home, far from the streets of Kerina Rut.

But the bells went on ringing. *Those* were real.

In Kerina Rut, she had been trained to fly from bed the instant the storm bells chimed their first note, ready to serve before she was fully conscious. But Yi-Nereen wasn't yet accustomed to Kerina Sol's storm bells; their timbre was different from the ones she'd been conditioned since childhood to obey. It was like dancing to a familiar tune and finding the chorus had changed. Her body stumbled over the missing steps.

Get hold of yourself. It was likely just another drill.

All they'd had in Kerina Sol for the past month were drills. The city had been in the grip of a bizarre storm-drought ever since the Second Storm of Centuries had torn through the city's shield and destroyed two districts. Most people were grateful for the reprieve. Rasvel's Mercy, they called it.

Yi-Nereen found it chilling. She was one of only three people in Kerina Sol who knew the truth about the Second Storm of Centuries. She had *been* the storm, its fury embodied, and she'd come within a hair's breadth of destroying everything.

She'd learned to never trust good news. A reckoning was coming; she felt the certainty of its approach in her teeth, in her bones.

Flight of the Fallen

Yi-Nereen dressed quickly. The whole point of a drill was to act as if it were real. No time for ornaments, makeup, or even to comb her hair; she slept in braids so she would be ready at a moment's notice. In Kerina Rut, an untimely arrival at her post would have meant a beating—after the storm was over, of course.

Opening the door to the hallway, she blinked against a sudden flare of candlelight.

Kadrin. He'd had no more time to rouse himself than she had, and he looked it. His hair was a dark mop of curls, rumpled from sleep, and he'd tied his robe too hastily; it gaped open, revealing an unseemly triangle of skin. Yi-Nereen averted her eyes. Her heart drummed in her chest.

A month of living under the same roof as Kadrin, and she still wasn't used to it.

"Reena. I was coming to wake you. Can I walk you to the Wall?"

Yi-Nereen nearly shivered. If a voice could sound half-dressed, in this moment Kadrin's did. It was a far cry from the way he spoke to her in the daylight with his parents and siblings watching: bright, warm but proper, respectful and a touch distant. They were so rarely permitted to be alone together, now that Kadrin's mother was making official arrangements for their wedding.

Wedding. Just the thought of that word made Yi-Nereen's stomach swoop, and not in an altogether pleasant way.

"If you wish," she said, trying to sound casual, as if walking through the streets with Kadrin in the middle of the night were of no great consequence—as if she were used to going where she liked at any hour, with no escort at all, a free woman of Kerina Sol.

She hardly felt free at all. Quite the opposite. She felt bound, tongue-tied by all she wanted to say and couldn't find words to express. Perhaps it would be easier to write them down. But wasn't it ridiculous, the idea of writing a letter to a man whose house she lived in?

They walked through the dark, hushed halls of the House together, a handspan apart. Close enough for Yi-Nereen to feel Kadrin's warmth, but not touching. She thought of taking his arm. But part of her balked, unwilling to risk shattering whatever fragile balance existed between them.

They'd kissed exactly once, on the balcony of a castle trembling in a storm. It had felt like a beginning, a prelude to the life Yi-Nereen had always longed for but never allowed herself to contemplate. But in the weeks since that kiss, Yi-Nereen had come to doubt everything. This new life of hers felt hollow, incomplete.

She knew exactly what was missing—or rather, *who*—but what could she do about it?

Yi-Nereen stepped over the House's threshold and tensed.

"It isn't a drill," she said.

The storm bells went on clanging, louder than ever. Kadrin frowned up at the dark sky. "How can you tell?"

"I just can."

The air felt charged and sharp; the hair on Yi-Nereen's arms stood on end. She could taste the approaching storm on the wind. It felt closer than it should. Had the stormwatchers given less warning than usual?

Kadrin was Talentless. He didn't have the connection to the storms that a shieldcaster or a sparkrider had; he couldn't sense them coming until they were upon him. Yi-Nereen's skin crawled at the thought, but she chastised herself for it. She had to unlearn the prejudices Kerina Rut had instilled in her, even the ones that were unconscious. *Especially* those.

Flight of the Fallen

"I need to get to the Wall," she said. "Quickly. Go inside, Kadrin."

She didn't wait to see whether he would do as she asked. Her assigned post was on the sector of Wall around Orchard District, seven minutes away from the House at a flat run. From the acrid, electric taste of the air on her tongue, Yi-Nereen sensed the storm would be here sooner than that.

By the time she reached the Wall, puffing hard, a stitch burning in her side, the shieldcasters had already raised the dome without her. The sky glowed blue; the city fell still, like the kerina was holding its breath. The bells had stopped.

Kerina Sol's Wall was a raised stone walkway that encircled the city, connecting the barbettes: circular platforms, one per district, where shieldcasters positioned themselves in a storm to raise the dome over the city. Three shieldcasters stood atop Orchard District's barbette, arms outstretched as they poured power into the shield. Yi-Nereen joined the two reserves seated behind them, a man and a woman who cast her sidelong glances but said nothing of her lateness. Yi-Nereen wished they would. She had an excuse—the House of Steel Heavens was located deep within the city, instead of close to the Wall like the compounds where the other shieldcasters lived—but she wouldn't have minded a light scolding.

In Kerina Rut, she'd served in the Shield Corps alongside her kin: a stable of uncles and aunts, cousins and nieces and nephews. All of them had the Shield Lord's ear, and so Yi-Nereen could trust none of them. Any stray word of hers could be twisted into something unbecoming of a First Daughter, a mark against her marriage prospects; it was safer to keep her lips sealed.

For as long as a storm lasted, all the shieldcasters were prisoners sentenced to the same fate, yet Yi-Nereen had always stood uniquely alone.

She'd hoped Kerina Sol would be different—that the shieldcasters here could be her confidantes, perhaps even her friends. But so far, they'd held her at arm's length. That was to be expected, Yi-Nereen knew. She was an outsider, the sole Rut-blood among their ranks.

"Couldn't last forever," the man next to her said. He was the older of the two reserves, bald but with enough gray streaks in his beard to mark him for nearing the end of his half-life. "The storms had to come back eventually. At least we're useful again, eh?"

The other reserve scoffed. She wore her hair in a short, shaggy cut that reminded Yi-Nereen painfully of—someone else's. "So much for Rasvel's Mercy. The Giver decided we were growing lazy, I suppose. A shame. I rather liked all the extra sleep."

Yi-Nereen racked her brain for their names: Brisen and Sofia. She'd listened to their banter for over a dozen drills, but never found the bravery to join in. Her isolated upbringing in the Tower had ill-prepared her for living among the loquacious, irreverent people of Kerina Sol. A comment like Sofia's would have bordered on blasphemy in Kerina Rut.

The storm was almost upon the city now. She heard its low, inconstant shriek beyond the shimmering blue barrier surrounding the ramparts. It pounded in her ears like blood. When Yi-Nereen closed her eyes, she found herself reliving memories: her own hand reaching through the storm to crush Kerina Sol's defenders and fall upon the helpless city like a predator swooping in for the kill.

She'd never felt so powerful. So blissful and unafraid. She craved that feeling again, hungered for it with an intensity that frightened and sickened her.

"You all right, Princess?"

Brisen and Sofia were looking at her. Yi-Nereen's hands were twisting in her lap; her face was cold and clammy. She tried to smile. "Oh, I'm fine—"

Thunder drowned her voice. The sky flashed white, bright enough to make Yi-Nereen flinch.

Good. She should fear the storm, not herself. Never again would she taste the might Tibius Vann had bestowed upon her, and thank the gods for that. No one could be trusted with such power.

It happened so quickly she almost didn't see it. One of the shieldcasters holding the dome collapsed. The woman's legs buckled and she sagged forward, stumbling over the parapet.

"Tela!"

Brisen dove for her. Yi-Nereen was a moment behind him. Together they pulled Tela down by the waist, back onto the safety of the Wall. The woman lay senseless on the stone, eyes rolled back in her skull. Yi-Nereen fumbled for a pulse in her neck and found one—thank Rasvel.

The other two shieldcasters hadn't so much as flinched. They stood in place, arms raised, blue tendrils streaming from their fingers into the shimmering dome. Yi-Nereen glanced at Brisen, who was crouched beside Tela's limp form.

"Go," he said. "I've got her."

Yi-Nereen straightened—but Sofia shouldered past her. "Let me." She took the spot between the two active shieldcasters before Yi-Nereen could argue.

Yi-Nereen had been the strongest shieldcaster in Kerina Rut, the product of a line of carefully bred Talent. She had tasted ambrosia and cast a shield so massive it could encompass an entire storm, shape it to her will. Now she'd been shoved aside by a Sol-blood woman who didn't trust her to hold rank. Treated like a novice.

They didn't know her, Yi-Nereen reminded herself. She'd have to prove her worth. After a month of drills, now was her chance.

"Rasvel have mercy," Brisen said, his voice flat with horror. "Curing District."

Yi-Nereen followed his gaze up and westward. A fissure had formed in the dome, like water parting around a rock. It could give at any moment, allowing the storm to roar in like a flood. Yi-Nereen knew the signs; she had seen a handful of dome failures in Kerina Rut. The shieldcasters could regroup and raise the dome again. But lives would be lost.

"Someone in that sector must have collapsed," Yi-Nereen said, though she doubted her own words. Even in Kerina Rut, with its dangerously undermanned Shield Corps, she'd never seen a shieldcaster collapse in the first hour of a storm. Tela could have been suffering from some ailment that weakened her, but the odds of another shieldcaster dropping at the same time were low.

"There was something different about that lightning strike," Brisen said. "I felt it. This isn't a normal storm. Listen."

Yi-Nereen willed her thundering heart to calm so she could hear the wind beyond the dome. Did it sound different? She couldn't tell. But she thought of that sense she'd had lately of a reckoning waiting in the wings, its hot breath on her neck.

It was *here*. Now. The realization washed over her in a chilling wave.

"Curing was short a shieldcaster," Brisen said. "They only had two reserves. Oh gods, if Tela wasn't the only one . . . If the dome fails and there's another strike like *that*—"

"I'll go to Curing," Yi-Nereen said. "They need reinforcement."

Brisen shook his head. "We're both staying right here until orders come. Shield Lord Tethris will handle redistricting. She'll send out novitiates if she has to."

"Curing doesn't have time to wait for novitiates!"

Brisen didn't understand. Kerina Sol was flush with Talent; he'd never faced a storm with half the complement of shieldcasters he needed to survive it, praying for Rasvel's mercy the whole dark night long.

If the Second Storm of Centuries had caused this, *she* had caused this. So it fell to her to make amends. She wouldn't allow Kerina Sol to be destroyed.

"Princess, wait—"

Yi-Nereen took off running.

The architects of Kerina Sol deserved a thousand humiliations for the inefficiency of the city's design: a sprawling honeycomb of districts all contained by a single outer Wall. Yi-Nereen cursed them all as she ran. She shouldn't have to circumnavigate the city to reach a district in trouble; it was a waste of precious time.

Her home, Kerina Rut, was built in the shape of a wheel: a central tower with raised spokes of Wall radiating outward, dividing the city into pie-shaped districts. Yi-Nereen usually served out a storm in the Tower of Arrested Stars itself. Her father rarely trusted her on the outer Wall, as if Yi-Nereen could find some opportunity for mischief while she was pouring all her blood and sweat into keeping her city safe.

She cursed him, too, for good measure.

Curing District was two sectors over from Orchard. Yi-Nereen ran through Jade District's barbette on the way without sparing a word for the shieldcasters there. Three of them standing, still—good. But a man lay slumped against the parapet, gasping for breath, and Yi-Nereen saw only a single reserve crouched beside him. Where was the other?

Her heart beat a fearful staccato against her ribs. The storm had barely begun. How much worse could it get?

Yi-Nereen stumbled onto Curing District's barbette. "I'm here!"

Three bodies in blue robes lay unconscious on the ramparts, scattered like dolls. Two shieldcasters still stood. "Who's that?" one of them demanded.

He couldn't see her, Yi-Nereen realized; he'd gone shield-blind, his vision darkened by the strain of holding a collapsing shield.

"Yi-Nereen. From Orchard."

The sound of her name—obviously Rut-blood—sank in the air between them like a stone.

"You shouldn't be here," he snapped. "Go back to your post. We don't need—"

Thunder roared. A blinding white flash filled the air. Yi-Nereen blinked furiously, hands over her ears, trying to restore her vision.

The man who'd spoken was gone. *Gone.* Over the parapet, just like Tela would have been if Brisen hadn't caught her.

"What's happening?" the other shieldcaster wailed. Her shoulders buckled, like someone had heaped a sack of bricks on her back. The blue light streaming from her fingers flickered. "I can't—I can't *see*—"

"Steady!" Yi-Nereen shouted. "I'm with you!"

She stepped up to the parapet, threw out her arms, and burned mana.

The weight of the shield crashed down on her. It was fire and ice, burning a trail through her veins. Her mind surged beyond her skin, out into the dome. At once, she felt every slash of wind and flung pebble as if her own flesh were under assault. But she wasn't one person anymore, trembling and vulnerable in the storm.

She was every shieldcaster who stood atop the Wall. Her strength was theirs, and theirs was hers. *We will hold.*

Her fear faded, erased by a lifetime of discipline. Under her dome slept an entire city of souls. No harm would befall them under her watch.

She was their shield and she would not break.

Yi-Nereen was still conscious when the storm ended, but only just.

Reinforcements arrived eventually, but they were barely trained novitiates. Just children, really. Yi-Nereen refused to let any of them replace her. Brisen was right; this storm was different, deadlier. If she had a choice, she would have borne its cost all on her own.

She stood, hour after hour, pouring herself into the shield while volunteers brought her fresh mana to infuse. Until finally the wind calmed and the dust receded. The storm had passed; now it moved east.

The moment the dome dropped, so did Yi-Nereen. She lay down right there on the stone tiles and closed her eyes. Her arms were leaden weights, her skull stuffed with cotton. *Breathe,* she told herself. *It's over.*

"Bravo," came a voice from above her. "What a *show.*"

Yi-Nereen forced her eyes open. The bony, angular face of Shield Lord Tethris swam into view above her. If Yi-Nereen hadn't recognized her on sight, the stars adorning her midnight-blue robes would have signaled her station.

"Where did you come from?" Yi-Nereen's exhaustion precluded politeness. Tethris was her distant cousin anyway, and she was finished with paying respects to her kin.

"I've been standing beside you for the past hour. You were too busy playing heroine to notice."

"What?"

"I assigned you a post for a reason, Yi-Nereen. If I don't know where my shieldcasters are, how am I meant to field reinforcements? Every man, woman, and child under my command knows better than to leave their post. Except one."

With a soft groan, Yi-Nereen pushed herself into a sitting position. Every muscle ached. She didn't have the stomach for this conversation, but she had little choice.

"The dome on this sector was about to crack. I made a decision—"

"If the dome cracks," Tethris said, "*I* handle it."

How many times had Yi-Nereen begged forgiveness for an error, even when she didn't truly believe she'd been wrong? In their crueler moments, her father and brothers had made a sport of breaking her. They'd perfected a whole host of techniques for making her doubt herself, pushing and *pushing* until they were satisfied her tears of remorse were genuine.

Part of Yi-Nereen knew that Tethris wasn't like that. In this instance, perhaps she was even right—perhaps Yi-Nereen owed her an apology.

Yi-Nereen would spit blood before she groveled in front of someone again.

"Why were only two reserves assigned to this sector?" Yi-Nereen asked coldly.

Flight of the Fallen

Tethris stiffened. "What?"

"You had access to reinforcements. Why weren't they posted on the barbette to begin with? If Curing had a full complement of shieldcasters, the dome would never have splintered and I would have had no reason to leave my post."

Out of the corner of her eye, Yi-Nereen saw movement. Someone had just climbed onto the barbette behind Shield Lord Tethris. Kadrin. He stood there, chest heaving, his hair lank with sweat. The relieved smile that split his face faded as Yi-Nereen spoke.

Stop this, she told herself desperately, *stop*. But her tongue had a mind of its own.

"This was a failure in leadership. Your mistake. Not mine."

Tethris's stare was flinty. "You're on leave," she said. "Two weeks. I don't want to see you on the Wall again until after you're wed. Perhaps by then, you'll have adjusted yourself to our customs. Your father may have tolerated your disrespect, but I certainly won't."

For one all-consuming moment, Yi-Nereen wanted nothing more than to shove Tethris from the ramparts and watch her fall, screaming, into the wastes below. Her father. How *dare* Tethris mention her father.

"Reena."

She flinched at the touch of a hand on her shoulder. It was Kadrin, gently guiding her from the ramparts.

"Come, let's go home."

Yi-Nereen was trembling, and Kadrin was warm, solid, and steady. He smelled like earth and bread. Part of her longed desperately to fall into his arms and sob away her rage and frustration. Another part wanted to push him violently away—to preempt the day when he would surely come to his senses and see her for what she truly was: a senseless, broken thing, a tangled mass of thorns that could only draw blood if he touched her.

It was why Jin had left. Yi-Nereen was sure of it.

"I heard what happened," Kadrin said as they limped slowly through the dark streets. "The shieldcasters who collapsed. I couldn't sleep a wink until I knew you weren't one of the dead."

"Dead?" The word wrenched itself from Yi-Nereen's throat. But of course. The shieldcaster who'd fallen over the parapet when she'd arrived in Curing District couldn't have survived.

One of the dead. That meant there were more.

Yi-Nereen stole a glance at Kadrin. There was a distant, glazed quality to his eyes, like he was reliving a waking nightmare. "One dead in Orchard District," he said quietly. "They couldn't give me a name, so I ran as fast as I could to the Wall. To *your* post. You weren't there, Reena. I . . . I thought . . ."

His voice tore at her, but her heart hammered for a different reason. "Someone died in Orchard?"

"A reserve whose heart gave out in the third hour. He was older, close to his half-life." Kadrin let out a rattling sigh. "It could have happened in any storm, but everyone's saying this one was different. Did you know him? Reena?"

He stopped walking, because Yi-Nereen had frozen in place.

Brisen. She'd left him with three other shieldcasters still standing. She'd thought him *safe.*

He'd joked about being useful again, after a month of drills. He'd noticed Yi-Nereen's silent horror at her own thoughts and asked if she was all right. When Tela fell, he'd been so swift to catch her.

He'd called after Yi-Nereen as she left, warning her not to go.

Yi-Nereen's head pounded. She had to *fix* this. But the only way to make amends for a death was to ensure it never happened again. How?

After tonight, she was certain of one thing: the Second Storm of Centuries had seemingly launched the wasteland into a new age of storms, even deadlier than the last. Even Kerina Sol's profusion of Talent wasn't enough to safeguard them any longer.

Yi-Nereen's treatise—only half-reconstructed a month after Falka had flung her research from the peak of Mount Vetelu—might succeed in repairing the bloodlines, but by then it would be too late.

Her thoughts whirled, caught in a windstorm. *I must save them. Save them all. I must—I must—*

Kadrin gazed at her, brow furrowed, then turned his face toward the blush of pink growing in the eastern sky. "I wonder if she's out there. Running from the storm."

Yi-Nereen felt a hand close around her heart, her thoughts scattering like ashes. She and Kadrin never said Jin's name anymore. But she was always *there*. Standing in the space between them, leaning against doorways and lurking in Yi-Nereen's dreams, a mana-cig between her lips and hands scarred with old burns.

Oh, they'd tried to find her. Kadrin had even posted false notices of courier work, hoping to lure Jin to a meeting so they could talk. He'd had the romantic notion that if only all three of them could sit down together, he and Yi-Nereen could convince Jin to be in their lives, in whatever role she wanted to play. But Jin had seemingly left Kerina Sol altogether.

Even Jin's mother, who worked in the House's kitchen now, claimed not to know where Jin was. She'd sounded distraught enough that Yi-Nereen believed her.

"That's what a courier does," Yi-Nereen said. "It's the life she wants."

But she never dreamed about Jin flying over the dunes on her bike anymore. Those had been good dreams, fantasies to comfort Yi-Nereen when she was a prisoner in her father's tower.

She had different dreams now. Darker ones.

Last night, Jin had been in the crowd outside her palanquin. But while everyone else was tearing through the wreckage, howling for Yi-Nereen's blood, Jin just stood in the background. Staring at her with those wounded dark eyes. As if she wanted something from Yi-Nereen, just like the screaming mob, but she'd die before she asked for it.

What do you want from me? Yi-Nereen wanted to plead.

But she was sure she'd never know.

CHAPTER TWO

LIVING SACRIFICE

Observation #479: Like Talentless humans, saurians lack mana affinity. They neither rely on consumption of mana nor suffer from its overapplication.

Hypothesis: Mana affinity requires possession of a soul.

Current temple doctrine in support. —O

Third Age of Storms, 1st Summer, Day 63

Kerina Sol – Curing District

Jin smelled like shit. That wasn't a figure of speech; she'd spent all day up to her knees in cow dung, mucking out livestock pens in Curing District. So it was no great surprise that when she trudged into the Chandru's Den, the rest of the clientele gave her dirty looks and made ample room for her at the bar.

Jin couldn't be offended. She was past that. Past feeling sorry for herself, even.

Laughter at a nearby table caught her attention. Two men and a woman, all of them dressed in rough-grain leather. Bonehelms rested on the table beside their drinks. Couriers, obviously. How far had they ridden to meet here? Jin wondered. Was it an appointment arranged months ahead of time, or happy coincidence?

The whiskey tasted metallic. Maybe the bartender had given her a batch that had languished too long on the bottom shelf, or maybe her senses were acting up again. Ever since she'd lost her Talent, her body didn't work quite right. She was forever getting headaches, seeing lights dancing in the periphery, hearing phantom sounds. Like a child's cruel laugh or a rovex's roar.

Talentless didn't normally suffer those problems, but Jin had the dubious honor of being special: she was the first person to ever survive the loss of their Talent.

Dwelling on the whiskey's metallic taste was dangerously close to self-pity, so she downed the cup and ordered another. The second tasted worse.

Jin eyed the shelves behind the bartender, lingering on the bottles of bloomfruit wine. Too expensive. The livestock pens hired Talentless, but at shit rates for shit work. There were always the tannery vats, right next to the pens, but Jin preferred cow dung to a combination bouquet of blood, shit, and urine.

The Chandru's Den felt subdued tonight. After a storm, people were usually eager to get sloshed and celebrate being alive, but last night's storm had been different. Jin's hand tightened on her cup. Word had it that two shieldcasters had died.

She'd felt a guilty surge of relief when she learned both of them were men.

A fresh cup thudded onto the bar in front of her. Jin sniffed. "I didn't pay for that."

The bartender jerked his thumb. "He did."

The space Jin's aroma had cleared for her wasn't empty anymore. Jin froze. On the stool beside her sat Kadrin, elbow propped on the bar, smirking at her in a most uncharacteristic manner.

Jin's gut clenched. He'd *found* her. How?

She'd spent a month avoiding all her usual haunts, hoping to fool everyone into thinking she'd left the city altogether. Had it all been a waste? Had Kadrin known the whole fucking time that she was here, frittering away her hard-gotten coin at all of Kerina Sol's dingiest watering holes?

Wait a godsdamn second.

"Elie?" Jin croaked.

Of course that wasn't Kadrin's smile. Because it wasn't Kadrin— it was his sister, Eliesen, lounging on the stool in her brother's clothes. The dim lights and mana-cig smoke wreathing through the tavern had fooled Jin. Just like it had on that night years ago, when she'd met a slim, curly-haired stranger in a different shithole and spent the loneliest hours of the morning getting lost in her lips and hands.

"Did you think I was him?" Elie asked, obviously delighted. She brushed a lock of brown hair out of her eye, and suddenly she didn't look like her brother at all anymore. Just Elie, rakish and wicked, the slant of her shoulders oozing confidence—and a lack of sobriety. "Sorry for the surprise. Just a little payback for worrying us all to death."

She didn't sound sorry at all. Jin's shock faded until a cold sort of numbness took its place. She raised her cup to her lips. Bloomfruit wine, the exact bottle she'd been eyeing earlier.

Damn it, Elie.

"So you found me," Jin said. "What do you want?"

"Now, now. I'll ask the questions." Elie scooted closer, as if she couldn't smell the stink on Jin's clothes. If she still smoked as much as she had when Jin was seeing her, maybe she couldn't. "Let's talk about why you left the House, hmm? Seeing my brother and Her Highness together must have been hard. But if you hadn't scampered off so quickly, Jin, my *darling*"—her fingers spider-walked up Jin's bicep, making her skin tingle—"they would have explained why you didn't have to go anywhere."

"Stop that."

"You used to like it." Elie pouted. "But fine. I can take a hint."

"Not historically, no."

"Oh, and you're one to talk. What does someone have to do to convince you they're in love with you, Jin? Scream it from the rooftops?"

"You're not in love with me," Jin said wearily. "You're just drunk."

"I wasn't talking about *me*." Elie wound a curl around her finger, smiling blithely. "Though I'll be honest, I've always been a little in love with you. Along with about a dozen other people. That doesn't bother you, I'm sure."

Jin rolled her eyes and glanced at the nearby table, where the couriers were sitting. One of the men looked a little familiar, but Jin wasn't worried he'd recognize her. In the five weeks she'd spent alone, no one but Elie had. Jin's leathers were packed away, her riding gloves and boots stashed where she didn't have to look at them anymore. She couldn't wear them without feeling like a child playing dress-up.

"Get to the point."

"*Fine.* I meant Kadrin and Yi-Nereen."

There it went. Jin's resolve not to feel sorry for herself anymore—gone. She clutched her cup of wine, her throat too tight to drink. "I know," she said, before she could think to say anything else.

"You know? You *know*? Jin, if you know, what the hell are you doing? They want to be with you, which is frankly so audacious I'm annoyed I didn't come up with the idea myself. Do you know how lucky you are?"

Flight of the Fallen

Lucky. Because losing her Talent was lucky. Being in love with two people who were better off without her: that was lucky. Finding out her first love was still alive, only to lose her all over again: lucky.

Jin set down her cup so hard she was surprised it didn't shatter. "You haven't got a clue what you're talking about. *Piss off.*"

Elie just rolled her eyes. "Your moods don't scare me, love. I know you're all bark and no bite. Whatever that phrase even means."

Jin stood, shoving back her stool. "It's about. Fucking *dogs.*"

She stormed out of the Chandru's Den, pursued by Elie's whining complaint that she'd never even *seen* a dog, so how was she supposed to know where a stupid turn of phrase came from? No doubt the rest of the tavern's patrons were happy to breathe slightly fresher air in Jin's absence. Elie's hurried footsteps pattered behind her.

"Jin, wait."

Suddenly Elie didn't sound drunk anymore. A lamp swung slowly in the air above them, shedding orange light across the dusk-darkened street. The sight of the lamp made Jin's heart twist; she felt angry tears prick her eyes. The careful wall she'd built around her heart had crumbled, destroyed by Elie's careless touch. Now any reminder of the Talent she'd lost was going to wreck her for Rasvel knew how long.

"I've been afraid," Elie said. "No one knew what happened to you. You just woke up that morning and ran off. I understand a broken heart, Jin, believe me I do—but not even saying goodbye to your mother? What are you running from?"

Jin steeled herself and turned to face her.

She couldn't tell Elie the truth. That would make its way back to Kadrin and Yi-Nereen, and they'd never stop trying to make things right: an impossible task that would ruin them both.

In her darker moments, Jin had contemplated confessing the

truth. Maybe there was a way to reverse what Yi-Nereen had done to her. But the chance was so slim, and the price of failure too high. Yi-Nereen would think herself a monster.

Elie wouldn't leave until she heard *something*. So Jin would have to give her a lie to chew on. A lie meaty enough that Eliesen wouldn't probe her further.

"It wouldn't work." Jin made her face hard, infused her voice with disgust. "The three of us together? It would be wrong."

She wasn't prepared for how rotten the words would taste.

Elie's eyes narrowed. "Do you really think that? You don't sound so sure."

"I'm sure."

"Good." Elie almost spat the word. "If there's even the slightest chance you aren't, better think it through quickly. The wedding's in three weeks."

The wedding? Jin rocked back on her heels, a phantom pain blooming between her ribs. Like she'd been stabbed, right in the same place where Falka's blade had pierced her. The wound had long since healed, but Jin could remember how it had felt with perfect clarity.

"I'm done with this." She turned before her expression could betray her. "Leave me be."

She walked unsteadily into the dark anonymity of the slums, leaving Elie alone under the orange glimmer of the streetlamp.

The Second Storm of Centuries had shattered two districts in Kerina Sol, stolen Jin's Talent and the two people she loved away from her, and destroyed her mother's home.

Flight of the Fallen

Jin picked her way through the rubble that had once been Forge District's main thoroughfare. During daylight hours, Forge District teemed with stoneshapers and metalcrafters working to repair the ruins that surrounded her. But at night, the place was empty and full of ghosts.

Jin liked it that way. The Second Storm had made her into a ghost, too.

She passed a twisted heap of broken masonry that had once been Eomma's bakery. Somewhere under all those stone slabs were the few belongings Jin and her mother had brought from fallen Kerina Tez: a pair of gold-plated earrings, a scroll case with a letter from Jin's father inside. A rusted gear from Lorne's workshop. Jin had spent a few nights digging through the rubble before, but all she'd gotten for her pains was bloody fingernails. A job for someone with Talent.

One of the knight ramps allowing quick egress from the district had collapsed in the Second Storm, leaving a hole in the Wall. The city guard had rigged a walkway from planks and shored up the gap, but they'd left a crack Jin could squeeze through.

Just like that, she was out of Kerina Sol.

With the dusk-dreaming city at her back, she leaned against the Wall and gazed upon her true first love—the wastes. The wind kissed her cheeks. The sand made little eddies at her feet. The horizon was a flat black line against the faint purple flush of sunset, studded with rocks and jagged wasteland cacti.

She couldn't see the highway from here, but she knew it was out there. The highways never changed.

They were the only part of the wasteland that didn't.

Glittering storm dust crunched beneath her boots as Jin strode toward the distant black shape of a rock outcropping. Normally it was a risk to venture into the wastes on foot; if a storm blew through, she'd have to scuttle back sharp-quick. But tonight she'd be safe. Storms never struck two nights in a row.

The first time she'd done this, she hadn't had the same guarantee. But that had been in the early, raw days of her Talentlessness, when she still wasn't sure it was something she wanted to survive. She'd hiked half a day through the wastes like an ant marching mindlessly across the sand, searching for something she couldn't name. A slow death, probably.

Her father had died in a city, at the hands of men. Jin had always been determined to die in the wastes. She'd just expected to do it on a bike, not on blistered feet.

On that day, she'd seen him. Not her father; Screech.

His shadow had fallen over her like a veil. She'd looked up, lips crackling from sunburn, to see the beast gliding far above her. Her gut had clenched in fear, the first real terror she'd felt since waking up Talentless. Pteropters weren't usually a threat to anyone on a magebike, but she was on foot, and this one was *big*.

In the black shadow of those wings, she'd glimpsed her end and realized she wasn't ready for it after all.

Then the pteropter shrieked, and she knew his cry. He'd wheeled away and was gone, a dark speck in the ether, before she could call out.

That fear had saved her. She'd turned around and gone straight back to Kerina Sol, arriving after dusk with nothing worse than a dry throat and sore heels.

The rock outcropping was a lonely place. Two boulders rose from the sand, jutting straight upward, sides scoured clean by countless years of exposure. Jin hoisted herself onto the shorter

Flight of the Fallen

boulder, grunting in exertion. The boulder was flat on top and almost square, its resemblance to a sacrificial altar only intensified by the smears of dried blood caked into its cracks and divots.

For a moment Jin imagined herself a living sacrifice, chained here for the wasteland to devour at its leisure. But that was silly fantasy, no more.

She shrugged off her pack and took out a lump of stinking offal wrapped in butcher's paper. Her time in the livestock pens had inured her to the smell; she barely wrinkled her nose. She slopped the sheep intestines onto the boulder and jumped down to retreat to a safe distance.

Then she waited.

An hour went by. Wasteland chill crept into her bones. Jin swallowed her disappointment—so he wasn't coming.

The moon winked out. Wind rushed over her, scattering her hair over her face. The hulking shape of a massive pteropter alighted on the boulder. Talons scraped against stone, a dull shriek that hurt Jin's ears and set her bones ringing.

Screech dipped his beak into the sheep guts and began the noisy business of slurping them down.

Jin cleared her throat. "You're welcome."

The saurian took no notice of her. He never did until he was finished eating. His appetite had ballooned along with his size; Jin was sure the scraps of meat she took him every few days were just a treat, not his main food source. Maybe he fed on other saurians or unlucky sparkriders.

He'd grown gigantic and gorgeous. The violet feathers in the crest fanning from his head were as long as Jin's arm; the last light of sunset lit his ridged back in streaks of bloody gold. She'd never seen a pteropter so large. Just a month and a half ago, he'd fit in her bonehelm; now he was bigger than a palanquin, with wings long enough to blot out the sky. And while pteropters tended to flock together, Jin had only ever seen him alone.

She was sure he was an oddity. A freak, just like her.

That was why she kept feeding him, even if he never showed an ounce of gratitude beyond not eating her. Maybe one of these days he *would* eat her. But until then, it cheered her ever so slightly to see him.

"Done yet?"

Screech snapped down one last slimy chunk, shifted his weight, and stared at her with one beady black eye. His beak clacked, a sound like rattling bones.

Sometimes Jin thought he was trying to communicate with her, even as the voice of rationality in her head—a stunted, pitiful thing—knew it was probably just a territorial gesture. A pteropter's way of saying *Keep your distance.*

Saurians weren't supposed to be intelligent. But people from the kerinas didn't know much about saurians at all. And the people who did—Faolin's people, the reclusive Talentless out in the wasteland—were now beyond Jin's reach.

"So, about what I asked last time," Jin said. "That relative of yours. The big guy who swims around in mana springs. You seen him lately? Think he fancies a chat?"

Screech swiveled his head to stare at her with his other eye.

Jin didn't know if what she'd seen back then was real, or if her dying, mana-drunk brain had hallucinated the giant saurian and her father's ghost. But if it *had* been real, then there were truths beyond anything the kerinas understood about mana.

One of those truths might tell her how to get her Talent back.

Jin crossed her arms. "Give me *something*, or I'll stop feeding you innards."

The saurian opened his beak and shrieked. Jin nearly jumped out of her skin. Up close the sound was earsplitting, skull shattering. Her head rang and her heart pounded. *Danger*, sang her instincts, *danger danger danger* run.

With a flap of those monstrous wings, Screech took flight. He was away and gone before Jin could remember how to breathe.

What a goddamn *fool* she was. He kept coming back because she kept bringing him food—that was all, the fucking end of it, case closed. She was wasting her time out here. Wasting her coin on half-rotted entrails.

One of these days he really would eat her, and that would be that.

Jin slung her empty pack over her shoulder and began the long, cold walk back to Kerina Sol.

Ducking through the gap in the Wall, Jin felt an icy hand grip her by the wrist. She cursed and tore herself free, panting. Eliesen glared back at her.

"What in the gods' names were you doing out there? On *foot*?"

"You fucking followed me?"

"Yeah, I fucking followed you. I've been waiting here for hours. I was *this close* to going after you." Elie's voice was sharp enough to cut Jin to the quick; guilt had always had that effect on her. "Risking the wastes without a bike? What were you thinking? Where have you been?"

"Leave me alone." Jin tried to push past, but Elie stood in her way.

"I'll tell Kadrin," Elie said. "Finding you in the Chandru's Den was between you and me. But if you're trying to get yourself killed out there, he deserves to know."

"Fine," Jin snapped. "Tell him."

Elie's eyes flashed. "I will. And your mother."

"Oh, that's low."

"Nothing's beneath me. Well, you were, once."

Jin felt an astonished smirk tugging at the corners of her mouth, even though she was still buzzing with fury. Gods, she'd been lonely. Even an argument with Elie was more fun than she'd had in weeks. But damn it, she still couldn't afford to slip.

"Don't you have better things to do than follow me around?"

Not the wittiest comeback, but nobody could claim that trophy from Elie.

Elie shrugged, her expression guarded. "I didn't come to Curing's sleaziest booze den looking for you. That was just a happy coincidence. Truth is, I've been scraping the barrel a bit lately."

Jin quirked an eyebrow. "Has the parade of lovers finally come to an end, then?"

"It's not them, it's me." Eliesen ran a hand through her curls. "Maybe it's Kadrin finally getting married. With the looks Mother's been giving me lately, I can tell she wants me tied down next. You're lucky, Jin. No one's coming after you to squeeze out an heir."

"You keep using that word," Jin said wryly. "It doesn't mean what you think it means."

"Lucky? Don't get cute. All I mean is that I wish I were like you. Free to roam *out there*." Eliesen stared dreamily through the gap in the Wall. "Where it doesn't matter what your name is or what you've got between your legs. I just want to feel like a person and not somebody's future wife."

Jin bit her lip. Elie was starting to sound a little too much like a certain someone else; the scar on Jin's ribs ached.

"I never said thanks," she said. "For the bike."

"You never returned it, either," Eliesen pointed out. "I had to charm my way out of that one."

"Couldn't have been too difficult. You're you."

"Always," Elie sighed, "much to my detriment." She dug into her pocket and came out with a mana-cig between her fingers. "Can I get a light?"

Jin's world narrowed. She'd lit hundreds of mana-cigs in her life with a lazy snap of her fingers, easy as breathing—*hundreds*, and this was the only one that mattered.

How simple her undoing was, in the end.

"Jin?" Eliesen's voice sounded like it was coming down a tunnel.

There was no reason, no reason at all, why she wouldn't light Eliesen's mana-cig for her. Jin lifted her gaze, slow and filled with dread, from the cig to Eliesen's face.

She knew. Somehow, she knew. The horror on her face said it all.

"Jin," Eliesen whispered. "What *happened* to you?"

"Don't tell them. Please."

Elie wrung her hands, apparently at a loss for words. The longer Jin looked at her, the sicker she felt. So she turned away and left Kadrin's sister there, standing in the ruins of a shattered district with only the ghosts for company, mana-cig still unlit.

CHAPTER THREE

THE CAPTIVE

Observation #535: Incidence of mindtalent is no higher than 1/400, according to genealogical records. Rarest of all Talents, or simply of those known to the public? No current hypothesis. —O

Third Age of Storms, 1st Summer, Day 63
Kerina Rut – Legion Barracks

The pale light filtering through the cell window did Sou-Zell's captive no favors. Lank hair fell over the sharp bones of her face like bleached grass; her eyes held none of the taunting spark that had so infuriated Sou-Zell upon their first meeting. A bowl of gruel sat untouched on the table between them.

"My patience wears thin," Sou-Zell said, though the words rang hollow. His patience had worn thin long ago and changed nothing between them. "How much longer do you think I'll keep you housed and fed here if you don't say a word? Your time is running short."

Falka stared through him and said nothing.

No change from yesterday, then, or the day before. Or every day since Sou-Zell had brought her back to Kerina Rut. He'd arranged for Captain Dev-Larai to keep her in a cell the Legion usually reserved for murderers awaiting trial. It was secure, removed from the public eye, and Sou-Zell had paid a handsome sum to keep the Legion from tipping off the High Houses about his prisoner.

If the Lords of Kerina Rut found out what Falka knew—what she could do—they would be swift to pounce. They would deem her knowledge heretical and bury its existence and Falka both.

Sou-Zell wouldn't let that happen. He needed the truth more than the High Houses needed order.

"You still eat," he said. "You still drink. I know you don't want to die. But that is all your stubbornness will amount to in the end, if you don't talk."

He kept his voice controlled, but desperation clawed at him. Falka wasn't the one running out of time. He was.

"If you think you would be better off in the custody of the High Houses, think again. I am the only man in Kerina Rut who can help you. What do you want? Money? Freedom? I can arrange it for you."

"Liar," Falka said.

Sou-Zell jerked in surprise. Had he imagined Falka's voice? No. It was the first word she'd spoken since he'd found her in the rubble of Mount Vetelu, covered in dust and staring at nothing.

"It's no lie," he said. "I can help you. All I need is information."

"You promised me freedom," Falka whispered. "All you gave me was madness. A dead man's voice in my head. What freedom can be found in a land of ashes?"

Sou-Zell cursed. She wasn't talking to him—but to a ghost, or perhaps someone who had never existed at all. Ravings, nothing more.

He leaned back and rubbed his temples. At first, he had assumed Falka's state was a ruse meant to frustrate him. Over time

Hana Lee

he'd reluctantly accepted that her madness was real. Whatever had happened at Mount Vetelu had broken her.

Even the insane could recover in time; Sou-Zell had seen it before. If only he had time to spare.

He'd tried threats. Bribes. Everything short of torture.

Sou-Zell stared at Falka, who was shivering in her chair, and imagined himself striking her. It should have been easy. A month ago, he would have killed her without a second thought—and she would surely have done the same. She was an enemy with information he desperately needed.

But he'd never struck a woman in cold blood before. Not even a heretical woman who'd stolen Talent and a purse full of Sou-Zell's coin.

Sou-Zell stood abruptly, left the cell, and shut the door. A knight standing guard nodded at him and slid the deadbolt back into place.

Another day wasted—but after all this time, she'd spoken. Perhaps tomorrow Falka would be saner, or Sou-Zell more resolute.

What freedom can be found in a land of ashes?

The question troubled him for the rest of the day, which he spent in the academy archives, searching through dusty scrolls for mention of Mount Vetelu. The ravings of a madwoman . . . but the words struck a chord. Like he'd heard them before.

The answer came to him as he was packing up his notes to leave.

Sou-Zell went straight to the biography shelf and plucked an unadorned metal scroll case from its niche. *A Life Unseen: Tibius Vann, a Biography.*

He'd read it repeatedly when he was young and entranced by magebikes. The biography contained little in the way of facts—no one knew much about the mysterious inventor's background—

but it did contain a number of quotes copied from Vann's own writings.

Sou-Zell pinned the scroll out on a table and ran his finger down the edge until he found the correct section.

Some say my invention is the key to unlocking the wastes. As if the wasteland were a prison, as if freedom lies beyond the walls of our cell. No, it is not so. There is no mythical Green Kingdom. It is the wastes that were once green but now lie in ashes. And what freedom can be found in a land of ashes? None—until we clear the embers and start anew.

Sou-Zell raised his head. "She isn't mad."

Falka must have read Vann's biography at some point in her life. If she could quote obscure texts, she must still remember how to transplant Talent. Sou-Zell had made progress by saying the right word: *freedom*. He'd unlocked the first compartment and gotten her to speak.

Now he just had to find more of the right words.

He smuggled Vann's biography past the archive guards and went home. His manor greeted him like a silent, joyless sentinel, eroded by years of neglect. Sou-Zell walked briskly under the peeling archway and made for the east wing for his first stop, his daily filial duty: visiting his mother. But she wasn't in the sunroom where he'd left her.

"Eomma?" His voice echoed through the empty wing.

He found her on the other side of the manor in the west wing, behind a door Sou-Zell swore he'd locked. She'd found one of his brother's old tunics and was sitting cross-legged on the rug in his bedchamber, methodically mending a tear.

Sou-Zell lingered in the hallway and watched her sew. Her fingers moved with a deftness he'd thought lost long ago. For a moment he let himself entertain the treacherous thought that, against all reason, she was better.

Then he saw a shiver run through her body. She gasped quietly; the needle had pierced her finger and drawn blood. Sou-Zell fought the urge to snatch the implement from her hands.

"Eomma. Min-Chuul doesn't need that tunic."

"He will when he comes home," his mother said curtly. "To-night, or perhaps tomorrow. I'll have his wardrobe ready for him."

Sou-Zell's throat tightened. "It's been a long day. I'm going to have a smoke. Will you come with me?"

Lady Ren sighed, as if Sou-Zell were six years old again and asking her to come see a saurian he'd drawn in the dirt. She rose from the floor, concealing her weakness well; Sou-Zell only guessed at her pain from the careful way she smoothed her skirt.

"Fine, fine. But you're going to give up that nasty habit before I'm through."

Sou-Zell smiled hollowly. He'd only begun smoking after his mother had grown too sick to infuse mana any other way. She refused to smoke unless Sou-Zell joined her.

"Here." His mother retrieved an envelope from her skirts and handed it to him. "This came for you today."

The envelope was sealed in dark blue wax, stamped with the symbol of a tower. A weight descended on Sou-Zell as he broke the seal and removed the letter.

My dear boy,

I am grieved to hear of Lady Ren's decline. It was my hope that she could attend my daughters' betrothal feasts, but alas. Some hopes are not meant to be.

As the dutiful son I know you to be, you can only be absorbed in attending to her. It must be a hardship for you to spare daily visits to your prisoner Falka; clearly she proves oddly resistant to your useful, singular Talent.

Never fear! I shall be happy to take over her interrogation, and will relay to you any information I discover.

Tomorrow I will send my personal physician with some tinctures to ease Lady Ren's discomfort.

At your disposal,
Lai-Dan, Shield Lord of the Tower of Arrested Stars

Captain Dev-Larai crossed his arms. "You're making a mistake, my lord. This woman is dangerous. You can't just lock her in your estate and hope for the best. Either she'll die of mana thirst, or you'll give her too much and she'll overpower you."

"Noted," Sou-Zell said. "Now hand her over."

Falka stood with her wrists bound in front of her, flanked by two knights in half-plate. Her eyes flickered between Captain Dev-Larai and Sou-Zell. Under the sunlight, she looked paler and gaunter than Sou-Zell remembered.

Dev-Larai nodded to his knights. "I'll have to inform the Lords of the High Houses. It was one matter when you were keeping her here. That was Legion business, and the Houses didn't need to know. But if she's loose in the city—"

"Inform whoever you like. Do what you must." Sou-Zell gripped Falka by her bony shoulder. "But rest easy, Captain. She won't be roaming the streets."

He led Falka out of the Legion compound.

In truth, taking her to his estate and keeping her around his mother was the last thing he wanted. But Lai-Dan's letter had been clear: he knew who Falka was, that she was Talented but somehow immune to Sou-Zell's mindreading. Sooner or later he would come for her, and Sou-Zell's last chance to save his House would be torn from his grasp.

Sou-Zell expected Falka to make a mad dash the moment they were out of the compound. It was the best chance she'd had in weeks, though she was mana-starved and Sou-Zell was ready for her. But she just let him lead her through back alleys and seldom-used avenues to his estate in her usual silence.

He'd been certain yesterday that her sanity was intact, but doubt gnawed at him now. The sneering bounty hunter he'd hired to track his lost betrothed would never in a thousand years have let Sou-Zell lead her around like cattle.

Captain Dev-Larai had been right on one count. Sou-Zell's estate wasn't designed for holding prisoners. The best Sou-Zell could think of was the wine cellar: it was underground, away from prying eyes, and he could lock the hatch from the outside.

Falka stood in the dimness of the candlelit cellar, looking around slowly, while Sou-Zell laid out bread, water jugs, and a wool blanket.

"No questions today." Sou-Zell cut the rope around her wrists. "I don't have the time. But if you'd like to do some reading . . ."

He set down Tibius Vann's biography before her and went upstairs to lock the hatch.

Another wave of doubt crashed over him. Sou-Zell leaned against a table and inhaled deeply. What choice did he have but to keep her here?

If Lai-Dan got his hands on Falka, he'd order his torturers to rip the knowledge from her head and never share it with anyone else. Sou-Zell had his Talent, but all Lai-Dan had to do was forbid him access, and he'd be helpless to do anything but watch as Lai-Dan wielded Falka's secrets to consolidate his own power.

"What are you doing?"

His mother stood in the kitchen doorway, her head cocked. A single earring flashed in her ear; she wasn't wearing the other. Sou-Zell straightened hastily. He'd expected her to still be in bed.

"Nothing."

"You were in the cellar." Her narrowed eyes flitted to the hatch. "Is someone down there?"

"Eomma."

Sou-Zell laced his voice with a warning. His mother should know better than to question him or his dealings. She must have an inkling of all the things Sou-Zell had done to maintain their House and stretch their fortune in the lean years since his father's death. He'd kept Min-Chuul from the drug dens, until his brother grew too headstrong to listen to him anymore. He'd arranged for a betrothal that had almost saved their bloodline.

Almost.

The whole time, Lady Ren had looked the other way and left Sou-Zell's business alone. But now, under her cold glare, Sou-Zell realized his mistake. This manor was her domain. He might be its lord, but she was still its lady.

"Come to dinner," she said. "We'll talk it over."

Sou-Zell watched her go, noting the stiffness of her gait.

How much longer? a voice within him asked, as it did several times each day. *How much longer can she survive?*

In his childhood, the Manor of Hushed Whispers had been a place of sunlit rooms and busy servants—his mother and father listening to musicians playing in the courtyard, dinner guests from every noble House in the city, invitations to every royal wedding, tutors in every subject.

Now his father was dead, his brother gone, his home crumbling, and his mother hobbling through its dusty halls and slowly dying of mana thirst.

It was Sou-Zell's fault. He'd let Yi-Nereen go.

The only way he could set things right, fix what still remained to be fixed, was sitting in his wine cellar. Falka knew the secrets of mana and Talent. If anyone knew how to stave off the inevitable—how to cure his mother's mana rejection and repair their bloodline—it would be her.

Falka's knowledge was the key to not only Sou-Zell's failing bloodline, but *all* the failing bloodlines. That knowledge would make him powerful beyond measure. It would clear the dust from his family name and secure his place in the history scrolls.

Whatever it cost, Sou-Zell would restore his House.

CHAPTER FOUR

A LIGHT IN THE WASTES

Observation #229: Mana cost basis of wasteland travel by
magebike v. inefficient with passengers in the equation.
Horses more optimal for traveling in groups.
Hypothesis: Kerinas were too hasty in culling herds. —O

Third Age of Storms, 1st Summer, Day 66
Kerina Sol – Council Chambers

A splash of boiling water hissed over Kadrin's hand and he cursed, nearly dropping the teapot. Then he glanced both ways down the corridor to make sure no one had seen. He was alone. Good.

Of late, Kadrin was rather tired of his family. Since Yi-Nereen's arrival, he'd begun to find the House of Steel Heavens a stifling place. It wasn't her fault, of course; it was only that Kadrin's mother had taken it as her latest crusade to see the two of them married as soon as possible. Which apparently wasn't an easy task.

Every marriage in Kerina Sol had to receive the temple's blessing, but obtaining permission for a marriage between a Talentless scion of a High House and a runaway princess from another kerina had proved a hugely complex undertaking, requiring dozens of holy rites and exhaustive interviews of both Kadrin and Yi-Nereen by temple priests—to make sure their union wasn't simply a matter of love, but one that was guaranteed to benefit the city.

In other words, Kadrin had been forced to endure some of the most awkward conversations of his life with both Yi-Nereen and his mother sitting in the room. They involved questions like *In the first year of your marriage, will you prioritize any duty more highly than creating a Talented heir?* and *If your efforts to create such an heir prove fruitless after three years' time, will you submit to physical examination and holy sacrament? What about annulment?*

Kadrin was fairly certain he'd blacked out during some of those questions. He had no idea what he'd said in reply, only that it had apparently satisfied his interrogator. He hadn't been able to look Yi-Nereen in the eyes for days afterward.

Yi-Nereen had been lucky enough to undergo her questioning in private, at least. The temple considered that to be a woman's right. She'd had no problems meeting Kadrin's gaze after those interviews, though Kadrin thought she seemed different after them. More distant, even troubled.

Then the storm-drought had come to an abrupt, violent end, and if Kadrin thought Yi-Nereen had seemed troubled before, she was downright brooding now. She'd barely said a word to Kadrin in three days.

Hence the tea. Kadrin knocked on the door to Yi-Nereen's chambers, balancing the tray in his other hand.

There was a rustling from inside; it sounded like paper. Then the door opened to reveal Yi-Nereen. Her hair was loose around her shoulders, a jet-black mane of glossy waves; there were ink stains on her hands and the corner of her mouth, as if she'd bitten the tip of a quill.

Kadrin felt a warm, pleasant flush suffuse his whole body at the

Flight of the Fallen

sight of her. It still seemed surreal that only a few corridors separated them at any given moment, instead of an entire howling wasteland. Kadrin wasn't used to it—and part of him liked not being used to it.

"I brought you tea."

The tray wobbled in his hands; the teapot, which Kadrin had probably overfilled now that he came to think of it, let out a threatening hiss of steam.

"Oh," Yi-Nereen said. "That was sweet of you." She inhaled, and Kadrin savored the way her face lit up, that crease between her brows banished if only for a moment. "Is it jasmine?"

Kadrin nodded. "In one of your letters, you said it helps you think."

"As long as it doesn't have any—"

"Sugar," Kadrin finished, and Yi-Nereen gave him such a glowing look he almost dropped the tray again.

"Well," she said, stepping back, "come in. I suppose I can't hide this mess from you any longer."

What she was referring to became apparent as soon as Kadrin stepped into the room. Yi-Nereen had transformed her parlor into a fever dream of a study. There were sheets of parchment and discarded books all over the floor and diagrams pinned to the walls; Kadrin cringed at the thought of his mother discovering Yi-Nereen had put pinholes in her wainscoting. For a long minute, he and Yi-Nereen stood in silence as Kadrin's gaze traveled over the room. He tried to count the number of half-empty inkwells in view but soon abandoned the effort.

"What is all this?" Kadrin asked weakly. "Is it for your treatise?"

Yi-Nereen shook her head. "I've put that on hold." A fervent, sleepless excitement simmered in her voice. "Kerina Sol doesn't need a treatise right now. It needs a tower."

Kadrin searched for an empty place to set down his tray, but every available surface seemed covered in parchment, ink, or wax drippings. "Tell me more."

"Do you remember my home in Kerina Rut? The Tower of Arrested Stars?" At Kadrin's nod, Yi-Nereen went on. "It isn't just a testament to my ancestors' vanity. It was built for a pragmatic purpose, too. The weakest point of a kerina's dome is the crown—but with shieldcasters in the center of the city, high above, it becomes the strongest."

Kadrin glanced around. Now he understood the diagrams pinned to the walls: they were different views, from the side and above, of a tower. The details were meticulous. Had Yi-Nereen studied architecture?

"If we build a tower in Kerina Sol's core, right on top of the spring," Yi-Nereen said, "the city will be ten times safer in the next storm. I guarantee it."

"We?"

Yi-Nereen bit her lip. "I need your help, Kadrin. Your father has a Council seat; we must convince him this proposal is sound. It's unlikely the Council will listen to me, especially given what Tethris thinks of me at the moment—but if it comes from Rain Lord Matrios—"

"Hold on." Kadrin finally settled for putting down his tray on the floor in front of the door, where he desperately hoped no one would unexpectedly come in and step on it. Then he turned to face Yi-Nereen. "If my memory serves, Kerina Rut has an *island* in the middle of their spring. That's where they built the Tower of Arrested Stars."

"That's true," Yi-Nereen said.

Kadrin spread his hands helplessly. "We don't have an island."

Flight of the Fallen

"No," Yi-Nereen admitted. "But that doesn't matter. Mana doesn't harm stone. The base of the tower can be built *in* the spring—or rather, on the bedrock beneath it. It means Talentless laborers will need to lay the foundations. No one else could do it safely."

Kadrin winced. "That'll be a hard sell. We aren't even allowed to touch the spring. The temple forbids it."

"I didn't know that." A chagrined flush spread across Yi-Nereen's face; it did interesting things to her complexion, making it difficult for Kadrin not to stare. "I thought Kerina Sol's restrictions on Talentless were rather lax. At least, compared to where I come from."

Kadrin almost brought up the battery of interviews he'd been subjected to for the past month, most of them focused on the topic of Kadrin's questionable capacity to produce a magical child—but no, that would be a terrible idea.

"Maybe, since it's an emergency, the Council could override that law," he said, though he secretly doubted it. "And it *is* an emergency. One storm and two dead shieldcasters? I'm not the keenest mathematical mind, but at that rate . . ."

Yi-Nereen made a soft sound. "You always do that."

"Hmm?" Kadrin looked at her. "Do what?"

"Demean your own capabilities. Not to distract from the issue at hand, but sometimes I wish . . . No, never mind." She sighed. "Thank you for the tea, Kadrin. Will you arrange an audience with your father? Tomorrow, if you can? We may not have long before the next storm."

"Of course," Kadrin said, his heart beating quickly. He didn't know if he wanted Yi-Nereen to continue down her earlier train of thought or abandon it forever. "I think it's a good idea. The tower, I mean. Of course it's a good idea, because it's *your* idea."

45

"I hope your father sees it that way," Yi-Nereen said.

Kadrin stepped over the tea tray and hesitated, his hand lingering on the door's handle. "Good night, Reena."

"Good night, Kadrin."

Kadrin had always been a light sleeper, but since the night of the last storm—when he'd spent a harrowing ten minutes knowing *someone* at Yi-Nereen's post was dead—he'd found himself almost unable to sleep at all. His body ached for rest; his mind felt even duller than usual. But as soon as he stretched out in bed, his heart began to race and he found himself hanging on the silence, anticipating the first ringing note of the storm alarm.

It had been bad enough worrying about Jin somewhere out there in the wastes. Now, for the first time in his life, Kadrin didn't feel safe in his city. And he was *still* worried about Jin.

So he'd taken to leaving the House at night and going to visit the only friend he had who would indulge midnight visits from an anxious prince: Orrin, an artificer who lived in Jade District.

Actually, Kadrin wasn't positive Orrin saw him as a friend. He was more of a patron, really. But maybe paying Orrin's rent and providing capital for materials and equipment entitled Kadrin to more tolerant treatment than friendship would have.

Kadrin knocked on the slightly charred door of Orrin's workshop.

"Orrin? Are you awake?"

"Of course I'm bloody awake," came an irritated voice from within. "You know I'm awake. Get in and close the door."

The workshop was smaller than it looked from the outside,

Flight of the Fallen

which was saying something; Kadrin had a generous allowance each month from his family's coffers, but Jade District wasn't a cheap place to rent land. Tables and machinery were jammed into every spare inch of space. Bell jars glowing with orange sparklight hung from the rafters, casting angular shadows on the walls. When Kadrin breathed in, he smelled grease and the faint, lingering odor of electricity. It was the same smell that had once clung to Jin's leathers whenever she'd come to him with a letter in hand. Kadrin swallowed down familiar sadness.

"Genius never sleeps," said Orrin's voice from somewhere in the crowded depths of the workshop. "That doesn't explain why *you* don't."

Kadrin craned his neck until he spotted the artificer hunched over a table. Tiny green jewels gleamed in Orrin's earlobes, catching the light as Orrin scowled at a pair of wires held together in one hand. As Kadrin watched, a spark jumped between the two wire ends, connecting them in a bright arc.

Orrin wasn't wearing gloves. White scars and old burn marks covered their hands, testament to the fact that Orrin thought very little of gloves and protective gear in general. Kadrin could smell the faintest hint of singed hair, too.

"Maybe I'm trying to become a genius," Kadrin said. "How long do I have to stay awake for that to happen?"

"Somewhere between two and three decades." Orrin slapped the wires down on the table with a frustrated noise. "Make that four."

"Still no progress?"

"Oh, there's been progress. Just not in the direction I'd like to go." Orrin massaged their temples, glaring at Kadrin through their fingers. "Remember when I told you Renzara was *this* close to completing a prototype before her untimely death by explosion?"

"How could I forget?"

Kadrin's very first meeting with Orrin, six or so months ago, had involved a thorough and gruesome recounting of Orrin's old master's death. Of course, Kadrin had already known about it. Renzara had been one of the most famous names in Kerina Sol, a young and brilliant master artificer whose magebike designs were the height of innovation. By all reports, she had been closer than anyone to building the first successful prototype of a sparkless magebike, one that didn't require Talent to ride. So of course Kadrin had been interested in her—right up until Kerina Sol woke one morning to find a smoking crater where Renzara's workshop had been and bits of the lauded artificer scattered up and down the street.

Orrin raked their hands through their dark, curly hair. "I'm even closer, Kadrin. But I still can't see exactly where she went wrong, and I don't fancy dying like she did."

"Is there anything I can do? Do you need more money?"

"That's sweet, but no. If you give me a single coin more, I'll spend it on drinking myself to death. Actually, Kadrin, would you mind standing there and letting me bounce a few things off you?"

Kadrin grinned. "As long as they're ideas and not rocks, sure."

Orrin didn't smile. They rarely did—which again reminded Kadrin of someone else. Gods, he missed Jin.

"Just keep nodding and humming every now and then so it doesn't feel like I'm talking to a wall. Not that you don't make a very charming wall, of course." Orrin eyed him. "All that muscle. Do you ever put it to use? Like, say, shoveling clay—never mind, that isn't relevant."

"Have I ever mentioned that you and my sister would get along splendidly?"

"Focus, Kadrin. You're distracting me. Now, about the prototype." Orrin paced, hands clasped behind their back. "The problem, of course, is that raw mana isn't stable. Mana fuel admixture is rendered inert, but then the power has to come from somewhere else: the rider. What I need is a form of mana that retains its power, but isn't so volatile that the engine's pressure will make it explode. A third form altogether."

Kadrin nodded and threw in a long *hmm* for good measure.

"Thank you, Kadrin. You're doing splendidly."

Orrin went on talking, and Kadrin let his mind drift. Standing here and listening to the artificer blather on was almost as restorative as a full night's sleep. He hadn't had one of those in ages. Not with marriage on his mind, and the terrifying prospect of *heirs*—and what it would mean if Kadrin couldn't produce one.

He'd known in the abstract that the temple had the authority to annul marriages between Talented and Talentless if those unions proved unfruitful. That was one of the injustices Yi-Nereen had often railed against in her letters, and a topic of her still-to-be-rewritten treatise. But Kadrin had dreamed of marrying Yi-Nereen since they were both children, and dreams always had a certain vague, pleasantly fuzzy quality to them. His imagination had never bothered to fill in all the details.

Now that his dreams had been dragged into the sunlight for scrutinizing, he was starting to see all the gaping holes in their fabric. Like the fact that Kadrin couldn't stop thinking about Jin—and judging from the wounded way Yi-Nereen danced around her name, he wasn't the only one.

"Kadrin. *Kadrin.* Have you mastered the art of falling asleep on your feet? I said you can go. I have experiments to run and you're taking up too much space."

Kadrin shook himself. "Sorry. Lost in thought."

"Imagine that," Orrin said dryly, before turning to rummage through a clinking cabinet behind them. "In any case, I appreciate your help. Take this." They held out a small corked bottle wrapped in brown cloth. "It'll help you sleep. Only two drops each night, mind you. No more, or your betrothed will find herself a widow—and quite upset with me, to boot."

"Thanks," Kadrin said, pocketing the bottle. He didn't think he'd use it, but it was a surprisingly kind gesture all the same. "See you around."

"I'm sure." Orrin showed him to the door.

The night was clear and balmy, with a breeze blowing eastward that wafted the sweet fragrance of Orchard District through the rest of the kerina. Kadrin leaned against the ramparts and closed his eyes. Faint singing echoed from a temple in the streets below; the delicate scent of pears mingled with incense.

On nights like these, Kadrin hardly believed in storms.

He looked over his shoulder at the dark expanse of the wastes. For the past three years, he'd spent many evenings standing here in this barbette, the closest point in Kerina Sol to Kerina Rut. He'd thought of Reena in her tower, of Jin coming or going with a letter, his chest hollow with wanting.

As if on cue, a light appeared out in the wastes. It was a tiny, steadily glowing pinprick, bobbing over the dunes. Kadrin rubbed his eyes to make sure the moonlight wasn't playing tricks on him. When he looked again, there were four lights.

Headlights.

Flight of the Fallen

A chill rushed over him. Multiple magebikes approaching Kerina Sol could mean only one of two things, and neither of them was Jin returning to swoon into Kadrin's arms.

They were either raiders, or knights.

Kadrin opened his mouth to shout a warning, but an archer posted somewhere on the Wall had already spotted the lights.

"Riders approaching!"

Guards who'd been lounging at their posts snatched up spear and shield and rushed to man the gates. Kadrin realized he should probably get out of the way, but he couldn't tear himself away from the ramparts and those glowing beams out in the wastes.

More of them now. Not just four, but ten. Twenty.

He was too young to remember a time of open hostility between kerinas. Flat-out war was impossible to wage in a land ravaged by deadly storms, but the invention of magebikes had made it possible to make quick strikes against an enemy kerina, to intimidate and sabotage. Kadrin had accompanied his father to Kerina Rut as a child to draw up a lasting peace treaty between their kerinas. As far as he knew, Yi-Nereen's flight from Kerina Rut hadn't jeopardized that treaty; her father, Shield Lord Lai-Dan, had sent a few threatening letters, but he'd made no formal move toward breaking the peace.

Were those Knights of Rut out there in the wastes? Was this Lai-Dan's reprisal, delivered without warning under cover of nightfall?

No, Kadrin realized. If they were enemy knights or raiders, they would have turned off their headlights.

He turned toward the nearest archer, his heart hammering in his chest, and shouted, "Don't shoot!"

"What? Who are you?"

"They aren't enemies!" Kadrin waved his arms, trying to get the attention of the archers in the nearest barbette. "Hey! Don't shoot at any of those bikes!"

In the dark, he couldn't tell whether anyone was paying attention to him. But the archer near him, at least, had lowered his crossbow a fraction and was squinting out into the wastes, trying to get a better look at the oncoming riders.

A gauntleted hand gripped Kadrin's arm.

"You don't give the orders here, young man. I do." It was a knight-captain judging from her armor, though Kadrin didn't know her name. She glared at him from under an impressively cliff-like brow. "Now get down from the Wall before I toss you down."

"With all due respect, ah, Captain—I don't think—"

"I'm not giving the order to shoot." Her fingers dug deeper into Kadrin's bicep, as if to remind him they were there. "There's no need. The gates of Kerina Sol are closed and our Wall is high. They aren't getting inside. But I don't need a civilian standing on the Wall telling my archers what to do and who not to shoot."

"I'm not a civilian," Kadrin said. "I'm the Rain Lord's son."

"Hmm." The knight-captain removed her hand with a swiftness that implied to Kadrin she'd mistaken him for one of his older brothers. "Sorry about that, Lord Raincaller. I'd still rather you didn't give my men orders, but you can remain on the barbette as long as you aren't in the way."

She didn't wait for Kadrin's response. The lights had grown brighter, and now both of them could hear the distant roar of mage-bike engines. The knight-captain moved to the edge of the ramparts and raised her hand. Sparks danced between her metal-clad fingers, bright orange against the dusky gray of the wastes.

In one smooth motion, the knight-captain twisted her arm and

Flight of the Fallen

fired a bolt of lightning from the Wall. It hit the ground a few yards out with a cracking boom, flinging sand into the air. The hair on the back of Kadrin's neck stood on end—whether from awe or the charge lingering in the air, he wasn't sure.

The headlights bobbed and stopped. They'd come close enough to the Wall that, if Kadrin squinted, he could see the dark shapes of the magebikes and their riders. They weren't wearing plate.

Kadrin let out a breath. He'd been right—they weren't knights.

"Name yourselves!" The knight-captain's voice carried clear through the wasteland air.

There was a pause. Archers on the Wall shifted and muttered. Kadrin crept closer to the ramparts for a better view.

He saw a figure approaching on foot from the cluster of mage-bikes. Whoever the person was, they were laden with bundles; they even had a pack strapped to their chest.

"We aren't foes!" the figure called. "I'm Chanh, of Kerina Lav."

"Refugees," the archer nearest Kadrin said. "Or exiles."

"Hail, Chanh of Kerina Lav," called down the knight-captain. "Is it Rasvel's Sanctuary you seek?"

"Yes." Chanh's voice shook with what was obviously relief. He reached down to lift away a flap of fabric from the bundle on his chest. Kadrin squinted. Even from a distance, under the moonlight, he could see the infant now—the tiny fists balled in Chanh's shirt. "We seek sanctuary. Myself and the others."

"How many of you are there?" Kadrin called out impulsively, ignoring the knight-captain's withering look.

Chanh hesitated, his hand cupped over the back of the baby's head. "I— I don't know. We were the first to flee, but there are more coming. Maybe a thousand—or more."

Gasps rippled across the ramparts. Kadrin gripped the parapet

53

for stability. A thousand! That was a tenth of a kerina's population, if not more. There had to have been a terrible cataclysm for so many to flee. Plague? Famine? Kerina Sol was used to welcoming refugees, but only when they trickled in over weeks and months. This would be no trickle.

It would be a flood.

The knight-captain was the first to find her voice, though it held a slight tremble. "Does Kerina Lav still stand?"

The baby in Chanh's arms began to cry, a thin, piercing wail. Chanh hugged the child to his chest like it was the last living thing left in the wastes and looked up at the Wall. Tears on his face gleamed under the moonlight.

"No," he said. "Kerina Lav is gone."

CHAPTER FIVE

THE SHIELD LORD'S WILL

Observation #304: Twinblessed live as long as single-Talented
individuals on average, but variance in lifespan is lower.
Hypothesis: Half-life and mana pool capacity are inversely
correlated. Two split pools in one person acts as
averaging function. —O

Third Age of Storms, 1st Summer, Day 66
Kerina Rut – Tower of Arrested Stars

Sou-Zell swept up the Tower stairs, his mood blacker than pitch. Lai-Dan's messenger had woken him before dawn. Roused from a deep sleep, Sou-Zell had had no patience for any more condescending notes or thinly veiled threats relayed from Lai-Dan; he'd pinned the unfortunate man to a wall and torn the message from his thoughts.

Thusly, he had learned of Kerina Lav's fall—of the refugees camped outside the Wall, waiting for the High Houses of Kerina Rut to decide their fate. Already they numbered in the hundreds, and more arrived every hour. The messenger hadn't known Lai-Dan's exact motive for summoning Sou-Zell, but it had to do with the refugees. So now Sou-Zell knew that much, too.

Sou-Zell knocked on a stone door engraved with butterflies and was bade to enter. Inside, the Shield Lord wasn't alone. The small, elaborately decorated room was host to three other men: two dressed in Tower robes and one whose clothes and hair were thick with dust. Sou-Zell eyed this last up and down.

The man's left hand was covered in rings: a Lav-blood custom. The more rings a man wore, the higher his stature in the Guildery, Kerina Lav's mercantile government. He was a refugee, then, but an important one.

"Welcome to the Tower, Lord Sou-Zell."

Lai-Dan's cheerful baritone sent ice surging through Sou-Zell's veins. He hadn't actually stood in the Shield Lord's presence since he'd returned to Kerina Rut without Yi-Nereen, five weeks ago. He had tried to arrange a formal apology, but the Tower guards had turned him away with ominous warnings: the Shield Lord would send for him when it was time to discuss his failure.

"My thanks." Sou-Zell would not bow and scrape before Lai-Dan, threats be damned. What purpose in restoring his House, if he sullied its authority by insinuating other Houses were his better? "I was gratified you sought my counsel."

That was a stab in the dark. He had no idea why Lai-Dan wanted him here.

Lai-Dan smiled. "Sou-Zell, meet Guildmaster Xua. Formerly of Kerina Lav. He and I were just discussing the situation outside the gates."

"Situation?" Xua's voice was chipped. "That's not how I would describe our plight. When Kerina Tez fell, every city took in their share of refugees, including Kerina Rut, Your Lordship. Now the time has come to do your duty once more—and not only do you refuse, you bar your gates and demand payment we don't possess. That isn't a *situation*. It's highway robbery."

"Such refreshing candor," Lai-Dan laughed, giving Sou-Zell a meaningful look. "My former dealings with the Guildery were a puzzle by comparison. Settling our trade routes six years ago took all the guile I possessed, but we reached an accord, did we not? I have faith in our collective powers of diplomacy."

"I don't have time for diplomacy," Guildmaster Xua said. "I watched lightning blast my city to rubble. People and animals flung into the wastes. An entire kerina destroyed in the span of five hours. And I lost a hundred more souls crossing the wastes to get here. *Do not test me.*"

Sou-Zell's mind defied him and replayed the horrors Xua described. *Rasvel's mercy.* His fingers twitched; he remembered clinging to a cliff's edge in a storm as the howling winds did their best to drag him into the abyss.

So that's that. Another kerina gone.

Sou-Zell remembered studying maps as a child, tracing his finger along the web of highways that connected the kerinas. Kerina Tez to the north had fallen three years ago, and now Kerina Lav to the east.

Kerina Sol remained, now Kerina Rut's only close neighbor. The other cities were far-flung, days away by magebike. Practically strangers.

"Well, Guildmaster, I'm certain we can come to an understanding." Lai-Dan sipped from a goblet; Sou-Zell noticed that neither he nor Xua had been offered refreshment. A cheap power play, but Lai-Dan never tired of those.

Xua said, "Enlighten me."

"Kerina Rut always welcomes new Talent. Your people need only submit to a simple test from our temple priests. Any who pass will be allowed through the gates to make my city their new home."

My city, Sou-Zell noted sourly. No mention made of the other High Houses; Lai-Dan assumed he spoke for them all. And he likely did.

"You speak of leaving children to die," Xua growled.

"Kerina Lav offered no refuge to Talentless born outside her walls," Lai-Dan said mildly. "You understand: it's a matter of resources. Every Talentless is a mouth to feed that gives nothing in return."

"Makela has cursed them, yes, but they do not deserve death!"

"None of us deserve death, but the wastes have other plans." Lai-Dan flicked his wrist. "It's your decision, Guildmaster. Save most of your people, or none."

Sou-Zell half expected Xua to launch himself at Lai-Dan in fury. But instead the guildmaster raised his chin and gave the Shield Lord a steady glare.

"Perhaps we can settle this another way," Xua said. "We can pay. Not in coin, but in something I believe Your Lordship will find even more valuable: information."

Lai-Dan's smile widened, and Sou-Zell felt his stomach drop. The Shield Lord had clearly awaited this moment.

"Ah, but Guildmaster, this Tower has a law. No guest may keep secrets from its master. The information you offer is, by rights, already mine—and I have the power to seize it."

"No," Sou-Zell said.

Both men turned to stare at him. Sou-Zell felt a wave of dizziness. He'd spoken too boldly; Lai-Dan was, after all, his social superior. But Sou-Zell would not, *could not*, surrender his Talent to Lai-Dan like this. He had made up his mind long ago.

Mindtalent was vanishingly rare. It manifested in only a few per thousand in each generation; those with the gift often spent their lives as pawns, spying for more powerful men. Sou-Zell would not become anyone's puppet, least of all Lai-Dan's.

"No?" Lai-Dan raised an eyebrow. "You speak in haste, Sou-Zell. After I sent my physician to treat Lady Ren, she wrote me with reassurances that she would seek to return the favor. I thought you would be more than willing to satisfy your mother's promise."

His words might as well have been: *Refuse me, and she will pay the price.*

How long had Lai-Dan coveted Sou-Zell's Talent? How long had he waited to use this weapon against him?

If he had used it half a year earlier, Sou-Zell would have been unmoved. His mother had been stronger then: a force in her own right, with allies among all the High Houses who would have condemned Lai-Dan's efforts to manipulate her. But as Lady Ren weakened, her friends had faded away like mist in sunlight. Sou-Zell's House stood alone.

If he submitted to Lai-Dan once, even just this once, it would never stop. Yet he couldn't see a way out.

Guildmaster Xua's eyes flickered between Sou-Zell and Lai-Dan, putting the pieces together. "This is beneath you, Lai-Dan. We are equals. If the winds of fate had blown a different direction, it would be *you* standing in *my* parlor, begging me to save your people."

Lai-Dan's eyes twinkled with amusement as he looked at Xua. "Are you begging me, my dear man? Is this what that looks like? Surely you can do better."

Xua stared, a rat caught in a trap. Sou-Zell could almost hear his teeth grinding.

"Please." Xua sounded like he might vomit. "Save my people. All of them. I *beg* you, in Rasvel's name."

Lai-Dan tutted softly. "Alas, I'm still not impressed. Sou-Zell, waste no more of our time. I shall have his secrets."

Sou-Zell's only consolation was that he wasn't the most beaten man in the room. That title belonged to Xua. But the thought did little to quell his hatred for both Lai-Dan and himself. Hatred and helplessness. There was no way out.

He burned mana, and Xua's desperation crashed over him in a choking flood.

I've failed them. Gods, I've failed them. Toraka was right. We should have made for Kerina Sol, all of us. Now our supplies are exhausted; we'll never make it there. I divided our people and damned us by halves.

Houses on fire. A boiling sky. Bodies in the streets.

Sou-Zell groped blindly for an anchor, something to cling to before the torrent of Xua's thoughts swept him away. Another mind to read. Lai-Dan's smug anticipation radiated from him in corrosive waves; Sou-Zell reached for one of the guards instead, and found himself able to breathe again.

The guard's mind was a placid lake; he was looking forward to breakfast.

Sou-Zell continued burning mana, holding fast to the guard's mind as his anchor, and spoke in a ragged voice. "Ask your questions."

"What is the secret you meant to use as barter?" Lai-Dan asked Xua. "What makes it valuable?"

A fleeting shadow flashed through Xua's thoughts, too quick to grasp. *The map*—then it was gone, replaced by memories of horror.

Gashes opening in the earth. Walls dissolving like sand. Screams of the trapped and dying.

No shield. No safety.

Xua had obviously received some training in resisting a mind-reader's power. He was flooding his surface thoughts with emotionally charged memories to push Sou-Zell out, like the body fighting an infection. Sou-Zell shivered. His vision grayed. But he held on; Lai-Dan would not be satisfied with his failure, and the last person in the world Sou-Zell cared for would pay the price.

"He's fighting me. Ask him—ask him about the map."

"What map, Xua?" Lai-Dan probed. "Where?"

Road Builder ruins. The vision came to Sou-Zell in between flashes of terror and destruction. A stone tablet, the markings on its surface faded with age but still legible.

A city beside a spring. Safe from the storms.

Sou-Zell sucked in a breath. "The First City."

Despair crashed over him—not his, but Xua's. Sou-Zell had found his quarry.

Sou-Zell let Xua's mind slip from his grasp. His vision returned slowly along with his breath. When he could see again, he saw Xua kneeling in front of him with a face gray as ash. Blood trickled from his nose. Sou-Zell felt warm liquid running over his own mouth, down his chin. They'd both fought hard—but in the end, Sou-Zell had crushed his foe.

"May you pass from Rasvel's sight forevermore," Xua whispered, his hateful eyes fixed on Sou-Zell. "May all your children be still-born."

Sou-Zell stood still. Behind Xua, Lai-Dan gestured carelessly and said, "Take him back to his people. I have no further need of him."

The guards moved to carry out his order. Sou-Zell averted his gaze, but he heard Xua's heels scraping the stone floor, his despairing cries.

Sou-Zell had seen Xua's mind. Felt his heart. Now they were bound, the way Sou-Zell was bound to everyone whose mind he had touched. And Sou-Zell hated him for it.

He hated Lai-Dan more.

Lai-Dan steepled his fingers. "Tell me everything you saw."

"I cannot be sure if I—"

"The First City, Sou-Zell." Lai-Dan's voice burned with eagerness. *"Tell me."*

It had been a careless mistake to say the words aloud. Sou-Zell should have thought faster, come up with a lie to satisfy the Shield Lord. Now it was too late.

"The Guildery believes they have found it," he said. "Or its location, at least. One of their scouts discovered a Road Builder tomb in the wastes to the east. When they broke open the tomb, they found a tablet among the remains."

"Most impressive," Lai-Dan said. "To have gleaned a full accounting of events, with Xua fighting you every step of the way. Your Talent is of the highest caliber."

Sou-Zell fought back a shudder.

"So, where is this tablet?" Lai-Dan continued.

Sou-Zell hesitated. But the flash in Lai-Dan's eye told him the Shield Lord had noticed his hesitation; he would pounce at once if Sou-Zell tried to hold anything back. The man was almost a mind-reader in his own right.

"Xua doesn't have it. He believes one of the other guildmasters took it when they fled the city: a woman named Toraka. She went

Flight of the Fallen

to Kerina Sol with half the survivors, but Xua hoped to barter with you using his recollection of what the tablet contained."

"Which was?"

"The map led to a location deep in the Barrens. It contained drawings. Detailed ones, of highways our knights have failed to chart."

Lai-Dan laughed. "Yes, the rovex certainly had other plans."

Now Sou-Zell did shiver, as Lai-Dan's words summoned an unpleasant memory to the forefront of his mind. He'd faced a rovex in close quarters before; it still stalked his nightmares. The Barrens were home to droves of the beasts, as well as other species of saurian who never roamed beyond its borders.

"The ruins of the First City," Lai-Dan said, his voice dreamlike. "What a gift Xua has brought me. *Whoever of mortal blood is first to set foot in the cradle of the divine shall be blessed with their gifts.* It must be providence that Kerina Lav fell before the Guildery could act on their discovery." He cocked his head with a smile. "Why are you looking at me like that, boy? Such contempt in those eyes—you wound me."

"I have never believed in fairy tales. I am surprised to hear you do. My lord."

Lai-Dan shook his head in mock disappointment. "What you name fairy tales, I call scripture. Where is your faith? But it matters not if you don't believe. You have done well for me today. I will remember your service."

Oh, he would certainly remember. Sou-Zell didn't doubt it, just as he was certain his own rage at being used like this would never fade. He made a flimsy attempt at a bow.

"The refugees from Kerina Lav should be informed of your offer," he said.

Lai-Dan cocked his head. "What offer?"

"Sanctuary for those who are Talented. I doubt Guildmaster Xua will pass it on, given how ill he took the suggestion, but his people should be allowed to choose for themselves."

"An excellent idea." Lai-Dan's eyes glinted. "I shall always welcome your counsel."

You are mine, those eyes said. *Your powers, your House, your mother's life. This is the price of failure.*

Sou-Zell swallowed an unwise retort and took his leave.

CHAPTER SIX

THE PRINCESS AND HER TOWER

Observation #156: Sol-bloods regard mana as divine energy
and resent mortal interference.
Related: Kerina Sol boasts fewer artificers than any other kerina.
Conclusion: I resent religious fools. —O

Third Age of Storms, 1st Summer, Day 73
Kerina Sol – The Spring

Yi-Nereen combed the banks of the spring, looking for Kadrin. When her gaze fell upon him, her stomach fluttered, a sensation that was disorienting but not altogether unpleasant. He had found a spot among the crowd thronging the banks, under an olive tree. Sunlight fell through the tree's branches, dappling his skin in moving shadows and bronzing his hair.

Yi-Nereen hadn't seen much of Kadrin this week, except for during meals. She'd forgotten how well daylight suited him.

"Reena!" Kadrin beckoned her closer.

Yi-Nereen picked her way through the crowd. Kadrin had spread a blanket on the ground; she sank onto it, arranging her skirts beneath her. "It's a lovely day for a picnic," she said, "but I'm not sure I'll be able to eat a bite."

Kadrin smiled. "Nervous?"

Yi-Nereen nodded, her throat clenching. She looked past Kadrin at the reason why the banks of the spring were so crowded with onlookers today.

It was the first day of construction on Kerina Sol's tower. *Her* tower.

To everyone's surprise, but Kadrin's most of all, Rain Lord Matrios had seized upon Yi-Nereen's proposal. He'd brought it to the Council the same day Yi-Nereen had presented it to him, with Yi-Nereen permitted to accompany him as his guest. And in the end, the vote to approve the tower's construction had been unanimous, save one.

High Priestess Edine, the temple's Council representative. When the white-robed, unsmiling woman had raised her slate marker in dissent, Yi-Nereen had nearly passed out on the spot. But then she'd learned that the temple didn't hold veto power in Kerina Sol, as it had in her home city. High Priestess Edine's vote counted the same as any royal's.

So the vote had passed without the temple's approval. The way Edine had looked at her afterward . . . The woman's gaze was like a chisel aimed to burrow through stone. Yi-Nereen was certain she'd made an enemy for life.

"Look!" Kadrin's voice pulled Yi-Nereen from her ruminations. He was pointing down the bank. "Those men there. Some of them are from yesterday's arrivals."

Yi-Nereen followed his gaze to a group of stoneshapers laboring over a pile of masonry. Their eyes gleamed amber as their hands moved, twisting and molding blocks of stone as if they were clay.

"You helped them settle in?"

"I didn't do much," Kadrin said. "Took their names down in

the registry, told them where to bed down for the night and where to collect rations. They were all on foot this time, poor bastards. Nearly dead of thirst."

Kadrin had been one of the first volunteers to assist the Lavblood refugees who were still flooding into Kerina Sol day by day. He spent almost all his time at a checkpoint in Forge District, where the Council had established a makeshift camp. Yi-Nereen would have joined him, but she had duties of her own, consulting on the tower plans with a team of stoneshaper architects from dawn till dusk.

She'd gone to bed exhausted every night this week. But it was a pleasant exhaustion, unlike any she'd felt before. She was on the right path; she could feel it. This tower would be her redemption. After nearly destroying Kerina Sol, she would be the one to save it.

"They're lucky to have you," Yi-Nereen said, looking at Kadrin fondly.

So am I.

Kadrin flushed and looked away, but she saw a smile dancing on his lips.

These were strange days in Kerina Sol, but Yi-Nereen was beginning to think they were good ones. Kerina Lav's fall and the refugees' arrival had changed everything. People were finally *listening* to her. The second draft of her treatise was coming along, written by candlelight late in the evening after she returned from the stoneshaper workshops. It was the second prong of her plan to save Kerina Sol; the tower was the first. Soon she would be able to share her findings with the Council.

Kerina Sol was becoming more than her sanctuary—it was becoming her home.

"Where did they get all the metal and stone?" Yi-Nereen watched a team of metalcrafters working on a dock that extended a quarter of the way across the spring. They would use it to access the tower's scaffolding once the foundations had been laid by Talentless.

"I'm not sure," Kadrin said. "I heard building materials were scarce. Everything was being used for repairs in Forge and Curing Districts. But the Council must have found something to use."

A faint quiver of doubt wormed its way past Yi-Nereen's self-satisfaction. Forge and Curing were the two districts she'd wrecked in the Second Storm. Suppose the Council had "found" their building materials by diverting resources away from reconstructing those districts?

Well, there was no point in ruining this sunlit picnic with Kadrin by bringing it up. She'd simply have to ask at the next Council meeting. Today was meant to be a good day; Yi-Nereen refused to let dark thoughts steal into her head.

That meant no thinking of Jin, either.

Beside her, Kadrin surged to his feet. "Someone just fell in."

Yi-Nereen didn't understand at first. "What? Where?"

"On the dock—one of the metalcrafters."

Kadrin wasn't the only one who'd noticed. All along the bank, people were shouting and pointing. Someone screamed. Yi-Nereen rose clumsily, almost tripping over her skirt. After so many days and nights poring over parchment by candlelight, her eyes were weary; she couldn't make out the details of the distant metalcrafters on the bridge, who were obscured by the fog rising from the spring.

"What's happening?" she asked. "Did they pull him out?"

"They've got his arm, but he's in up to his waist—oh, Rasvel." Kadrin sucked in a pained breath. "It's already been too long. Hasn't it?"

Yi-Nereen's head spun. She licked her dry lips as bile crept up her throat. "I need to go out there."

Kadrin tore his gaze from the spring and looked down at her, wide-eyed. "Can you save him?"

Selfish thoughts darted through Yi-Nereen's head like bloodsucking flies. What would happen if everyone found out she could siphon Talent? If the Council branded her a freak, a heretic, what would become of her tower? Her pending marriage?

But Kadrin wasn't concerned with consequences. If he saw someone in danger, his only question was whether they could be saved. Yi-Nereen's chest surged with affection for him—and hatred for herself.

"I don't know," she said. "But I— I can try."

Kadrin nodded and took her hand. Yi-Nereen picked up her skirts in her other hand and ran. Kadrin elbowed his way through the crowd, using his broad frame to clear a path for them to the shore. Yi-Nereen's temples dripped with sweat; a stitch burned in her side. But then her feet were on the skeleton dock, the metal supports rattling beneath her. She slowed, picking her careful way across.

Shouts rang out from the shore behind her. "Who is that? What's she *doing*?"

"She's crazy!"

My fault, sang Yi-Nereen's pulse in her ears. *My fault if someone dies. My tower.*

Her foot slipped. For one sickening moment, she lost her balance and teetered on the edge. Then Kadrin's hand was under her elbow, holding her fast. "I've got you," came his voice in her ear. "We're almost there."

The metalcrafters had finally pulled their fallen comrade out of the spring. The man lay on the dock, moaning, eyes burning silver. Steam hissed from his skin. His fellow workers sprawled around him, panting and looking miserable. One of them waved Yi-Nereen and Kadrin away.

"It's not safe. What are you doing out here?"

"I can help him." Yi-Nereen knelt beside the dying man. No time to explain—she didn't know how long she had to save him. If she could save him at all.

What if rescuing Jin had been a fluke, a one-time miracle?

Perhaps it would be better if it was. Then Yi-Nereen wouldn't have to explain her unnatural abilities to anyone. People were only just beginning to look at her like she belonged in Kerina Sol, like she wasn't a complete outsider—and she was about to destroy all the hard-won progress she'd made.

She brushed those doubts away like clinging cobwebs and bent down. As she pressed her mouth to the dying man's, it occurred to her that perhaps she didn't need to kiss people to siphon their mana. Just because her father preferred to do it that way didn't mean it was necessary. But now wasn't the time to experiment.

A hand grabbed her shoulder. "You'll burn yourself! Get back."

"Let her be," Kadrin said. "Trust me. She won't hurt him. Or herself."

The hand released her. "What in Rasvel's name is she doing?"

Yi-Nereen's lips were burning and blistering, but the mana she drew from the metalcrafter's body was ice-cold. It filled her, sand in an hourglass, whispering through her veins. The man writhed and moaned into her mouth.

Too much. Yi-Nereen's skin tingled; her vision trembled. She

Flight of the Fallen

knew this feeling and what to do. Instinctively, she burned mana, shaping her shield to herself like a second skin.

At once she knew something was wrong. Different. This shield was more malleable than it should be—and sharper. Like a weapon, something that could strike and cut.

When she'd siphoned Jin, she hadn't noticed a difference in her shield. But she'd been rather distracted by other sensations, like Jin's lips and the warmth of the courier's hand on the small of her back.

The man's writhing stilled until he lay limp and silent in her arms. Yi-Nereen hesitated but didn't draw back. She could sense the mana still searing him from the inside, coursing through his blood. She had to take more—but not too much.

This was so *difficult*. Both times she'd drained Jin, she'd almost gone too far. Almost taken her Last Breath. She had to stop at just . . . the right . . . moment.

Now.

Yi-Nereen wrenched herself away, panting. Her body burned—but it was a painless fire, euphoric. She felt like a rag soaked in pure, liquid power.

If the storm bells rang at this very moment, she could cast a shield to shadow the whole of Kerina Sol. It would be child's play. Tethris could bluster all she wanted; she'd never hold a candle to Yi-Nereen's power.

Kadrin's arms encircled her, but Yi-Nereen shook them off. She couldn't be restrained right now, not even by an embrace.

Yi-Nereen rose. The other metalcrafters' faces swam into focus around her. They were staring at her like she was Rasvel made flesh. "He probably won't wake for a few days," she said, and her voice echoed strangely in her own ears. "But he'll live."

"Impossible," one of them said. Her tone was sharp. Accusatory.

Yi-Nereen shivered. No, they weren't staring at her like she was a god; they looked at her warily, like she was a demon. She'd seen only what she wanted in their eyes.

"Reena." Kadrin's voice, subdued. He didn't try to touch her again. "We should go."

"Go where?"

She wanted to climb the Wall and spread herself over the city; she wanted to show Tethris the dreadful mistake she'd made in dismissing Yi-Nereen from the Corps. Or better yet, show High Priestess Edine her folly in voting against her at Council.

"Home," Kadrin said, sounding uncertain.

She certainly did not want to return to the House of Steel Heavens. What could she do there, with all this power locked inside her?

But no, Kadrin was right. Everyone in the city would know what she'd done by nightfall. They would want explanations—the temple and the High Houses would question her. Yi-Nereen needed to come up with a story that would satisfy them without damning herself.

She let Kadrin lead her back to the shore. Yi-Nereen felt the crowd's stares, heard its whispers. It was like her recurring nightmare, pulled inside out; instead of mobbing her, the crowd parted of its own accord, making a path for her.

She'd *saved* a man today. They should all be grateful. But no—they would fear her until they understood her. Until she made them understand.

Kadrin walked swiftly, and Yi-Nereen had to hurry to keep up. Was he afraid of her, too? Doubt pierced the heady fog of her power. Once they were away from the crowded banks, Yi-Nereen pulled him into an alley.

"Kadrin, wait. You *told* me to save that man."

"It was the right thing to do." Shadows clung to the familiar planes of his face. "But I wasn't thinking, Reena. Once people hear about this, they might get the wrong idea. It'll be safer once that man wakes up. Then everyone will know you saved him."

"He's still alive, isn't he?" Yi-Nereen shook her head in irritation. "No, you're right. I'll stay away from the spring for a few days."

"Better if you stay inside."

Kadrin's serious expression didn't suit him at all. Yi-Nereen's stomach clenched at the sight of it.

"All right." Yi-Nereen forced a smile onto her face. That was easy. She'd spent years smiling for her father, for her House and her people, even while she shriveled into rot at her core. "I will."

She'd erred somehow. But what could she have done—refused to even try to save that man? Surely that wasn't what Kadrin wanted. But he was looking at her with something akin to caution, like he wasn't sure he liked whatever he saw in Yi-Nereen's expression.

He was all she had. Jin was gone, and only Kadrin remained, the steadfast anchor who'd kept her alive in the darkest hours of her life. She couldn't lose him.

Yi-Nereen forced herself to breathe. Ordered tears not to fall from her eyes.

Be still. Be stone.

Be a shield.

CHAPTER SEVEN

THE VULTURE

Observation #340: Hallucinations common symptom of acute mana poisoning. Survivors report similar motifs: flying or moving at great speeds through the sky, speech-capable saurians, sensations of emptiness and existing in a void. Future study: Interview drug addicts for comparison. —O

Third Age of Storms, 1st Summer, Day 74
Kerina Sol – Forge District

Knapsack slung over her shoulder, Jin wove through the crowded streets of Forge District, stepping over bedrolls and around cookfires. The neighborhood was far from the ghost town it had been a week ago. Filled with refugees from fallen Kerina Lav, it bore a striking resemblance to the ghetto Jin and her mother had lived in when they'd first come to Kerina Sol after the destruction of their own home city, Kerina Tez.

Everywhere she looked, memories from that time struck her like darts to the heart. But Jin shook them off. She had work to do.

As twisted as it was, Kerina Lav's fall had been a godsend for Jin. Suddenly there was more work than ever for a Talentless with no particular skills. Someone had to hand out rations, run messages between checkpoints, break up fights over sleeping space. It was like a faded, shadowy replacement for being a courier.

The pay wasn't much better than the livestock pens, but at least Jin smelled better nowadays.

She had to be careful, though. A few days ago, she'd been distributing waterskins when she'd spotted a familiar figure across the street. Eomma, doing exactly the same thing as Jin: helping. Jin had ducked behind a wall to hide until her mother was gone.

She knew she couldn't avoid Eomma forever. But, Rasvel help her, she just wasn't ready. The moment Eomma saw her face, she would know something was terribly wrong. Jin never could keep anything from her.

Gods, Elie's face still haunted her dreams—that look of dawning realization and horror. A born Talentless was one thing, but Jin was an abomination, a husk whose essence had been torn from her body. The temple didn't even have a word for someone like her.

Raised voices caught her ear. Jin peered through the haze of smoke and clay dust that fogged the refugee camp, looking for the source of the fuss.

Refugees thronged around a man in saffron-yellow robes who stood with his back to a ruined wall, flanked by a pair of stocky guards. None of the refugees were empty-handed; they clutched bits of jewelry, cookware, colorful scarves.

Jin swallowed hard. Three years ago, she'd been one of those dusty, haggard people, hawking whatever she and Eomma could bear to part with for a bit of coin. Anything to get them a leg up, a foothold in this place where they knew no one and had nothing.

That man in the yellow robes. He was what the refugees called a *vulture*: an old Dirilish word for a scavenger. A Kerina Sol native who had hired guards and come to the refugee camp to make unfavorable deals with desperate people.

There was nothing Jin could do to help. The refugees probably knew perfectly well that they were beggaring themselves, but their needs today outweighed whatever losses they'd mourn tomorrow.

She was on the verge of walking away when one of the refugees, a woman with braided brown hair, opened a small wooden chest. Blue light spilled from within: a spectral glow that didn't belong here in the dust of a ruined district, far from the shores of the mana spring.

By the time Jin had crossed the street, the vulture and the refugee with the chest were neck-deep in an argument.

"You expect me to believe this donkey shit?" The vulture plucked a glowing blue bottle from the chest and held it to the sunlight. "You must have filled these up at the spring. I'm not paying for something I can get myself."

"No touching unless you're buying," the refugee snapped. "It's special mana. Preserved. It never loses its glow."

Jin shouldered her way through the crowd and stepped between the vulture and the woman. "Where'd you find it?" That mana could have come from only one place: the ancient Road Builder ruins.

The vulture's bodyguards shifted menacingly toward Jin, but the vulture waved them back. "She's lying," he said. "I've seen a hundred counterfeits this week—mostly jewelry. Imagine trying to pass off mana from the spring as something valuable."

Jin fought down her rising temper. "She's *not* lying. I've seen preserved mana before."

"Oh?" The vulture sized her up. "You're probably in on her scheme."

That look in his eyes: dismissive, contemptuous. Had Jin ever looked at a Talentless that way? Gods, she hoped not.

Flight of the Fallen

"I don't know her," the refugee said, giving Jin a narrow-eyed stare. "But it's real. How do you think so many of us made it here from Kerina Lav? Walking through the wastes for days on foot, we should have died in droves. But our knights had plenty of these bottles. We used almost all of them on the way here."

So Kerina Lav's knights had stumbled on a set of intact Road Builder ruins, like the Temple of Makela that Jin had visited with Yi-Nereen and Faolin. And of course they hadn't shared their windfall with the other kerinas; that wasn't how things worked in the wastes. Jin understood now why the Lav-blood refugee camp was so much larger than the Tez-blood ghetto she remembered. More of them had survived their journey across the wastes, thanks to this extra resource.

She knew she shouldn't feel envious of these people just because they'd lost slightly less than her. That was absurd. But she felt a pang of resentment anyway.

The vulture tightened his grip on the bottle in his hand, an avaricious gleam entering his eyes. "How about this? I'll take the whole chest. If it's glowing in the morning, I'll pay you then. Can't be sure you're telling the truth otherwise."

"I kept inventory for the granaries in Kerina Lav," the refugee retorted. "I know a thieving rat when I see one. Give it back."

"Don't sell him anything," Jin said. The vulture shot her a murderous glare. "Take it to a courier bunkhouse. They'll give you a much better price."

"And what's in it for you?" the vulture demanded. He turned to the refugee woman and said, "Watch yourself. I think this vagrant plans to lure you down an alley and take the bottles off your corpse."

Jin didn't bristle at *vagrant*. She'd been called worse. But when one of the guards laid an insistent hand on her arm, her poorly contained temper boiled over.

"Back *off.*"

Instinctively, she tried to burn mana that wasn't there—and felt its sick, hollow absence in her gut. Instead of a shower of sparks, she thrust an empty palm in the guard's direction. The man stepped back. Then he grinned. She probably looked ridiculous.

Jin punched him.

It wasn't her best moment. She wouldn't be proud of it later. But at least her mother wasn't here to see it.

The guard bellowed and came at her with his fists. Jin surged to meet him with a kind of fierce pleasure. She wasn't usually one for scraps in the street, but after six weeks of utter shit, she was tired of being humbled and ready to humble somebody else for a change.

"Hey!" someone shouted. Jin didn't see what happened—but she heard a crash, the tinkle of bottles rolling across the ground. The vulture had tried to take advantage of the scuffle by snatching the coveted chest.

Then suddenly Jin and the guard weren't the only ones throwing fists. Angry cries filled the air. As Jin fought to pry off a pair of hands around her throat, she saw refugees pelting the vulture with pebbles. His other guard was making panicked sweeps at the air with a truncheon.

Someone hit the guard strangling Jin. He let her go. She took the opportunity to kick him in the balls.

Back when she'd been a refugee newly arrived in Kerina Sol, she'd stayed squeaky clean. She'd let people heap abuses on her head, tread all over her. As long as she and Eomma were safe, what did it matter?

Those days had ignited a fire in her belly that Jin didn't think had ever stopped burning. She had nothing to lose now. She was no one's protector these days.

Flight of the Fallen

She'd brawl until they locked her up. No difference between a cell and this prison of a walled city, not for her. Home was out in the wastes, the only place she'd ever felt free. She'd never roam there again.

The guard she'd punched had clearly had enough. He dove for Jin with a roar, catching her off guard, too slow to react in time. All the air exploded out of her lungs as she hit the ground. She couldn't breathe; his hands were on her neck again. Her vision shivered, going black.

"Get your hands off her!"

A thick arm snaked around the guard's neck, dragging him off Jin, leaving her gasping and heaving in the dirt. As oxygen poured back into her brain, she abruptly went cold. She knew that voice.

In the broad daylight of Forge District, Kadrin looked nothing like his sister. He made a tall, muscular shadow across the street while sunlight toyed with the brown curls swept across his forehead. His long robes, pale blue as the desert sky, were belted with a golden sash and thick with dust at the trailing hem. And he had the guard who'd been choking Jin in a headlock.

For a moment all Jin could do was stare—at the guard struggling and kicking in Kadrin's grasp, at the blank look on Kadrin's face. She'd never seen him look like that before. Ever.

"Kadrin," she rasped. "Kadrin! Let him go."

Kadrin loosened his grip almost at once, and the guard scrambled to his feet. Looking around, Jin realized the rest of the scuffle had already died away. The vulture and his other guard had made a hasty exit; the other refugees had scattered, save for the woman who'd been trying to sell her mana bottles. She was crouched over their glass remains, sifting through the dust. All the mana had leached into the ground.

"You didn't need to get involved," she snapped at Jin. "What do you care anyway?"

Kadrin crouched in the dirt, his chest heaving. He glanced between Jin and the woman. "I'll pay for those."

"Kadrin," Jin said, "that's not necessary—"

But Kadrin was already digging out his coin purse. Jin looked away as the money changed hands, hot with shame. This reunion was already off to a worse start than she'd ever pictured. If she could just crawl into the nearby gutter and die, that would be lovely.

There was a tiny silver lining, though. Jin had heard about the metalcrafter who'd fallen into the spring, the one whose life Yi-Nereen had saved. Last she'd heard, he hadn't yet regained consciousness—which meant Jin was the only person alive who knew what was waiting for him when he did. A life without Talent.

For now, Kadrin didn't know the truth. Which would make this reunion ever so slightly easier on Jin.

She turned her head, sick with dread, and her stomach flipped at the sight of Kadrin's face. He was watching her with a beaming smile, utterly absent of anger or grief. Like he'd never been so glad to see anyone in his life.

"So—" Jin said, at the same time that Kadrin said, "You're—"

"You first," Jin said quickly.

Her heart was pounding. If he was looking at her like that, then he truly didn't know. Eliesen hadn't told him about her Talentlessness. Good, but now what?

She hadn't been prepared for the beast of longing to rear up inside her as soon as she laid eyes on him, but there it was. Rattling her rib cage, roaring at her to go and be close to him again. To ask after Yi-Nereen.

In a city of ten thousand, it had always been only a matter of

Flight of the Fallen

time before their paths crossed. But Jin had hoped, foolishly, for more time to heal.

"You're here," Kadrin said, his voice as incongruously soft as if they were alone in a room together instead of standing on a sun-baked street in the aftermath of a brawl. "I didn't know you were in Kerina Sol. I was worried . . . we were worried you might have been in Kerina Lav."

Kerina Lav had been one of Jin's regular stops in her previous life—the one that had ended abruptly a little over a month ago.

"Luckily I wasn't," she said without meaning it. "Have you, uh— Have you been well?"

Kadrin opened his mouth and Jin waited for the answer he always gave, their call-and-response of three years of letter deliveries. *Can't complain*, he'd say, and then he'd launch into descriptions of whatever amusing thing Eliesen had done lately or what he was thinking about telling Yi-Nereen in his next letter.

"I . . . ," he said instead, and Jin froze. "I'm not sure."

Jin's mouth was dry. Like so much else lately, this was unknown territory. "What's wrong?"

Kadrin's gaze slid from Jin's off to the side, at the ground, anywhere but on her. "It wouldn't be right to burden you," he said finally. "But, Jin, I really have missed you."

Jin's heart twisted. Sometimes she hated how honest he was. "I have a few more deliveries to make. I should get going."

Oh, she was a coward. The vilest coward ever to slink through the streets of Kerina Sol. She felt split in two, one half railing at the other for going about this all wrong. For not even thanking Kadrin for pulling that asshole off her.

But Kadrin was supposed to be happy. He was getting married.

"Wait." Kadrin trotted to catch up with her as she walked away.

81

Like his sister, he had long legs. "Jin, please, can we talk? When you're free. That tea shop you like in Jade District—would you meet me there?"

Jin stared down at her empty hands. Kadrin didn't know the truth yet. But when that man Yi-Nereen had saved woke up, everyone— including Kadrin—would know exactly what had happened to Jin. The hours were slipping away until her secret was revealed. And Jin didn't have to be there to see their horror unfold; she could stay well on the periphery, safe from the immediate fallout.

And then what? Was there any reason not to give Kadrin an inch or two, let him and Reena step back into her life? Maybe she could do it—strike a balance between being their friend and guarding her own heart.

The fact that she was considering it at all was a testament to just how fucking lonely she'd been lately.

Jin turned. "How about three days from now? Sixteenth bell?"

Kadrin's eyes softened. He grinned. "That sounds lovely."

Gods, Jin hoped she wasn't making a mistake. "Then I'll see you there."

She couldn't risk staying in his presence a minute longer; Kadrin had always had an uncanny talent for bringing down her guard, making her say more than she should. It was that damned conta- gious earnestness of his.

She felt his eyes lingering on her back as she walked away. Jin swallowed her doubts and tightened her grip on the strap of her knapsack. Her throat ached; she'd have bruises there later. But bruises were nothing compared with the hollowness of these past weeks alone.

CHAPTER EIGHT

A SECRET TABLET

Observation #189: Blood transfusions only possible between individuals of like Talent. Exception: Talentless. Universal donors, can only receive from other Talentless.
Hypothesis: In event of mass catastrophe, Talentless survivors more valuable than suspected. —O

Third Age of Storms, 1st Summer, Day 74
Kerina Sol – Forge District

Jin was *alive*.

Kadrin could sing it from the ruined rooftops.

Jin wasn't dead in the wastes somewhere, flattened beneath rubble in Kerina Lav, or meat in a saurian's belly. She was alive and well and in Kerina Sol, and she'd agreed to meet him for tea.

Whatever had gone wrong between them, he would find a way to repair it. If Kadrin had failed her in some way—which seemed more than likely—he would make amends. If Jin wanted to be part of Kadrin's life again, in any small fashion that pleased her, he would take it, and if she *didn't*, well . . .

He'd weather that storm when it came. For now, no clouds could darken his sky.

Hana Lee

"Are you the Rain Lord's son?" asked a polite voice. "The volunteer?"

Kadrin blinked and came back to earth. He was still standing in the dusty street where Jin had left him. A tall man had appeared before him as if from nowhere; he must have come from one of the nearby alleys. Dark braids ridged his scalp; he had the confident stature of a knight in full plate, though he wore the same threadbare traveling clothes as the other refugees Kadrin had met.

"That's me," Kadrin said. It was unexpectedly pleasant for someone to recognize him on sight—not as "the Talentless prince," but as "the volunteer." "Do you need help with something?"

"Not me, but I know someone who does." The man studied him, smiling faintly. "I'm Celwyn. Are you free at the moment?"

It wasn't uncommon for a refugee to ask Kadrin for help other than what the checkpoints provided: extra blankets for a sick grandmother, directions to the nearest drinking hall, or—once, memorably—a backup harmony for a song of prayer. Kadrin did his best to be all things to these people who had almost nothing. It was his way of trying to make up, in a single week, for the burden he'd been all his life.

But it was certainly odd for someone who needed Kadrin's help to be so vague.

"I am," Kadrin said. "Is your friend nearby?"

"Yes—I can take you to her. Will you come with me?"

Kadrin nodded, and Celwyn turned and walked away without another word. Kadrin followed him. There was something about the way Celwyn moved that made Kadrin think his earlier impression of him as a knight wasn't so far off. But he could be a courier, too; he moved like Jin, like a sure-footed but wary animal.

84

Flight of the Fallen

Then again, everything reminded Kadrin of Jin these days. It was a sickness.

Kadrin followed Celwyn into a part of Forge District he hadn't visited recently. Like the rest of the camp, it was thick with refugees who'd claimed space on every patch of dirt that wasn't covered in rubble. But the Second Storm's hand had touched this part of the district more gently than the rest; a few buildings still stood. It was one of these buildings that Celwyn led Kadrin toward, a smithy with one wall torn away and replaced slapdash with sheets of corrugated metal.

Inside, the air smelled fragrant, floral and sweet. Kadrin's eyes took a moment to adjust to the dim. Then he stared, taken aback.

It was a garden. Flowering bushes and trees sprouted directly from the smithy's packed-earth floor. They had to be bloomwoven—there was no sunlight in here, and no space for the plants to have grown naturally. Strangely enough, Kadrin's mind produced no names for the plants he saw; strange, because—despite not being a bloomweaver—he had made himself familiar ages ago with almost everything that grew in Kerina Sol. These were specimens from Kerina Lav, then.

"I found him," Celwyn said.

Kadrin realized with a start that he and Celwyn weren't alone. A woman was standing so still among the plants that Kadrin hadn't noticed her. Even in the dim light, Kadrin noted fine wrinkles around her mouth, crow's-feet at the corners of her eyes. She was middle-aged—which, if she was Talented, meant she might be nearing the end of her half-life.

"It's an honor to meet you, young prince," she said, bowing with the vigor of a youth. "My name is Toraka."

85

"Oh, there's really no need for that." No one in Kerina Sol ever bowed to Kadrin despite his rank. It wasn't something he ever missed. "Did you grow all of this?"

Toraka dusted dirt from her hands and smiled at him. Kadrin felt tension he hadn't realized he was carrying begin to leach out of his body. Toraka's smile was kind and serene, with none of the desperate uncertainty that permeated Forge District like a fog.

"I did. Do you like them?"

"It's quite nice," Kadrin said, which was an understatement.

"You aren't like the other volunteers," Toraka said. "Kadrin, yes?" At Kadrin's nod, she continued, "Kadrin. Few of them are Sol-blood natives, I've noticed. Many must have been refugees themselves three years ago when Tez fell. None are royal."

A little frisson of shame wormed through Kadrin's belly. Not for himself, but for all the other royals whom Toraka had implicated with her observation. "My duties are much lighter than those of the other royals. I'm sure you've heard why. It gives me plenty of time to come here and help. And speaking of help"—Kadrin glanced over his shoulder at Celwyn—"what can I do for you?"

Toraka's smile faded. "I am—was—a guildmaster in Kerina Lav. Our city no longer stands, so our government is defunct, but I still speak for the survivors who came here. I meet with members of your Council on a daily basis to keep them apprised of what my people need. But among other things, there is one request they refuse to grant: an audience in the Marble Palace, before all the Lords of the High Houses."

Kadrin cocked his head. "That's odd. Why wouldn't they grant that? The Council allows petitioners."

"Only citizens of Kerina Sol may make petitions. The Council has been *kind* enough to offer an exception, but . . ." Toraka sighed.

Flight of the Fallen

"The wait would be months long, and I don't have that kind of time."

Kadrin had the familiar, niggling feeling that he'd failed to understand something.

"I'm sorry, I still don't quite follow. You said you're already meeting with members of the Council every day—can't you ask them for what you need? Why a formal audience?"

Toraka and Celwyn exchanged glances. "A secret is like a coin," Toraka said. "The more hands it passes through, the less brightly it shines." She drew closer, looking searchingly into Kadrin's eyes. "Let me put it this way: I have information to share with the Council. It's too valuable to risk giving away to a single lord. They could use it for themselves, and my people would gain nothing. But if the entire Council hears what I have to say at once, their opportunities to work against each other will be limited. They will be forced to use this information to everyone's benefit."

Ah. Kadrin swallowed. Well, Toraka certainly wasn't wrong in her estimation of the Council and its individual members. In fact, she'd managed to sum up in a handful of sentences exactly why Kadrin despised politics.

"All right," he said. "I see now. But I'm not sure how I can help. I'm afraid I've used up my share of the Council's goodwill already, on a similar problem."

"So I've heard," Toraka said. "That's why I decided to trust *you* with this information, and you alone."

Kadrin stiffened. "What? Why? Forgive me, but we hardly know each other."

"That's not quite true," Celwyn said from behind him. The man was leaning against a wall, looking casual, like a predator at rest.

"I apologize if this causes you alarm to discover," Toraka said.

"I've had Celwyn tailing you for days. He's given me accurate reports on your movements: who you speak to, what they ask of you, and—of course—your charity."

Well, that was certainly alarming. But also oddly flattering.

"Did you tail all the other Council members, too?"

"If they had come to Forge District to assist as you did, I would have." Toraka smiled again. "The fact that not a single one did told me half of what I needed to know. You yourself gave me the rest."

"All right, then." Kadrin could hear his pulse thudding in his ears. He wasn't sure if he was in danger; he might well be. But he wasn't going to walk away now. "I'm listening."

"You must tell no one what I am about to share with you. Will you give your solemn vow?"

Kadrin brought his fist to his heart. "I do so vow, in Rasvel's name."

His skin prickled. What he was doing was against temple edicts: Talentless weren't supposed to invoke Rasvel's name for vows. No contract signed by a Talentless person could be witnessed by divine will. But he had the feeling Toraka wouldn't object.

"Excellent," Toraka said. "What do you know of the First City?"

Kadrin hadn't expected to be quizzed on childhood stories. But he had a feeling Toraka had a point to make, and he didn't mind being used for it. "Let me think."

The First City was like the Lost Highway: a mythical creation of the Road Builders, a place of legends. But, Kadrin realized with sudden discomfort, the Lost Highway had turned out to be real. It led to a Road Builder laboratory hidden in the Barrens, at the top of a mountain that no longer existed. He hadn't considered what that might mean for the other stories of his youth.

"It's a city the Road Builders made for their gods," Kadrin said, choosing his words carefully. "For Rasvel, above all. No mortal was ever supposed to set foot there once it was complete. When the Road Builders betrayed the gods, the gods sent the storms to punish them. They destroyed everything the Road Builders had made except the highways—and the First City. It was a special place, too sacred to ruin, protected forever from storms."

Toraka and Celwyn exchanged glances. "Remarkably similar to our temple stories," Toraka said. "Though still full of holes and contradictions, of course."

Celwyn's jaw twitched. "What part of scripture isn't?"

Kadrin winced. "Sorry. I've only heard it secondhand. They don't allow Talentless into the temple to listen to sermons. I don't even know what the Road Builders' betrayal was supposed to be, exactly. Just that it was—well, bad."

"Oh, no," Toraka said. "I meant no slight to your recollection, Kadrin. You've heard the tale exactly as it was intended to be told. The priesthood of Kerina Lav refused to speculate on the nature of the Road Builders' betrayal. They believe that to speak of the sins of the past is to risk committing them again in the present. A sentiment they share with your High Priestess, by the sound of it—and one I could not disagree with more strongly."

Kadrin's skin was prickling. Swearing a vow in Rasvel's name was one thing; standing here while Toraka skirted the line of heresy was another. Yet again, she wasn't wrong, but that didn't mean it was a good idea to criticize the High Priestess aloud.

"In any case," Toraka went on, "I can finish the tale. The gods abandoned the First City all the same. They were too bitter to dwell there any longer. The place is known to still contain traces of divinity, and legend claims that the first mortal to tread there will assume the mantle of the gods."

Kadrin grinned despite himself. "That was always my favorite part. Those exact words: *mantle of the gods*. I always imagined it as a great big warm cloak full of stars."

Toraka laughed. "I think I did well to choose you, Kadrin."

"So you've found it, then? The First City? Is that your secret?"

Toraka's eyebrows shot up. "I didn't expect anyone in Kerina Sol to be so swift to accept the First City's existence as more than myth."

"It's a long story," Kadrin said, "but I do have my reasons for believing in legend."

"Even I wasn't so quick to believe," Celwyn said from behind them, suspicion darkening his tone. Kadrin tensed as Celwyn pulled away from the wall and stalked toward him, his face unnervingly blank. "And I'm the one who brought Toraka the tablet."

Kadrin remained still, only his eyes moving from Celwyn to Toraka. "What tablet?"

Toraka reached inside her cloak and drew out a thin stone slab. "This one."

She held it out for Kadrin to see. The slab was square, only as wide across as the span between his pinkie and thumb. It was carved from impossibly smooth, opalescent gray stone that shimmered in the daylight filtering through the smithy's cracked ceiling. Etched on its surface were characters Kadrin couldn't read, though they looked familiar. He'd seen similar script on other artifacts retrieved from the wastes, and on the walls of the ruined Temple of Makela while he and Jin were searching for Yi-Nereen.

"It's beautiful," Kadrin said. "But what does it have to do with the First City?"

Toraka stroked a line of script on the tablet and said in a clear voice, "Show me Avi'Kerina."

Flight of the Fallen

Cold blue light bloomed from the tablet's surface. And Kadrin watched, dumbstruck, as the carved lines under Toraka's finger smoothed into a featureless, blank plane, only to re-form seconds later into a different pattern: a hatching of crossed lines that snaked into a familiar shape. A map of the wasteland highways.

"What happened?" Kadrin asked hoarsely. "Did you use your Talent to do that?"

He'd seen Jin use her sparktalent to light sconces and raise a moving platform before—but Toraka wasn't sparktalented as far as Kadrin could tell, and she was already shaking her head.

"The First City's gifts are real, and they are not for the Talented alone."

Only a single point on the tablet was glowing blue now: a four-pointed star buried in the tangle of highway lines. Toraka touched the star.

"This is where it lies, deep in the Barrens. The kerinas haven't mapped the roads in that region. They're far too dangerous."

"Where did you *find* this?" Kadrin asked.

"The Guildery has long taken a special interest in Road Builder artifacts," Toraka said, sounding guarded for the first time. "Celwyn made this particular discovery: the most significant by far, but hardly the first."

The bottled mana. Of course. Kadrin still had the chest of broken bottles tucked under his arm; he doubted either Celwyn or Toraka knew what it contained. And they definitely didn't know how familiar Kadrin already was with Road Builder artifacts. Maybe when everyone in this room trusted each other a little more, he'd tell them about Mount Vetelu.

"Celwyn also discovered how to awaken the tablet," Toraka added.

Celwyn shifted in place, arms crossed, and said only, "Trial and error."

Kadrin nodded slowly. Gods, he was hopelessly out of his depth. It should be Yi-Nereen or one of the royal scholars here in his place. He'd have to convince Toraka to trust someone else, someone smarter than he was—possibly multiple someones. But that could wait.

"Avi'Kerina. Does that mean 'first city'?"

"In the language of the Road Builders," Toraka replied. "Yes."

"You obviously want to find it. So why not follow the map?"

"The Guildery voted to send an expedition as soon as we understood what the map was pointing to," Toraka said. "But that was the night of the storm."

She didn't need to specify which storm. Kadrin fought a shiver.

"Some say it was the will of the gods," Celwyn said darkly. "Rasvel's fury at those who would trespass in the place where mortals are forbidden."

"I don't believe that," Toraka said. "If it were Rasvel's will that we should not go, He would have destroyed us all. No. He destroyed Kerina Lav, but He spared our lives. It was a message—but not the one Xua's faction thought it was."

"Xua?" Kadrin echoed, feeling lost.

"Another guildmaster. He and I parted ways in the desert after the storm. Half of our people followed him to Kerina Rut." Toraka sighed. "I understood why: their ways are more similar to ours. But I believed only Kerina Sol would accept us. Time will tell which of us was right."

Kadrin looked down at the tablet again. "This *is* valuable. I hate to say it, but you were right not to show this to anyone else. Why the rush, though? It's a pain, but if the First City has survived this

Flight of the Fallen

long, it'll surely still be there when the Council grants you an audience as a petitioner."

"No, Kadrin." Toraka's voice sent a chill down Kadrin's spine. "I'm afraid there is no time to spare."

"What do you mean?"

"Rasvel destroyed Kerina Lav because it was no longer our home. We know the way to our new home: Avi'Kerina."

Toraka's words smoldered like embers, like they might burrow into Kadrin's flesh and burn him from the inside out.

"Now, for better or worse, we have brought that knowledge to Kerina Sol. So. Where do you think He will address His next message?"

CHAPTER NINE

DEVASTATION

Observation #421: Hunger decreases incidence of intelligent observations. —O

Third Age of Storms, 1st Summer, Day 74

Kerina Rut – By the Wall

It was daylight when the storm bells began to toll. Sou-Zell was in the drill yard of a Legion compound, sharpening his sidesword on a whetstone. All around him, men fell still in the middle of training bouts, faces turning as one toward the Wall. Someone near Sou-Zell muttered about *damned shieldcaster drills.*

Sou-Zell sheathed his sword. A premonition, not unlike the whispers of another mind brushing against his own, told him this wasn't another drill. The storm-drought that had ended for the rest of the wastes was about to end in Kerina Rut as well.

Another vision came to him: the refugee camp sprawled outside the kerina gates. Guildmaster Xua and his people had stood firm over the past week, refusing to enter the city if it meant abandoning their Talentless in the wastes. And the High Houses of Kerina Rut had refused to budge in turn. The royals had decided they could simply wait the refugees out; sooner or later mana thirst would force

Flight of the Fallen

Xua to bow to the High Houses' demands. It was a miracle they'd lasted this long.

Now they would be slaughtered by default, Sou-Zell realized, his blood turning cold. All of them.

The Legion compound stood in the shadow of the Wall. Sou-Zell climbed the ramparts in a daze. When he reached the summit, he expected to see the city's gate swinging open to let the refugees in. Surely the High Houses would not waste so many lives for the sake of obstinacy. There were hundreds of Lav-blood Talented out there, scores of the bloomweavers, raincallers, and shieldcasters that Kerina Rut so desperately needed.

But when he gazed over the parapet, he saw tents still littered below the Wall like a child's scattered playthings. People ran back and forth, small figures in the distance. Thin cries floated up to Sou-Zell's ears.

"Please let us in!"

"Have mercy!"

The storm bells went on ringing. Sou-Zell looked out over the wastes and saw the skies darkening in the north, in the direction of ruined Kerina Tez. A minute later came the first flash of lightning.

Any moment now, Sou-Zell thought. The gates would open.

A man in blue robes jostled past Sou-Zell without a care for whoever he might be. The shieldcasters were arriving on the rampart. The next to arrive was a woman who cast down her eyes demurely when she saw Sou-Zell. She took her place at the parapet with practiced, drilled calm.

"This is ridiculous," Sou-Zell said aloud, gaze fixed on the refugee camp.

His voice was almost drowned by the desperate shouts of the people below. They had formed a heaving mass at the nearest city gate and were beating at the metal panels with their fists. As Sou-Zell watched, a tall man with eyes burning silver marched through their ranks. A Lav-blood metalcrafter. He laid his hands on the Wall and began, slowly, to pull it apart.

For a moment, nothing happened. Sou-Zell narrowed his eyes. No one had given the order to let the refugees into the city, but would anyone stop them from entering by force?

He heard a barely audible *twang*. The metalcrafter collapsed with an arrow in his neck.

Sou-Zell's fists clenched to the point of pain. Along the Wall, archers stood with crossbows pointing down at the camp in silent warning. They *had* received orders, then.

So the High Houses had decided to make an example of the refugees. But for the eyes of whom? The pointlessness of this, the needless death. All to punish the refugees for refusing to abandon their Talentless.

The pact that was law between the kerinas forbade denying refuge to anyone during a storm, unless they were a branded exile. But the compact was dead, Sou-Zell realized in a bitter flash. Kerina Tez and Kerina Lav had fallen. Only Kerina Rut and Kerina Sol remained as signatories. By breaking the pact now, the High Houses of Rut were declaring that they feared no reprisal.

Sou-Zell wondered whether Lai-Dan had bothered to convince the other Houses to cooperate or simply made the proclamation unilaterally.

He's mad, said a voice in Sou-Zell's head, while another, colder voice argued, *No. He's perfectly sane. Kerina Rut now stands alone.*

"My lord! My lord, please!"

Sou-Zell glanced down. Directly below him stood a woman at

Flight of the Fallen

the base of the Wall. She held a swaddled babe above her head in trembling arms.

The baby wasn't making any sound. Its dust-covered face seemed half-filled with its large, blinking eyes. Sou-Zell looked into those eyes, felt his throat constrict, and looked past them at the mother. She was calling out to him, but the shrieking wind stole her voice. Clouds gathered swiftly overhead.

He remembered hanging over a screaming, dark void, his only salvation the warm hand of a Talentless prince clenched around his wrist. Sou-Zell felt the void below him now, though he stood on solid ground. He saw Kadrin's face. The vision was accompanied by a surge of shameful hate.

That *wretched* man. Sou-Zell would not bow to him any more than he would bow to Lai-Dan. But he couldn't tear his eyes from the woman below the Wall.

She was straining at her fullest height. The Wall was almost twelve spans high: there was no reaching the top. But then another woman and an older child came running to her side. The child took the baby in her arms, and the two women hoisted her up by her feet.

And now, now Sou-Zell could reach down. He hesitated for only an instant.

His fingertips brushed against the baby's swaddling cloth.

"Shield Corps!" The wind had swelled high; Sou-Zell barely heard the cry. "Raise!"

He jerked back, nearly losing his balance. A shimmering blue barrier seared the air in front of him. If he'd waited a moment longer, it would have forced him headfirst off the Wall.

Dazed, he reached out with curled fingers to touch the shield itself, something he'd never done. It was like brushing flesh, warm and pulsing. Completely solid.

And on the other side, directly in the storm's path, were the women, the child, and the baby he had almost had in his grip.

Bitterness writhed across Sou-Zell's tongue. He stood there for a long moment, motionless, his mind turning. In the absence of his ability to alter the outcome in any way, it only made sense for him to leave—to turn away and spare himself the sight of the inevitable.

He had already seen children crushed and incinerated in Guildmaster Xua's memories. Those visions were a fever dream of grief and guilt. Unreal. Stolen. Sou-Zell's now, to keep for as long as he drew breath.

He sank to his knees, resting his forehead against the parapet, and through an arrow slit he watched the storm descend upon Kerina Rut like a howling beast. It beat itself against the dome and, finding it solid, vented its wrath on the soft creatures outside the city.

It was carnage, sickening waste, and it woke an anger in Sou-Zell's belly he had never known before. A dark burning ember with a single name at its core.

Lai-Dan.

When Sou-Zell stepped into the manor, his mother was waiting for him just beyond the threshold. For a moment, he pictured her with open arms and himself falling into them, shamed and trembling and aching from his hours kneeling atop the Wall.

He didn't know the last time he'd sought her comfort like that. Perhaps he never had. His brother had always seemed to need it more, and by the time Min-Chuul was gone, Sou-Zell had lost the instinct to ask.

His gaze slid past his mother, and shock jolted through him. Falka was standing behind her.

"What's the meaning of this?" Sou-Zell demanded coldly.

Falka wasn't bound. Her stained clothes had been replaced with a beaded gown from Lady Ren's wardrobe. Her hair was combed. She was still gaunt, paper-skinned, but the moment Sou-Zell met her eyes, he knew something was different. Those eyes were clear, lucid. All traces of her madness gone.

But she wore no smirk of triumph, which surprised him. Wasn't this exactly what she must have planned—to trick Sou-Zell's elderly mother into letting her out of the wine cellar as soon as he was away? But her lips were set into a thin line. She looked guarded, watchful. Waiting to see what he would do.

"My House," Sou-Zell's mother said calmly. "Looking after guests is my purview, Sou-Zell, not yours. I'm not so far gone that you should have forgotten that."

Sou-Zell was in no state to have this argument. If Falka hadn't killed his mother and run off yet, she was hardly likely to have waited for him to do it.

"I'm going to bed," he muttered, and stalked past Falka without a second glance.

Keeping her locked up hadn't worked. Interrogating her hadn't worked. Maybe his mother was onto something.

Perhaps he'd been going about this all wrong.

PART TWO

CHAPTER TEN

THE APPRENTICE

Observation #561: Stable cycling of artificial sparks through treated
mana vital for successful sparkless magebike prototype.
Obstacle: Electricity unstable without a sparkrider's control.
Result: Frequent explosive mishap. —O

Third Age of Storms, 1st Summer, Day 75
Kerina Sol — Jade District

Kadrin opened his eyes to see a slim, dark-haired figure standing over his bed. He bolted upright, heart hammering. "Jin?"

"Interesting," came Orrin's familiar, dispassionate voice. "I assumed an insomniac would be a much lighter sleeper."

Kadrin groaned and cast himself back down upon his pillows, throwing a hand over his face. "Orrin. What in all blazing hell are you doing here? Hang on—how long have you been standing there?"

"Only one of those questions is relevant, so I'll answer that one. Though you should be able to guess the answer yourself, given what you dropped off at my doorstep yesterday."

Kadrin racked his sleep-muddled brain. *Ah*—Orrin was talking about the chest of bottled mana Kadrin had bought from that refugee woman in Forge District yesterday. He'd been at a loss over what to do with a chest containing eleven broken vials and a single intact, glowing one; in the end, he'd decided Orrin would want to take a look. But Orrin hadn't answered when Kadrin knocked on the workshop door, so Kadrin had left the chest behind with a note.

"Right. So was it useful or—?"

"Useful?" Orrin stared at him, unblinking, their eyes deep shadows of black. Kadrin imagined himself as an insect squirming under one of the odd glass lenses in Orrin's workshop. "Kadrin. My dear, sweet, innocent man. Do you know what you brought me? Is there a solitary, faint inkling in that beautiful head of yours?"

Gods, Kadrin was too tired for this. "Bottled mana. I've seen it before, in Road Builder ruins. It stays good for years. Centuries, probably." He squinted at the curtains drawn over his bedchamber window. "It's still *dark* outside. What time is it?"

"A completely irrelevant question, which I'll politely disregard. Kadrin, what you so blithely dropped off at my doorstep is none other than *the third form.* Mana that retains its power without the addition of any of the stabilizing agents that we artificers mix up to fuel magebike engines. I'm not sure I could have forgiven you if you'd known of its existence before and didn't tell me."

"Wait." Kadrin rubbed his eyes. "Are you saying—?"

"Yes," Orrin said patiently. "The third form of mana is exactly what I need to finish Renzara's prototype. *My* prototype."

"The sparkless magebike?" Kadrin sat up again, energy suddenly buzzing through his body. He was wide awake. "You can build one?"

"No."

"I thought you just said—"

"Kadrin, in your infinite wisdom, you brought me eleven broken bottles and only one that was of any use. What happened to the

Flight of the Fallen

others? And where in all of creation did you find the stuff to begin with?"

"I can get more," Kadrin said. He was already pulling his boots out from under the bed. "I'm sure the refugees have more. I'll ask Toraka."

Orrin stopped him with an outstretched palm. "When *I* ask questions, you can assume they are all extremely pertinent to the matter at hand. So I'll repeat myself and add one more: What happened to the other bottles? Where did you find the chest? And who is Toraka?"

Kadrin frowned, backtracking to make sure he didn't miss a question. "The rest of the bottles were smashed in a street fight. I bought them off a refugee who was trying to hawk them for coin. And Toraka is a guildmaster from Kerina Lav. She said that the Guildery was very interested in Road Builder artifacts. I think they must have found the bottles in a ruin like the one I've been to before."

Orrin's nose twitched. "Hmm. You're telling me that Kerina Lav had access to the third form before you or I got our hands on it. Which means their artificers have had time to experiment. I should have heard about this. The fact that I haven't is concerning."

"Why does that matter?" Kadrin tugged on his boots. "Let's just go talk to Toraka and ask."

"No." Orrin snapped their fingers decisively. "We must operate under the assumption that the artificers of Kerina Lav didn't know what they had. Perhaps the Guildery kept them in the dark. This is *our* discovery, Kadrin—yours and mine. Not Kerina Lav's. Not Renzara's."

It was difficult to level a proper glare at Orrin, given that it was so dark Kadrin could barely see them, but he did his best. "You're being ridiculous. There's no reason to keep this a secret. If it works, it will benefit everyone."

"Kadrin." Orrin perched on the edge of his bed and steepled their long, scarred fingers. "You are a prince. A Talentless one, granted, but a royal nonetheless. What am I?"

Kadrin had the feeling this was a trick question, but he was already well accustomed to playing the fool in interactions with Orrin. "An artificer. A smart but very conceited artificer, if we're being specific."

"Wrong," Orrin said. "I am an artificer's *apprentice*. Renzara never graduated me from her service, and now she never will. Before you became my sponsor—a kindness I shall never forget—not a single master artificer in Kerina Sol was willing to take me on. I was tainted with Renzara's failure. Someone even went to great pains to spread nasty rumors that my contributions were responsible for her untimely death. Hurtful and entirely untrue, but there it is. Now I have the chance to rise beyond Renzara's shadow and make every master artificer in the wastes green with envy. Would you deprive me of that pleasure, Kadrin?"

"I—"

"Keep in mind that a share of the glory is yours as well. The Talentless prince and the masterless apprentice, architects of the greatest invention since the days of Tibius Vann."

Kadrin winced. One of these days, he would have to tell Orrin that he'd actually *met* Tibius Vann and hadn't exactly come away with a glowing respect for the man.

"You make a good argument," Kadrin said. "But we just can't keep this a secret. I have to tell Toraka. Especially since she's trusted me with *her* secret."

Orrin released a long, world-weary sigh. "You know, with your looks, I would really expect you to be a great deal less honest."

Whatever *that* could mean, Kadrin didn't pursue it. "I'm sorry. But, Orrin, the faster you can finish your prototype, the better. Even if you let Toraka and the Lav-blood artificers help, the credit will still be yours."

"The faster the better?" Orrin gave him a sharp look. "Why? What do you know?"

Kadrin gave an awkward, jerky shrug. "Oh, you know. The storms. They're getting worse."

"Don't *lie* to me, Kadrin, I'm much better at it than you are, and it's painful to watch an amateur. This secret Toraka is holding over your head—it's about the storms, isn't it?"

Well, Kadrin reasoned, it was all about to come out in the open anyway. He had secured his and Toraka's Council audience for two hours after dawn. Soon the entire Council, and by extension all of Kerina Sol, would know about the First City and the pressing need to send an expedition into the Barrens.

He eyed Orrin. "I can trust you, can't I?"

Orrin offered him a small, rare smile. "Not many can. But you happen to be my favorite person in Kerina Sol by quite a long distance. So. Yes."

Kadrin shook off the warm, fluttery feelings that statement had given him, filing them away for later. Perhaps it was empty flattery, but he thought it was unlikely, given how matter-of-fact Orrin tended to be about Kadrin's faults.

"All right, then. Have you heard of the First City?"

Toraka was waiting on the broad marble steps to the Council chambers when Kadrin arrived, sweating through his silk robe. There was no one else outside the chambers except for Celwyn, who leaned against a pillar and fixed Kadrin with a piercing stare as he approached.

"You made it," Toraka said with obvious relief. "They wouldn't let me in until you arrived."

"Sorry," Kadrin panted.

Stupid Council and their stupid rules. He'd cashed in the goodwill he'd earned from Yi-Nereen's tower proposal to get Toraka this hearing in front of the Council, but of course they still wouldn't treat her with the respect she deserved; it was their way of saying Toraka's status in the leadership structure of Kerina Lav didn't matter here. She was a refugee like any other.

He led Toraka into the chambers and escorted her to a seat in the highest tier alongside the other petitioners. Celwyn came slinking in after them.

Kadrin glanced down the tiers and stiffened. His seat next to his father was occupied—not by a member of his House, but by a woman in white robes.

High Priestess Edine's profile could have been carved from granite; she was beautiful, but there wasn't a hint of softness to her. Her pale hands were folded in front of her as if she were praying. It always seemed to Kadrin that there was a bubble around her, an invisible shield people instinctively kept their distance from, the way one might avoid a cactus covered in poisonous thorns. Kadrin's father was the only one who seemed immune.

Then Edine turned her face ever so slightly in Kadrin's direction, and her cool eyes found his. Kadrin felt the chill he always did in the presence of a temple acolyte, but magnified tenfold. A Talent-

Flight of the Fallen

less under the eye of the High Priestess . . . he knew suddenly what it was like to be a beetle crawling in the relentless glare of the sun.

He sat down next to Toraka, even though the highest tier was no place for a royal's son. The servants and commoners around him tittered. An hour passed, then two. Kadrin's palms never stopped sweating, but Toraka sat as still and serene as the High Priestess.

"Next on the agenda!" It was Bloom Lord Feyrin's turn to run the Council meeting, and he looked as eager as anyone else for it to be over. "Guildmaster Toraka of Kerina Lav wishes to speak on behalf of the new arrivals."

Ears perked in interest as Toraka rose smoothly from her seat. She had all the self-possession that Kadrin had always longed for; he wondered if she'd been born with it, or if it was a skill he could learn.

"Thank you for welcoming me into your Council," Toraka said, as if she hadn't had to beg Kadrin to use his limited favor with the Council to arrange five minutes for her to speak. "First I would like to—"

"A moment, please."

Heads turned. Down in the lower tiers, High Priestess Edine remained seated, but somehow she drew every eye. Maybe it was the blazing white of her robes, such a brazenly pure color to wear in the inescapable dust of a kerina. Or else, Kadrin thought, it was because people saw something else when they looked at her: Rasvel's divine authority made flesh.

"The matter Guildmaster Toraka intends to discuss is not part of the Council's purview," Edine said. Her voice was like a silk scarf cooled in the shade. "It is religious in nature. By Kerina Sol's custom, it is my sole right to hear her petition and decide as I see fit."

Kadrin sat still, stunned. He hadn't even known such a custom existed. But he was woefully inexperienced at Council, as events kept conspiring to remind him, and judging from the expressions of the other royals, Edine wasn't making this up.

How had Edine known the nature of Toraka's secret? Did the temple employ mindreaders, as gossip would have it? Had someone been listening in on Kadrin's meeting with Toraka and Celwyn in that run-down shack in Forge District?

"No one's invoked that particular custom in decades," Shield Lord Tethris pointed out. She was looking at Edine with well-masked dislike; Kadrin only recognized it in her expression because he'd seen it directed at himself before. "Surely we need to hear out the guildmaster to know whether her petition is in the temple's jurisdiction, or ours."

Kadrin glanced at Toraka, but she was silent, her hands clasped over her stomach. He felt a pang of guilt. She had no argument against Edine because Kadrin hadn't warned her about the temple. Maybe Edine wasn't doing this because of Toraka at all, but because she was still sore about being overruled on the tower proposal.

It didn't seem in character for the High Priestess, speaker for the gods and interpreter of their wills, to hold a grudge over something so petty. But what did Kadrin know about divine law anyway? He was a Talentless.

"The temple allows her to speak," Edine said after a brief pause, which she had probably spent considering how gracious she wanted to be. "You may proceed, Guildmaster. But it will be Rasvel who judges your words, not mortal men."

Toraka smiled blandly; Kadrin couldn't tell if she was relieved. "My gratitude, High Priestess."

Titles, Kadrin thought, could just as easily sound like cutting insults if said in a certain tone of voice.

Flight of the Fallen

As Toraka began to speak, following much the same script as the speech she'd given Kadrin, he had the odd sensation he was watching himself from the outside. He'd stood where Toraka stood now, spoken eloquently and passionately about something that mattered to him deeply—and received only the blunt edge of the Council's indifference in response.

No. Not indifference. Yes, the royals listening were *pretending* to be unmoved, but from the vantage of his high seat, Kadrin saw the hands twisting in laps, the sidelong glances at their neighbors. Toraka and Edine were two candle flames in a dark room, burning tall and dignified and in utter opposition to each other. There was only so much air in the room; one of those flames would be snuffed out.

The moment Toraka finished speaking and Edine's lips curved into a smile, Kadrin knew which one it would be.

CHAPTER ELEVEN

UNFORGIVEN

Observation #374: Lightning strikes common, but genesis (formation of new mana springs) rare. Majority of new springs too small to support settlements. All kerina-scale springs fall on highway lines.
Hypothesis: Possible to predict location of future springs? —O

Third Age of Storms, 1st Summer, Day 75
Kerina Sol – House of Steel Heavens

Yi-Nereen paced the halls of the House of Steel Heavens like a trapped ghost. It was the third day of her self-imposed house arrest. The servants had begun to avoid her, as if she had a contagious illness. And perhaps she did. Her thoughts were darkening in a way they hadn't since she'd escaped Kerina Rut.

For twenty years she had been locked in a tower, suffocating in her own despair. For a single month she had been free: dizzyingly, gloriously free. Now she was trapped again—and all because she'd tried to help an innocent man.

Footsteps echoed behind her. A young servant hurried down the hallway, sleeves fluttering, breathing hard as if he'd run halfway

Flight of the Fallen

across the city. "Lady Yi-Nereen. My apologies, but do you know where the Rain Lord is?"

Yi-Nereen eyed him, wondering if he feared her. "He's at Council."

Kadrin was at Council, too, presenting Toraka's case. Yi-Nereen longed desperately to be at his side. The First City! Just the thought made her ribs ache, like she'd heard a name lost to a childhood memory. And why shouldn't it be real? The Lost Highway had been real, even if the stories had greatly exaggerated its ability to wash away the sins of those who traveled it—to Yi-Nereen's dismay.

The servant looked put out. "I see. If you see him, would you please tell him to come to his office right away?"

It was unusual for one of Kadrin's servants to make a request of Yi-Nereen, even a small one. She cocked her head. "Is something happening in the city?"

The boy hesitated. He glanced around, and Yi-Nereen waited for his obvious eagerness to win out over prudence. To her satisfaction, it took only moments.

"It's about the spring. I just heard from a runner in the Shield Lord's household that the mana level dropped again at the latest measurement. By six handspans."

Yi-Nereen stared at him, too shocked to speak. Each lunar cycle, Kerina Sol tested the depth of its mana spring and recorded the value in the temple logs. It was more formality than anything else, from what Yi-Nereen understood. A mana spring large enough to support a city would never deplete. Mana ran like blood through the veins of the entire wasteland.

She only knew of the measurements because the last one Kerina Sol had taken, one month ago, had stirred alarm as well. The spring had measured a handspan and a half lower than the cycle previous, slightly outside historical norms. And now . . .

She flashed back to standing atop Mount Vetelu, arms spread, embodying the Storm of Centuries. Stripping away Kerina Sol's defenses and descending on the mana spring like a predatory beast.

She'd stopped in time. She *thought* she'd stopped in time. She'd pulled away at the sound of Jin's voice and aborted Tibius Vann's plan to rule the wastes. But what if the damage was already done?

"My lady?" The servant's voice sounded like it came from far away. Or perhaps the hallway had lengthened, unfurling between him and Yi-Nereen like a snake.

Yi-Nereen found one of the many beautifully carved wooden benches that lined the House's hallways and sat. She tried, without much success, to breathe.

If the spring ran dry, it could only be because of what she had done.

If the spring ran dry, it meant death for an entire kerina.

Gods, her treatise. There were notes in her quarters that spelled out in damning detail everything she'd done at Tibius's command. If they were found, Yi-Nereen would surely be exiled, or worse. And wasn't it monstrous for her own safety to be the first thought to cross her mind? Wasn't *she* monstrous?

Yes. She was. But it was better to be a monster than to be a victim.

Back in her quarters, Yi-Nereen gathered her notes into a loose heap atop her writing desk and stood staring down at them. She was breathing hard. A candle flickered near at hand, but she couldn't risk starting a fire. Perhaps an ink spill?

What was she doing?

Her treatise was the reason she'd come to Kerina Sol. Everything she had learned about mana, about Talent, about storms and souls and what it meant to be born with magic running through one's veins—she had always intended to make it public one day. No scholar worth her salt carried secrets to the grave; it was the antithesis of progress, of the pursuit of knowledge Yi-Nereen had always held sacred above all else.

But she had found a home here. She had found safety. Perhaps even a family.

Haven't I done enough? a voice within her cried out. *Can't I be forgiven?*

"Yi-Nereen?"

Yi-Nereen spun around.

Eliesen stood in the open doorway to her chambers. Yi-Nereen had been so absorbed in her thoughts she hadn't heard her footsteps.

"He's awake," Eliesen said. "The metalcrafter."

Yi-Nereen had moved on instinct to block Eliesen's view of the desk with her body. She didn't know if Eliesen had noticed.

"Is he all right?"

Eliesen looked at Yi-Nereen for a long moment before answering. There was a strange light in her eyes; was it Yi-Nereen's guilty conscience, or did Eliesen look accusatory?

"No. He's Talentless."

Wind threatened to tug Yi-Nereen's veil from her face as she struggled through the streets of Kerina Sol. So much the better: the veil was a half-hearted gesture toward concealing her identity, but it wasn't working. Whispers and stares had followed her from the moment she left the House of Steel Heavens.

If her miraculous healing of the man at the spring had unsettled the people of Kerina Sol, they were in an uproar now. News was spreading faster than Yi-Nereen could walk.

She'd left the House over Eliesen's protests, heedless of the danger that awaited her in the streets. Her notes and the draft of her treatise lay untouched on her desk. None of it mattered. She had to find Jin.

This was why Jin had left. To protect Yi-Nereen from the truth at her own expense. Yi-Nereen had saved her life but stolen her power, her freedom. She'd drained away the very essence of Jin and she hadn't even known.

How terribly, awfully alone Jin must have felt all this time.

A dark knot writhed in Yi-Nereen's chest. What right did Jin have to keep this a secret? She'd robbed Yi-Nereen of the chance to even try to make things right. She'd made *herself* the victim.

Yi-Nereen had thought there was something wrong with her. Some irredeemable lack that had given Jin reason to lose all affection for her. But this wasn't something she *was*; it was something she'd done. And she could fix it—if only Jin would let her try.

Kadrin had found Jin in Forge District. So that was where Yi-Nereen would go, if she hadn't gotten turned around already. Born and raised in a tower and seldom allowed to leave, she'd never had much of a head for directions.

She stood on her toes and scanned the rows of crooked buildings and billowing canopies around her for a landmark. Perhaps she should ask someone for help getting her bearings—but the faces staring back at her from alleys, doorways, and windows looked less than friendly.

Flight of the Fallen

Yi-Nereen was alone in an unfamiliar part of a city that still considered her a stranger—a city now buzzing with rumors of her heretical abilities. She felt a sudden fierce longing for the steady presence of Teul-Kim, her old bodyguard. Then she realized she had no idea if he was still alive after her escape from Kerina Rut, and numbness washed over her.

A man stepped out from a nearby doorway and approached her. He was certainly no Teul-Kim: instead of an elegant robe belted at the waist, he wore a stained smock and sleeves rolled up to the elbow to reveal work-blackened hands.

"What are you doing here, Princess?" His voice was harsh. "Go back to the Rain Lord's House. We don't need any more misfortune in our district."

Yi-Nereen had no idea what to say. Should she apologize? Ignore him?

"I think I'm lost."

The man's mouth twisted. "What *are* you? How could someone do what you did?"

"Isn't it obvious?" called another voice. Yi-Nereen looked up to see a gangly girl perched on a rooftop, staring down at her. "It's like the High Priestess says. The princess is Makela made flesh. The Herald of the One Who Takes."

"What?" Yi-Nereen asked, stunned.

She'd had no idea the High Priestess was giving sermons about her. Nor that Edine had cast her in the role of Makela's Herald, a figure as ancient as any of the stories of the Lost Highway or the First City. Utterly ridiculous—yet Yi-Nereen felt her breath stolen by the fact that, actually, it made *sense*.

She'd always secretly wondered if her family's ability to siphon was a gift from Makela, the Talent Thief, in spite of her father's claims to the contrary. The prophecies that foretold the end of the world always spoke of storms and devastation and the gods imbuing mortal heralds with their power so they might battle one another for a claim to the next world.

Now there could be no doubt. Yi-Nereen could siphon not just mana or life, but Talent itself. Even if she wasn't Makela's Herald, these powers could have only one source.

"The High Priestess warned us about the tower," said someone else. "She warned us that sending Talentless into the sacred waters would anger the gods."

"We invited Makela into our hearts! Into our city!"

"You need the tower," Yi-Nereen said helplessly. "The storms will destroy the city otherwise. Please, I—"

"And did you come to save us?" a new voice asked. "Or deliver us into destruction?"

Yi-Nereen's heart plummeted at the sight of the woman walking toward her. Sofia. The third reserve from Orchard District, the one who'd shoved past Yi-Nereen and taken her place at the parapet during the last storm.

"Brisen died because you left your post," Sofia said bitterly. "His heart couldn't take the strain. And you know what? Before you arrived, I'd only seen lightning like this once. During the Storm of Centuries."

Yi-Nereen was struck voiceless. How could she argue? They were right. The storm. The waning spring. Jin. The fallen metalcrafter.

It was all her fault.

Doors opened along the street. People who'd been watching from windows strode onto the road, emboldened by the growing clamor. Yi-Nereen couldn't even hear individual voices anymore. They surrounded her, a heaving mass of angry, accusatory faces.

Flight of the Fallen

This was a nightmare. At any moment, Jin would appear in the crowd, and Yi-Nereen would finally know what she wanted.

Her Talent. And Yi-Nereen would give it back, whatever it cost.

A hand touched her veil. Ripped it away. After that first touch came dozens more. Fingers scratching at her skin, tearing at her hair, her clothes.

This *wasn't* a dream. No one ever touched Yi-Nereen in her dreams.

She burned mana on instinct. A shield flared around her, repulsing those who were nearest. People who'd been touching her screamed—in fear, Yi-Nereen thought at first. But then she realized they were shrieks of pain.

Inside the pulsing shelter of her shield, she looked down at the ground. There was *blood* on the cobblestones. And— And pieces of flesh in sickeningly familiar shapes.

Severed fingers.

What in Rasvel's name—the *metalcrafter*. She remembered the sensation she'd felt right after siphoning the man. Like she could mold her shield, use it to form a cutting edge instead of a barrier. She'd forgotten.

Now she felt that rush of power again, like it had never truly left her. But instead of giddy vitality, it filled her with horror.

What was she becoming?

The mob resorted to pelting her shield with rocks and shoes and all manner of projectiles. Their voices roared like thunder. Nothing compared with the force of a storm, yet Yi-Nereen almost let her shield fall.

Being torn apart was no less than what she deserved.

Through the translucent blue shimmer, she saw the crowd part. A tall, broad-shouldered man was forcing his way through. Kadrin?

No—it was someone Yi-Nereen didn't recognize. A dark-skinned man with braids and a strong, sure stride. Behind him, farther down the road, waited a woman with silver hair.

The man leaned in close to Yi-Nereen's shield, his mouth almost touching the barrier. "Come with me, Princess." His voice was distorted. "I'll take you somewhere safe. My name is Celwyn."

Yi-Nereen didn't want to be safe. She just wanted Kadrin and Jin. She wanted Jin to curse her, forgive her, slap her, kiss her. She wanted Kadrin to hold her and promise a future where everything was healed, fixed. She'd never let herself want anything so much.

But she'd have to do without them both.

The crowd raged on. People were beating Celwyn now, trying to drag him away from her shield, but he weathered it like a tower in the wind. His dark eyes were fixed on hers. And, for only a moment, Yi-Nereen thought: *Do I know you?*

Then the feeling passed, and she was sure she'd never seen him before.

"All right," she said. "I'll come."

CHAPTER TWELVE

A REUNION

Observation #65: Saurians never observed eating wasteland flora.
An anti-observation, if you will. No other obvious food sources.
Hypothesis: Saurians not a form of animal life. Plant?
Photosynthesis a possibility? —O

Third Age of Storms, 1st Summer, Day 76
Kerina Sol – The Spring

J in crouched behind a cart ten paces from the bank of the mana spring. She watched the pale shapes of the guards moving along the shore under the moonlight. The market square at her back was dark and quiet, devoid of movement. The High Priestess had declared a curfew.

Edine had also declared strict rationing of mana until the spring's levels returned to normal. Hence the guards posted at the spring. Jin had spotted them earlier when she'd escorted a group of refugees to collect their rationed mana; she'd been disturbed to realize they weren't reassigned metalcrafter guards, but temple acolytes, garbed in white hooded robes and hemp-rope belts.

Yesterday's temple proclamation had forbidden nonessential use of Talent. Repairs in Forge and Curing were on pause. No bloomweavers sold flowers in the marketplace anymore; they were either working in the orchards or not at all. Wherever it was possible for a Talentless to do the work of a Talented, even if it was ten times slower, the temple commanded it.

But even Jin could see the problem: for a Talented, even moving and breathing burned mana at a slow, constant rate. So if Kerina Sol's mana spring had somehow stopped replenishing itself from the great well below the wastes, they were all living on borrowed time.

Somehow, that concerned Jin less than the fact that the temple had seemingly commandeered Kerina Sol's governance from the Council, taking over rule of the city in the span of a single day.

It seemed far-fetched to Jin that anyone would try to steal mana one day into the crisis. No one would be that desperate yet. But clearly Edine wasn't taking any chances.

This is stupid, Jin reminded herself. *A stupid, stupid idea.* The latest in a long dynasty of stupid ideas.

She'd tried to talk herself out of it. But her mind couldn't let go of a memory: floating in the mana spring at Mount Vetelu, drifting between life and death. That massive saurian swimming through the blue.

She'd dreamed of it almost every night since.

Jin didn't have much faith in the gods. She'd never believed, like some people did, in a planetary consciousness or a divine presence that could be tasted in mana. Mana was the thing that made Jin's bike run and her sparks fly. But if recent events had taught her anything, it was that what she didn't know about the world could fill a library—and then some.

There.

She'd watched the guards long enough to spot a gap in the patrolling pattern. This would work if she was quick.

Go.

Jin darted forward. She didn't take a breath until she was splashing into the shallows of the mana spring. Then a light swung toward her—and she saw, for a harrowing second, the ghostly figure of an acolyte glancing in her direction.

Fuck.

No time to back out now. Jin sucked air and dove under the surface.

If she hadn't been certain she was Talentless, this moment would have been proof. Once, mana had felt unlike anything else: hot and cold at the same time, an electrifying shock that sank deep into her skin and bones and blood. It was life—but taken too far, it was death.

Now it felt like nothing. Like sinking into a bath, but cooler. If there was a planetary consciousness, Jin wasn't part of it anymore. If the gods lived in mana, they viewed Jin as no better than a rock or a stray grain of sand.

Jin opened her eyes. It was night, but down here the whole world glowed soft blue. She floated in perfect stasis, neither rising nor falling.

The mana was opaque. It gave the impression that it filled the whole world and stretched into nothingness. Holding her breath, Jin turned her head, searching for signs of movement—for a glimpse of a rippling, patterned back.

Nothing.

Did she have to be dying? Had it all been a hallucination? The mana saurian had appeared to her on two occasions, and on the first she'd been very much alive and hale. But no one else had seen anything. Not Kadrin, who was Talentless, and not that prick Sou-Zell, though he'd probably lied.

Why would she have dreamed of the mana saurian every night if it refused to appear to her now? Why did Screech keep turning up to save her life if he was really just a dumb beast and their bond meant nothing?

Who was Jin to think she was special anyway?

She'd just always been in the wrong place at the wrong time.

Chest burning, she kicked and rose to the surface—only to immediately submerge again. There was an acolyte kneeling beside the spring, not six paces off. Maybe they were checking the depth of the mana, or perhaps they'd heard a splash.

Jin couldn't stay down here forever. Fortunately there was cover in the spring: the partially built skeleton of Yi-Nereen's tower, hunched in the mist. The High Priestess had ordered construction halted, of course. She probably meant to disassemble it after the crisis, but in the meantime Talent couldn't be spared.

Jin hated the idea of Yi-Nereen's hard work amounting to nothing. But part of her was relieved, too. She'd heard the rumors in tavern after tavern: people thought the tower was the reason the spring had stopped producing.

She'd heard less flattering things said about Yi-Nereen, too—and she had the bruises to prove it.

Saurian shit. Makela's Herald. Even when Jin had been allowed to attend sermons, she'd never believed those stories.

Jin propelled herself through the mana in long, smooth strokes. It was easier than swimming through water, like she sometimes did in the bathhouse. She didn't have to worry about sinking or bobbing to the surface. But she couldn't see where she was going, and because the mana was half gas, half liquid, some of it flowed into her nose and down her throat as she swam, tasting of nothing.

Finally her questing hand hit stone. She'd reached the tower's

Flight of the Fallen

foundation, a pyramid of quarried blocks that rested on the bottom of the spring. Jin pulled herself up by her fingertips until her face broke the surface.

Metal struts rose up before her, a shadowy structure that formed a ring and ended in a jagged, unfinished crown far above Jin's head. She found a gap in the struts and pulled herself into the tower's heart. Now she was out of sight of the bank. If she climbed up into the supports, she could find a place to watch the patrols, figure out their pattern, and find another chance to slip by.

Above her, in the circular opening of the tower's crown, the moon shone down. And . . . Jin squinted in confusion, treading mana.

There was someone up there. A person, clinging to the precarious supports at the top of the tower. A figure in a dark, flowing gown.

Yi-Nereen.

Jin was hallucinating again—the wrong kind. Yi-Nereen couldn't be out here in the mana spring at night, having climbed her own unfinished tower. Why would she do that?

Then a dark thought struck Jin, possibly the darkest she'd ever had, and she opened her mouth to scream Yi-Nereen's name.

In that same moment, Yi-Nereen let go of the supports and fell.

The sound that came from Jin wasn't a name at all, but a strangled, wordless cry. There was nothing, *nothing*, she could do. She couldn't catch Yi-Nereen. Couldn't stop her from plummeting into the mana spring to her certain death. She could only watch.

Watch as a shield bloomed around Yi-Nereen, a perfect blue bubble, and her descent slowed until she was suspended in midair.

Jin had forgotten to keep treading mana. Gas and liquid rushed into her mouth as she slipped beneath the surface. Spluttering, she rose again and hauled herself halfway onto one of the platforms built inside the tower ring.

This was impossible. Shieldcasters couldn't use their shields to *fly*. But when she looked up, Yi-Nereen was still floating there.

Jin caught sight of Yi-Nereen's face; she looked almost as shocked as Jin felt.

"Jin?"

"Gods, Jin." Yi-Nereen dragged her fingers over her face, smearing black lines of galena down her cheeks. "I don't even know where to begin."

They were sitting, side by side, on one of the rickety platforms inside the half-built tower. There wasn't a great deal of room. Jin could feel the heat of Yi-Nereen's body beside hers, a burning line all the way from shoulder to knee. She could smell Yi-Nereen's perfume; apparently she still favored sandalwood. Maddening, all of it. This wasn't quite a dream *or* a nightmare, but something far more visceral and frightening.

"What are you doing here?" Jin could think of nothing else to ask. "You weren't trying to—?"

"Practicing," Yi-Nereen said, too quickly. "I wanted to see if I could."

That wasn't an answer to Jin's unasked question—and yet it was. Yi-Nereen hadn't known her shield would work like that. Hadn't known, but she'd still jumped.

A gust of wind blew a lock of Yi-Nereen's dark, fragrant hair into Jin's face.

"Sorry," Yi-Nereen said. Her hand brushed Jin's cheek. A fleet-

Flight of the Fallen

ing touch, just enough to gather her hair away from Jin's face, but a sweet ache lingered on Jin's skin like sunburn. "I'm sorry," Yi-Nereen repeated, her voice barely more than a whisper, and when Jin turned her head she saw that Yi-Nereen was crying.

Jin's hands clenched in her lap. "You didn't know." Some deep, twisted part of her loved the sight of those tears glistening on Yi-Nereen's cheeks. She'd never consciously wanted anyone to weep for her. But now that someone was, she felt real again. Loved.

"All this time." Yi-Nereen's breath hitched. "You were *alone*, and I— What I've done to you, Jin, I can't ever . . . I'm so furious you never told me. But at the same time, I understand completely. I've never given you a single reason to trust me, have I?"

"You saved me." Jin's throat hurt; it was hard to get the words out. "And I would have let you. I would have said yes."

She didn't know if it was true. Death or Talentlessness—it should be an easy choice, but somehow it wasn't. Not when everything Jin knew about herself was wrapped up in her Talent and what she could do with it. Being a sparkrider had given her freedom, made it possible for her to save her mother, to bring Yi-Nereen and Kadrin together.

She didn't know what she *was* now. But that wasn't Yi-Nereen's fault.

Yi-Nereen made a gasping noise that was part sob, part laugh. "Jin, you pretty fool, don't you realize? You saved me first. I'm not talking about when you brought me out of Kerina Rut. I would have been dead long, long before that, if not for your letters."

"They weren't my letters," Jin protested, heart hammering. "They were Kadrin's."

"And you were the one who brought them. Recited them to me. Not only that—you forced me to listen."

Jin remembered. It had been three years, but few of her memories were clearer than the first handful of times she'd met Yi-Nereen. The princess had almost turned her away the second time, Kadrin's letter still sealed and unread, until Jin had stumbled onto those magic words: *He's been waiting for you all this time.*

She'd been thinking only of her coin. Kadrin had paid her well to deliver the first two letters, and the thought of a consistent income at last was too tempting to pass up. Selfish from the very start. And Yi-Nereen thought *she* was the one who couldn't be trusted?

"It's not . . ." Jin swallowed, considered her words carefully. "It's not a contest. Which of us owes the other more, I mean. Who saved who how many times. It's not about debts. I knew you wouldn't see it that way." Damn—that sounded like an accusation. "That's why I left. Not because I blamed you, but because I couldn't watch you blame yourself."

"It drives me absolutely mad," Yi-Nereen said with a deep shudder, "how noble you are. Both of you."

"You have completely the wrong idea about me, but you're right about Kadrin."

"I can't marry him." The words emerged from Yi-Nereen in a desolate rush. "I *love* him, Jin, gods I do, just as much as—as anything, but I simply can't. I haven't been able to tell him."

"Why not?" Jin's heart was in her mouth. The world was falling down around her with every word Yi-Nereen spoke. *No, this can't be true.* "It's not me, is it?"

"No. And yes. Rasvel help me." Yi-Nereen dragged in a shaking breath. "I'm not so foolish as to think I deserve you both. It isn't even that. It's children. *Heirs.* I don't want to be a mother, Jin. I think I'd rather die."

Jin sat still, stunned. She shouldn't have been surprised; hadn't

Yi-Nereen told her as much, the day before they'd fled Kerina Rut together? But Jin had always supposed her reservations had everything to do with her unwanted marriage and the horrors of being a childbearing woman in Kerina Rut. *My daughters will be used as broodmares, and my sons will be taught to control their sisters*, she'd said. But Jin had thought Yi-Nereen would feel differently in Kerina Sol. With Kadrin.

"No one will force you," Jin said. "Will they?"

Yi-Nereen laughed harshly. "I won't be killed or exiled, no. But the conditions under which the temple will bless a marriage between a Talented and Talentless are quite clear. *Every effort must be made*. It'll be annulled otherwise."

"Plenty of people love each other without getting the temple involved," Jin said. "If you told Kadrin how you felt—"

"I know," Yi-Nereen said with a ragged sigh. "You must think I'm awful for stringing him along like this. But you can't think any less of me than I do myself."

"That *might* be true," Jin said, frowning hard. "But hang on—"

"Look." Yi-Nereen sniffed. "I meant to beg for your forgiveness and here I am, confessing even more of my sins. I thought I'd run out of ways to feel sorry for myself. But no matter what I do, I hurt someone. You. Kadrin. Faolin. That poor metalcrafter. Those people yesterday."

"I heard," Jin said. She kept her voice neutral, though the horror of what she'd *actually* heard still coiled deep in her veins. Jin might be one of a handful of people in Kerina Sol who didn't believe Yi-Nereen was a demon sent by Makela to usher in the end of days, and still the secondhand description of those severed fingers on the ground had stolen her breath. "But I know none of it is your fault."

Useless words. It didn't matter if it was Yi-Nereen's fault or not.

129

Jin happened to know a thing or two about guilt, and it was never that easy.

"Too much is happening," Yi-Nereen said, as if Jin hadn't spoken. "And it's happening too quickly. I thought I would have more time."

"Time for what?"

"To do what I came to Kerina Sol to do. To persuade the temple and the High Houses to repair the bloodlines by changing the way marriages are arranged. That won't work fast enough, I know that now. It's already too late for Kerina Lav. I don't even know anymore if a stronger shield is enough to keep a kerina safe." Yi-Nereen made a strangled sound of frustration. "I don't know how to keep everyone safe."

"Who says that's your job? You aren't the Council."

But that sentiment was hollow, and Jin knew it. By all appearances, the Council wasn't even in charge of Kerina Sol anymore. The temple was, and Jin knew where that led. All it had taken was a brutal storm and a six-handspan drop in the spring, and Jin was seeing Kerina Tez fall all over again.

No matter how many shrines to the Talent Thief the temple in Kerina Tez had destroyed or how many Talentless women they abducted in the night, they'd only hastened their city's destruction.

Jin had gotten herself and Eomma out in time. But now? She had nowhere to go, no way to get there, and far too many people to save.

"No." Yi-Nereen stared straight ahead into the darkness, her face carved from stone. "I'm not. But I can't give up. No matter how terrible things become, I'll do what I can. What I must."

I know, Jin almost said. Yi-Nereen would never stop trying to fix what couldn't be fixed. She was a royal, and more worthy of the

Flight of the Fallen

title than anyone else Jin knew, save one. That was why she was so goddamn impossible. Why Jin was still in love with her.

Yi-Nereen didn't look at Jin, but her voice quavered as she said, "It was so much harder after you left."

"Never again," Jin said.

Technically it wasn't a promise. You only needed to make a promise, Jin thought, if there was a chance you might break it. But what she'd just said was something she couldn't break if she tried, any more than she could grow wings and soar through the sky.

It didn't matter that she lacked a bike or anyplace to go. She could have her Talent and the fastest bike in the wastes, and she still wouldn't step an inch from Kerina Sol.

Not while the people she loved were still here. Not while they needed her.

CHAPTER THIRTEEN

HOUSE IN DECLINE

Observation #460: Twinblessed more common in failing bloodlines (high rates of stillbirth, Talentless birth incidence of 1 in 5 or higher).
Supplemental observation: Twinblessed generally less powerful than single-Talented counterparts.
Hypothesis: Twinblessed and Talentless both symptoms of bloodline degeneration. —O

Third Age of Storms, 1st Summer, Day 76
Kerina Rut – Manor of Hushed Whispers

Two days had passed since Sou-Zell had returned home to find Falka a free woman in his manor, unchained and dressed in his mother's clothes. It still gave him a cold shock to walk into his dining room in the morning and see her sitting at his marble-inlaid table, eating chicken porridge across from his mother.

For a moment, no one spoke. Sou-Zell began to simmer. Who did Falka think she was, taking breakfast in his house like she wasn't a degenerate criminal? The only reason he hadn't thrown her out in the streets was because he couldn't risk Lai-Dan getting his hands on her.

Then he glanced at his mother's bowl. It was half-empty.

Flight of the Fallen

"You're eating," Sou-Zell said.

For two weeks, he'd watched helplessly as his mother's skin hung looser on her bones, eyes sinking into her skull, all the unmistakable signs of starvation as she refused to eat, even when Sou-Zell or one of the few servants he'd kept on coaxed her through each meal. Now a burden he hadn't noticed lifted from his shoulders.

Lady Ren pursed her lips, like she always did when Sou-Zell drew attention to her infirmities. "Sit down and eat, Sou-Zell. You look famished."

Sou-Zell glanced at Falka. It was only half a bowl of porridge. Perhaps it was a trick, intended to lower his guard.

Cautiously, he sat. A covered tray waited for him on the table. These days, his staff weren't paid enough to remain in the manor all day; they cleaned, cooked meals, and left them waiting while they went to other jobs across the city.

"So," Lady Ren said conversationally. "Are you ready to explain why you were keeping this young woman locked in our cellar? I've heard her side of the story already."

"Is that so?" Sou-Zell asked. "And what did she tell you?"

"That you were fool enough to empty our House's vaults in payment for her to retrieve your lost bride. That you failed to predict she would betray you. That you came after her in revenge, together with a Talentless prince of Sol and a woman courier. That when all was said and done, you locked her up and interrogated her for weeks in search of heretical knowledge."

It was a thorough and shockingly honest accounting. Sou-Zell was left momentarily speechless. Finally he gathered himself and said, "You shouldn't have spoken to her."

"I don't need permission to speak to a guest in my own home."

Falka was dangerous, and Lady Ren was frail. "That's not what I—"

133

"Oh, shut up, Sou-Zell." Falka splayed her elbows on the table like a pale spider. "You'll never win an argument with your own mother. Believe me, I've tried."

Sou-Zell's blood ran hot again. "How dare you."

"Just offering my advice." Falka shrugged.

She sounded like herself. Insolent, crude, everything Sou-Zell had been raised to despise in a woman. And yet . . . Sou-Zell glanced at his mother, noting the tiny smile on her face. Falka had charmed Lady Ren somehow, despite being her polar opposite.

It would do no good to fly into a rage at his own table. This was Sou-Zell's House, his territory. He would make Falka understand his authority.

"Tell me," he said. "Why did you maintain that ruse of madness for so long? You almost brought disaster on both our heads."

Falka sipped tea. "Who says it was a ruse?"

She was a good liar. But Sou-Zell was a skilled reader of people even without his gifts. He heard the too-casual drawl of her voice, saw the twitch of her fingers on the cup she held.

Falka was afraid. Afraid of him, or of the madness that might claim her again? Surely she wasn't aware of the true danger that loomed over them both: the towering shadow of Lai-Dan.

It was time for that to change.

"You should know you aren't safe here." Sou-Zell watched Falka's expression. "Princess Yi-Nereen's father knows who you are. He may even suspect the nature of the information I've attempted to extract from you. Wherever you go in Kerina Rut, he'll find you."

"Then I'll leave the city." Too casual still, a veneer of carelessness that would crack if Sou-Zell tested his weight against it. "All I need is a magebike. Would you stop me?"

Yes.

"No," Sou-Zell said after a moment.

He needed her. But she was still here because she must need him, too. Why?

"Forgive my son's manners," Lady Ren said coldly. "I'm sure I raised him better than this."

Falka smiled. "I'm sure you did."

That smile—it made Sou-Zell's breath catch. Not because Falka was beautiful; she was repulsive inside and out, with her sneering eyes and waxy skin. But she looked like a different person when she smiled at Sou-Zell's mother. Like a real, *human* person. Just for a heartbeat.

Was *that* why she'd stayed? Could it be so simple?

It had been years since three people had sat together and eaten a meal in this room, but suddenly Sou-Zell was right back there in his memory, watching his mother laugh and half-heartedly scold Min-Chuul for an off-color joke he'd made.

Sou-Zell shook away the memory, disturbed.

"Now, Falka, you've barely eaten," Lady Ren said. "Don't tell me . . ."

Sou-Zell waited for her to finish her sentence, but the rest of the words never came. He turned his head in alarm. "Eomma?"

His mother sat stiff and straight-backed in her chair, her jaw slack, staring at nothing. Sou-Zell took it in. The moment stretched into eternity. Then he saw her arm beginning to slide off the table, her body slowly pitching sideways, and time unfroze.

He and Falka reached her side at once. Sou-Zell eased his mother from her chair, lowering her gently to the floor. His heart beat an off-tempo rhythm against his ribs. Sweat slicked every inch of his skin.

He had never been less in control.

"Eomma," he rasped, touching her neck to take her pulse. It was faint against his fingers. He transferred her weight to his lap and realized that strands of her hair were catching on his clothes, separating from her head like they were hardly attached.

She was so light—she felt hollow. Half a bowl of porridge hardly made a difference in the end.

"Tell me what to do, Sou-Zell," Falka said. Her voice sounded peculiar, though Sou-Zell barely noticed. Only later would he realize that it was the first time she'd ever said his name without condescension dripping from every syllable.

"Mana-cigs. There's a pack—on the table next to the door."

In no time at all Falka was back, pressing the small paper carton into his hands. Sou-Zell took out a mana-cig and lit it with a shaky snap of his fingers. He sucked in a mouthful of cold, tingling mana-smoke, bent down, and blew the smoke into his mother's nose.

Lady Ren's body convulsed. A cough tore from her throat, and for a second Sou-Zell thought she was conscious again. But then she choked, gasped for air, and went limp. Hands shaking, Sou-Zell took her pulse again. It hadn't changed.

"How long?" Falka asked quietly.

Falka shouldn't be here in this intimate, dreadful moment—but Sou-Zell himself had brought her here, into his House. She'd smiled at his mother; they had become friends. He couldn't make sense of any of it.

"About a month," he said at last. "Mana-cigs were the last source she could handle."

"Then she has about a week left," Falka said.

Sou-Zell didn't ask how she knew. Words were unnecessary; he had already guessed from the moment he'd seen that smile. How strange it was that he and this woman he despised were bound in this way. How utterly wretched.

Still, he couldn't bring himself to send her away.

Making his way through the crowded, dirty streets of the Sub-Ring, Sou-Zell found his destination quickly: a sprawling, dilapidated complex of shanties surrounding an inner courtyard. All the outer windows were draped in faded red cloth. Sou-Zell wasted no time lingering outside. He pushed through a curtain of beaded strings and entered the inner courtyard.

Bodies lay everywhere, along raised verandas and in the bare dirt, as if Sou-Zell had entered a scene of bloodless carnage. But the bodies were alive. Some of them moaned; others lay quietly and twitched. The air was thick and cloying with incense. Sou-Zell was sure to reek of it long after he left.

He moved slowly through the courtyard, scanning faces. It would be useless to burn mana here; he'd simply be overwhelmed by the addled thoughts of the drug users around him. But it wasn't long before he saw a familiar maroon robe, tattered and stained.

"Min-Chuul," Sou-Zell said.

His younger brother rolled over at the sound of his name, and Sou-Zell grimaced. Min-Chuul's pupils were blown wide, his skin coated in a thin sheen of sweat. He was high, which would make this conversation unpleasant.

Yet when he spoke, Min-Chuul sounded lucid, his voice bright. "Elder brother! How kind of you to visit." He patted a straw mat beside himself. "Would you like to sit?"

Sou-Zell's skin crawled. He hated this place, hated the people here, hated his own brother for the choice he'd made years ago at Sou-Zell's ultimatum: either give up his habit, or leave the manor for good.

Min-Chuul had chosen to leave. And in some ways, it was better. Their mother didn't stay up anymore, waiting for him to come home. She no longer had to bear the shame of a younger son who not only lacked Talent, but spent his time with the dregs of society, getting high to forget the pointlessness of his life.

"Eomma is dying," Sou-Zell said. He wanted to see the words strike his useless younger brother like a knife. But to his frustration, he heard his *own* pain trembling in his voice.

Min-Chuul was silent for a moment, though that damned smile stayed on his face like it was stuck there. "What else is new?" he asked eventually. "She was dying a month ago."

"It means that you should be a dutiful son for once in your life and come say farewell."

"A dutiful son?" Min-Chuul's smile only widened, until Sou-Zell could see nearly all of his teeth. "Like you? The dutiful son who is obsessed with restoring a legacy that was already bones and dust before you were born? The son who was so resentful about missing his chance to be a commander in the Knight Legion that he vowed to claw his way to royalty instead? I've had to find satisfaction in a meaningless life, elder brother. It looks like I learned my lesson before you did."

They were only words. Sou-Zell had heard them all before. Instead of the burning desire he'd once had to kick his brother in those gleaming teeth, he felt only the dullest flicker of resentment. "Will you come see her?"

"Better for both of us if I don't," Min-Chuul said. "Better to remember each other the way we were when we last met. Hopefully Mother is too far gone to remember the screaming match we had back then."

Sou-Zell was silent. He would never come to this place again. Never see Min-Chuul again. After all these long, bitter years, he had simply forgotten how to care about his brother. It should have been a relief, but still he felt nothing.

As he walked away, Min-Chuul called after him.

"I heard about the people who died outside the Wall. Is that your idea of power, Sou-Zell? To decide who deserves to live and die?"

The question hung in the air between them alongside the stench of incense and stale vomit. Sou-Zell stepped over an unconscious body and left the courtyard without giving his brother an answer.

At the manor, Sou-Zell found Falka standing in the music room. Surrounded by cases draped in white cloth, she gazed up at a painting of Lady Ren playing the harp.

Sou-Zell stalked up behind her. She turned, and in a moment he had her pinned to the wall beside the painting, his forearm pressed into her throat.

"Tell me," he said, voice a cold snarl. "Tell me how to transplant Talent."

Falka's nails dug into his arm, though Sou-Zell hardly felt the pain. He loosened his grip a little so she could breathe and speak.

"It won't help her," Falka gasped.

"Don't lie to me."

Sou-Zell curled his free hand into a fist. Part of him reveled in the uncertainty of what he would do next. Falka's madness had passed. He no longer had to feel any guilt about striking her, because she would surely give as good as she got. This woman had deceived him, humiliated him, kept from him answers he desperately needed—he had every right to hurt her.

That was the last thought he had before Falka made a swift, sharp jab to the sensitive place under his armpit. Sou-Zell's arm fell back from her throat to defend himself, but before he could draw his knife, Falka kicked him in the knee—*hard.*

He went down with a strangled yell, and in a moment Falka was on top of him, straddling him with his own knife at his throat.

"You still have a magebike, don't you, Lord Sparkrider?" Her breath was hot on his face; her eyes gleamed like embers. "Do you keep it around here somewhere? I could use a ride."

"You'll never make it out of the city."

"Jin-Lu did. And with precious cargo, to boot." Falka leaned down, the knife edge pressing into his neck, until she and Sou-Zell were cheek to cheek. The touch of her skin made him shudder. It was worse than the smell of that courtyard full of moaning addicts; it was wrong, profane, for a Talentless-born woman to be so near to him. "I'm going to ask you an important question now, so listen closely. *Is she alive?*"

"The courier?" Sou-Zell squirmed, but he could move only so much without cutting himself on the blade. "Yes. They took her back with them—Yi-Nereen and that prince."

Abruptly, Falka drew back. A cascade of expressions tumbled across her face, beginning with relief and ending in a sort of grim satisfaction. "I saw her go into the spring. So Yi-Nereen pulled her out—and did as her father taught her."

As furious as Sou-Zell was to admit it, he couldn't see a way out of his current position without risking a slashed throat. Even though Falka was smaller and weaker than him, she'd caught him off guard. He'd underestimated her a second time. There wouldn't be a third.

"I wasn't lying," Falka said. "Transplanting Talent won't help your mother. She's already Talented, so all the procedure would do is augment her abilities, increasing her dependency on mana. She would only die more quickly."

He wanted to call her a liar again. But part of him knew that she was telling the truth. Sou-Zell felt something inside him flicker and die.

"Besides, I can't do it. I don't have the equipment. All of it got destroyed along with Mount Vetelu and that bastard Tibius Vann."

Sou-Zell blinked. Tibius Vann had been at Mount Vetelu? He'd had no idea. He had assumed Falka was the leader of her bandits, the mastermind. But now it made sense. She could never have learned all of these secrets on her own without the help of a smarter, more competent man.

Falka licked her lips. "How badly do you want to save your mother's life?"

Sou-Zell considered the question. In the end, it seemed pointless to lie to someone who had been in the dining room that morning, who had seen him trembling while he held his dying mother in his lap.

"Badly."

"Her Talent is what's killing her," Falka said. "Logically, if you take that away, she'll live a long and healthy life—and die Talentless."

Sou-Zell scoffed reflexively, and the knife edge stung his neck. He was probably bleeding, but that didn't matter. "Impossible. And blasphemous."

"It's not impossible, and blasphemy seems a small price to pay for her life." Falka looked at him coldly, without a trace of her usual mocking grin. "If I'd had the chance to make that trade, I would have done it in a heartbeat. So don't whine to me about the cost, Sou-Zell. What's more important is that there's only one person in this city who can take your mother's Talent, and it isn't me."

"Who, then?" Sou-Zell spat. "Who do you claim can do this impossible thing?"

Falka's smile returned. "Lai-Dan, of course."

CHAPTER FOURTEEN

CONSPIRACY

Observation #29: All wasteland maps notoriously inaccurate.
Distances approximate, sometimes to a shocking degree.
Hypothesis: Couriers make poor cartographers. —O

Third Age of Storms, 1st Summer, Day 77
Kerina Sol – Jade District

J in sat cross-legged on a cushion at a low table, nursing a cup of
strong red tea. A novelty, to be somewhere other than the Chandru's Den and drinking something other than bottom-shelf swill.
But the tea wasn't bitter enough to calm her nerves.

It was half past the sixteenth bell. Kadrin was late.

She'd agonized over keeping this appointment at all. Gods, but
that encounter with Yi-Nereen had rattled her—she couldn't imagine having this conversation all over again, the hellish rehashing of
all she'd lost, with Kadrin's wounded eyes looking at her the whole
time. And now it was worse; she knew Yi-Nereen didn't want to
marry him.

It drove Jin mad. They were supposed to have gotten their fucking happy ending—without her, like she'd intended all along. But
she couldn't blame Yi-Nereen one bit.

143

The beaded curtain at the tea shop's entrance rustled. Jin looked up.

Today Kadrin's robes were a storm-cloud gray; a floral design picked out in silver thread glittered along his sleeves. He scanned the shop. The moment his gaze found her, he grinned broadly. "Jin! You came."

Why did he look so cheerful? Not only must he know the truth about her Talent—but the mood in the tea shop, the city at large, *everywhere*, was grim. Mana restrictions had trickled down into every part of life in Kerina Sol, especially for the refugees. Half the city was convinced Yi-Nereen was Makela's Herald. And everyone lived in constant, mind-numbing fear of the next storm.

"I invited *you* here," she said as Kadrin knelt on the cushion opposite hers. "Of course I came." Though she very nearly hadn't.

Kadrin airily waved away the attendant who approached to take his order. "I'm so sorry to do this, Jin." His smile vanished and became a look of contrition. "Something's come up. Is there any way I could convince you to accompany me to Forge District to—ah, meet some friends of mine?"

"Excuse me?"

Did he know how desperate she was to escape this conversation? Was he giving her an out?

Kadrin winced and glanced over his shoulder. "I've been instructed not to talk about this in public." He looked back at her, his eyes wide and earnest. "But it would mean a lot to both me and Yi-Nereen if you came."

Now Jin's interest was well and truly piqued. Kadrin had always had a flair for the dramatic, but this felt different. Had he become some kind of cloak-and-dagger agent in the weeks she'd been absent from his life?

"All right." She tossed back the rest of her cooled tea. "Lead the way."

It was a damn good thing she trusted Kadrin with her life, or she would have balked at the sheer number of dark, stinking alleyways along their route. Conditions in Forge District had gone from bad to worse in the past few days. Jin heard Sol-blood natives calling the neighborhood the "Refugee Quarter" these days, in the same tone of disgust that royals and their ilk used for Curing District and its unique olfactory signature.

Kadrin's destination was apparently a smithy on the outskirts of Forge. Jin had once made regular deliveries to its previous owner, a talkative metalcrafter who specialized in elaborate jewelry. Now the building was gutted and had clearly been repurposed as a command center for something.

Two burly men in stained clothes lounged outside the entrance, watching the streets. They nodded at Kadrin, obviously familiar with his face, and stared unblinkingly at Jin.

Jin was no stranger to places and people like this, but Kadrin? What had he gotten himself mixed up in?

She followed him into the smithy—turned-garden, apparently—and then she *did* balk.

Yi-Nereen sat at the base of a bloomwoven peach tree with a writing pad in her lap. Beside her was Eliesen, who had stolen a calligraphy brush and was painting characters along her forearm. Jin's heart stuttered—her *mother* was here, picking peaches. And Renfir, majordomo of the House of Steel Heavens, as well as her mother's suitor, stood nearby.

Jin took a step backward in panic, but it was too late. Behind her, a metal panel shrieked as one of the men outside dragged it back into place over the door. Everyone in the smithy turned to stare at Kadrin and Jin.

There was a dull thud as a basket hit the floor and peaches rolled everywhere.

"Jin?"

Jin had time to shoot Kadrin a look of utter betrayal before Eomma crossed the room and clasped her in the tightest embrace she'd ever endured. Eomma's muffled sobs shook them both.

In hindsight, it had been awful of Jin to avoid her mother for six weeks. She'd been an animal sitting in her own pain, heedless of anyone else's suffering. For a moment she thought the guilt might drown her.

But when Eomma pulled back, Jin saw her mother smiling through tears.

"Oh, Jin. I'm so happy to see you. You look— You look well."

"I do?" Jin asked, nonplussed.

Eomma gave her hands a brief squeeze. That beatific smile still glowed on her face. What in Rasvel's name was she so happy about? She must have put it together that Jin was Talentless now.

Oh. *Oh.*

Jin had never once considered that her mother might be *happier* if Jin was Talentless. Her father had believed their shared Talent more curse than gift, but he'd been strange in many ways—though Jin had loved him for it. To Jin, sparktalent had been a blessing. It had saved her and Eomma from Kerina Tez, kept them safe and somewhat prosperous in their new home.

But it had also kept Jin in the wastes, away from her mother and risking her life almost every day.

So Eomma preferred her this way: toothless but, in some ways, safer.

Jin set her jaw and looked over Eomma's shoulder.

There were unfamiliar faces in the room, too. A gray-haired woman in emerald robes, her fingers heavy with rings. A tall, good-looking man with braids and suspicious eyes. A shifting, dark-haired person who was watching Jin more intently than anyone else; Jin only had to glance at their scarred hands and grease-stained clothes to mark them for an artificer. And the most mysterious of all: a wide, fleshy figure sitting on a trunk in the corner whose face was completely obscured by an opaque veil.

"Friends of yours?" Jin asked Kadrin.

Kadrin nodded brightly. "We're all here now, so perhaps introductions are in order?"

"Allow me." The gray-haired woman's voice—calm, commanding—told Jin she was in charge. She approached Jin with a beringed hand outstretched. "I'm Toraka."

Jin, who knew the customs of Kerina Lav, touched her fingertips gently to the other woman's palm instead of shaking her hand. "I'm Jin."

"A pleasure to meet you at last, Jin. And now, to business." Toraka smiled. "I have a proposal to make."

"Well, shit," Jin said.

It was fortunate the smithy was full of sweet-smelling foliage that kept the air clean, or she would have panicked long ago and fled outside. Too many bodies in here, too many faces watching Jin as she listened to Toraka's explanation of what they were all doing here. She missed the bare, empty wastes.

"High Priestess Edine has the city in a chokehold," Kadrin said with uncharacteristic ire. "The temple will never sanction an expedition to Avi'Kerina. Especially now, with the mana crisis. They won't spare the supplies—or the protection of the knights."

"So your idea," Jin said, "is to put together your own expedition from scraps? You know this is the Barrens we're talking about, right?"

Kadrin nodded. "I know. That's why I told everyone we needed you."

"For what?" Jin crossed her arms. "You don't need me to tell you the Barrens are dangerous and this is suicide. The roads there aren't mapped. No springs to refuel. And that's not even mentioning the saurians."

"But there is a spring," Yi-Nereen said quietly. "Mount Vetelu."

Jin bit the wall of her mouth. Yi-Nereen was right, and Jin had forgotten. The Barrens were devoid of any known springs, but that had changed six weeks ago, when the Second Storm of Centuries had birthed a new spring from the rubble of Mount Vetelu. There was no reason it wouldn't still be there.

The only source of mana in hundreds of miles of desolate, mountainous terrain.

Toraka held up the tablet again. It wasn't glowing anymore, like it had during her little demonstration, but Jin's skin still prickled at the sight of it. Genuine Road Builder technology. She'd seen enough of it for a lifetime.

"The bottled mana we have is enough for a small expedition to reach Mount Vetelu. They can refuel there, ride that infusion to

Avi'Kerina, stake a claim, and return to Kerina Sol. I think it can be done in six days."

Jin frowned. "Assuming the map is accurate and we don't run into anything that tries to kill and eat us."

"We won't know until we go and check it out," Kadrin said reasonably.

"Give me one good reason we should even try," Jin said, perhaps a bit unreasonably.

No one had yet mentioned the obvious: neither she nor Kadrin would be part of the expedition. A Talentless would be a useless burden, two even worse. So if Kadrin had brought her here to poke holes in the plan, then she would. And she didn't know how to do it nicely.

"Jin, sweetheart," Eliesen said. "Maybe you've noticed the situation here. If Kerina Sol's spring is running dry, we're all fucked. The High Priestess wants us to pray to Rasvel and hope everything will turn out fine, but if it doesn't? We're fucked. We need a new place to live. And when Kerina Rut is the only walled city left standing, I don't think they'll take kindly to twelve thousand heretics showing up on their doorstep. So I repeat: if we don't try, we're fucked."

"Watch your mouth in front of my mother," Jin said.

Her heart was pounding. Why was everybody looking at her like this was her call to make? Toraka had come up with the plan, Kadrin had gathered them here, Yi-Nereen wanted a grand scheme to save everyone, Eliesen loved to be part of anything dramatic, and Eomma . . .

"Eomma." Jin turned to her mother. "Who made you part of this?"

Eomma gave her a loving, exasperated look. "I did, dear. Even in Tez, I knew running from kerina to kerina wouldn't solve our problems forever. Your father knew it, too. He always talked about taking us out of the wastes, to somewhere the storms would never touch. He believed in the First City."

Jin sat still, trying to conceal her surprise. "He never told me that."

"I'm not fully convinced, either," Celwyn said. He'd spoken little so far, but Jin had already taken the best measure of him she could: he was definitely a sparkrider, with the telltale calluses and tan lines, and his scars said knight rather than courier. "I don't have Toraka's faith. But even if Avi'Kerina is nothing more than a ruin, it might contain something of use. Some piece of technology that will save us."

"Like the magebikes," Orrin said. "Their discovery unlocked the wastes and changed the kerinas forever, just in time for the First Storm of Centuries to make other forms of travel impossible. Now the Second Storm has changed the game yet again. We need another miracle. Another Tibius Vann."

Orrin's tone left no doubts about who *they* believed Vann's successor would be. Artificers and their egos. Some things never changed.

"You two haven't had much to say." Jin gestured toward Renfir and the mysterious veiled figure. "Obviously we're doing this in secret; the temple would put a stop to this right away if they knew. I can't trust anyone unless I know where they stand."

Renfir adjusted his cuff links. "The raincallers of Kerina Sol are responsible for thousands of lives. As steward of the House of Steel Heavens, I am responsible for the *raincallers* and their kin." His gaze flickered to Kadrin and Eliesen. "Sometimes that duty must be carried out without the Rain Lord's express approval. Or knowledge."

"Fair enough," Jin said, impressed despite herself. Perhaps Renfir wasn't as poor a match for her mother as she'd originally thought. She nodded at the veiled figure. "And you?"

Slowly, the person raised their hands to doff their veil. Jin found herself looking into the perpetually frowning, mustached face of one of the last people she'd expected to see here: Bloom Lord Feyrin.

Feyrin blinked owlishly at the rest of the circle. "Toraka is an old friend. We've corresponded regularly over the years. I trust her judgment—a great deal more than I trust our own High Priestess, in fact."

Jin rubbed her temples. This was *not* how she'd imagined her day going. For a while there, she'd been grateful to Kadrin for sparing her a difficult, emotional conversation over tea—her worst nightmare. Clearly she lacked imagination.

"If you're here," Yi-Nereen said, guarded and respectful, "does that mean this expedition *is* sanctioned by the High Houses?"

"No," Feyrin said. "It's sanctioned by me. Privately. I won't support this in front of the Council until you return with proof that the First City exists. All I can provide is discreet material support: rations to get you there and back."

"Enough of this," Jin burst out. "Who's *actually* going to Avi'Kerina?"

She hadn't expected her outburst to trigger such a heated discussion. But in the end, there were few surprises.

"So that's the optimal configuration," Renfir concluded. He'd taken notes on a clipboard, like they were assigning shifts in the House kitchens. "One shieldcaster, one raincaller, and two sparkriders. The expedition will require water; one raincaller can produce enough for all four. The shieldcaster's necessity is obvious."

"With the spring rationed," Toraka said, "and our dwindling supply of bottled mana, we can't fuel more than two magebikes and four Talented overall. I've asked my people to stop using the bottles and turn in all they still have to me."

"I'll keep a sample," Orrin said. "I expect I can isolate the stabilizing compound and produce more, but it's unlikely to happen in time. Scientific discovery so rarely adheres to a sensible schedule."

"Four people." Kadrin frowned. "For an expedition to save everyone in Kerina Sol? That's so few."

He was looking at Jin; she could feel the heat of his gaze, though she avoided meeting it. What did he want from her? She'd barely spoken for the past few minutes. *She* wasn't going, after all. At this point, it was obvious who was.

"I'll be the shieldcaster," Yi-Nereen said.

Very fucking obvious, indeed.

"And look at that," Eliesen said. "I'm the only raincaller in the room. I could say no and leave you all out to dry, but this sounds like great fun. I'm in."

"Celwyn?" Toraka asked quietly, and the man nodded.

"Regrettably," Orrin said, "though I *am* sparktalented, I can't volunteer my own services for the expedition." For the first time today, Jin thought the artificer looked ill at ease. "A physical issue that prevents me from riding for any length of time. I'd prefer not to discuss it."

An uncomfortable silence followed; Jin sensed people trying not to look at her. She sat still, stewing, and refused to speak up.

Finally Toraka spread her arms and said, "I'll ask around for another volunteer sparkrider. We can't approach any Knights of Sol;

Flight of the Fallen

they answer only to the High Houses. Jin, could you check with your fellow couriers?"

"Sure," Jin bit out. "It'll cost, though. Couriers don't work for free."

Only she had, once. And she was still paying for that decision.

"Then we all know our tasks," Toraka said. "No one can know what time remains to accomplish them, but we know what must be done. Rasvel help us all."

Jin didn't care for being dismissed. It made her feel petulant; she wanted to decide when it was time to stay or go. But obviously it was time for everyone to go. And maybe she just felt like being a bitch.

While everyone else drifted off in various directions into the sticky evening, Jin stopped in the street to unpick a pebble from her shoe. When she straightened up, she saw that Kadrin had lingered.

"You hate this, too," Jin said without preamble. "Elie and Reena going into the wastes with a pair of strangers. Don't you?"

Kadrin nodded. He was standing in the shade of a dead, gnarled tree that the bloomweavers had abandoned when Forge District fell. Branches cast twisting shadows over his face, segmenting his features in odd ways.

"Part of me wishes I'd never tried to help Toraka," he said. "I didn't think it would turn out like this. I thought I would be part of something grand, a plan to save everyone. I certainly didn't plan on sending my little sister and my bride-to-be into the most dangerous place in the known world. But we have no choice, Jin."

Jin waved off a fly that seemed determined to land in her ear. "Did you bring me into the fold just so I could suffer, too?" She was hot, angry, and hardly in a state of mind to be fair. "You didn't need

153

me to tell everyone how dangerous the Barrens are. No one gives a shit. If it was do-or-die all along, what was the point?"

"You're right," Kadrin said. "Maybe I just didn't want to suffer alone."

Gods, it killed her when he was like this, sad and honest and oh-so-fucking-vulnerable. It made her want to tuck that stray curl back behind his ear and watch him smile. But she wasn't allowed to do that. She'd never been allowed.

"You weren't supposed to be alone," Jin said bitterly. "You have Reena."

Kadrin barked a laugh. "That's like cutting a man in half and telling him to go on with his life." He passed a hand over his face and looked at Jin through his fingers. "How am I supposed to be enough for her, when half of me is somewhere else? *With* someone else?"

Jin licked her lips. Her mouth was suddenly dry. "We're too different."

She cringed as soon as she heard herself say the words. It came off as a terrible excuse, but wasn't it true? Royals married below their stations, sure, but never into the literal slums. Kadrin and Yi-Nereen had their childhood romance, a decade-long love story, and Jin had memories of a hundred dusty letters. It wasn't nearly the same.

"Different?" Kadrin laughed again. "Look at us now."

Jin scowled, stung. "We might both be Talentless, but the last time I checked, I wasn't a prince."

"It doesn't count for as much as you think."

"No?" She felt like she was watching herself on her bike, careening toward a yawning chasm, out of control. Kadrin didn't deserve this. "Have you slept in any gutters lately? Spent much time shoveling cow shit?"

Flight of the Fallen

Kadrin went still. "You could have come back."

"Oh yes." Jin paced, back and forth, her hands in her hair. "I could have become one of your Talentless servants. The ones your parents keep around to show off how enlightened they are. I could have served drinks at your wedding, helped Reena with her hairpins, played nanny to all those screaming children she doesn't want—"

"What?"

Jin stopped, horrified. "Shit."

"Reena doesn't want children?" Kadrin didn't move a muscle.

"I shouldn't have—" Jin fought down a wave of bile. "I shouldn't have said a damn thing." She swallowed. "That's between the two of you."

She had to get out. It wasn't enough to have left the sweltering air of the smithy—there were still far too many bodies in Forge District. She needed the wastes. The horizon.

Or the bottom of a bottle. The next best thing.

"Jin, wait—"

It was too late. She was already outside, heels pounding away, and nothing in the world could call her back.

CHAPTER FIFTEEN

THE HERETIC

Observation #255: Talents divided between the elemental
(Metal, Rain, Bloom, Stone) and the ephemeral (Shield, Mind).
Latter group smaller than former.
Unresolved: Placement of Spark? Shit, I'm not sure about
Bloom, either.
Conclusion: Categories may be bunk. —O

Third Age of Storms, 1st Summer, Day 78

Kerina Sol – House of Steel Heavens

Yi-Nereen was soaking in a tub of cool water Eliesen had filled for her, idly detangling her hair with a long-toothed comb, when someone hammered on the door to her quarters as if they meant to knock it down.

"A moment, please," she called out.

The door flew open and through it charged Kadrin, scroll in hand.

"Reena? Are you—?"

He turned and his eyes fell upon her, frozen in the act of rising from her bathwater. Stark naked, of course.

For a moment, neither of them moved. Then Kadrin made an

unidentifiable sound, halfway between curse and apology. The door slammed shut. Yi-Nereen sank back into the water with a splash.

Her heart was racing. Nothing like this had happened previously during her stay in the House of Steel Heavens. Or ever before. In fact, the only man who'd ever seen her in a state of undress was her bodyguard, Teul-Kim.

Had Kadrin been frozen like her, or had his eyes lingered on her body? Yi-Nereen tried to recall the exact expression on his face—

Yes. He had looked. She was almost sure of it.

She had to think of something else. The scroll in his hand. It must have been important.

A few minutes later, freshly dressed with her hair wrapped in a drying cloth, Yi-Nereen opened the door. Kadrin held out the scroll, red-faced.

"It isn't good." His eyes were fixed on the wall beside her. "Just don't be afraid. I won't let anything happen to you."

That didn't bode well.

Yi-Nereen unrolled the parchment and read in silence. The world faded around her as she did, retreating into darkness until she and the scroll were the only things in existence. The characters on the scroll blurred together; Yi-Nereen blinked. Her eyes were watering.

"I've been declared a heretic," she said. "The temple is placing me under suspicion of causing the Second Storm of Centuries and corrupting the mana spring. There will be an investigation."

"Reena . . ."

"If I'm found guilty . . ." Yi-Nereen heard her voice distantly, from somewhere else. "I'll be put to death."

"You spineless, backstabbing *worm*—"

"Kadrin!" Rain Lord Matrios's voice boomed through the study. "That's enough."

There had been a portrait hanging in one of the inner staircases of the Tower of Arrested Stars. Yi-Nereen had observed it countless times from the corner of her eye, but she'd never studied it closely. All she could recall was an array of colorful figures standing around a stone table, embroiled in heated argument. Some pointed accusatory fingers; others shrank away or shouted back.

The scene in the Rain Lord's study was eerily familiar. Kadrin and all three of his siblings were here, along with their mother and father. Yi-Nereen had never seen all five in the room at the same time. Kadrin's mother was rarely in the House at all except when planning Kadrin and Yi-Nereen's wedding; she spent most of her time at temple, or at salons, banquets, and performances across the city.

"You went into Yi-Nereen's quarters," Kadrin snarled. "You intruded on the privacy of a guest. My *fiancée*."

"The door was open, and there were candles burning." Devros crossed his arms over his chest. "I only went in to blow them out. The papers were in plain sight."

Devros, the eldest of the Rain Lord's sons, was the shortest and stockiest of the trio: a water ox to Kadrin's stallion. Not that either of those beasts existed outside paintings; the kerinas had culled their herds long ago, after the First Storm made it impossible to cross the wastes without magebikes.

"Still," Eliesen said with uncharacteristic coldness, "it was poor manners to read them. Wasn't it?"

Devros flushed dark. "Poor manners? We've been harboring a heretic, a woman who almost destroyed our city—Kadrin knew what she did, all this time, and said nothing—and *I'm* the one with poor manners?"

Kadrin seized his brother by the collar. Yi-Nereen froze, her heart pounding; for a moment she thought Kadrin was about to strike Devros in the face.

But he only said, his voice strained but level, "None of it was her fault. Tibius Vann forced her into it. If you read all she wrote, you must have understood that. And yet you went straight to Edine—"

"I did no such thing." Devros stared evenly back at Kadrin. "I went to Father."

Kadrin staggered back from Devros and rounded on his father. "But . . . Father, did you—?"

Matrios raised an eyebrow. "You ask if I betrayed a guest in my household by revealing their secrets to the temple? Knowing those secrets would result in violent persecution? No, Kadrin. And you shame me by asking."

"Then how did that cow Edine find out?" Eliesen asked, ignoring her mother's angry hiss. "*I* didn't know about this before now."

"Does it matter?" Satriu asked. He was the middle brother; Yi-Nereen had spoken only a handful of words to him in total, but he'd given her a sympathetic look when she'd entered the study. "We need to protect Yi-Nereen from the inquisition. She's a refugee with no legal status; she's vulnerable. The wedding needs to happen as soon as possible."

Yi-Nereen felt a familiar, sick jolt in her stomach. And to her surprise, Kadrin looked at her sharply. As if he knew.

Kadrin's mother shook her head. "No, no. That isn't an option anymore. The temple won't bless the marriage, and we *cannot* bind heresy into our bloodline."

Yi-Nereen went cold. She should have seen it coming, and yet she hadn't.

She'd spent weeks dreading the prospect of marriage, and now the entire possibility had slipped through her fingers in an instant. Until now, every future she could imagine contained both Kadrin and Jin: a distant promise of happiness, achievable if she somehow made all the correct choices.

Now those futures were gone. She was left with nothing. Just a void.

"We can't do *nothing*," Eliesen said. "This isn't her fault."

Matrios sighed. "The temple will investigate Yi-Nereen and render judgment. We will cooperate. Fully. If Yi-Nereen did summon the Second Storm under duress, High Priestess Edine will take that under consideration and her punishment will be tempered."

"Talk to the High Priestess," Kadrin snapped. A small current of shock went through the room; Yi-Nereen was sure no one had ever heard Kadrin speak to his father that way. "You're friendly with her. Make sure she understands Reena is under your protection. That a guilty verdict isn't an option."

There was a long, pregnant silence.

"Everyone is dismissed," Matrios said. "I need to think. Alone."

Kadrin's siblings dispersed, casting Yi-Nereen troubled looks. And then she was alone in the hallway with Kadrin.

Yi-Nereen drifted to the nearest window. Beyond it lay a courtyard with a marble fountain. A few days ago, the fountain had run with splashing water, blazing under the sunlight: a frivolous use of mana. Now it was dry.

Flight of the Fallen

"Reena," Kadrin said, his voice low and thrumming. "I won't let this happen to you. I *promise*. You won't be put to death. The High Priestess won't find you guilty."

"It was over the moment the temple declared me a heretic. I've seen hundreds of these investigations in Kerina Rut. Even if the High Priestess doesn't find the evidence she's looking for, she'll find enough to be suspicious. That's worthy of exile."

For a non-sparkrider, *exile* was just another word for *death*.

"Kerina Sol isn't the same," Kadrin protested. "The High Priestess—"

"The High Priestess hates me," Yi-Nereen said, flat and final.

For a moment neither of them said anything. Despite the warm air, Yi-Nereen shivered before she continued.

"The kerinas exiled my great-uncle. He was supposed to die in the wastes without changing the course of history. But don't you see, Kadrin? He had to be cast out. He never would have found his destiny otherwise."

"Your destiny isn't in the wastes. It's here, with me."

Yi-Nereen tilted her head. "It doesn't matter. In a few days the expedition departs and I'll be gone. Once I find Avi'Kerina, this investigation won't matter."

As she turned to leave, Kadrin caught her by the wrist. His fingers were so warm they seared her skin, like fire licking her flesh. Or perhaps that was the memory of how he'd looked at her in the bath. Like a man who'd only just understood the vehemence of his own desire.

"I'm part of your destiny," he said. "No matter where you go or what happens. Am I wrong about that?"

Yi-Nereen couldn't look at him, for fear he'd see the lie in her eyes.

"No."

161

Yi-Nereen had come to Kerina Sol for one purpose: to publish her treatise and lay bare the truth of the bloodlines. When Falka had scattered her writing to the four winds, Yi-Nereen had first fallen into despair; then she'd resolved to start again. But the last month had been full of distractions. Kadrin, the spring, the tower . . .

Now the expedition loomed before her. Within days, she would be in the deadliest region of the wastes—this time without Jin to depend on. If Yi-Nereen were a gambler, she would think long and hard before staking coin on her return to Kerina Sol.

And if she did? There was still the temple. No matter what she told Kadrin, Yi-Nereen knew Edine wouldn't simply give in.

So she needed a fail-safe. She needed to finish her treatise.

Yi-Nereen locked herself in her quarters and didn't leave for three days. Time passed in a frenzy of ink and parchment, candles burning low, food and tea growing cold in a forgotten corner of the room. She turned away all visitors, even Kadrin and Eliesen. If the temple ever sent priests to interrogate Kadrin's family, Yi-Nereen heard nothing of it. She was sequestered, consumed. No distractions.

All that could have broken her concentration was a storm. But Rasvel was merciful. The bells didn't stir.

When she slept, Yi-Nereen dreamed of the Tower of Arrested Stars, of climbing an endless spiral staircase in search of something she desperately wanted but could not name. Was it a person, an object, or some ineffable divine truth? Her hands were empty. Her heart ached. Without that which she sought, she was nothing.

Then she woke, her fingers tangled in the sheets, and went back to work.

"Look who's back in the land of the living!" Eliesen poured Yi-Nereen's tea with the sort of glee she usually reserved for stealing food from her brothers' plates. "At last."

Yi-Nereen was back at the breakfast table for the first time in days. Sunlight streamed through the windows; motes of dust danced in the light. It was a fine morning. Yi-Nereen told herself to enjoy whatever peace remained to her.

"Did you finish what you were working on?" Kadrin asked. He'd smiled with relief when Yi-Nereen entered the dining hall, but now he watched her with an expression she couldn't identify. That was unusual. Kadrin's feelings had always been plain to her.

"It's done," Yi-Nereen said.

She had finished her treatise the previous evening. Then she'd crept out of the House after dark and gone to the Refugee Quarter with a satchel stuffed full of scrolls. Toraka had been waiting for her, like she'd known exactly what Yi-Nereen was going to do all along—or at least, since they'd spoken after the riot.

Footsteps struck the tile as Renfir entered the dining hall and cleared his throat.

"The Rain Lord would like to see all three of you."

Eliesen yawned. "Can't it wait until after breakfast?"

"I'll go now," Yi-Nereen said. She felt strangely calm. Of course she had hoped for more time, but she had only what Rasvel saw fit to give. "You two finish eating."

"What's the point of that?" Eliesen asked irritably. "If you're going, we'll all go."

Kadrin said nothing, but his gaze burned into Yi-Nereen like embers.

Hana Lee

They entered the Rain Lord's study to find Matrios seated at his desk. In front of him lay a scroll, unfurled and pinned to a board.

So soon. Yi-Nereen was impressed. Toraka had promised hundreds of copies, with dozens of transcribers working through the night, but Yi-Nereen hadn't expected those copies to make their way to Jade District so swiftly. Perhaps other royals in other Houses were reading her treatise at this very moment, their hearts hardening and their brows furrowing in incredulous fury—like Matrios's was right now.

"Kadrin. Eliesen." Matrios's voice was level. "Were you part of this?"

"Part of what?" Eliesen asked, the picture of innocence. Yi-Nereen gave her a look. In fact, Eliesen *hadn't* been part of this, but she certainly sounded guilty.

"No, they weren't," Yi-Nereen said. "They knew I was writing a treatise, but not what I planned to do with it."

Matrios steepled his fingers and turned a withering gaze on her. In her early days in the House, Yi-Nereen would have been cowed by such a stare. She had been so desperate to please Kadrin's family and earn a place here in the House of Steel Heavens. But now she finally understood: she would never have everything she wanted. A long and painful lesson that had begun the day Jin walked out of that garden.

"I refused to turn you over to the temple, Yi-Nereen. I gave you shelter. And in exchange, you've spread *this* through the city. In this time of crisis—when everyone should look to us for guidance—you call for the dismantling of the High Houses. You call for the royals to step down from the Council and for an end to marriage blessings. You argue that because Talent can be stolen or transferred, it is no sign of Rasvel's favor. Just an accident of birth."

164

Matrios unpinned the scroll, one corner at a time. It sprang back into a rolled cylinder and he tossed it into the fireplace.

"I never believed the imbecilic rumors that Kerina Rut sent you as a spy to destabilize our city from within. Or that you are Makela's Herald." Matrios stared at her, his dark eyes impenetrable. "No, Yi-Nereen, you are simply young and foolish. And you have betrayed my trust."

"Father—" Kadrin said.

"You are no longer welcome in this House."

Yi-Nereen nodded. "I understand. Thank you for sheltering me."

She turned on her heel and left the study. Behind her, the room erupted into a storm of raised voices. Kadrin and Eliesen were both shouting, and she didn't wait to hear Matrios's reply.

She had already packed her belongings, scarce as they were, this morning.

Celwyn met her in the avenue outside the House. Trees that had once been resplendent with pink blooms swayed around him, branches black and bare. Yi-Nereen again felt the fleeting sense that she recognized him. But then it was gone.

"The main streets aren't safe," Celwyn said. "But the alleys are quiet for now. We'll take the back way to the Refugee Quarter."

"Have you heard from Jin?"

"No, but Toraka is negotiating with another courier to join the expedition. We'll leave soon. Two days from now, I think."

Yi-Nereen's heart was pounding now. As calm as she'd been in Matrios's study, it was only because that was how she faced the certainty of a storm: head-on, rock steady, braced to endure as long as she could.

What came next was anything but certain. She'd thrown a spark into the seething belly of a city split between Talented, long-suffering Talentless, and refugees with nothing to lose and everything to gain. She'd called for unrest. Uprising.

"You'll be safe with Toraka," Celwyn went on. "The temple won't find you. They'll be looking, I'm sure—but they don't know how little time they have."

Yi-Nereen steeled herself and nodded. "Lead the way, then."

CHAPTER SIXTEEN

BLOOD, SWEAT, AND PRAYER

Observation #325: "Mana-drunk" is colloquial, but anecdotal evidence suggests psychoactive effect more similar to drug high than alcohol intoxication.
Supplemental observation: Most drug users are Talentless.
Inference: Mana-drunk named as such by those more familiar with effects of alcohol. —O

Third Age of Storms, 1st Summer, Day 82
Kerina Sol – House of Steel Heavens

Kadrin moved his lips slowly, mouthing the words as he read them. *Kadrin, I'm safe. I'll send word. Don't look for me today.*

When he'd read the note thrice, he put it back on the table in Yi-Nereen's study. Then he stood there for a long while in silence. It had been only six hours since Yi-Nereen's departure from the House, yet hardly any trace of her presence remained. She'd gathered all her diagrams and loose notes and taken them with her. She'd left behind an armoire full of clothes, most of which Kadrin was certain she hadn't worn at all during her stay.

Where could she have gone? Her only kin in Kerina Sol were Shield Lord Tethris and her family, and Kadrin couldn't imagine Yi-

Nereen seeking refuge with them. Worry knotted in Kadrin's chest; he couldn't draw a full breath.

Yi-Nereen hadn't told him of her plans to disseminate her treatise. Why? Didn't she trust him to help her? Had she simply not thought of him at all?

Kadrin turned abruptly and stalked out of the room. If he stayed there a moment longer, surrounded by those blank spaces and pinholes on the walls, he'd go mad.

His favorite place to sulk—the garden—wasn't empty. Eliesen knelt among the dying flower beds, working a trowel under the roots of a drooping plant with gray-blue flowers. She was cursing quietly.

"It's already dying," Kadrin said. "No need to kill it."

Eliesen sniffed and looked up. Her eyes were red-rimmed. "It wasn't ever really alive."

"What do you mean?"

"I read Yi-Nereen's treatise. Don't look at me like that—I mean just now, not before. Jin's mother gave me a copy." Eliesen stabbed at the dirt. "There's so much I didn't know. Things I never thought about. Did you know they sterilized Talentless women in Kerina Tez? Or that Talented women in Kerina Rut are sold like animals to the highest bidder?"

Throat tight, Kadrin shook his head.

"It makes me sick," Eliesen said. Kadrin could see the plant's roots splintering under her trowel as she dug. "And it's no different here. Oh, we won't be killed or cut open, but the temple rules what we can do with our bodies all the same." Eliesen gave a sharp cry and tossed the trowel to the ground. She turned on Kadrin, her eyes wild. "I fucking *hate* being a woman. It's all shit. I'd rather be anything else. A beetle. A cactus. A cloud in the sky. *Anything.*"

Flight of the Fallen

"I . . ." Kadrin wrung his hands, helpless. "I don't know what to say. I'm sorry."

Eliesen rubbed tears from her cheeks, sharp and jerky. "Just come here and give me a hug, idiot."

Kadrin didn't need telling twice. He gathered Eliesen into his arms and tucked his chin over the crown of her head. He felt her shaking, heard her quiet sobs into his chest. "Stupid flowers," she said. "I liked yours better."

"Mine?"

"The ones . . . you grew . . . from seeds."

Kadrin wanted to look at her face, but she hadn't given him permission to stop hugging her yet. "Why did you say the plant wasn't real?"

Eliesen took her time answering. Her breathing slowly steadied. Finally she said, "It can't survive without Talent. Without mana. It's just a pretty thing that'll die once no one's around to keep it alive."

"Elie, that's people. You're describing people."

"*You'll* be fine without mana." She gave his chest a rough nudge. "You can live in Avi'Kerina. Where it's safe and you never have to worry about storms."

"Aren't you jumping too far ahead? We haven't even found Avi'Kerina yet. And once we do, we'll all start over there. Together."

"No spring, Kadrin." Eliesen pulled back, straining against the cage of Kadrin's arms, and he let her go. "We haven't talked about it. Toraka didn't say anything. But if there's no mana spring, then how are the Talented supposed to live there?"

Kadrin scratched his day-old beard. "We'll figure something out."

"Wrong," Eliesen said. "*Yi-Nereen* will figure something out. And we're all stuck waiting here until she does. That treatise—I'm scared, Kadrin. Every single word was right and justified and a fucking long time coming, but I'm scared of what happens next. You should be, too."

"You know me." Kadrin grinned, though it was harder to summon a smile than usual. He kept thinking of those blank spaces on Yi-Nereen's walls. "It takes a lot to scare me."

Eliesen's lips thinned; she was clearly in no mood for games. "Read the treatise, Kadrin. See how brave you're feeling afterward. I burned my copy. Didn't want Mother to find it. Remember your flowers? The way she cried? This is so much worse."

"Okay," Kadrin said. "I will."

It wasn't difficult to find a copy. Kadrin had hardly left Jade District before a grubby boy darted from an alley and shoved a scroll toward him with one hand, holding the other out expectantly. Kadrin dug in his pocket for a coin.

"How many of these have you sold today?"

"Dunno. A lot?"

Kadrin watched the boy scamper off into the restless streets. Glancing around, he saw Yi-Nereen's treatise clutched in hands everywhere: a craftswoman lounging against her closed stall, two men arguing in a doorway, a young man in student's robes who was reading with a quill pressed between his teeth and taking notes.

Kadrin unfurled the scroll. He read the first line once. Twice. *My name is Yi-Nereen, and until my father sold me into marriage, I was First Daughter of the Tower of Arrested Stars in Kerina Rut . . .*

The characters were already swimming across the parchment. He let the scroll snap shut. Sweat beaded on the back of his neck.

Flight of the Fallen

Gods, this wasn't going to work. He couldn't even read his own letters without help.

Half an hour later, Kadrin stepped into the Chandru's Den. His chest was tight as he scanned the smoky room; just because Eliesen had found Jin here once didn't mean she spent *all* her time here, surely. But it was Kadrin's only lead.

There. His pulse skipped. A familiar, short-haired figure slouched over a table in the corner. At Kadrin's approach, Jin's eyes flashed up to meet his.

"Kadrin. That *is* you, right?"

"Of course it is." How much had she drunk, exactly?

"I wanted to find you. Apologize." Jin swept a hand over the room. "Came here instead. See? Can't even keep a promise to myself."

Kadrin sat. "You don't have anything to be sorry for."

"I've been an ass." Her eyes bored into him. "That's worth an apology. You're a good man, and I haven't treated you like one."

Kadrin had never seen Jin drunk before. At least, he was almost sure he hadn't.

His plan—ill-conceived from the start—to track Jin down and beg her to read Yi-Nereen's treatise aloud was dissolving into pieces, scattered before a strong wind. He'd been so distracted by Yi-Nereen's departure that he'd forgotten the way he'd parted from Jin almost a week ago. Now it came back to him in a rush of guilt.

"Jin," Kadrin said, "I don't have any complaints about how you've treated *me*. But I am worried about how you treat yourself."

Jin threw up her hands. "See? This is exactly what I mean."

This was going nowhere. "My father kicked Reena out. I have no idea where she is now. Have you seen her?"

Jin's chair scraped across the packed-earth floor as she rose.

171

Hana Lee

"Fucking hell, Kadrin. We have to find her. It's not safe in this town after what she did. What she said. Have you read it?"

"She left me a note saying she had somewhere to go," Kadrin said, choosing to ignore Jin's question. "I don't think you should traipse around looking for her, especially not—"

"Drunk?" Jin bit out a laugh. "Would being sober make me any more useful? Ah, fuck. See, that's exactly the kind of thing I'm trying not to say to you."

Kadrin gazed down at her face. He could see the faint tan lines her bonehelm had left on her cheeks, not quite faded still, and he burned with the urge to rub his thumbs across them. Like the evidence of what she'd lost were a smudge he could clean away, make better with his touch. He was such a fool.

He opened his mouth and a string of words came out that he hadn't planned to say at all. "I don't think I'm getting married."

Jin swayed. "Don't say that."

Kadrin caught her. It felt like a crime to hook his arm around her waist and pull her flush to his side, but what else was he going to do—drop her?

"Where are you staying, Jin?"

They left the wine-scented din of the Chandru's Den behind, and Jin led him down the street to a magebike garage, leaning on his shoulder. Kadrin was in shambles and trying not to show it. In one way, the last seven weeks of his life had been the best, and in another they'd been the worst. Now Yi-Nereen was who-knew-where and Jin was right here in his arms, piss-drunk. The gods were laughing at him.

"Here," Jin said. She pulled him into the garage, past rows of gleaming bikes and a few couriers cleaning or refueling their machines, to a door in the back that led to the quiet dark of a bunkroom. At first Kadrin thought it might be empty; then he heard a snore and saw a figure shift under a blanket.

"You've been staying here?" he asked.

Jin hadn't looked at the magebikes as they'd passed; she'd kept her eyes averted. He thought of her sleeping here, week after week, surrounded by reminders of the life that had been stolen from her. All that time he'd assumed she was far away, riding from city to city. Free.

"Don't give up on her," Jin said. She clung to Kadrin's shirt, her face pressed to his chest like she couldn't bear to let go. But she wouldn't look at him, either. "I know you need each other. Fuck the temple. My parents were never married, you know."

"What would you do?" It was a stupid question, but he had to ask.

Jin made a sound of confusion. "If I were you? Or her?"

"Either."

"I'd find a way."

Kadrin threaded his fingers through her hair—it was dangerous, he could sense it, but Jin made no move to shake him off. "So why haven't you?" Rasvel help him, words were hard. "I know you have feelings for Reena still."

Jin sighed into his shirt. "That obvious?"

"And, well." Kadrin laughed, low and helpless. "You seem a little glued to me right now."

"I liked that." Jin tightened her grip. "That laugh. Do it again."

Kadrin swallowed. "All right, clearly you need to sleep this off."

It was the hardest thing he'd ever done, but he gently tugged her free, and she went without a fuss. He watched her crawl into a bunk and collapse face-first into a pillow. Then he turned to go, a lump in his throat—but her voice called him back.

"I'm trying," she said, almost too softly for him to hear. "To find a way."

He waited, but all that came after was the sound of her slow, rhythmic breath.

※

Don't give up on her, Jin had said. Kadrin had absolutely no plans to do so.

The first place he went to find Toraka was the smithy where they'd met to discuss the expedition, but Kadrin was half a street away when he realized something was wrong. Two acolytes in white robes stood outside the building, talking in low voices. No sign of Toraka's sentries. Heart pounding, Kadrin beat the most casual retreat he could manage.

So the temple had already traced the distribution of Yi-Nereen's treatise here, to the Refugee Quarter. Kadrin didn't feel quite as clever anymore for putting that together. He'd realized that Yi-Nereen *did* have friends in Kerina Sol, apart from Kadrin and Shield Lord Tethris. The Lav-blood refugees were the only people in the city who hadn't been swayed by High Priestess Edine's sermons about Makela's Herald.

Fortunately, Kadrin's weeks spent as a volunteer in the Refugee Quarter meant he knew his way around better than the temple did.

The district's shrine to Rasvel had been blasted to pieces in the Second Storm of Centuries. Blocks of masonry and statue limbs were still scattered up and down the street. But the refugees had rebuilt the shrine into a small open-air cathedral. Candles burned around bowls of polished, multicolored glass beads engraved with

Flight of the Fallen

names: memorials to the dead. Kadrin's heart stilled. There were *so* many more bowls today than the last time he'd been here.

Toraka was there, standing with head bowed in front of one of the memorials. Kadrin joined her.

"I carved a bead for Guildmaster Xua today," Toraka said. "Word came from Kerina Rut. He and many others were denied sanctuary there."

"He's dead?" Kadrin blinked. "They're *all* dead?"

"By the cruel hand of the High Houses, yes. The compact is no more."

"Shit. Did you know him well? Xua?"

Toraka chuckled. "He was my greatest rival in the Guildery. We both spent the better part of our time and energy trying to ruin the other's reputation. It was a game, Kadrin. I would poach a marriage contract from his House, he would spread rumors about my children . . . He was a stubborn fool who refused to ever give an inch, even from the losing position. No ability to adapt whatsoever."

"I didn't think you were the type to play games like that," Kadrin said. He winced at his own comment. "I mean—I'm sorry. It sounds like you did know him well."

"You needn't console me, Kadrin. Kerina Lav's priests taught that we exist on a knife's edge. Rasvel tugs one way, Makela tugs the other, and the rest of the nameless gods watch and wait." Toraka placed her hand on her heart. "No one can balance like that forever. That's what survival is: spending every day trying not to fall. Forestalling the inevitable by any means at hand—that was Xua's favorite tactic. I prefer to embrace my fate with open eyes and a willing heart."

"I want to know where Yi-Nereen is."

Toraka smiled. "She's safe. Celwyn is watching over her. I have a message from her for you."

She hadn't answered his question, but Kadrin had known she wouldn't. "What is it?"

"Don't renounce your father. Use every privilege your family has for as long as you can. Kerina Sol needs your voice in the Council chambers, not on the streets."

Heat swelled in Kadrin's chest. "Of course she would ask me to do that. Everyone loves to make my decisions for me." Even Yi-Nereen and Jin. "I'll never be lord of my House, and she knows it. Let me help in a way that actually matters. Let me carry any burden except that one."

There was silence as he held Toraka's gaze. He felt the weight of her judgment as she measured his words and intent. His skin prickled.

"A burden you ask for is no burden at all," Toraka said at last. "I understand how you feel. Neither of us can help find Avi'Kerina—not by blood, sweat, or prayer. That isn't where our talents lie. But the work we do here is still important. We must ready the way for when they return."

"How? The Council won't listen. They're under Edine's thumb."

"It isn't the Council who needs to hear us. It's the people. We are only two, Kadrin, but there are so many more hearts in Kerina Sol waiting for the chance to be swayed. Yi-Nereen's treatise is only the beginning. Will you help me with the rest? Will you help *her*?"

Kadrin swallowed his anger. If this was his burden, the only one he could carry, then of course he would do it. And who was he to complain anyway? He wasn't the only person without a choice. Eliesen, Jin, Reena . . . all of them were prisoners in their own way.

It all had to change.

"I'll do it," he said.

CHAPTER SEVENTEEN

RASVEL'S WILL

Observation #349: When scientific evidence conflicts w/ temple
doctrine, doctrine always wins.
Possible area of further study: Can science be dressed up as
theology, and thus made more palatable to the masses? —O

Third Age of Storms, 1st Summer, Day 83
Kerina Sol – Refugee Quarter

In her former life, Jin had often woken just like this. Tangled in the sheets of a bunk in a courier safehouse, head pulsing to the beat of a hangover, skin prickling with the certainty that a storm was on its way. She never felt safe behind walls in a storm, unlike most people. Walls hadn't saved Kerina Tez from destruction. Neither had shieldcasters.

She couldn't sense storms anymore. She'd lost that ability along with her Talent. Now her skin was prickling for a different reason.

"Kadrin?"

Her only response was a rattling snore from the bunk above her. No, of course he wouldn't be here. He'd walked her home like the gentleman he was, then left.

177

Never mind that Jin didn't have a home, and she hadn't wanted Kadrin to be a gentleman.

Jin swung her legs from the bunk and went in search of water to soothe her dry throat. There was a half-full basin outside the dormitory; she filled a ladle, resisting the temptation to dunk her entire head under the surface.

Two couriers, freshly coated in wasteland dust, walked past.

"—wouldn't go by Temple Square tonight, there's talk. Something's happening."

"I heard. Toraka and Maķela's Herald—"

Jin dropped the ladle in the water with a splash. The couriers ignored her and made their way into the garage. Jin considered chasing them down—but no, she'd spent the last seven weeks trying not to draw attention to herself and the fact that she slept here almost every night.

In the haze of waking, she'd forgotten until just now that Yi-Nereen had left Kadrin's House. She was somewhere in the city, doing Rasvel knew what. And apparently something was going down tonight in Temple Square.

Reena, what are you doing?

The moon was full and rust-orange, floating in a sea of red stars. Jin had called these lantern-moon nights when she still rode across the wastes; she hardly needed her headlamp to navigate the highways. In cities, though, a lantern moon didn't make the night safer. It brought malcontents out onto the streets to play.

Jin joined a slow-moving current of people moving toward Temple Square. She'd heard a dozen different stories of what was going to

Flight of the Fallen

happen tonight from fifty different mouths. Clearly nobody knew shit, except that Toraka was planning some kind of demonstration.

Jin's sense of danger was on high alert, screeching in her ear like an agitated pteropter. It was long past curfew, and the High Priestess had to have heard the whispers. Yet the streets were suspiciously empty of temple acolytes or city guards.

Temple Square was a large, open-air pavilion below the polished stone steps of the Basilica Sol. Statues lined the square: intricately detailed carvings of people, saurians, and animals, all of them from scripture Jin had never bothered to read. At the base of the temple steps stood the largest statue of all: Rasvel the Talent Giver, dressed in flowing robes and wooden sandals. Opposite him was an empty plinth.

Jin thought of the statue of Makela in the ruined temple out in the wastes and shivered.

The crowd in the square swelled with each passing moment. Jin's trepidation rose, and sweat trickled down her neck. The High Priestess must be watching from somewhere hidden. Waiting.

"Jin?"

Jin whirled, heart pounding. But it was just Kadrin. Somehow he'd found her in the crowd.

"I hoped you'd be here," he said, drawing close.

Jin had hoped *he* wouldn't be. Her throat was dry with dread of whatever was about to happen; her brain had spent the entire day screaming at her not to come. The air in Kerina Sol tasted just like the air in Tez days before its fall. Dry, hot, crackling with tension. But Yi-Nereen was here, and Jin had to know she was safe—or at the very least, not dead.

"You should go home." Jin had to raise her voice to be heard above the muttering crowd. "This isn't a good place for you to be."

Kadrin touched the hilt of his sword with a smile. "Don't worry. I came prepared."

That was exactly why Jin was worried. Kadrin's sword and fine clothes instantly marked him for a royal, and people nearby were already staring and whispering through their hands at him. Hadn't he noticed how many refugees were part of the crowd? *They* didn't know he was Talentless. Gods, the man had no sense of self-preservation.

Kadrin lowered himself to speak into Jin's ear. "We've got to get close enough to talk to Reena. The more she shuts us out, the worse it's going to get. I know she doesn't think she needs anyone. But she does."

Jin shivered again. This time she didn't know if it was dread or the warm sensation of Kadrin's breath. "I know."

"Something's happening." Kadrin straightened, tall and remote once again.

The crowd was clearing to make way for a trio of figures striding purposefully into the center of the square, carrying lanterns. Jin recognized their leader at once: Celwyn, his loping stride distinctive, a sword bobbing at his belt. Behind him came a pair of tall figures in white robes and long, gauzy veils.

Jin raised herself onto her toes. She'd lost sight of all three of them; the crowd was too thick. "Kadrin, what's—?"

A gasp rippled through the crowd. From the middle of Temple Square, a tree was growing, unfurling and stretching up from the ground—but unlike any tree Jin had ever seen, it split into two thick boughs that curved over and grew parallel to the ground. The white-robed figures stepped onto the boughs, rising above the crowd, and removed their veils.

Toraka and Yi-Nereen. Jin's heart began to race.

Flight of the Fallen

Kadrin cursed. "We're too late, aren't we?"

"Friends and fellows!" Toraka's sonorous voice filled the square, cutting through the gasps. Silence fell at once. "You are people of two kerinas, equal under Rasvel's eye. Talented and Talentless, we are all children of the gods. When has that ever been more obvious than now? In this time of hardship, we rely on each other. For safety. For shelter. For resilience."

At any moment, Jin was sure, the doors of the Basilica Sol would swing open and High Priestess Edine would emerge with a small army of acolytes in tow. Toraka couldn't have chosen a more conspicuous—or blasphemous—location for this little display. Even the tree she'd bloomed from the paved stones was spit in the face of the temple's mana edicts, given how dry the kerina's well had run.

"When the Road Builders' empire fell, our people were in their infancy. We had no cities, no springs, no magebikes. We were wanderers, scattered across the wastes. But the storms were not so deadly then. We learned to build walled cities on the banks of springs. We came together in hundreds, then in thousands. Our Talents flourished. We believed Rasvel intended the wasteland for our home. We believed the Talent Giver had provided us everything we needed to thrive."

Toraka paused. The yellow lantern she carried lit her face from below, the orange moon from above. The entire square held its breath.

"We were wrong. The wastes are not our home. Our Talents are fleeting gifts, a sacrifice to sustain us until our true home is found: the First City."

Whispers flowed through the crowd. Jin doubted anyone was surprised; Yi-Nereen's treatise had made all of Toraka's arguments already, at length. But hearing Toraka say the words aloud was a spell of its own kind. The woman was a fine orator. And Jin didn't trust her one bit.

Toraka gestured toward Yi-Nereen, who stood silently in her white robes, her dark hair unplaited and streaming over her shoulders. Jin had never seen her in white before. It was unsettling, like seeing a skull stripped of flesh and skin.

"Some of you believe this woman is Makela's Herald. In Kerina Sol, the temple teaches that Rasvel and Makela stand opposed. A hand that takes and a hand that gives. In Kerina Lav, we know them to be two sides of the same coin. Makela's Herald and Rasvel's Herald are one and the same. Yes, Yi-Nereen can take Talent away. But it isn't theft. It isn't heresy. It is necessary, for what we must do and where we must go. It is Rasvel's will."

Yi-Nereen raised her head. "There is no mana in the First City. So there can be no Talent."

Well, shit. Jin's world narrowed to a single certainty: Yi-Nereen had just said the words that would spark the fire, and she was standing in the middle of the powder keg.

She had to stop this. She had to get Reena out of here.

But Kadrin's hand closed on Jin's shoulder, holding her back. "Wait." His voice was rough. "She's right."

"What?"

"Have no fear!" Toraka called out, but her voice was nearly swallowed by a roar of voices.

The crowd was starting to turn; the faces around Jin looked more furious than frightened now. A man near Kadrin was shouting, his fist raised. The crowd was closing in on that divided tree at the square's center. They'd have a mob on their hands soon if something didn't give.

"Have no fear!" Toraka shouted again. The lamplight caught her wide, beatific smile. "I am not afraid. Rasvel will guide us to our true home. Did we think it would come without sacrifice? Nothing in this life comes for free. But I— I will gladly pay the cost. I give freely what I no longer need."

She joined hands with Yi-Nereen and they stood above the crowd, their foreheads pressed together.

What had it looked like when Yi-Nereen had taken Jin's Talent? She'd been dying, hallucinating, only conscious enough to remember heat and agony and Yi-Nereen's lips on hers. Toraka didn't look like she was in agony. She looked blissful, rapturous. Her eyes glowed the bright, living green of a peach tree's foliage. Yi-Nereen's glowed electric blue. Their mouths weren't quite touching; Jin thought she could see wisps of something flowing between them, half liquid and half gas, just like mana.

Toraka swooned into Yi-Nereen's arms. The crowd roared, a great noise that swept over Jin like a battering wave. And across the square, the doors to the Basilica Sol flew open, and High Priestess Edine stood silhouetted at the top of the steps, flanked by acolytes.

Jin's trance broke. What was she *doing*? She had to get Reena.

She shoved two men aside but fell back, staggering, as the crowd surged against her. For a terrifying moment she thought she'd lose her footing. She'd go under the mob, crushed to death. Like all those bodies in Tez.

The crowd pressed in on all sides. Jin was tossed this way and that, between walls of sweat and heat and screaming noise.

"Reena!" she cried out. "Kadrin!"

She stumbled. And then, in an instant, her cold fear came true: she fell to one knee and people immediately began stepping on her. Someone kicked her in the side. Jin tried to burn mana that wasn't there, to clear a space with hot sparks. But she was empty. Empty.

She sank down and curled into a ball, shielding her head with her arms.

Hands grabbed her. Not the flailing hands of the crowd, but two purposeful grips that hoisted her upright. Kadrin—and Celwyn. Jin sagged between them as they pulled her from the crush. She didn't know how they'd found her, but she was relieved. So relieved.

The crowd thinned at the edge of the square. Jin leaned against a statue and vomited. People ran past her, but she was vaguely aware that Kadrin and Celwyn remained close, flanking her with their height and bulk. She was trembling like a pebble in an earthquake, skin cold and clammy.

"Jin?" Kadrin's voice. "Are you okay? We can't stay."

Jin wiped her mouth and nodded. A lie, but that didn't matter. "Where's Reena?"

"I saw her with Toraka," Celwyn said, low and gravelly. "They made it out. I know where they're headed. We should go there, too. Before the High Priestess finds them."

"You asshole." Jin's gratitude melted as she rounded on him, fists raised. "You and Toraka both. How could you bring her here, right to Edine's doorstep? How could you make her—make her *do* that?"

"Jin," Kadrin said quietly, "no one made her do anything."

He was right. Some part of Jin knew that. But she was seething, burning from the inside, sick with fear and rage. Yi-Nereen despised her abilities; she hated what she'd done to Jin. What had changed? Did she really believe this was the only way forward?

It all stank of Tibius Vann's plan for the wastes, even though he was dead and gone. No more Talented. Everyone equal—or dead.

"Fine," Jin spat. "Take us to Reena."

CHAPTER EIGHTEEN

THE RIDERS DEPART

Observation #115: Renzara, master artificer. Brilliant, not too young or too old, respected but aloof. People expect greatness from her but can't see behind the curtain.

Hypothesis: Excellent smoke screen for my own devices.

Conclusion: Will apply to become her apprentice. —O

Third Age of Storms, 1st Summer, Day 83

Kerina Sol – Below the Wall

Yi-Nereen held out a damp cloth, but Toraka waved her off. "That isn't necessary," she said. "I feel fine."

The ceiling trembled. Dust rained down on them both in a brief shower. Yi-Nereen had spent the last day and a half constantly brushing dust and dirt from her clothes; Toraka's safehouse, a basement beneath a destroyed house in the Refugee Quarter, left much to be desired in terms of creature comforts. But it *was* well hidden. Even as hordes of people ran through the street above, fleeing the High Priestess and her acolytes, no one had yet stumbled on the trapdoor leading here.

Yi-Nereen studied Toraka. Was she telling the truth? She was conscious, which was a marked improvement over the last two people Yi-Nereen had siphoned. But she hadn't been dying from mana poisoning at the time. That had probably helped. Her skin was paler than usual, her eyes a touch duller. Still, for a woman newly made Talentless, she did look unexpectedly hale.

The trapdoor creaked. *That* was a new sound.

Yi-Nereen leaped to her feet. "They're here."

She was brimming with Toraka's power. It simmered in her veins, yearning to be set free. Part of Yi-Nereen had hoped the acolytes would find this place. Not because she craved violence, but because she wanted an end to the waiting. The dread. The fear of reprisal.

She'd wanted change at any cost. But no one could live like this, not for long.

Three sharp raps rang out, muffled through the ceiling. Yi-Nereen flinched as disappointment and relief surged through her in equal measure.

"It's Celwyn," Toraka said.

The trapdoor opened. Celwyn was first down the stairs, but he wasn't alone.

"Reena," Kadrin exclaimed. "Thank the gods you're safe."

Jin stalked across the bare earthen floor until she and Yi-Nereen were face-to-face. She looked more ill than Toraka. "That was the most idiotic thing I have ever seen someone do. Why? *Why?*"

Yi-Nereen took an involuntary step back. She'd been more ready to fight for her life against a dozen temple acolytes than one pissed-off Jin. As painful as planning to leave Kerina Sol without saying farewell to either Jin or Kadrin had been, it would have been easier than this.

Toraka rose to her feet. "We needed a public demonstration of Yi-Nereen's power. The High Priestess's sermons have branded her a monster, a demon who preys on the unwilling. How better to reject that image than to show everyone the beauty of her gift—with a willing volunteer?"

"In other words," Jin growled, "this was all *your* idea."

Yi-Nereen found her voice at last. "That's not true."

Jin opened her mouth, but Kadrin laid a hand on her shoulder. "Let her talk," he said quietly.

Yi-Nereen gave him a silent look of gratitude. "Realizing what I did to you was the worst moment of my life. But Toraka helped me see this power as something Rasvel meant for me to have, not just another sick thing my grandfather made. Once I understood that, I knew we had to make others see it, too. But I would never have done it again without a willing subject. Toraka and I decided to do this together. As equals."

"I'm not young anymore," Toraka said. "My half-life couldn't have been more than a handful of years away. But now, who knows what will happen? I might live to see my grandchildren fall in love and marry."

Jin stood still, her expression unreadable. Yi-Nereen's throat was tight; she *needed* Jin to understand. To forgive her a second time.

"I hate to ask," Kadrin said, "but what's the plan now? The High Priestess has already declared Yi-Nereen a heretic and placed her under investigation. I can't imagine what happened tonight will help her case."

"For now, the plan is the same as before," Toraka said. "Find Avi'Kerina. In fact, the expedition leaves this very night. The timing couldn't be better; Yi-Nereen will be safe, beyond the High Priestess's reach."

Jin's eyes flashed dark. "You found another sparkrider?"

Toraka nodded. "One of your fellow couriers. The price was steep, as you warned me, but with Bloom Lord Feyrin's help we'll be able to afford the charge."

"No," Kadrin said. "There's no need to hire another courier."

Yi-Nereen turned to stare at him. She wasn't the only one; even Celwyn, who'd been lurking under the staircase and listening in silence, looked taken aback.

"Explain," Jin said through gritted teeth.

Kadrin nodded, his face flushed. "Orrin and I may not have been *entirely* honest about why we needed all those bottles of mana from Toraka's people. I didn't want to say anything earlier because I wasn't sure we would have enough, or if Orrin would be able to finish the prototype in time—"

"Kadrin," Yi-Nereen said gently, because Jin was rocking back and forth on the balls of her feet and looking like she might throttle him. "Your point?"

Kadrin coughed. "I'm only letting you and Eliesen go on this expedition if you're with someone I trust. Sorry, Celwyn."

"Dare I ask *who*?" Jin asked.

Kadrin grinned at her. "You, of course."

Kadrin led Jin through a twisting maze of alleys, out of the Refugee Quarter and back into the depths of Jade District. Twice they had to stop and keep still in the shadows as a band of armed acolytes stormed past. Kadrin's heart was in his throat. He didn't think he and Jin were truly in danger, despite both being Talentless; Edine's lackeys would surely recognize him on sight as a royal heir. But he could feel the anxious energy buzzing through Jin's body every time

Flight of the Fallen

their shoulders brushed. He didn't know what *she* would do if they crossed paths with anyone from the temple.

Finally he saw the glowing window of Orrin's workshop. "Here." He bundled Jin over the threshold without knocking.

Orrin was waiting inside. "There you are. I expected you hours ago."

Kadrin's heart thudded. "Is it ready?"

"Is *what* ready?" Jin demanded.

Hadn't she put it together yet? Kadrin glanced at her. His heart broke at her stone-faced expression; for perhaps the first time in their entire acquaintance, he could see right through the mask. He felt her desperate hope and her refusal to believe. Of course she knew why Kadrin had brought her here. But she had to hear it spoken aloud. Had to see it for herself.

"Show her, Orrin," Kadrin said.

Orrin's lip curled; it was obvious enough to Kadrin that the artificer thought this moment should have a sort of ceremony to it. But Orrin moved aside, revealing a shape draped in white cloth. A familiar shape, even to Kadrin.

"Here it is," Orrin said. "My masterpiece, risen from the ashes of Renzara's failure. And no, Kadrin, I haven't forgotten your contributions. Yet another study in the efficacy of great wealth and generosity paired with great ambition and intellect."

Orrin gave the cloth a tug. Steel and chrome glittered in the orange light of the bell jars hanging from the rafters. Kadrin saw it out of the corner of his eye. He couldn't look away from Jin's face.

He could almost see the bike's reflection in her dark, staring eyes.

"How does it run?" Her voice was strained.

"The fuel tank is divided into sections." Orrin indicated a trio of intake valves. "Ordinary mana fuel admixture, stable, unstable. All three forms. There's an injector—here. Introducing raw first-form mana to treated second form tends to cause explosions, which is how my old master met her unfortunate end. But a series of small, controlled explosions is actually what powers this entire machine."

A frisson of alarm crawled through Kadrin. "Um. The bike runs on explosions? Isn't there a chance that—?"

"That it will explode while she's riding it?" Orrin nodded, unsmiling as ever but still with slightly more enthusiasm than the question warranted, in Kadrin's opinion. "Of course there's a chance. I've calculated it to be quite low, so no need to worry."

Jin moved. She walked a circle around the bike, ghosting her fingers along the handlebars and the leather seat. Kadrin watched her, transfixed.

"When?" she asked. "Kadrin, when did you commission this?"

"*Commission* isn't exactly the right term," Orrin said acerbically. "Did he sponsor my work? Yes. Offer the occasional insight in between taxing questions? Yes. Bring me the raw materials that led to a breakthrough? Yes. But the original concept was—"

"About six months ago," Kadrin said.

Jin exhaled slowly. "Then it wasn't meant for me."

Kadrin didn't respond. How could he? Of course it hadn't been. When he'd met Orrin and agreed to become Orrin's sponsor all those months ago, he'd had no inkling that Jin would ever wind up Talentless. All he had wanted was a way to accompany her into the wastes and see Yi-Nereen for himself.

Even now, he wanted that so badly he could taste it like blood in his mouth after a punch. *He* wanted to be the one to keep Yi-Nereen and Eliesen safe. To see Avi'Kerina with his own eyes. To be the one leaving, not the one left behind.

Flight of the Fallen

Finally, he found his words. "It is now. It's yours, Jin."

She turned to him. There was a fire in her eyes, a glow unlike any spark he'd seen there before. That was all the warning he had before she took two long strides toward him and pulled his face to hers to kiss him.

Kadrin's thoughts fled and his body responded on instinct. He wrapped his arms around her, nearly lifting her off the floor. Gods, what sweet torment this was, for all these hollow weeks to end with his courier returned to him—knowing she'd be gone again in a moment. He never wanted to let her go.

Jin pulled away, just an inch. "Thank you," she whispered. Her nose brushed his. "I'll keep her safe. I swear."

Kadrin closed his eyes and imagined Jin's scent, her warmth, the touch of her skin soaking into him and becoming part of the fabric of his being forever.

"Elie, too. I know she's a royal pain, but please don't let her get eaten."

Jin laughed. It was a delighted, genuine sound, nothing like the harshness he'd felt from her ever since their reunion in the dusty streets of Forge District.

"It'll be like we never left."

Yi-Nereen stood in the shadow of the Wall, clutching a satchel containing a six-day complement of rations. Her riding boots were new and already rubbing her ankles raw. For the second time in her life, she was about to enter the wastes.

"There they are," Eliesen whispered beside her.

Yi-Nereen peered through the dark. Two figures were moving

down the ruined street with a magebike between them, navigating the broken stones. Jin and Kadrin.

He'd done it. Yi-Nereen had hardly dared to believe it. But somehow, Jin was coming with them. Kadrin and his hired artificer had created a miracle.

"I saw one guard on the Wall," Jin hissed as soon as they were within earshot. Straight to business, of course. "I doubt they'll stop us from leaving. There's nothing but death out there as far as they're concerned. But let's not take chances. Once we're out, ride and don't look back."

Eliesen flew into Kadrin's arms. "If any uncommonly beautiful people show up at the House to read me poetry or drop off flowers, kiss them for me, would you? They'll hardly know the difference."

"Oh, I think they'll be able to tell." Kadrin squeezed Eliesen against his broad chest until she was wriggling and laughing breathlessly, demanding to be set free.

"All right, Celwyn." Eliesen extricated herself from her brother's arms and held out her hand to Celwyn, wrist bent daintily. Yi-Nereen could see the smirk on her face under the moonlight. "Show me a good time. I've been on rides before, but six days is rather a long while for one of my entanglements to last."

Celwyn removed a bonehelm from the handlebars of his bike and nudged it gently toward Eliesen. "If you want to last six days, you'll need this."

Impressive, Yi-Nereen thought with a measure of amusement. He'd been quick to learn how to handle Eliesen. To the extent she could be handled, anyway.

Her own goodbyes loomed before her. One goodbye, really.

Kadrin stood in silence. Yi-Nereen felt keenly for him—and for herself. How fervently she wished she could go back and do everything over again. She'd rewrite the past, make the most of every moment, and in the end she'd still leave him behind tonight. Whatever happened in the wastes, at least she would know Kadrin was safe.

As if he'd heard her thoughts, Kadrin reached out and took one of Yi-Nereen's hands and one of Jin's. His smile, when it came, was wounded and beautiful. "Come back to me. Both of you."

Jin brought Kadrin's knuckles to her lips with a conviction that surprised Yi-Nereen. "We will."

Yi-Nereen swallowed. All the unsaid words of the past several weeks hung in the air like smoke. A small voice inside her said, *This might be the last time you ever see him.* And she broke; she staggered forward and fell into his arms. "We'll meet again," she said. "It won't take twelve years this time."

"Six days at the outside." She felt his hand stroking down her hair.

Before she and Jin slipped through the gap in the Wall, Yi-Nereen sent one last lingering look back. Kadrin stood there, a barrier against the dark, his hands empty at his sides as he watched them leave the city. And Yi-Nereen imagined him standing there every day for six days, with his gaze fixed on the wastes—watching for the plume of dust that would signal their return.

No two magebikes were the same. And Jin's heart had room for only one: her most cherished lover, the rusted hauler that currently lay under the mound of rubble that had once been Mount Vetelu. She'd never replace the familiar wear of its leather or its habit of leaning into a turn almost before she did.

But maybe she could love again. Even if this new bike was

saddled with an awful name: *manacycle.* A term Orrin had invented, apparently; the artificer claimed that the word *mage* came from an old term for someone who was Talented, which wouldn't be appropriate for a bike built for a Talentless rider.

Jin straddled the bike with Yi-Nereen pressed close behind her. Fortunately Jin was too distracted for the dizzying scent of Yi-Nereen's perfume to rattle her; she had to focus.

"Throttle," Jin muttered. The little lever that would start the engine and control her speed was attached to the left handlebar, where she could work it while she rode. She positioned her hand over it but didn't squeeze.

Blowing herself and Yi-Nereen into pieces would be a fine way to start this journey. Jin's stomach roiled with nerves. But wasn't that a familiar feeling? She'd been stranded on the highway once, with raiders and a storm on her tail, a broken intake valve, and a pteropter squawking in her bonehelm. She could've blown up then. That was what being a sparkrider was.

She wasn't one anymore. But she could still ride again.

Heart racing, Jin squeezed the lever. The bike responded with a glorious growl that shook her bones—and leaped forward.

It took Jin utterly by surprise. She'd controlled her old magebike instinctively, its engine an extension of her Talent. She could stoke the engine and produce that ready rumble before the bike actually *went.* Not so with the manacycle. The bike raced forward at incredible speed, plowing up a huge cloud of dust.

She couldn't see. Who knew if Eliesen and Celwyn were behind her, or if the guards on the Wall had opened fire? But none of that mattered. Yi-Nereen's arms were tight around her waist, and she was riding again. Flying.

Jin laughed, her voice lost in the roar of the manacycle's en-

Flight of the Fallen

gine, dissolving into the delightful riot of sound she'd missed so much.

"*Fuck* yes."

✺

Sou-Zell pulled his bike to a stop. "Someone's leaving the city."

He and Falka waited atop the sandy ridge overlooking the flickering lights of Kerina Sol and watched two dark shapes flit across the wastes, plowing up clouds of dust. Whoever was leaving Kerina Sol, they weren't taking the highway that led toward Kerina Rut, or even the lesser-used roads that led into the distant southeastern stretches of the wastes toward the other kerinas. Their magebikes turned a wide curve around the city and sped west. Toward the Barrens.

Sou-Zell's jaw tightened. For someone to willingly flee one of the two remaining bastions of safety in the northern wastes for the unspeakably dangerous badlands where few had ever ventured and survived . . . what did that say about conditions in Kerina Sol?

Had he made a mistake?

He glanced at Falka's bike and the sidecar attached to it. His mother sat hunched in the sidecar, wrapped in a blanket and secured by a harness Sou-Zell and Falka had fashioned from cattle straps. Sou-Zell couldn't tell if she was conscious, but he hoped she was still breathing. They'd ridden from Kerina Rut as swiftly as he'd dared.

Sou-Zell looked down at Kerina Sol again.

He'd made his choice. His mother would rather have died than live Talentless and indebted to Shield Lord Lai-Dan. Pleading for Lai-Dan's aid would have sacrificed any chance Sou-Zell had of seeing his House restored.

195

Now his only hope lay somewhere in the city below, on the shoulders of a woman Sou-Zell had once intended to marry—the only other person in the wastes who had the power to save his mother.

Lai-Dan's daughter, Yi-Nereen.

PART THREE

PART THREE

CHAPTER NINETEEN

DOUBTS

Observation #492: Sabotage suspected in Renzara's mishap.
Suspects: Husband, lover, rivals, apprentice.
Hypothesis: This will get ugly. —O

Third Age of Storms, 1st Summer, Day 84

The Wastes – West of Kerina Sol

Jin's body ached. The initial burst of exhilaration had faded, and she was swiftly discovering the true nature of the beast between her legs: it wasn't a bike at all, but a devil incarnated in steel and leather. It refused to do what she wanted unless she applied exactly the precise amount of pressure, shifted her weight in just the right way. It balked at turning in the critical moment. She'd nearly flung herself and Yi-Nereen headfirst into a cactus ten times already.

Celwyn was riding ahead; he cut the familiar, relaxed profile of a sparkrider on the open road. Jin was a hunched bundle of nerves, hot, angry, and embarrassed. No doubt Yi-Nereen was comparing this with all the rides she'd had from Jin before. Jin wanted to shout that it was the godsdamned bike's fault, but she knew that would make her sound like a child.

Two hours west of Kerina Sol, Celwyn raised his gloved hand, signaling for a break. Jin's legs trembled like jelly as she swung off the manacycle. She was drenched in sweat and burning with humiliation.

"That was *amazing!*" Eliesen hopped off Celwyn's bike and stretched like a cat. The wind had blown her hair into a frizzy brown cloud around her head. "Why are we stopping?"

"We're far enough from the city that pursuit is unlikely," Celwyn said. "At some point before dawn, we'll need to rest. Now is as good a time as any."

He didn't look at Jin. But surely it was obvious to everyone *why* they'd stopped. Jin couldn't keep up. They had six days' worth of mana and a vast amount of land to cross, and she was slowing them down.

"Out here in the middle of nowhere?" Eliesen squinted around at the rocks and dirt like she expected to find a complement of servants ready to tuck her into bed. "How long before we get going again?"

Jin walked away without waiting for Celwyn's reply. She felt Yi-Nereen's eyes on her back, but no one asked where she was going.

She shouldn't be here. There should be another courier on this trip, one with a real magebike. Seeing the manacycle had sparked hope in her for the first time in almost two months; she'd glimpsed her old life again. But that was stupid. Nothing had changed.

She was still Talentless.

Jin glanced over her shoulder. She'd already put a good distance between herself and the other three. They were dark shapes moving under the moonlight, pulling things out of packs and making temporary camp.

Jin's stomach grumbled. She could swallow her pride and rejoin

Flight of the Fallen

them for a bite to eat. But then she'd probably blow up at some innocuous comment and ruin everybody's night. No, better to get out of sight and kick rocks until her temper simmered down.

A cactus garden bristled a few hundred paces from where they'd stopped, spiny black shapes against the night. Jin slipped between them, grateful for a bit of cover. The hard knot in her gut relaxed with every breath she took of crisp, cool air. She'd never been able to come this far on foot. Gods, she'd missed this: the silence, the dark, the breeze. Living in a kerina was like sticking her head in a chamber pot every day.

But the city had its upsides, too. Like Reena and Kadrin.

Who *weren't* getting married, apparently.

Jin had left them in the House's garden that day because she was broken, and she wasn't foolish enough to think that she could be fixed. But she'd left expecting Reena and Kadrin to put themselves together without her. Somehow they'd fucked it up, and now Jin wasn't actually sure who was the most broken out of the three of them.

Maybe their unhappiness was her fault, too. Or maybe not.

In the distance, a magebike engine roared. Jin's blood ran cold.

She'd been slowing them down—and now they were leaving her behind.

No, she was an idiot, and that engine didn't sound like hers or Celwyn's. It had a different voice. Throatier, feral.

Jin turned and sprinted back to the campsite. She didn't have a weapon besides her utility knife; she never carried one in the wastes. Fleeing was the first and best option in any scenario. But like an absolute fool, she'd gone and separated herself from her bike—and from her companions.

Her head pounded with images of Yi-Nereen and Eliesen grappling with shadowy figures in tattered leather. The two of them held down and gagged while the flesh was flayed from their bones. Or motionless already, impaled by a raider's lance. The thirty seconds it took for Jin to sprint back fit an eternity of gory possibilities.

As she drew close, she saw a tight circle of bikes pulled in close around her bike and Celwyn's. Typical raider tactic, cutting off retreat. Celwyn was on his feet, a blade flashing in his hands, surrounded by five or six raiders. But even in the dark, Jin could see they weren't fighting. Celwyn's free hand was raised in a gesture of parley.

The next thing she knew, there were lances bristling in her direction.

"No closer!"

"Who the fuck is this?"

"One step and I'll—"

"Wait, just wait." Celwyn's voice, deep and arresting. "She's no threat."

That stung, but Jin couldn't deny it. She skidded to a stop, breathing hard. The moon wasn't bright enough to reveal important details: whether there was blood on anyone's clothes, whether the raiders looked crazed or reasonable, or even where Yi-Nereen and Eliesen were.

"Reena? Elie?"

"Here," came Yi-Nereen's voice, and Jin saw her—sitting on the ground, back-to-back with Eliesen. Like they'd been ordered to get down and stay still.

Which was all rather civil for a band of raiders. And they *had* to be raiders. Their bikes were far too scrappy to belong to knights,

Flight of the Fallen

and couriers didn't travel in groups. But that didn't explain why no one was screaming or dying or getting flayed.

"Just keep calm, Jin," Celwyn said. "Don't move."

He sounded calm himself. And suspicion rose in Jin's throat like bile. She'd assumed he had been part of the Knights of Lav; his familiarity with a sword was suggestive evidence. But she'd never actually *asked*.

It had been Celwyn's decision to stop here. Right here, in this exact spot.

Now he and one of the raiders were speaking, their voices too low for Jin to make out what they were saying. She took one careful step forward, but the nearest raider hefted their lance and Jin got the message. Her hackles were raised.

If Celwyn was in the process of betraying them, there was nothing she could do about it. The thought made her want to throttle someone.

Celwyn's sword slid back into its sheath with a metallic rasp. He and the raider shook hands. Jin's blood boiled as the other raiders, save the one whose lance was trained on Jin, bent over and rifled through the packs strewn across the ground.

Their supplies. Nothing she could do. Jin ground her teeth and waited.

Finally it was over. There was no exchange of farewells; at a whistle from their leader, the raiders hopped on their bikes and tore away in a thunder of snarling engines. They were gone in moments, out of sight over the hills.

Celwyn hadn't gone with them. He stood staring across the wastes as if he wished he had. Jin advanced on him, simmering with heat—but Eliesen beat her to the punch.

"What the hell was that? You let them take our food! Our maps! You and that raider knew each other—don't bother lying about it. Did you fucking *set us up?*"

"Elie!"

Jin caught up and grabbed Elie's arms before she could hit him. If Elie started a fight, Celwyn would surely best them all. Yi-Nereen was still on the ground, clutching one of the satchels the raiders hadn't stolen. Knowing her, it probably contained her notes on Avi'Kerina and absolutely nothing of material use.

Celwyn stood like a statue under the moonlight. "I can explain."

"Don't bother." Yi-Nereen climbed to her feet and turned to Jin. "Those raiders. I recognized their voices. They used to be with Falka. And so did *he.*"

Jin froze, her hand still clenched on Eliesen's wrist. "Are you sure?"

"He wasn't with the group that ambushed us at the temple. But I saw him later, at the castle." She cast a scornful look at Celwyn. "Do you deny it?"

Celwyn glanced between the three of them like a hunted animal. He'd made no move to draw his weapon, which was Jin's sole comfort. "No. But I swear, I didn't set a trap for you. I had no idea Falka's freebooters were in the area. I haven't had any contact with them since Mount Vetelu fell."

"You bastard," Eliesen seethed, tugging at Jin's grip. "You lied to Toraka. You lied to us all."

"It's worse than that," Yi-Nereen said coldly. "You helped kill someone I cared for. A boy named Faolin. Did you even know his name?"

Celwyn flinched, as if Yi-Nereen had slapped him. His mouth opened, but he said nothing.

Flight of the Fallen

"Answer the question!" Yi-Nereen shouted.

The hair on Jin's arms stood on end. Yi-Nereen raised her hands and a glowing blue shield bloomed from her fingertips, but it was like no shield Jin had seen her cast before. Blue light darted forward like a lance, honed to a razor-sharp tip. It came to a halt inches from Celwyn's chest, humming audibly.

"What in Rasvel's name?" Eliesen hissed in Jin's ear. "How is she *doing* that?"

Celwyn staggered backward. His fingers clutched uselessly at the air, but still he didn't reach for his sword. Then, for no reason Jin could see, he fell to his knees.

"I couldn't stop her." His voice had changed. Jin's skin crawled; he sounded *wrong*. Younger, almost like a child. "I *tried*. They all jumped me. Falka put me in the lift and sent me down from the mountain. I couldn't—couldn't save him."

"You liar," Jin snarled, letting go of Eliesen's arm. "You expect us to believe you just happened to be the only one of Falka's goons who didn't go along with what she was doing? Saurian shit."

Yi-Nereen's shield-lance trembled in midair. "Wait—Jin. I don't remember seeing him when the mountain fell. I saved the others. They ran off. He wasn't with them."

Jin took a step forward, her fingers on the hilt of her utility knife. "Maybe you just forgot."

"No, Jin." Yi-Nereen let her arms fall. The shield dissipated into nothingness. "I don't think I did. Celwyn, who was Faolin to you?"

Celwyn shivered, arms wrapped around himself. "My brother."

Jin blinked. What? She'd sat next to Faolin under the sunlight in the green canyon where his people lived and watched him draw every sparkrider he knew on a piece of parchment. Three people: him; his sister, Amrys; and his unknown progenitor, who'd turned out to be Tibius Vann. There certainly wasn't room for Celwyn in that family tree.

But Yi-Nereen was staring at Celwyn like she'd just seen the sun for the first time.

"You're Amrys," she said.

CHAPTER TWENTY

A DEAD GIRL'S SECRETS

Observation #612: Options running short. List of potential patrons dwindling by the day. No one wants to finance Renzara's rumored murderer.

Next move: Look into younger High House heirs for someone coin-foolish and naive. —O

Third Age of Storms, 1st Summer, Day 84
The Wastes – West of Kerina Sol

The moon hung like a bright lantern over the wastes, but Yi-Nereen's mind transported her back into the churning dark of the Storm of Centuries. Ambrosia burned in her veins; a dead boy's voice fogged her thoughts. Faolin had lived in her for those brief moments, after she'd consumed his Talent at Tibius Vann's behest. It was Faolin who had convinced her to stand down and listen to Jin.

It was thanks to Faolin that she hadn't destroyed the world.

Celwyn knelt on the ground before her now. His shoulders trembled. He hadn't reacted to Yi-Nereen's voice. She took a step toward him, her hand hovering near the crown of his head.

"Amrys," she repeated. "Is that you?"

She knew Amrys had met the same fate as Faolin: her soul

harvested for her Talent, to bestow power on one of Falka's raiders. But she hadn't known which of the raiders had killed and absorbed the girl, and she'd certainly never expected to *meet* her . . . like this. Her skin was crawling.

Celwyn looked up, his eyes dark and hollow. "It was." His voice was back to its normal depth and roughness. "She can't speak through me often. It hurts us both. But how did you know?"

"The same thing happened to me. Tibius Vann's procedure. He used Faolin."

She'd never acknowledged it aloud before. Hearing Faolin's voice in her head in the grip of ambrosia was the only part of her ordeal she'd never spoken about to anyone, not even Jin or Kadrin. It was too unbelievable, too possible to dismiss as a hallucination, even though Yi-Nereen knew it was real.

Celwyn's fists tightened. "Is he still . . . ?"

"No. I was already Talented, so it didn't last. He's gone."

Yi-Nereen could only imagine what was going on in Celwyn's head right now. It struck her that Amrys didn't know she and Yi-Nereen were cousins. Yi-Nereen had no idea what she was like, really; she hadn't exactly been able to ask Faolin. Gods, this was strange. Yi-Nereen had mourned the death of this girl she'd never met, and now she'd come face-to-face with her living ghost.

"Um," Eliesen said from behind her. "So what's happening? Who's Amrys?"

"It's difficult to explain." Yi-Nereen swept a hand across her sweaty forehead. "Tibius Vann used living Talented sacrifices to transplant Talent into Falka's raiders. One of the side effects of his procedure is hearing that sacrifice's voice, even after they are gone. In my case, only for a short time. For people who were originally Talentless, it seems permanent."

Flight of the Fallen

To Yi-Nereen's surprise, Jin nodded. "Falka mentioned hearing a voice. I think it drove her mad."

She'd never talked about that final confrontation between herself and Falka in the castle, at least not to Yi-Nereen. All Yi-Nereen knew was that the encounter had ended with Jin gut-stabbed and bleeding to death. Maybe Yi-Nereen wasn't the only one who'd kept the most traumatic, inexplicable parts of that day to herself.

Celwyn rose to his feet. "Toraka and I should not have kept you in the dark about my history. In truth, I was exiled from the kerinas years ago. I was only permitted to reenter Kerina Lav because of what I brought with me. The tablet."

"And then you gained Toraka's trust," Jin said. "A fine job of it, too. She trusted you enough to send you on this expedition. And look where we are."

"I admit I've made mistakes," Celwyn said coldly. "I went along with Falka's schemes for far too long. But the kerinas abandoned me to die in the wastes, and she saved my life. She gave me a home and a purpose. Toraka understood everything: why I was loyal to Falka, and why I turned on her."

Jin clenched her fists. "She should have told the rest of us who you were."

"Why do that?" Eliesen shrugged. "Seems like that would have pissed everyone off and set us back even further. We didn't exactly have a legion of sparkriders raring to go."

"Whose side are you *on*?"

"Oh, calm down, Jin. We're all still heading toward the same goal. Celwyn didn't have to help us find Avi'Kerina. He's risking his life out here, same as us."

"He just handed most of our food over to his old friends. Didn't waste much time arguing about it, either."

"They're starving," Celwyn said, his tone sharp. "I know what that's like. Don't worry; we still have enough to survive the journey. It just won't be pleasant."

Jin shook her head. A familiar obstinacy burned in her dark eyes. "We need to go back. I'm not riding into the Barrens with someone who was willing to murder a girl for her Talent."

"Jin, don't you realize?" Yi-Nereen asked wearily. "It isn't just Celwyn you're talking about. It's Amrys, too."

"That doesn't make it better," Jin snapped. "She's not really alive, is she? She's just trapped inside her killer's head. Damn it, I promised Faolin I'd help him rescue his sister. And by the time I got there, he was already—"

Her voice broke. Yi-Nereen wrestled down the urge to go to her, to put her hands on Jin's trembling arms and comfort her. She didn't know what Jin would do. Yi-Nereen hardly had the right to touch her, after everything she'd done.

"We can't go back," Eliesen said. "The second we step into the city, High Priestess Edine's going to be all over us like flies on cow shit. Sorry, Jin, but we need him. Them. Four bodies, two bikes. I can do that math."

"What about our maps?" Yi-Nereen asked. "They're gone. Stolen. We'll never find our way through the Barrens without those."

Celwyn sighed. "I wouldn't have let them take the maps if I hadn't already memorized them. I can lead us there."

"Well, good." Eliesen smiled. "Jin, darling, any further objections? Otherwise, Avi'Kerina awaits."

Seconds ticked by in silence. Jin stared at the ground, her expression molten. Finally she raised her head and gave Celwyn a glare so dark Yi-Nereen felt her hackles rise. "When this is over, you'll be siphoned like everyone else. Amrys will finally be free of you."

Flight of the Fallen

"She isn't trapped," Celwyn said in a low voice. "At first she was, yes. But she stayed with me because she wanted to. We've been working together for some time now."

"Pardon me if I don't believe you," Jin said.

Eliesen clapped her hands. "I'm so glad everyone's getting along. Now, why don't we get going? I don't feel safe here."

For a moment Yi-Nereen thought Jin and Celwyn would simply stand there glowering at each other until dawn, both refusing to be the one to break eye contact. Then Celwyn turned with a gruff sound and began helping Eliesen retrieve the supplies the raiders had strewn around the campsite. Yi-Nereen moved to help—but then she felt Jin's hesitant touch on her arm.

"Are you all right?" Jin's voice was rough. "Did anyone touch you?"

"I'm fine. Are you okay?"

She knew better than to mention the way Jin had stormed off earlier, but from the visible flush on Jin's face even under the moonlight, she was thinking about it, too.

"I'm fantastic. Thrilled to have an ex-raider on the team. He and Falka must have kidnapped and murdered dozens of sparkriders together, not just Amrys and Faolin. Probably other couriers I knew."

"I know," Yi-Nereen said. "But Eliesen is right. We do need him."

Jin snorted. "Should have known better than to join an expedition with *two* princesses. She might be worse than you are." She eyed Yi-Nereen, and something in her face softened. "No, I can't decide. You're both awful in your own way."

It would have sounded like an insult on anyone else's tongue. But Yi-Nereen felt a rush of warmth. She knew how much Jin cared for Eliesen; there was history there, and it was obvious in the way they spoke to each other. If Yi-Nereen was honest with herself, she'd been the tiniest bit jealous.

Yi-Nereen swallowed. "I told you Faolin was my cousin. You know what that means."

Jin stared at her. "Shit."

"I know."

"I hadn't put that together. But I suppose that means I can't kill Celwyn."

"I'd really prefer if you didn't." Yi-Nereen laughed shakily. "And I'm not the only one. Eliesen might take issue."

"Yes," Jin said, her lip curled. "I've noticed. She always did have terrible taste in men. Much better taste in women, though."

"I can see that," Yi-Nereen said softly.

She was rewarded by an even deeper flush that spread across Jin's angular cheekbones. They were standing a few inches apart, but Yi-Nereen felt a sudden, almost irrepressible urge to reach out and touch her. She couldn't, of course. It wouldn't be fair. Not to Jin or to herself.

She hadn't earned Jin's forgiveness yet. Perhaps that would come only once they reached Avi'Kerina.

Two days passed in a dusty haze. Celwyn was their guide, but Jin had unequivocally taken the lead. She chose each and every place they stopped, whether for a quick break or a night's rest, and set the watch order at random herself.

When it was Yi-Nereen's turn and the rest were sleeping, she sat near Jin and attuned herself to the steady rhythm of Jin's breath. Her world had been so small for so many years; the infinite emptiness of the wastes threatened to send her into a panic. At least in the Tower, she'd known what to expect from each monotonous day of her life.

Now she didn't even know herself. Her head ached, growing worse by the hour. The aborted attack she'd made on Celwyn had drained more mana than she'd expected, but she refused to take more than her share from their dwindling stores. She'd take only enough to sustain herself, however miserable an existence it was.

Once they reached Mount Vetelu, this torment would end, at least in part. The plan was to refuel at the spring there. If they ran into any bloodthirsty saurians—which Jin seemed to treat as a given—Yi-Nereen would be ready. No harm would come to the others.

At dusk on the second day, they camped on a bluff strewn with reddish rocks. A lone cactus grew above the overlook, its arms wispy with white fluff that Celwyn warned them all not to touch. "You'll get a nasty rash. And don't even think about putting it in your mouth."

"Why would anyone think of doing that?" Eliesen asked acerbically. Two days of strict rationing had put everyone in a foul mood, but Elie most of all.

She was setting up their water collection system, which was nothing more than a large oilcloth draped over pegs driven into the ground, with a hole cut into the center and an attached funnel. Yi-Nereen watched Elie raise her arms and tilt her face to the sky. Her eyes glowed misty white. The air above her fogged, and droplets pattered down onto the oilcloth, collecting in rivulets.

Yi-Nereen's skin prickled. She wasn't the only one watching Elie. Celwyn leaned against his magebike a few paces off, arms crossed. He was frowning slightly, but the look in his eyes was anything but disapproving.

"Reena," Jin called from the overlook.

Yi-Nereen's pulse skipped. She craved the sound of her nickname on Jin's tongue; it was even stronger than her hunger for food, despite days of near starvation. "Coming."

She joined Jin at the edge of the west-facing bluff. Sunset painted Jin's tanned skin orange, tinting her dark hair and softening the lines of her face. Yi-Nereen found it hard not to stare. In the city, she thought of Jin as handsome in a way few women were; she dressed plainly and wore no jewelry or cosmetics, not even a streak of galena on her eyelids, but her bone structure drew the eye and she moved with a taut, ranging surety that seemed entirely unselfconscious.

But out here, with the wild wastes as her backdrop, Jin was beautiful. The dying sunlight draped her like a gown; she was radiant in it.

"We'll be in the Barrens tomorrow," Jin said. "Not that there's an exact border, but you can see it, can't you? That yellowish fog. We'll want to cover our faces."

Yi-Nereen blinked. She hadn't actually been listening. She was behaving like a lovestruck fool, and for what? Jin had barely spoken to her since the demonstration in Temple Square, and she'd been furious then.

Maybe she'd come on this expedition only as a favor to Kadrin, or because she didn't trust Yi-Nereen with a task of this importance. Yi-Nereen had no business mooning over her.

"Sorry, what——?"

A scream cut her off. Yi-Nereen whipped around.

Huge, dark wings loomed over Elie. A massive pteropter had landed on a rock inches away from her; it *dwarfed* her. Its long,

Flight of the Fallen

toothy jaw was open, emitting a rattling hiss that made Yi-Nereen's hair stand on end.

She reacted on instinct, reaching into herself to burn mana. Shaping it as it flowed from her fingers into a humming blue lance. Her temples throbbed with mana thirst.

"Celwyn!" Eliesen scrambled backward so quickly she tripped and fell on her rump.

Celwyn raced over, his sword drawn, but Jin threw herself into his path.

"No, don't! He's not—"

The saurian's shriek drowned her voice. It reared up and flared its wings again. Eliesen was screaming, too, her arms raised to cover her face.

Yi-Nereen's eyes darted from the saurian to Jin and back. Could it be?

Screech?

She remembered Jin's story of the pteropter absorbing lightning at Mount Vetelu. Her insistence that the saurian had grown before her eyes. Yi-Nereen had forgotten that bizarre little detail in the wake of everything else.

"Stay where you are," Jin snarled at Celwyn, her arms outstretched. "I know this pteropter. He's just hungry. He won't attack if you stay calm."

"How sure are you about that?" Eliesen demanded.

Celwyn's drawn sword gleamed in the light of sunset, but he didn't move. "This isn't good. Pteropters don't fly alone, especially not this close to the Barrens."

"This one does," Jin said. "Ask Amrys, all right? Her people know not all saurians are dangerous. This one is mine."

Celwyn gave her a strange look. "You command it? You know the words?"

"What? No. I feed him."

Yi-Nereen watched with equal parts terror and fascination as Jin lowered her arms and turned toward the pteropter. A few cautious steps, and she was beside Eliesen.

The saurian cocked its head. The colorful feathers on its back rippled in the breeze. Yi-Nereen's brain painted a picture of it lunging forward and clamping its beak on Jin's neck in one violent motion. Dear Rasvel, but it was *gigantic*.

Jin put her hand in her pocket. "I thought you might show up. Been saving this for you. Easy now, all right?"

One of Yi-Nereen's uncles had kept a dog: a hulking white hound he'd imported from Kerina Tez when it was a pup. There weren't many of the animals left, and the ones that remained were raised as ostentatious companions for the wealthy and inbred to the point of malfunction. For years, Yi-Nereen had never seen the beast do anything but bark at her uncle's visitors and stagger about on the verge of collapse. But her uncle had spoken to it sometimes in the same tone Jin was using now: calm, low, soothing.

It had worked, until the day the dog took her uncle's hand off at the wrist. Then Yi-Nereen's father had made her and all her siblings watch it die.

Yi-Nereen trembled. Her knees were weak, but she kept her power focused on Jin and the saurian. If it moved, she'd be faster.

Jin dangled a strip of meat in the air and tossed it on the ground, past Eliesen's cowering form. In a blur, the pteropter lunged. It snapped up the morsel in an instant and rounded on Jin once more.

"Shit," Jin said. "I guess he's hungry."

Flight of the Fallen

"Give him more," Eliesen gasped from the shelter of her arms. "All the fucking rations. I don't care. Don't let him eat me, Jin."

"Oh, for Rasvel's sake."

Celwyn stepped forward. His eyes burned orange and a stream of sparks shot from his outstretched hand. Jin made a feral sound and whirled on him, but before she could reach him, the pteropter opened its beak and *swallowed* the sparks.

Jin froze. Screech chirped. He took several ungainly hops toward the edge of the bluff and his massive wings beat once, twice, carrying him away.

Yi-Nereen released her power only once the pteropter was nothing more than a black dot against the sun. A wave of weakness washed through her, so intense her knees nearly buckled. Blood roared in her ears. She barely heard what Celwyn said next.

"It's the storm-drought. I should have known. Saurians are lightning eaters; they must have been starving all this time. Though it seems like *that* one has a taste for meat. Was that your doing?"

"What are you, a saurian expert?" Eliesen asked sharply before Jin could reply.

Celwyn rubbed his temples. "In a manner of speaking."

"Not you," Jin said. "Give credit where it's due."

"Oh, will you two stop sniping at each other for one fucking second?" Eliesen rolled to her feet. "That damn beast made me spill our water. It's going to cost mana we don't have, filling up those bottles again. You could have warned me you had a pet, Jin."

"He's not my—"

"Can I talk to you?" Yi-Nereen said in a low voice, head turned toward Celwyn.

She led him to the edge of the bluff. Out in the Barrens, the sun was sinking slowly into a soup of yellow fog. The sky was darkening quickly—or perhaps that was Yi-Nereen's vision. She was terribly thirsty.

"I've been among her people. Amrys's." Yi-Nereen glanced at Celwyn, searching his face. "Can she hear me right now?"

"Always," Celwyn said.

"Does she have anything to say?"

Celwyn sighed. For a moment, his features twisted with something Yi-Nereen could only recognize as pain. "It isn't quite that simple. We don't exactly . . . have conversations. There's no clear separation anymore. When I open my mouth, it's usually me. But sometimes it's her. And sometimes it's both of us."

"I want her to know I made her brother a promise. He asked me for something at the end, and I've done my best to keep my word ever since."

"What did he ask for?"

"He asked me never to go back to the canyon where his people lived and not to tell anyone else where they were. I don't know whether he wanted to protect them or their secrets. I assumed Amrys would want the same."

"I don't know what she wants," Celwyn said coldly. "I have memories that aren't mine and I know things I shouldn't know. There's hardly two of us in here anymore."

Yi-Nereen's hands worked, restless and frustrated. "I'm sure she'd feel the same as Faolin. Jin already knows, but Eliesen—you shouldn't tell Eliesen about the herders. She loves to gossip."

"I won't spend the rest of my life keeping a dead girl's secrets," Celwyn said. "For better or worse, she lives with the kerinas now." He gave Yi-Nereen a dark, tired smile. "Before you criticize me, think about all the decisions you've made for other people. Keep-

Flight of the Fallen

ing your word to one person won't absolve you of everything else. Believe me, I know."

Disquiet stirred in Yi-Nereen's chest. She wanted to argue, to defend herself. When she *could* ask for consent, she did. And she always acted to save lives.

But if she had what Celwyn had—the secrets of the Road Builders' descendants rattling around in her head—would she be able to keep it to herself?

Perhaps it didn't matter. They were on their way to plunder Avi'Kerina of its secrets and change the wasteland forever. Perhaps Yi-Nereen *should* have broken her word to Faolin and gone to visit his people again. Maybe they knew about the First City and could have led them there—or warned her away.

It was too late now. But once they located Avi'Kerina, Yi-Nereen would find Faolin's people. Her kin. She'd invite them to share in the richness of whatever it contained.

Celwyn turned abruptly, as if he'd grown weary of Yi-Nereen's silence. "Good talk."

She watched him rejoin Eliesen and Jin around the oilcloth. Jin regarded him with narrowed eyes, but under a shower of freshly called rain, Eliesen smiled.

CHAPTER TWENTY-ONE

AN INTERROGATION

Observation #630: Found him. Kadrin, Third Heir to Rain Lord
Matrios. He's perfect.
Conclusion: Talentless are good for coin as well as blood, it seems.
—O

Third Age of Storms, 1st Summer, Day 84
Kerina Sol – House of Steel Heavens

Someone knocked on the door to Kadrin's bedchamber.
"What?" he croaked, disoriented. It felt like mere minutes
had passed since he'd staggered back from seeing off the expedition at the Wall and collapsed into bed, but sunlight was pouring
through the windows.

"It's Wexler, Your Highness. There's a courier here to see you in
the parlor."

What?

Kadrin slid out of bed. At least he didn't have to get dressed.
He'd fallen asleep in clothes still stained with Refugee Quarter
grime and riot sweat.

"Is it Jin?" he called out.

No reply. Wexler must have gone away already.

Flight of the Fallen

If the expedition had returned already, that could only spell disaster. And why wouldn't Eliesen have come directly to wake him up? Kadrin paused just long enough to buckle on his sword before leaving his bedchamber and hurrying to the parlor.

For a moment he thought it *was* Jin standing stiffly beside the cushioned divan, staring up at the gilt-framed painting. Then the figure turned.

It was Sou-Zell. He wore a leather coat with a high, buttoned collar; his dark hair was braided away from his angular face, revealing a long, still-healing scar that snaked down his cheek to his jaw. Kadrin had last seen that scar as a wound; a raider had cut Sou-Zell's face while he and Kadrin were fighting at Mount Vetelu. A thin layer of wasteland dust coated his slim figure, head to toe.

Kadrin gaped. He'd never expected to see Sou-Zell again, much less in his own House. His hand found the hilt of his sword.

"What are you doing here? Is Kerina Rut—?"

"Fallen? No." Sou-Zell's voice was a shock, too. The man sounded hoarse, exhausted. This was not the haughty, sneering nobleman Kadrin remembered. "That isn't why I've come. Where is Princess Yi-Nereen?"

Kadrin stiffened, instantly on guard. Sou-Zell had given up his claim to Yi-Nereen's hand over a month ago, but what if something had changed? Kadrin didn't relish the thought of crossing blades with him again, especially not if Sou-Zell actually meant to win.

"Don't tell me you're still working for her father."

"Don't waste my time." Sou-Zell's jaw twitched, as if he'd just swallowed an insult. "This has nothing to do with you. It's between the princess and myself. I simply assumed she would be *here*, with her husband."

Kadrin reached for words, but found none. Apparently his face gave him away. Sou-Zell's eyes widened almost imperceptibly; then that old, mocking smirk Kadrin remembered made its reappearance.

"Ah. She thought better of marrying you, did she?" His voice was low and silken. "Good for her."

Kadrin's face burned. "Do you always resort to petty insults when you don't get your way? Or is this what it sounds like when you're asking for help?"

He'd touched a nerve. Sou-Zell's nostrils flared. "The wastes will burn to ash before I ask for *your* help, Talentless."

"Funny. I don't recall you complaining when I saved your life."

"A debt long since repaid. How predictably gauche of you to mention it."

"*Was* it, though?" Kadrin pressed, sensing a weak spot. "I think it was Jin who saved us both, actually."

Sou-Zell inhaled sharply, as if to steady himself. And Kadrin noticed something odd: Sou-Zell's hands were trembling, ever so slightly. It couldn't have been anger; Kadrin didn't have that much power over him. It had to be exhaustion. Had he ridden straight here from Kerina Rut? Even Jin was tired after making that trip, and she'd been a much stronger sparkrider than Sou-Zell.

Kadrin bit his lip. "Do you want something to drink?"

Sou-Zell's eyes flashed; now *that* was anger. "If Yi-Nereen isn't here, I'll find her myself." He swept past Kadrin and into the hallway, his head held high.

"Wait," Kadrin said.

He'd never really had a chance to hate Sou-Zell. At least, not the way the man seemed to despise him. Kadrin hadn't even known he *existed* until he found out Yi-Nereen's life was in danger, which had overshadowed every other thought. Now he realized that though Sou-Zell would never admit it, he must have suffered; he'd known

Flight of the Fallen

there was never a chance Yi-Nereen would love him, and that she'd risked her life to get away from him. That didn't excuse his actions—but it did explain why he would latch on to Kadrin as the source of all his woes.

And that was nothing new to Kadrin, truly. Half of Kerina Sol probably felt the same way Sou-Zell did about the Talentless, but at least Sou-Zell's hatred of Kadrin felt personal. It was almost refreshing.

For a moment he thought Sou-Zell wouldn't stop. Then he did, turning his head just enough to glare at Kadrin with one eye, so all Kadrin could see of his face was that half-healed scar.

He'd received it fighting for the very same things Kadrin valued above all: Yi-Nereen's life, and Jin's. Surely that mattered more than an obsolete rivalry.

"Yi-Nereen isn't here," Kadrin said. "She's not in Kerina Sol at all. Long story, but she went into the wastes with Jin, looking for—something. They're due back in six days."

There was a beat of silence. Then Sou-Zell asked, his voice carefully level, "When did she leave?"

"Last night. If you tell me where you're staying, I can let you know when—"

"That won't be necessary." Sou-Zell sounded abruptly distant. His voice was beyond feeling entirely. "We won't meet again."

He went on walking, and this time Kadrin had no reason to call him back before he was gone.

Kadrin rubbed the back of his neck, bewildered. What could Sou-Zell want so desperately that he'd ride all the way to Kerina Sol to get it, yet wasn't willing to wait six more days? It didn't feel right to let him leave. But Kadrin didn't have the words he'd need to convince Sou-Zell to confide in him. It was likely they didn't exist.

Later, perhaps, he'd find out where Sou-Zell was staying and press him again. But right now, Kadrin was late for Council. Attending those meetings was the one thing he could do to help Kerina Sol. Even if none of the royals would listen to him, they couldn't keep him from using his allotted time to speak—and speak he would. He'd ensure not a single one of them could forget about the refugees and Yi-Nereen's treatise. In time, he might even wear a few of them down.

That was more important than whatever Sou-Zell's problem was.

Kadrin had wondered if the streets would be empty after last night's riot in Temple Square, but that had been a foolish thought. Life had to continue, even under all the new restrictions and curfews. He passed through streets filled with people going about their daily business, though the hushed mood he'd sensed before the riots had shifted perceptibly. Kerina Sol felt like a pot simmering over a fire.

He had a gnawing feeling the city wouldn't see another peaceful night for some time.

A voice called to him from an alley. "Prince Kadrin? Is that you?"

A young woman wrapped in a threadbare shawl stood with her hand on a filthy brick wall. Her eyes were wide; her lip trembled in obvious distress.

"It *is* you. Please—I'm from Kerina Lav. My brother was just attacked. He's hurt. We need help getting back to our family in Forge District. No one will help us."

Kadrin felt a guilty surge of relief. He hadn't been looking forward to spending hours in the stuffy Council chambers today,

Flight of the Fallen

taking clumsy notes so he could report back to Toraka later. He'd always preferred to help with his own two hands.

"Of course. Where is he?"

"This way." The woman led him down the alley, her movements quick and urgent. "I had to leave him alone. But I'm scared they'll come back."

"Who attacked him?"

"I don't know. Sol-bloods. He's Talentless—they saw his brand."

Gods, had it really come to this? Talented attacking Talentless in the streets? Kadrin felt a cold sweat rise all over. How was he supposed to stop this—convince a whole city not to turn on their neighbors?

Maybe Yi-Nereen and Toraka were right, and the only way to save them all was to turn them all Talentless. But it would take more, much more, than one public act of heresy to overturn centuries of religious doctrine.

One step at a time. First Yi-Nereen and Jin had to prove Avi'Kerina existed. Then Kadrin could help them figure out how to convince everyone to go there.

"In here." The woman ducked through a faded green curtain, into a doorway. Kadrin followed.

A sharp blow to the back of the knees sent him to the floor. Kadrin caught himself on his palms, but a heavy weight—a boot?—flattened him. He twisted, reaching for his sword.

"Don't move or you'll get hurt." It was the young woman's voice, but she didn't sound scared anymore. Her voice had gone cold.

Kadrin twisted his head, trying to see. His eyes were still half-blinded by the transition from light to dark, but it was obvious they weren't alone. Two burly figures flanked the young woman. The weight on his back had to be a third captor.

Hana Lee

"What is this?" Kadrin could barely breathe.

The woman ignored him. "Bag him."

Kadrin had no time to react. The person sitting on his back shoved a rag in his mouth, and then someone else yanked down a burlap sack over his head.

He thought about fighting back. But his captors were obviously experienced; he'd lost his opportunity the moment he stepped into their trap. Kadrin knew, of course, that kidnap and ransom were risks every royal heir faced. But he'd never been afraid to walk the streets without a personal guard. Of all his siblings, he'd surely fetch the lowest ransom. Clearly he'd been foolish to rely on that fact for protection.

Breathe, Kadrin told himself. Not that doing so was easy while gagged. Cooperating with his captors would be the quickest way out of this mess, so long as his parents coughed up the ransom. This was an inconvenient time to be kidnapped, but all things considered, he was in little danger.

A hand yanked him to his feet. Kadrin made a sound of protest, which was predictably ignored. Sunlight fell over him. His captors were marching him out of the building.

The march went on for a long time—not just through alleys, but buildings and basements as well. Kadrin couldn't keep track past the first turn. His captors yanked him to a stop, dragged him forward, and forced him through narrow openings too many times to count. Until finally he fell to his knees on a hard stone floor, in a chamber that echoed.

The sack was yanked off his head; Kadrin sucked in a greedy lungful of clean air.

Then he looked up. High Priestess Edine stood before him.

With a flick of her hand, Edine commanded the man standing

beside Kadrin to remove the gag from his mouth. Kadrin spat. He could still *taste* it.

"Dear gods," he gasped. "If you wanted to see me, High Priestess, you could have sent an invitation."

Edine said nothing. In the silence, Kadrin's heart began to race. This couldn't be good. She *did* have any number of more civilized ways to summon him, yet she'd chosen a method that meant no one knew Kadrin was here, in what must be the temple basement.

Even Kadrin could put two and two together occasionally.

Edine looked at him a moment longer. Her dark eyes were chillingly remote. Then she said, "Put him in the chair."

Forced to his feet, Kadrin took in the room for the first time. There wasn't much to see. Stone walls, floor, and ceiling, all bare. The room echoed not because it was large, but because it was empty. Save for the High Priestess, two silent men in plain clothes, and a single steel chair.

Kadrin noted with a spike of dread that the chair had an additional feature: leather cuffs, one for each limb.

It struck him then. High Priestess Edine had no reason to hold a royal heir for ransom. That wasn't why Kadrin was here. Which meant cooperation was no longer his safest option.

Kadrin threw his weight backward, into the man pushing him toward the chair. He'd been disarmed, of course, but he'd trained in unarmed combat. The man staggered, and Kadrin swung a roundhouse kick into his ear with a brutal crack. Now he was down.

Where was the exit? The walls were featureless. There—the rectangular outline of a door—

The second man drew a short, thin metal rod from his belt. Kadrin's brain screamed a warning. If the man was a metalcrafter, he could fashion himself a deadly weapon in an instant.

What was Edine doing? Standing by the wall. She hadn't even moved to block the door. She wore an expression of vague disapproval.

The man with the rod lunged toward Kadrin, eyes burning orange—orange?—and Kadrin raised his hand instinctively to block the blow.

He caught the rod in his bare hand, and the world exploded into pain.

Flames seized his entire body. An unbearably high-pitched buzzing filled his ears. He could see nothing but white. This must be what it felt like to be struck by lightning. Kadrin could even smell the stench of burning skin and hair.

He felt himself screaming—his throat vibrated—but he couldn't hear it.

Then he was on the floor. His muscles wouldn't answer his demands. Hands dragged him into the metal chair and buckled the cuffs over his wrists and ankles.

"My dear boy." A tall, blurry figure in white approached him. "I hoped not to have to resort to such measures. We needn't have even used the restraints. This can still be a civil conversation, if you can behave yourself from now on."

"What do you think you're doing?" Kadrin slurred, his tongue thick. "I . . . I am a royal son of the House of Steel Heavens . . ."

"Indeed you are. But had I approached you at your House, you would not have been as forthcoming as you will be in this room. What I need from you is simple, Kadrin. You have knowledge of a conspiracy to undermine the temple and throw all of Kerina Sol into chaos."

Kadrin laughed, the sound a touch hysterical. "A conspiracy? That's absurd."

Yi-Nereen's plan wasn't a *conspiracy*. She and Toraka were just

Flight of the Fallen

trying to save everyone. They had to be secretive about it because of Edine's blasted sermons and accusations of heresy. Sure, they'd had a clandestine meeting in the Refugee Quarter to plan the unauthorized expedition to the Barrens, and Yi-Nereen and Toraka had staged a demonstration after curfew, but . . .

Oh. It *was* a conspiracy.

"Kadrin." Edine's tone softened. Her face shivered into focus before Kadrin's teary eyes; for a moment she looked motherly. "Your parents are personal friends of mine. I believe you're a well-intentioned young man who has been misled. Misled by Princess Yi-Nereen and her co-conspirator, Guildmaster Toraka of Kerina Lav. Perhaps Yi-Nereen herself is even a victim. It isn't too late for her to be treated leniently, but you must tell me where I can find her before she does any more damage."

"I haven't—haven't been misled. This is all happening because the Council didn't listen. Because of *you*. If they would just—"

Edine's eyes flashed violet. "Where is Yi-Nereen?"

A moment passed in breathless silence. Then Kadrin said slowly, "That doesn't work on me."

He'd never known the High Priestess was a mindreader. Of course, she had to be Talented; Talentless weren't allowed past the temple steps. But since Edine and her acolytes were exempt from the duties of ordinary Talented, there was no reason for anyone to know what their Talents were.

"I had to be certain," Edine said. "After all, your father once lied to the Shield Lord of Kerina Rut, claiming you were Talented. Now I know. I'm sorry, Kadrin."

"It doesn't bother me really." Kadrin was growing more confused by the second. "I am what I am."

"You misunderstand me." Her voice was soft. "I'm sorry because

229

this won't be quick and painless after all. I can't know if you're being truthful. I can't simply ask you questions and send you on your way. This would have been easier if you had never fallen prey to the Talent Thief. Many things would have been easier."

Kadrin had never considered himself particularly quick at forming conclusions. But he was coming to one now, perhaps far too late.

He was in deep trouble.

"Where is Yi-Nereen?" Edine asked, her face suddenly blank.

"She isn't in the city. Not anymore."

"Are you claiming she returned to Kerina Rut?"

"No."

"Where else? Kerina Tez and Kerina Lav are fallen. The other cities have no promise of sanctuary."

Was there actually any point to concealing the expedition's existence? They'd already left. The temple and the High Houses couldn't fetch them back. At worst, Kadrin would be punished for not speaking up sooner, but he was surely in for much worse if he said nothing at all.

"The Barrens," he relented, sick with guilt. "She went to the Barrens to find the First City. The place she and Toraka talked about in Temple Square last night."

"I'm sorry, Kadrin. That's quite implausible, not to mention convenient. If you gave me a location within Kerina Sol, I could verify it swiftly. Telling me Yi-Nereen is in the wastes is a much cleverer answer. It's impossible to disprove."

"Trust me." Kadrin's mouth was dry. "I'm not that good of a liar."

"We'll see," Edine said. "Again, I am truly sorry."

Never had a softly delivered apology struck such fear into

Flight of the Fallen

Kadrin's blood. Edine nodded to the man standing beside him, the one with the metal rod. Kadrin had forgotten he was there.

The memory of that all-consuming flame overtook him. He'd never heard of sparktalent used that way. Talents were supposed to be *gifts*. They were meant for survival. Not torture.

"No," he said. "Wait. There's no need for that. I'm telling the truth. I swear it to Rasvel, Reena isn't in the city anymore, she's on her way to the Barrens—"

The cool tip of the rod touched his cheek, even as he strained away from it, and a moment later he felt the flame.

CHAPTER TWENTY-TWO

THE WRETCH

Observation #323: Renzara is a disappointment. Coddled all her life
by royal relatives, handed every discovery she's credited.
Hypothesis: When she accepted my application, she planned to
shake my brain upside down and snatch everything that fell out.
—O

Third Age of Storms, 1st Summer, Day 84
Kerina Sol – Refugee Quarter

Sou-Zell returned to the hovel with fire in his veins.

The hovel—that was enough reason for rage on its own. When he'd arrived at the city gates, he'd learned that Kerina Sol was overrun. Guildmasters, common folk, and Lav-blood Talentless alike had been packed together into a single district with no regard for social stature. The gate guard had brusquely informed Sou-Zell that there were no rooms available to let in the entire city, not for love or coin, but he could stake a claim in the Refugee Quarter.

The Refugee Quarter was an overcrowded slum. Foul smoke permeated the air; the refugees had long since run out of fuel and were burning clothes, debris, and offal for their cookfires.

Flight of the Fallen

Apparently a storm had reduced the district to rubble and it had never been rebuilt. Kerina Sol's ineptitude would never cease to amaze.

Sou-Zell had found a Lav-blood physician who'd set up shop in one of the few remaining buildings: a squat mudbrick dwelling without a roof. *The hovel*, Sou-Zell called it. The physician was a gaunt man with a minor Talent for relieving pain. He'd reluctantly agreed to give Lady Ren a cot. *A kindness not to let her die in the streets*, he'd said. *But there's nothing more I can do for her.*

As if Sou-Zell weren't already aware.

Falka was perched on a step outside the hovel, smoking a mana-cig. When she saw Sou-Zell coming, she stood and flicked ash to the ground.

"Well? I don't see a princess."

"She's gone," Sou-Zell said. "Jin-Lu spirited her away on a mage-bike. I heard it from her ex-fiancé's lips."

Falka snorted. "He was lying to you. Jin's Talentless now."

"*Was* he lying?" Sou-Zell drew closer. "Or are you?"

Doubt flickered in Falka's eyes, almost too swift to see. "Look, Jin fell into a spring, didn't she? And the princess siphoned her to save her? Then she's Talentless. No other way she could have lived. It works just the same way as the defuser Tibius built, though he didn't bother keeping the victims alive."

"I only have your word that Yi-Nereen has this power at all."

"You witless bastard," Falka said. "I almost feel sorry for you. You're so proud of your Talent, but you're too stupid to use it when it counts—or use your fucking ears. Have you been listening to anyone in this city? They're calling Yi-Nereen Makela's Herald. She demonstrated her power in *public*."

No, Sou-Zell hadn't thought to listen to street rabble. He'd gone straight for Kadrin, certain that the prince would help him. Why had he done that?

Those magebikes Sou-Zell had seen leaving the city under cover of darkness, just as he and Falka had arrived. That had to have been Yi-Nereen.

He'd missed her by minutes.

He'd dragged his dying mother all the way to this city of infidels for nothing. The only way he could have saved her life was to swallow his pride, his ambition, and beg for Shield Lord Lai-Dan's help. He'd been too stubborn to do it.

His mother was going to die. Sou-Zell's pride had killed her.

He'd been running on fumes, and now the strength left him abruptly. Sou-Zell half slid, half collapsed to the ground, inches from a stinking gutter that ran brown with blood and other bodily fluids. He stared down at his own hands in a daze.

For nothing. All for nothing.

There was nothing waiting for him in Kerina Rut, no future except becoming Lai-Dan's pet mindreader. No family besides a brother whose name was ash on Sou-Zell's tongue. A House with empty coffers drained to pay a bounty Falka claimed was lost in the ruins of Mount Vetelu.

"Get up," Falka said. "You're embarrassing both of us. You look like a drunk."

"Leave my sight. I have nothing else to say to you."

He should kill her. She'd stolen from him and dangled the cure to his mother's ailment in front of his face, only to snatch it away. But living as a refugee in this godforsaken city might be a fate worse than death anyway. Sou-Zell didn't think *he* would choose it. Would Falka?

"You look like your brother," Falka said. "I followed you that

Flight of the Fallen

day. What useless, hateful excuses for men you both are. I thought you had at least one quality to recommend yourself: you were trying to save your mother. But this looks like you giving up, doesn't it? I suppose you and he are exactly alike."

Sou-Zell staggered to his feet. "What the hell do you *want* from me?" His fingers found the hilt of his sidesword; he was breathing hard, like a hunted animal on its last legs. "You have your freedom. You lured me out of Kerina Rut. You have the satisfaction of knowing a woman who was nothing but kind to you is going to die—"

"That doesn't bring me any satisfaction, believe it or not." Falka's mana-cig dripped a steady stream of ash. "I'm not that wretched."

"Just go."

"I lost everyone I ever cared about. Jin-Lu included. You might be a sorry excuse for a person, Sou-Zell, but I won't watch you squander the last chance you have at not being alone in this world."

Sou-Zell shook his head, bewildered. Gods damn her, why did she care?

"There's nothing more to do."

"You've never been truly desperate, then. There is always something else to try. For example." Falka's eyes gleamed. "One of Yi-Nereen's latest victims lives in this very district. Word has it she volunteered to have her Talent stripped away. The only person to ever willingly submit to such a fate. Don't you think it might be worth finding out what she knows?"

Falka sounded calm. She looked lucid. But Sou-Zell wondered if her madness had ever truly left her. No sane person would commit themselves to such a hopeless cause. If the tables were turned, Sou-Zell would take his freedom and go in a heartbeat.

Did she want *redemption*? He was the last person who could give that to her.

"Who is this person?" Sou-Zell asked, his voice low.
"Her name is Toraka."

"She wasn't dying," Falka said. "At least, not publicly."

Sou-Zell was silent. He and Falka had joined a line of petitioners winding down the stairs to a basement where this Toraka held court. Sou-Zell could only picture someone like his mother: days away from her half-life, frail of mind and body, desperate for survival in any form. Who else would willingly relinquish their soul and remain in this world a husk?

Toraka had been a confident leader, someone the refugees from Kerina Lav had trusted enough to follow her from their crumbling city and across the wastes. Yi-Nereen had destroyed her. Sou-Zell found it hard to reconcile that with what he remembered of the woman who had almost been his bride.

Finally he and Falka were the next ones ushered into the basement.

A woman with long, pin-straight hair stood with her beringed hands folded over the back of a chair. She smiled as they came in: a warm smile that tinged her fair cheeks with pink.

"Welcome. I apologize for the clutter; I only moved in last night."

"After your demonstration?" Falka prowled along the edge of the room, glancing over the sparse furniture. "You must have needed somewhere the temple wouldn't find you."

"Just so." The woman's smile never faltered. "I am Toraka. You are?"

This woman could not be Toraka. She looked bright and youth-

Flight of the Fallen

ful. Sou-Zell had thought, from the whispers he'd heard while standing in line, that she was aged.

He reminded himself that born Talentless didn't look like ghosts. Their appearances were deceptive; they resembled ordinary people. Like Kadrin, with his boisterous step and constant gesticulating. It was all to disguise their soullessness.

"I am Sou-Zell," he said. "This is Falka. We hail from Kerina Rut."

Using both of their names in the same breath felt wrong. But were their stations so different now? In Kerina Sol, they were both refugees. Both Talented. That was an unnerving thought.

"Where we come from matters little now," Toraka said. "I am no longer a Guildmaster of Lav. But what we brought from our old lives can still be useful. I have connections, resources, friends. So, what can I help you with?"

Sou-Zell felt instant distrust. Would his mindreading work on Toraka now? It was ineffective against born Talentless and those who'd stolen Talent, like Falka. He itched to know. But there was no way to use his Talent surreptitiously in such close quarters.

"What *can* you help with?" Falka asked.

She'd removed her scarf, and her Talentless brand was clearly visible on the nape of her neck. It nauseated Sou-Zell to see, but perhaps it would earn Toraka's trust.

"Kerina Sol's Council used to provide supplies to anyone entering the city, but recently they've stopped sending volunteers into the Refugee Quarter." A touch of bitterness colored Toraka's tone. "So I facilitate trade for the things people need and settle disputes when they cannot agree. I can put you in touch with others who can help in more specific ways than I can."

"Like the Herald of Makela?" Falka asked innocently. "We wanted to meet her in person, to know if the gods have truly imbued her with their power."

"Regrettably, that won't be possible." Toraka's smile faded. "With all the risk I face from the temple, Yi-Nereen's position is far more precarious. People fear what she represents."

"And what is that?"

"Change," Toraka said. "Like the storm that reshapes the wasteland, Yi-Nereen has come to reshape the kerinas. When her work is finished, nothing will remain as it was. But we will all be better for it."

Ah. Sou-Zell understood now; Toraka was a zealot. That was why he'd distrusted her.

"I heard the Herald has left Kerina Sol," Sou-Zell said. "If that's true, I suppose my *companion* and I are wasting our time here."

Toraka glanced at him. "You have the look of a Rut-blood noble, Sou-Zell. What was your House?"

"The Manor of Hushed Whispers."

Falka snickered. In response to Sou-Zell's glare, she smiled insolently. "It's an incredibly pretentious name."

"The name of a very old House," Toraka said, "and one I know. Your father corresponded with the Guildery by courier, but I haven't heard from him in years."

"He's dead," Sou-Zell said.

"My condolences."

"Enough." Sou-Zell burned now, his simmering rage ignited by Falka's insult and the reminder of all the alliances that had died with his father. "Yi-Nereen is no Herald. Her power doesn't come from the gods. It comes from her father."

Toraka stared at him, clearly taken aback. "Shield Lord Lai-Dan shares her ability?"

Flight of the Fallen

"Not only that, but he uses it to kill. A better fate for those he drains than being left Talentless—but clearly you don't agree." Sou-Zell burned hotter with every word. He knew, faintly, that his temper had assumed control and made his rational mind its slave, but he found himself incapable of stopping it. "The only difference between Yi-Nereen and her father is that Shield Lord Lai-Dan rules a city and his daughter is in hiding. But make no mistake. They are both heretics."

The basement was beginning to spin around him. He was breathing hard. He grasped for his Talent; it was time to end this, time to expose Toraka's thoughts and find out whether his quest was truly over.

But instead of burning mana, his body rebelled. Sickness boiled in his veins instead of power. Sou-Zell keeled over to vomit on the dirt floor.

This—this was the thing that had prevented him from becoming a knight. The weakness of his sparktalent, his eternal shame. He'd ridden too long and too fast without rest. All the mana infusions in the world wouldn't help him recover; only sleep would heal him.

"Goodness. Sit down, my dear man. I'll fetch some water."

Sou-Zell caught Toraka by the sleeve as she stepped past him. "There isn't time. I need—"

"He needs to save his mother," Falka said. "She's at the end of her half-life, on her deathbed as we speak. The Herald is the only one who can save her. As she saved you."

The room spun on, but Toraka fell still. "I'm sorry. Truly sorry. But Yi-Nereen has left Kerina Sol. She will return, but not in time."

Sou-Zell didn't need to read her mind to know she was telling the truth. Unless Toraka was the greatest performer he'd ever met, her sorrow was genuine. He wiped his mouth and straightened. "Then we have nothing more to discuss."

"Shut up, Sou-Zell, you useless heel-stain." Falka's knuckles whitened on the back of a chair. "A courier named Jin-Lu took Yi-Nereen into the wastes, correct?"

Toraka blinked. "How did you know that?"

"Jin-Lu and I are old friends. I also know she's Talentless. So tell me, Toraka, how exactly did she take the Herald anywhere on a magebike? Restoring her Talent is impossible. Which means there's an artificer in Kerina Sol who's finally accomplished the *other* thing that's supposed to be impossible."

"The sparkless magebike." Toraka dipped her head. "You're right. There is."

Falka grinned, triumphant. "Wonderful. If you'll tell us where to find this artificer, then we'll be on our way."

Sou-Zell trailed after Falka, back up the stairs and into the blinding sunlight aboveground. His first breath of fresh air steadied his shaking hands, restored a little life to his blood. "Why in all hell does it matter if we find the artificer?"

"I'll be charitable," Falka said, "and assume you're a great deal more intelligent when you aren't about to pass out. Otherwise, it's a mystery why Yi-Nereen didn't jump into the spring and end it all the moment she found out the two of you were engaged."

As a matter of fact, Yi-Nereen nearly had done just that, but Sou-Zell wasn't about to share that with Falka. "Tell me what you're planning."

Flight of the Fallen

"Why should I? I've done all the work so far. Perhaps you should go and sit by Lady Ren's deathbed and let me finish saving your precious House."

She was toying with him. Sou-Zell wrestled his anger into submission. For all he despised her, she'd been right; there *was* something left to try for his mother's sake, however hopeless.

"I beg of you," he said bitterly, every word a knife between his ribs. "Help me help her."

For a moment, Falka looked disconcerted—like the last thing she'd expected was to hear Sou-Zell plead for help. In truth, it was the last thing Sou-Zell had expected to hear from his own lips, too. But Falka recovered swiftly.

"It's a long shot. But Tibius Vann built a defuser out of scraps of Road Builder technology, using nothing more than his own genius and a bunch of unproven assumptions—and it *worked*. Apart from the tiny flaw of killing half the people he used it on, of course. I've seen his machine. I know a little about how it works. Unfortunately, I don't have a genius intellect or access to Road Builder technology. However." Falka bared her teeth in a feral grin. "We know where to find someone who has both."

Sou-Zell stared at her. "You believe this artificer can build a defuser?"

"I can't think of a better person to try besides Tibius himself. And *he's* a skeleton at the bottom of a spring."

Falka wasn't only duplicitous and insolent. She was clever, in the way Sou-Zell knew Yi-Nereen was, the way he'd always thought himself to be.

It shouldn't be possible. Just as it shouldn't be possible that Kadrin, a Talentless whose very existence sullied his House's name, was the only person not related to Sou-Zell by blood who had ever looked at him with something in his eyes besides fear or contempt. The only person who—gods knew why—seemed to care whether Sou-Zell lived or died.

Sou-Zell wasn't sure how much *he* cared anymore.

"Fine," he said, voice rough. "We find the artificer."

CHAPTER TWENTY-THREE

INTO THE BARRENS

Observation #755: The power exhibited by Makela's so-called
Herald is one I long theorized was possible. But I expected a
sparkrider to wield it, not a shieldcaster.
Hypothesis: At some point over the centuries, there was a switch.
—O

Third Age of Storms, 1st Summer, Day 86
The Barrens – The Ruins of Mount Vetelu

Through the yellow fog, Jin caught a glimpse of blue. A mana spring, burbling quietly in a jagged stone cauldron, surrounded by the shattered remains of a mountain. It was even larger than she remembered. Bigger by far than any spring the kerinas had built themselves around.

They'd been in the Barrens for only half a day. Incredible to think that in all Jin's years of crossing the wastes, she'd only ever been a fuel tank away from Mount Vetelu and Tibius Vann's laboratory. From Falka.

And now that was gone.

"Be careful," Jin called ahead to Celwyn and Eliesen. "Lots of places for saurians to hide here."

Yi-Nereen's grip on her waist tightened. Jin's pulse quickened. A familiar call-and-response.

They hadn't seen any saurians yet. Was it because of Screech? Had he cleared the way somehow? No, that seemed unlikely. If the tales of the Barrens were true, even Screech was far from the biggest or most dangerous thing that lived here.

"Look at the spring," Yi-Nereen said. "That isn't normal."

Jin didn't have to ask for clarification. The springs in the kerinas were still, peaceful. Mount Vetelu's spring churned and bubbled as if it were freshly made. The sight filled Jin with unease. Legend had it that storms rarely touched the Barrens, but Falka's storm had tapped this vein and brought mana to the surface. Maybe the land had responded to that incursion with an aberration of its own.

"Well, we don't have a choice. We have to draw from it."

Jin's fuel tank was running low. So was Celwyn's. They'd brought the chemical treatment they needed to stabilize the spring's mana and turn it into second-form fuel. The other three—not Jin—could fully infuse here, too. Jin would need the rest of the bottles of third-form mana to keep her bike going.

Fortunate indeed that Falka's Second Storm of Centuries *had* created this spring. Otherwise they'd never have had a chance to make it to Avi'Kerina.

Celwyn and Jin parked beside the spring. Yi-Nereen hopped off Jin's bike and paced slowly along the bank. Her sleeves fluttered in the warm wind that wafted upward from the mana's surface. Jin watched her, caught in a familiar trance, until Yi-Nereen stopped.

"It was here," she said. "Where you almost died."

Jin joined her. It was a patch of dirt like any other; she didn't know how Yi-Nereen recognized it. "I don't remember much."

Flight of the Fallen

Yi-Nereen wasn't staring at the dirt, but at her own hands. She lifted her head, and Jin's heart caught at the sight of her anguished expression.

"Jin, if I hadn't . . . if I hadn't . . ."

Jin shook her head. "Don't. I'm alive. I'm still me."

The aching hole her Talent had left behind was fading. Day by day, scarring over as she became accustomed to this life. It hadn't truly changed her, no more than losing a limb. It had changed what she could *do*. Not who she was.

As much as Jin despised the manacycle, she had to admit she felt more like herself now that she had it. She hadn't been grieving for her lost Talent. She'd been grieving for the freedom she'd lost with it.

Yi-Nereen still looked forlorn. Her shoulders were slumped; she stared into the spring with beautiful, downcast eyes. Jin groped for the words to explain the realization she'd just come to. But as ever, she couldn't find them.

In the end, all she could do was what Kadrin had done for her once. Jin drew Yi-Nereen into her arms. Yi-Nereen made a choked sound but didn't resist. Jin cupped the back of her head in one sweaty palm and wrapped her other arm tightly around Yi-Nereen's back. She willed her body to speak for her—to say *I'm here. I'm with you.*

I love you.

A wolf whistle split the spring's tranquil bubbling sound. Jin pulled away from Yi-Nereen, bristling. "I swear to Rasvel, Elie—"

She froze. The whistle had come from a jumbled heap of stones looming from the yellow haze, but Eliesen wasn't over there. She was next to Celwyn's bike, laughing at something he'd just said.

Jin opened her mouth to shout a warning.

Figures emerged from the rubble, all around the spring, converging on Jin and her companions. Blades and lance tips flashed.

An ambush. The whistle had been a signal.

"Get down, Jin!"

Jin hit the dirt. A burst of azure light flew overhead. She looked up to see a glowing blade of blue slice through a man who'd been about to descend on her, sword drawn. Two cauterized halves of him toppled to the ground.

"Holy shit," Jin gasped.

She turned her head. Yi-Nereen was crouched, fingers outstretched, panting with a wild look in her eyes.

Steel rang out in a metallic cacophony. Celwyn had leaped to Eliesen's defense, sword spinning in blurred silver circles. Jin took the briefest of moments to admire his agility and obvious skill. It was more than practiced; it was surgical.

Then a crossbow bolt whizzed past her ear. Someone was shooting at her from the rocks. Jin curled into a ball, trying to make herself a smaller target.

Yi-Nereen threw herself down beside Jin with a thump. A shimmering blue dome enclosed them only an instant before another bolt made contact: a white scorch mark that faded quickly.

"I can't get to Eliesen," Yi-Nereen said.

Jin's brain worked furiously. "You can move with a shield, right?"

"Yes, but it'll drain me. Quickly. I don't have enough. All the bottles are with the bikes."

"What about the spring?"

Yi-Nereen blanched. "Yes. If Celwyn can hold them off while—"

Eliesen screamed. A chill shot through Jin's bones. She scrambled to her hands and knees, squinting through the pulsing blue

Flight of the Fallen

barrier. *Fuck!* She couldn't see anything. The clanging of blades had fallen silent.

"Shit," Jin said. "I think we're too late."

"Rasvel's blood, who *are* they?"

That was a damn good question. There were no raiders in the Barrens, not since Falka's lot had cleared out. There was nothing for them to eat out here. No water to drink. They had to stick close to the trade routes between kerinas to survive.

Yi-Nereen shrank down. "Someone's coming."

Outside the shield, a tall, broad silhouette drew closer. With every step the distortion lessened until Jin could see them clearly. But Yi-Nereen gasped in recognition before Jin had an inkling of who it was. Jin felt her body go rigid.

The man was tall, his straight black hair drawn halfway back from his face, graying at the temples. His high cheekbones and angular jaw were a mirror of Yi-Nereen's; his skin was scraped clean of stubble. He wore half-plate, like a knight's squire, over a midnight-blue riding tunic. Embroidered stars shone on his cuffed sleeves.

Jin had seen him only in passing on her visits to the Tower. But she'd never forget those keen, lingering eyes.

Lai-Dan, Yi-Nereen's father.

Oh, they were so screwed.

"My daughter," he said with obvious delight. "At long last. What fortune to find you here."

"Father." Yi-Nereen's voice was almost a whimper. She clung to Jin's arm. "Why are you here?"

"I'm here on the same quest as you, of course." Lai-Dan smiled. "The First City. I may not have a map to its location, but when I heard the tablet had found its way to Kerina Sol, I knew it was only a matter of time before the High Houses of Sol sent an expedition.

Where would they stop to refuel, if not the only mana spring in the Barrens? Now be a good girl, Nereena. Lower the shield. Haven't you missed your father?"

"No." Yi-Nereen's fingers tightened in Jin's jacket. "Not until you promise not to hurt her."

"Reena," Jin said quietly. "That doesn't matter."

"And who is this?" Lai-Dan asked. "A new friend of yours?"

Relief rushed through Jin. He didn't recognize her. Not as the courier who'd smuggled Yi-Nereen out of Kerina Rut, or the one who'd brought her hundreds of letters. She'd pretended to be a man on all those trips to Kerina Rut. Her foresight might just delay her death by a few more minutes.

Yi-Nereen said nothing. Perhaps she'd realized how close she'd come to a critical mistake.

Lai-Dan sighed. "My girl, this is pointless. I've waited for your expedition for days. Do you think I can't wait for you to exhaust yourself?"

"Perhaps not, Father." Yi-Nereen let go of Jin and rose into a half crouch. Her voice thrummed with darkness. "But you've forgotten that in a few steps, I can be free of you."

Her eyes flickered to the spring. Jin's blood ran cold. Yi-Nereen was right; she could almost certainly make it to the bank before her father caught her. Jin was Talentless—she could cartwheel under the surface for hours without dying. But Yi-Nereen stepping into the spring would be the last defiant act she ever performed.

Jin's reason fled. She grabbed Yi-Nereen by the arms. "Don't you dare."

"Let me go," Yi-Nereen spat, struggling.

Lai-Dan raised his hand. More blurry figures approached the

shield. Two knights in half-plate, dragging two bound figures with them.

Celwyn was spattered with blood but seemed unharmed. But Eliesen—Eliesen's hand was clamped to her shoulder. The feathered end of a crossbow bolt protruded between her fingers. Her face was drawn and sheened with sweat.

"Do you care about these ones?" Lai-Dan asked lightly. "Or only the girl in there with you?"

"It doesn't matter what I do," Yi-Nereen bit out. "You won't let them go. Not when they might beat you to the First City. I can't win, Father, but I won't lose. Not to you."

"Damn it," Jin swore. Her heart was racing. Yi-Nereen might have given up, but all that meant was that Jin had to pick up the torch. "Listen to me, Shield Lord. You can't hurt them. Celwyn is the only one who knows the way. Kill him, and you'll never find the First City."

She never thought she'd be grateful for the raiders who'd stolen their maps, but there it was.

"Celwyn?" Lai-Dan repeated, his tone soft.

"That's me," Celwyn growled.

The two men faced each other: the Shield Lord in his regalia, only slightly dusty from days spent in the wastes, and the bloody, panting former raider.

"I recognize you," Lai-Dan said. "Though I don't believe we've met. Why is that?"

Celwyn's nostrils flared. "The outlaw notice, I expect."

Jin could have kicked herself. Of course—she should have realized sooner. Every time a kerina exiled one of its own, notices were sent by courier to every other kerina in riding distance: a sketched portrait, a name, and a list of the exile's crimes. She'd delivered her fair share of notices. Perhaps even Celwyn's. It wasn't much money, but it was steady work.

"Hmm. A strange choice, for Kerina Sol to send an exile and my runaway daughter on such an important mission. But I suppose the High Houses of Sol have always been unorthodox." Lai-Dan reached for a pouch at his belt. "What do you say about joining my expedition as a guide? I would compensate you well."

Celwyn tilted his head. "How well?"

Jin cursed quietly. She should have seen *that* coming, too.

Lai-Dan wordlessly held out a coin purse. Celwyn hefted the weight in his palm. "The women live," he said with an almost careless glance at Eliesen. "She's a raincaller. Of course you know your daughter's Talent. If I'm taking you to the First City, they're coming, too."

"What about the other sparkrider?" Lai-Dan indicated Jin.

Celwyn hesitated. "Her as well. No point in letting a bike go to waste."

Well, that was something. He hadn't revealed that Jin was Talentless and her bike didn't require the spark. Perhaps he was only saving that reveal for more coin down the line, but Jin would take what she got.

Celwyn and Lai-Dan grasped each other's forearms. Jin's heart was slowing slightly, her panic lessening. For now, they had an agreement that kept everyone alive. As long as they were still alive, they could find a way out.

"Reena," she whispered. "I think you should let down the shield. Save your mana."

Yi-Nereen was still trembling. "I can't." Her voice was ragged. "He'll take me back there. I can't ever go back."

"I won't let him take you."

Jin put her arms around Yi-Nereen and buried her face in Yi-Nereen's hair. Her blood was boiling. She didn't feel like a human, but like some kind of beast. A monster who'd tear asunder anyone who put their hands on Yi-Nereen. Rage tasted like copper in her mouth.

Yi-Nereen gave one last shudder, and the shield evaporated. Jin tore herself away, ready to swing at anyone who came close. But Lai-Dan held his men back with a calm, upraised hand. Jin's eyes darted back and forth. When she was satisfied no one was going to approach, she took two steps forward to Eliesen's side.

"Gods, Elie." The crossbow bolt had buried itself in the meat of Eliesen's shoulder. Jin felt queasy at the idea of how much that must hurt, but at least it hadn't pierced through, and it wasn't bleeding much. Jin cupped Eliesen's sweaty cheek. "You're going to be okay. I've got you."

"Hurts like a bitch, Jin," Eliesen snarled. "Don't you dare pull it out or I'll kill you."

"We can't remove it yet," Celwyn said. "Not until we have a way to stanch the bleeding and close the wound. That shot was aimed for me."

That last sentence was rich with some emotion Jin couldn't decipher, but a deep part of her shivered in recognition. One beast to another.

"Lucky for you I was in the way, then," Eliesen said with a choked laugh.

"Lucky indeed." Celwyn brushed his knuckles against Eliesen's.

Jin fought the urge to roll her eyes. Well, she couldn't begrudge Eliesen two facts: Celwyn was good-looking and he knew how to handle a sword. He might also have the soul of a teenaged girl riding along in his skull, but Eliesen had still done worse before.

Yi-Nereen hadn't moved a step from where Jin had left her. Her thick black hair was speckled with yellow dust; her arms hung loosely by her sides. She stared with haunted eyes at her father and his men, who were huddled in discussion by the rocks.

Jin knew little about Yi-Nereen's childhood in the Tower. But she could guess from the darkness that had seeped into her letters that it had been a special kind of hell. She sought something comforting to say but came up empty-handed.

Yi-Nereen spoke first. "I knew he'd find me. I only hoped I would have more time. With Kadrin. And with you."

"We'll have more time," Jin said.

Her heart fluttered like a moth before a light. They'd wasted so much time already, and it was her fault.

"We *will*," she said. It was as much a promise to herself as to Yi-Nereen.

CHAPTER TWENTY-FOUR

SYMPATHIES

Observation #699: Finding myself growing fond of Kadrin,
lunkhead that he is. Another idiot raised in wealth, yet he's
nothing like Renzara.
Hypothesis: None at this time. —O

Third Age of Storms, 1st Summer, Day 86
Kerina Sol – Jade District

Sou-Zell snapped awake. He'd fallen asleep in a wooden chair with his head on a table. A pendulum swung gently, inches from his nose. Above him, orange sparks flickered to life in bell jars.

He was in the artificer Orrin's workshop. For the past two days, he'd shuffled between two places: here, and the hovel in the Refugee Quarter where his mother clung to life. Falka's clever tongue had worked its magic on Orrin, not that much magic had been necessary. The artificer wasn't merely willing to help build a defuser. They were *eager*.

Sou-Zell lifted his head just as Orrin shut the workshop door with a click.

"Where's Falka?" Orrin asked without preamble.

Sou-Zell curled his lip, irritated as always by the artificer's

253

brusque manner. "How should I know? It was your errand she left to run."

"Don't sound so envious," Orrin said dryly. "I have work for you, too, if you're amenable."

Sou-Zell wasn't particularly. But now that he was fully awake, his hands itched to do *something*. He, Orrin, and Falka had spent two days working by sparklight in the cramped confines of Orrin's workshop; they were making progress on the defuser, but not quickly enough.

Lady Ren's life was in Rasvel's hands. If she breathed her last before the defuser was complete, then Sou-Zell would know he'd angered the gods with this blasphemous plan to save her by stealing her soul. If she survived . . .

Then he *was* doing the right thing. A more terrifying prospect than any other.

He'd spent so many years trying to find a way to restore power to his bloodline. His family had once been strong in the Talent; restoring that strength was simply a matter of correcting an imbalance, not usurping the gods. But taking Talent away, robbing his mother of the power she'd been rightfully born with, was different.

Sou-Zell's divine punishment could strike at any moment. He didn't want to be asleep or idle when it did.

"What would you have of me?"

"It's Kadrin," Orrin said, and Sou-Zell's stomach twisted. "I believe you're acquainted? Charming fellow, a bit dim, but excellent taste in investments and an endearing fondness for pretty women. I've just been to his House to see him, but he wasn't there. His serving staff haven't seen him in two days."

Sou-Zell scowled. "And?"

Orrin spread their scarred hands. "We're short on coin. I need a few more materials. The way I see it, there are two options. Rustle up at least fifty mun on short notice in a city under martial law, or find dear Kadrin and ask him to open his purse. One seems easier than the other, don't you think?"

"What makes you think I know where to find him?"

"Nothing at all," Orrin said languidly. "But you aren't useful for anything else right now. Falka and I are needed here, working on the machine that will save your mother's life. So go on, little lord. Fetch."

Sou-Zell seethed. He was a breath away from drawing his sidesword and forcing it down Orrin's throat. All the cleverness in the world wouldn't protect them from physical violence.

But—Sou-Zell was forced to admit—Orrin's cleverness was *exactly* what was protecting them from him now. He couldn't do a single thing with his mother's life on the line and Orrin being the only one who could save her.

"Fine," he said through gritted teeth. "Where should I begin?"

"You're the mindreader," Orrin said. "You tell me."

Four hours later, Sou-Zell knelt in the echoing heart of the Basilica Sol before a multicolored tapestry of the Giver of Blessings and lit a bowl of incense. Beads clinked gently against his face and neck. Fragrant smoke curled from the bowl. Sou-Zell breathed deep of the smoke and opened his mouth, ready to shape the familiar words of prayer. A prayer for guidance, forgiveness, mercy.

His tongue stilled. Who was he to ask for such gifts, when he was in the process of committing two blasphemies at once—giving aid to a Talentless, and conspiring to steal his mother's soul?

Sou-Zell rose to his feet and turned away. As he left the worship chamber, an acolyte glided past him. Her robes whispered against the temple floor; her arms were piled with folded prayer shawls.

"A moment, please," Sou-Zell said. "How many rooms are there in the temple?"

The acolyte gawked at him. "I—I don't understand the question."

"It's quite simple. In this temple, how many rooms are there? Think of as many as you can." Sou-Zell turned his back on her and burned mana.

Is this a test? The senior acolytes said there would be more tests of faith, even after initiation.

The acolyte brightened; she'd always been good at games of memorization. Her mind flew through the halls of the temple at dizzying speeds, taking Sou-Zell on a thorough mental tour of prayer chambers, vaults, storage rooms, and cells where the acolytes slept.

Oh, and the basement. Who knows how many rooms are down there? It's off-limits, so it must not count.

"Thirty-two," she said confidently.

"Hmm," Sou-Zell said. "Close enough. Keep working on it."

The acolyte was so distracted by this statement she didn't seem to notice as he swept off, navigating the winding halls of the temple toward the nearest supply closet. He'd left the public chambers of the Basilica Sol behind, so it was conceivable someone would stop him and ask what he was doing there, but he walked with purpose and received no questions.

The inner halls were eerily empty. Perhaps that had something to do with all the priests Sou-Zell had seen patrolling the streets of the city: the High Priestess's personal army, sanctioned by the High Houses of Sol.

Flight of the Fallen

The supply closet was unlocked. The inside smelled of cleaning herbs. Sou-Zell took a set of freshly laundered robes from a shelf and donned them over his clothes.

Then he made his way to the nearby staircase he'd glimpsed in the acolyte's thoughts. He made the descent to the basement by flickering torchlight.

Inwardly, a part of Sou-Zell railed against what he was doing. He'd spent four hours using his Talent to retrace the idiot prince's steps across the city two days prior, a staggeringly unsubtle display that left Sou-Zell more exposed and vulnerable than he'd felt since Lai-Dan had ordered him to read Guildmaster Xua's thoughts. That trail had led him to the Basilica Sol, where Sou-Zell had been sorely tempted to give up the chase. That blasted artificer surely didn't expect Sou-Zell to move against the High Priestess herself for the sake of access to Kadrin's coin purse.

Yet something drove Sou-Zell on. Something intensely irritating and impossible to forget. Words that lingered in his memory no matter how hard he tried to excise them.

Funny. I don't recall you complaining when I saved your life.

Clearly Kadrin, Orrin, and Falka were all cut from the same cloth: manipulative heathens who'd somehow coerced Sou-Zell into a position of weakness. He would have his vengeance against them all in time, once Lady Ren was safe.

If Prince Kadrin was being held in the temple against his will, it must be somewhere acolytes weren't permitted access, else Sou-Zell would have seen it in that girl's mind. The question of *why* Kadrin was here against his will was a puzzle. The man's whole life was an abomination. What more could he have done to anger the priesthood?

The acolyte's mental map ended at the bottom of the stairs. Sou-

257

Zell opened a door and found himself in a dimly lit hallway. The ceiling here was low, the walls rough. It was a far cry from the sumptuous dressings of the temple above.

Left or right? There were no telltale splashes of blood on the floor, no signs of an errant prince. Sou-Zell went left.

He'd gone only a few steps when a door at the end of the hallway opened. A tall, stately woman in white emerged, followed by a man holding an unfamiliar metal implement: a slim, blunt-tipped rod.

No time to turn around. Sou-Zell continued forward, walking at a steady, confident pace. The hood of his robes fell low enough to shadow his face.

The two figures moving toward him wore no hoods. The woman drew Sou-Zell's eye. She was beautiful in a cold, remote way—like an older, more self-possessed Yi-Nereen. Her skin was almost as porcelain pale as her robes, a rarity in Kerina Sol. She passed within inches of him.

The skin all over Sou-Zell's body tingled at the most proximal moment, like he'd brushed the edge of a storm. Once she was past, he released the breath he'd been holding.

"Stop," came a woman's steely voice from behind him.

Sou-Zell froze midstride. A dozen thoughts raced through his head; the first, as always, was to burn mana and search her mind for a likely excuse for his presence here. But something stayed him. Instinct, perhaps.

"Yes?" he asked, turning just his head.

"Clean and dress the prisoner's wounds. Bring a change of clothes. You are not given leave to speak with him."

Fortune smiled on Sou-Zell today; his disguise had worked. She'd mistaken him for an acolyte. But *he* still had no idea who she

Flight of the Fallen

was, other than a superior. He couldn't risk using the wrong title, and he wouldn't get away with failing to use one twice. So he simply turned, bowed low, and waited with his head bent.

At last, he heard a door open and footsteps retreat up the stairs. They were gone.

Sou-Zell made straight for the room the woman and her companion had left.

The acrid stench of sweat and urine struck him the moment he opened the door. Sou-Zell stopped short. The only furnishing in the chamber was a chair, and strapped into that chair was Prince Kadrin.

He was unconscious. His face shone with bruises. Blood trickled slowly from a fresh cut on his lip. Someone had opened his robes to the waist and left red burn marks all over his chest.

Something in Sou-Zell's chest snapped. He was utterly unprepared for the flame that kindled within him. For a moment, he thought Kadrin was the object of his rage. How Sou-Zell loathed him, this coddled child who'd seduced Sou-Zell's fiancée into a life of blasphemous exile.

Then his hands twitched and he realized he wanted to wrap them around the High Priestess's throat. Now, *that* was odd.

The prince stirred, his eyes fluttering open to focus blearily on Sou-Zell where he stood in the doorway, rooted to the spot.

"I've told you a thousand times," he whispered. "She's in the wastes."

In a flash of insight, Sou-Zell understood. Kadrin wasn't trapped in the bowels of the Basilica Sol because of *his* sins. He was here for exactly the reason Sou-Zell had sought him at the House of Steel Heavens: his connection to Yi-Nereen.

Sou-Zell went to the chair and began undoing the buckles around Kadrin's limbs in swift, seething movements. "Be silent. Someone might hear you."

Fresh blood dripped from Kadrin's mouth. *"Sou-Zell?"*

Sou-Zell's fingers hesitated on the straps. Perhaps it was hasty of him to set Kadrin free. He hadn't come here to make an enemy of Kerina Sol's priesthood.

Could this be a test? Did Rasvel wish to see if Sou-Zell had fallen so far as to commit treason in the Giver's own temple? What did Sou-Zell truly have to gain by freeing Kadrin?

Coin was cheap. Sou-Zell could surely acquire it by less heinous means.

"Please." Kadrin's voice broke. "Get me out of here."

Gods *damn* him.

Sou-Zell went back to the buckles. As he worked, he noted Kadrin's broken fingernails—and that strange, sick flame howled inside him again. Again his thoughts turned toward violence and destruction. This time, to his horror, he imagined taking a hammer and chisel to the statue of Rasvel at the base of the temple steps and smashing the marble visage to pieces.

Once Kadrin was free, Sou-Zell lifted him from the chair and walked him to the door. Not long ago, his skin would have crawled at the prince's touch, but at the moment he couldn't bring himself to care. There were more important problems at hand, like getting Kadrin out of the temple without being caught.

"I think they brought me underground," Kadrin said. His face glistened with tears, some of them fresh. He trembled against Sou-Zell's shoulder like he was freezing to death. "The temple must connect to some basements nearby, though I can't imagine why that would be necessary."

Sou-Zell could. The Rasvelite priesthood was a ruling power in every kerina, and all powerful entities had business that needed conducting in secret. But he supposed Kadrin would know little of such things. The man was a naïf, ignorant of how the world around him functioned. He had probably walked straight into his kidnappers' arms with a smile on his face.

"Come," Sou-Zell said harshly, pulling Kadrin into the hallway. The prince was right. Sou-Zell searched three rooms before he found a door into a corridor that smelled of must and earth. By then, Kadrin had regained some of his strength—enough to close his robe and wipe the blood from his mouth.

Sou-Zell closed the door behind them, casting the tunnel into pitch black, and summoned a single spark to light their way. In the flickering orange glow, Kadrin's bruise-mottled face turned toward him.

"How . . . how many days has it been?"

"Two."

"Gods. Did my family send you? They must be frantic."

His serving staff haven't seen him in two days, Orrin had said. The artificer had made no mention of Kadrin's family.

"What did they want from you?" Sou-Zell asked brusquely.

If Kadrin noticed that Sou-Zell had ignored his question, he was uncharacteristically wise enough not to mention it. "To make a long, painful story short, High Priestess Edine is desperate to find Yi-Nereen. I told her over and over again that she isn't even in the city, but she wouldn't believe me. She's a mindreader, by the way. Like you. But that doesn't work on me, so they went with other methods."

Sou-Zell recalled the tingle he'd felt as the woman earlier had passed by. That must have been the High Priestess. He'd felt a similar sensation in the proximity of other sparkriders, but only when they were actively using their Talent or had just stopped.

Never before had he knowingly entered the presence of another mindreader. Sou-Zell's skin crawled; he wondered suddenly if *that* was how others felt when they learned of his Talent. The queasy feeling in his stomach worsened.

"Why should I care?"

Kadrin stopped walking. "Because if you ever meet her, she'll know it was you who helped me escape. Stay away from her, or she'll hurt you."

Sou-Zell clenched his fists—and the spark floating above him winked out, plunging them into darkness. That hadn't been intentional. He was losing control; he had to regain it any cost, no matter how determined Kadrin was to drive him to madness.

"Sou-Zell? Are you all right?"

"Don't ask me that, you cretin. Be silent."

"I was just trying to warn you—"

"Are you incapable of following simple directions?" Sou-Zell snarled. "If you must know, your family neither knows nor cares about your whereabouts. I am here because an artificer called Orrin needs more of your coin. I will be *compensated* for this, so I have no need of your warnings—or any other useless tokens of your gratitude."

There was a beat of silence, during which Sou-Zell's hands twisted at his sides and he felt sick relief for the darkness.

"All right," Kadrin said. "One more thing, and then I'll shut up."

He sounded shaken; his voice was colored by pain. Both of those things should have brought Sou-Zell a sense of satisfaction, but neither did.

Flight of the Fallen

"What?"

"Thank you."

Sou-Zell inhaled sharply through his nose. One day the prince would pay for his insolent tongue. Perhaps Edine *had* believed his claims eventually, and had chosen to continue torturing him out of spite. Sou-Zell could hardly fault her for it.

He summoned his spark again and strode down the tunnel, leaving Kadrin to limp slowly behind him. The passage ended in another basement under an empty house; it was dusk when he and Kadrin emerged onto the streets of Kerina Sol. From the nearby Basilica, temple bells chimed the hour—and curfew.

"This is where we part ways, I suppose?" Kadrin asked.

Sou-Zell eyed him. Some of his anger had fled during the walk through the tunnels—enough, apparently, to make room for reason. "Are you going home?"

Kadrin nodded. "I suppose so. Oh." He reached wearily for his belt pouch. "They took my sword, but not my coin. Here. For Orrin."

Sou-Zell's stomach churned anew as he gingerly took Kadrin's coin purse. Kadrin had taken his claim about Orrin at face value. Sou-Zell could go straight to the nearest tavern and fritter away the prince's mun on mana-cigs and wine, and he would be none the wiser.

The godsdamned *fool.*

"Don't go home," Sou-Zell said, despising himself. "That's the first place the High Priestess will look for you. I know a physician in the Refugee Quarter who can tend to your injuries."

He gave Kadrin the address. The prince nodded; his lips quirked into a smile. Sou-Zell would have taken it for a mocking smirk if he didn't unfortunately know better.

"Give Orrin my thanks, too, will you?"

Sou-Zell turned on his heel and stalked away without a reply.

"Oh," Orrin said, frowning at the coin purse Sou-Zell had dropped on the table. "So you found him? That's a relief. Now you can hurry along and give that back to him. I don't actually need it."

Sou-Zell stared. *"What?"*

Orrin wiped sweat from their forehead, replacing it with a streak of black grease. "The explanation is rather obvious, isn't it? I hope so, since I don't have time for this conversation. Good thing it's quickly drawing to an end. Go *away*, Sou-Zell. I'll send Falka to fetch you in a few hours, once the defuser is ready."

Sou-Zell struggled to speak. Finally he asked, "So soon?"

"Indeed." Orrin smiled, and yes—*that* was a mocking smirk, no two ways about it. "Your mother's life will be saved. Assuming she's still alive. So you'd better go and check, hadn't you?"

CHAPTER TWENTY-FIVE

A BURDEN SHARED

Observation #66: Gloves dull the senses, make it impossible to conduct a spark.

Upside: Lower risk of injury to digits, less pain.

Conclusion: When the stakes are high, ditch the gloves. —O

Third Age of Storms, 1st Summer, Day 86

Kerina Sol – Refugee Quarter

Kadrin was no stranger to pain. He'd spent his childhood roughhousing with Satriu, whose favorite pastime was introducing Kadrin's face to the dirt with gusto. As he'd grown, he'd learned to stretch his body to the limit. He'd run laps around the Wall until he was bent and gasping. Then, with his body screaming for relief, he'd go home and practice his lunges in the garden.

If someone had asked him a few days prior whether he could withstand torture, Kadrin would have said yes, he probably could. Especially if it meant protecting someone he loved.

After all, pain was pain. A body could get used to anything.

Then High Priestess Edine had strapped him into a chair, and Kadrin had learned how wrong he was.

It didn't matter that he had no secrets to admit. Somewhere

between screaming his throat raw and wetting himself, after the interrogator had moved from his neck to his torso with the spark-baton, Kadrin's brain and tongue had conspired to spin a dozen confessions, each more damning than the last.

He'd taught Yi-Nereen to siphon Talent. He was the spawn of Makela herself, swapped for the Rain Lord's true heir at birth. He didn't believe in Rasvel or his divine gifts to humanity. He wanted the kerinas to fall, every last one, because if he couldn't have Rasvel's love, no one could. He loved two women at once—and sometimes he even thought he was worthy of both of them.

And while Kadrin's mind spun in useless circles like a rat gnawing its own tail, Edine held fast to a single question.

Where is Yi-Nereen?

Far away from me, Kadrin had sobbed. *I let her go into the wastes, I let both of them go, and now they're both dead, and gods help me, I'm going to die here. I'll never see her again.*

All his life he'd understood instinctively that if he hurt himself enough, he'd beat everyone else to the punch. He'd made an old friend out of suffering—taught himself to smile when it knocked, to invite it in.

Pain, it turned out, was impossible to get used to if he wasn't the one controlling it.

Edine must have realized at some point that Kadrin had nothing useful to tell her. She didn't even seem to enjoy watching him suffer. On the rare occasions when Kadrin was able to focus his blurred vision on her face, he couldn't find a trace of satisfaction in her cold stare. Maybe she was training herself, the way he'd tried to inure himself to pain.

Maybe she was training herself not to be bothered by the act of causing it.

Kadrin lay on a threadbare blanket stretched over a clay tile floor. Coughing and moans of discomfort echoed around him. Candles guttered in alcoves along the walls of the hut, illuminating the gaunt figure of a man who moved between beds.

The doctor had touched Kadrin's burned chest for only a moment, eyes smoldering pale yellow, before he'd pulled his hands away with an irritated huff and handed Kadrin a pot of salve instead. Apparently his Talent for alleviating pain didn't work on the Talentless.

In truth, Kadrin didn't hurt much anymore. It was the memories that dogged him. Every time he blinked and the world fell away, part of his brain screamed in horror. He was certain he would open his eyes to see the High Priestess's torturer standing before him again.

The door to the hut opened, and Sou-Zell entered. He crossed the room, ignoring Kadrin completely, and knelt beside a different mat.

The old woman who lay on that mat was almost skeletal, her bones sharp under her skin. Her eyes moved restlessly beneath their lids. Every few seconds, all the muscles in her body contracted at once, pulling her hands into claws.

Sou-Zell glanced at one of those hands like he wanted to hold it. He didn't.

Kadrin raised himself into a sitting position with a wince. "Sou-Zell?"

The man didn't react to his name. He was lost in some private torment; his jaw worked as he stared at the old woman's face.

Kadrin limped to Sou-Zell's side and sat down.

Hana Lee

"It's mana rejection, isn't it? Is she your mother?"

Slowly, Sou-Zell turned his head in Kadrin's direction. Kadrin shivered at the sight of his eyes. There, like a grim reflection, he saw his own horror. The same helpless suffering.

Sou-Zell had come to rescue Kadrin from his torment, but no one was coming to save Sou-Zell from his.

"You'll never know what this is like," Sou-Zell said. "To die poisoned by the thing that gave you life. Count yourself fortunate."

"It's true—I won't. But I'll know how *you* feel. I have a mother and father, too."

And brothers. A sister. A woman I love.

He expected vitriol from Sou-Zell, or at least a scathing glare. But the fight he'd sensed in Sou-Zell earlier, in the tunnels, had fled. Sou-Zell looked at his mother's face again. His own expression seemed carved from stone.

"Yi-Nereen's family had no inkling," Sou-Zell said. "No knowledge that she was being seduced under their noses. But *I* knew. It only took a single moment of listening to her thoughts, on the rare occasions that our paths crossed. She was thinking of you, princeling. Constantly." Sou-Zell shuddered. "Do you know how many times I considered telling her father about your secret correspondence? But I was sure Yi-Nereen would be punished and you would remain unscathed. A lover in a faraway city pouring promises into her ears, promises he would never keep. How I loathed you."

Stunned, Kadrin said the first words that came to mind.

"I didn't even know you existed."

Sou-Zell laughed harshly. "You don't know how pleasant that sounds."

"Did you love her? Reena."

"Did I love her?" Sou-Zell echoed. "I don't even know what that's like."

It wasn't exactly a question, but Kadrin answered it anyway.

"It's like . . . the rest of the world is less interesting without her in it. I'm always holding my breath, waiting to see her again. When she's out there in the wastes, I can't even think about something happening to her, or I start getting crazy ideas about jumping off the Wall."

His throat was on the verge of closing up; he had to force the final words out. In his mind, he remembered his own voice babbling in a mad fever of agony. *Gods help me, I'm going to die here, I'll never see her again.*

"That sounds almost as exhausting as hating someone," Sou-Zell said.

Kadrin felt his lips twitch into a smile. "It's all the same thing, really."

The minutes became hours. Sou-Zell said nothing more, and Kadrin's mind drifted. Still, he retained enough presence to wonder why Sou-Zell hadn't told him to leave. Kadrin was intruding on a private moment—Sou-Zell's mother was mere hours from death.

All Kadrin could think was that Sou-Zell was lonely. Even Kadrin's company was better than none. And that only spoke to the depths of the grief Sou-Zell must be feeling: something worse than what Kadrin had undergone at Edine's hand.

The door to the hut opened again. A warm, fresh breeze gusted inside.

Kadrin looked up, and his pulse quickened.

Falka's narrowed eyes scanned the dark interior until they fell on Sou-Zell. She looked more lucid than the last and only time Kadrin had seen her before: sitting in the rubble of a collapsed mountain with her knees drawn to her chest, face streaked in tears and clothes stained with blood, staring blankly into the distance.

Kadrin's mind whirled with questions. Had she come to Kerina Sol with Sou-Zell? Was she looking for Jin, to exact the revenge she'd failed to complete at Mount Vetelu? Did she remember Kadrin's face?

"It's time," Falka said.

Sou-Zell leaped to his feet. "It's ready?"

Falka nodded, eyes bright with excitement.

Sou-Zell scooped his blanket-shrouded mother into his arms and staggered out the open door without another word. Falka followed. Clearly she hadn't recognized Kadrin, and Sou-Zell seemed to have forgotten he existed.

Kadrin wavered. Whatever Sou-Zell and Falka were doing together was none of his business. Falka was dangerous—she'd hurt people, murdered people, and she was obsessed with Jin. Better for everyone if she didn't know Kadrin's face.

But then he remembered what he'd seen in Sou-Zell's face. The certainty that no one cared enough to save him, or even shoulder some of his burden.

To hell with what Sou-Zell thought of him. When Kadrin saw someone dangling over a cliff, he would always reach out for them.

He limped out the open door.

Flight of the Fallen

Kadrin trailed after Sou-Zell and Falka through the darkened streets. It was easy to tail them while keeping out of sight; Sou-Zell was wholly occupied with his mother, and Falka stalked along with an eagerness crackling around her like electricity, oblivious to everything else.

He shouldn't have been surprised by their destination: Orrin's workshop. Sou-Zell had mentioned the artificer had sent him to Kadrin's rescue. But why were Falka and Sou-Zell's dying mother here?

Kadrin stepped behind a wall and watched Sou-Zell and Falka disappear into the workshop. He waited a minute, counting out the seconds with bated breath, and went to the door to knock.

A moment of silence. Then Orrin's voice called out, "Go away. I'm not taking visitors."

"It's Kadrin."

After another delay, the door opened a crack. Kadrin blinked at the sight of Orrin dressed in a strange outfit: a heavy leather apron that covered them from the neck down and a sparkrider's bone-helm that hid their face.

"Well, I'm glad to see you're alive. But you've chosen a poor time to visit, I'm afraid. I'm on the precipice of changing the world— again—and I don't need your help this time. So run along home, Kadrin. I'll send for you when I need you."

Kadrin crossed his arms. "First: I'm not your errand boy. Second: I don't care if you need me. Sou-Zell's here, and *he* does."

Orrin raised an eyebrow. "I didn't think he particularly liked you, my dear."

"I didn't say he liked me. I said he needed me."

Orrin sighed. "Well, who am I to stand in the way of such a beautiful friendship? Come in. Try not to ask too many questions."

The door swung open and Kadrin stepped inside. All the mechanical clutter he'd seen on his previous visits to the workshop was gone, swept away to make room for two things: a surgeon's table equipped with two broad leather straps, and a contraption Kadrin couldn't puzzle out at a glance. Valves and tubes, wires and a clear glass cylinder, a hand pump attached to an air tank. He hadn't the faintest idea what it was.

Sou-Zell's mother lay on the table, unconscious, and Sou-Zell stood beside her with one of the leather straps in his hand. "Are these necessary?"

"I think they will be, yes." Orrin strode over to stand by the table.

Kadrin took a step closer—then stopped, his heart quickening. He felt the cold press of a blade to the side of his neck.

"So you're Kadrin," Falka said softly from the shadows beside the door. "It's a pleasure to make your acquaintance. Imagine that—a Talentless royal heir who wasn't drowned at birth. What a charmed life you must have led. Now, kindly keep your hands and tongue to yourself, and I won't have a problem with you being here."

"Agreed," Kadrin bit out, and Falka pulled back her knife and moved past him without another word. She rested her hand against Sou-Zell's mother's cheek with surprising tenderness. Kadrin had clearly missed a lot.

"If it's like the defuser Tibius built, it'll be painful for her," Falka said, looking at Sou-Zell. "But it'll be worth it in the end."

"It had better *not* be like the one Tibius built," Sou-Zell growled. "That one killed every single one of its subjects, or so you told me."

"But clever Orrin found the flaw in Tibius's design. She'll survive."

Flight of the Fallen

It had been a matter of seconds, but Kadrin couldn't *not* speak up.

"Am I hearing this right?" he asked. "You built a machine that can do what Yi-Nereen can do? Take someone's Talent away and give it to someone else?"

Orrin coughed. "Well, we were pressed for time. What I built can extract a person's mana without killing them, but it won't be usable afterward. Quite sufficient for our purposes, and still a revolutionary instrument."

Kadrin turned to Sou-Zell. "You're letting them do this to your mother?"

Sou-Zell stared back at him, his eyes flat and dark. "It's the only way to save her life. Frankly, *you* are the last person I expected to object."

"Because I'm Talentless?" Kadrin frowned. "It's different, don't you think? I didn't choose this, but no one else made the choice for me. I know you want your mother to live. Truly, I understand. But does she want this?"

He'd hit a nerve. A muscle jumped in Sou-Zell's jaw.

"Get out of here, Kadrin. I never asked you to come."

It was true. He hadn't. But Kadrin was rather of the opinion that he hadn't asked because he was incapable, not because he wasn't in need.

The wastes will burn to ash before I ask for your *help, Talentless.*

On the table, Sou-Zell's mother shifted and drew a rattling breath. Falka hissed. "Now or never, Sou-Zell."

Sou-Zell turned away from Kadrin with a tight nod and began buckling the restraints over his mother's gaunt frame. Nausea welled in Kadrin's chest at the sight of those leather straps. He felt the phantom shock of a spark-baton against his flesh. And suddenly, despite all his protestations on Sou-Zell's behalf, *he* couldn't stand to remain in the workshop a moment longer.

He stumbled outside and slid down the wall until he was sitting in the dirt. He smelled burning flesh. *His* burning flesh. His hands twitched, nails scraping at the arms of an invisible chair.

Inside the workshop, he heard Orrin's voice. "There, that mana injection will keep her breathing for a few more hours—until her body rejects it. By then we'll be finished. Keep the needle steady, Sou-Zell. Falka, I need you here on the pump."

A low, weak moan. And then Sou-Zell saying, "She's conscious. Eomma, I'm here."

"No need to worry, there's a paralytic in the mix. She won't move."

Kadrin buried his fingers in the cool dirt. Edine wasn't here. He wasn't in the chair anymore. But maybe he *should* still be there. In two days, no one had come looking for him besides Sou-Zell. Not his parents, not his brothers.

"But she'll feel it." A note of panic had entered Sou-Zell's voice.

"We can't stop now, Sou-Zell. It's already started. Keep that needle where it is—this will take time. All the blood in her body needs to pass through the defuser for extraction. Falka, I'll take over when your hand gets tired."

"Min-Chuul," moaned an unfamiliar voice. "Where are you? It hurts."

"Stop this," Sou-Zell said. "It isn't working. She's in pain."

"That means it *is* working," Falka snapped. "Weren't you listening? Do you want her to live or not?"

The silence stretched, broken only by a steady rushing noise that might have been the blood pounding in Kadrin's ears. He staggered

Flight of the Fallen

to his feet. The instinct almost overtook him to flee into the dark, away from the workshop and whatever was happening inside. But something rooted him in place.

Sou-Zell hadn't left him under the temple. He'd gotten him out.

"What happens if we stop now?" Sou-Zell asked.

"I injected her with ten times more mana than her body can process. If I don't filter it out, she'll die of mana poisoning. It isn't a painless death. You know what it looks like, Sou-Zell. You watched it happen to a courier."

"I don't know what to do. I don't know. Eomma? Tell me what you want."

"She can't hear you, Sou-Zell. She's too far gone."

"Min-Chuul . . ."

Kadrin was sweating; his vision frayed around the edges. But he pushed his way into the workshop. He hardly saw what Orrin and Falka were doing, apart from a few confusing flashes of metal tubing, Falka's hand squeezing a pump, and a glass chamber filled with dark red liquid. Orrin's eyes glowed orange.

Kadrin stumbled toward the table, where Sou-Zell stood hunched over his mother. He put his hand on Sou-Zell's shoulder, expecting the man to flinch away or strike him. But Sou-Zell only turned to him, his pupils blown wide like a distressed animal.

"It's okay to let her go," Kadrin said.

"Are you mad?" Falka's voice dripped with venom. "We've come this far. She'll suffer either way. It makes no sense to stop now."

Kadrin ignored her. His eyes were on Sou-Zell. "We can take her back to the doctor. He can help ease her suffering. Think about what *she* would want—not what you want. This isn't the time to be selfish."

Sou-Zell's mouth flattened into a thin line. That was Kadrin's only warning before Sou-Zell *did* hit him. It was a weak punch, all things considered, but it was enough to send Kadrin reeling against the wall.

Strangely, it hardly hurt. Kadrin's jaw throbbed, but the sensation was muted, remote, as if all the other pain he'd felt recently had numbed him. Anyway, it didn't matter. The punch was proof that Sou-Zell had heard him.

"It doesn't make you a bad son if you can't save her," Kadrin said.

Sou-Zell shut his eyes and made a soft, strangled noise. Then he turned toward Orrin. "No more."

"Sou-Zell—" Falka snarled.

"I said *no more*."

The scorching orange glow faded from Orrin's eyes. Falka's hand stopped squeezing, and the steady rushing noise of the machine died away. Silence fell over the workshop. The only remaining sound was Sou-Zell's mother's labored breath.

"Come on," Kadrin said. "I'll help you carry her back."

CHAPTER TWENTY-SIX

A FATHER'S LOVE

Observation #765: Shocked that I didn't realize this the moment
Makela's Herald revealed herself; it's now glaringly obvious how
the shieldcasters of Kerina Rut have endured despite horrific
levels of population loss. The Talent she steals is absorbed,
transmuted into pure power.
Further study: Would kill to obtain a blood sample. —O

Third Age of Storms, 1st Summer, Day 86
The Barrens – Somewhere West of Mount Vetelu

Embers danced in a black column of smoke rising from the
Shield Lord's campsite. Seated on the dusty ground, Yi-Nereen
imagined her lungs filling with smoke and ash: the vapors of a flame
and the scraps of its destruction. That was how it would feel to stand
in a dying city when the storms came and the defenders were fallen.

She had to make it to Avi'Kerina so no one else would know
what it felt like.

"Your Highness."

Yi-Nereen shivered. No one had called her by that title in almost
two months. She'd risked everything to flee those words; hearing
them again felt like the cold kiss of metal shackles around her wrists.

The knight standing above her shifted his weight. "Your father requests that you join him for dinner."

Dinner. As if nothing had changed. As if she were back in the Tower, a sullen girl bound by the wishes and whims of her father. Maybe it had all been a long, vivid dream: escaping with Jin, reuniting with Kadrin, those few precious moments in the sunlit garden. The dream had had its dark stretches, but waking from it was worse than any nightmare.

She rose numbly to her feet. Jin stepped between her and the knight.

"You don't have to go, Reena. He can treat you like a prisoner, but he can't force you to be his daughter."

Yi-Nereen wanted to take Jin's hand and seek comfort in the warmth of her calloused skin, but that would only make it harder to let go and walk away.

"I'll always be his daughter," she said. "Don't worry. I'll be fine."

"Stay with us," Jin persisted. "It's safer if we're together."

Beyond her, Eliesen lay on the hard ground with a rolled-up sleeping mat as a pillow. They still hadn't extracted the bolt, since they had nothing to stitch the wound closed. The feathered end stuck out from a mass of bandages. Eliesen's face shone with sweat, even in sleep. Celwyn sat beside her, his shoulders hunched.

No, Yi-Nereen couldn't do anything to upset her father. He would be delighted that for the first time since her childhood, Yi-Nereen had people in her life she loved and cared about. Knives he could twist in her flesh until she begged forgiveness.

"I lived under his roof for twenty years," Yi-Nereen said. "I can handle one more conversation with him. His expedition is better equipped than ours; I'm sure he brought medical supplies. I'll ask for something for Eliesen."

Flight of the Fallen

She knew that would persuade Jin to let her go. After all, Jin also suffered from the incurable weakness of caring about other people.

Sure enough, a muscle in Jin's jaw clenched and her eyes darted to Eliesen. "All right. But I'd rather we just made a run for it."

It was a hollow sentiment. There were archers perched in the rocks, and the bikes were guarded. They'd be killed within seconds of the attempt. But Yi-Nereen had no doubt that Jin would try, even knowing the odds.

She followed her father's errand knight to the other side of camp, where the smoke rising from the fire had concealed an unlikely scene. Lai-Dan sat in a lordly chair with arms that curved back like the limbs of a winged statue; across a stone table was another, less ostentatious chair.

He'd brought a stoneshaper on his expedition just so he wouldn't have to eat on the ground like everyone else. Yi-Nereen felt a surge of hatred.

"Nereena, please, sit. How I've missed you."

A platter of sliced fruit rested on the table. Yi-Nereen's favorites: Rut plums, their flesh dark bluish purple and glistening. Her stomach growled.

"Kerina Rut is dying," Yi-Nereen said. "Bloomweavers, stoneshapers, shieldcasters. Your city needs them all. Every last one. How many did you bring on this expedition, Father?"

Lai-Dan smiled at her, as if she'd said something simpering. "You used to call me Appa. Your sisters still do. I'm surprised you haven't asked after them."

It was a needle to the heart, the kind of precise assault her father exulted in. Yi-Nereen had buried her love for her sisters so deep that it only welled up in moments like this—like blood from a wound. Most days she didn't think of them at all. It only hurt more when she did.

"Sit down, Nereena." Her father's tone made it clear he wouldn't ask again.

Yi-Nereen sat. Her sore muscles cried out in relief; after days of riding, the stone chair felt softer than all the cushioned ottomans in the House of Steel Heavens. Yi-Nereen remembered Eliesen sweating on the ground with a bolt in her shoulder and choked down a wave of guilt.

"I wondered if the First City would call to you," Lai-Dan said, "the way it did to me. I'm pleased you answered its call. Like father, like daughter."

He bit into a plum slice; the violet juice ran obscenely through his fingers.

"I haven't been the best father to you, Nereena, not always. In my defense, I never had the luxury of *only* being your father. I was your lord and ruler as well."

In theory, the lords of Shield, Bloom, and Rain ruled Kerina Rut in tandem. But Yi-Nereen knew her father had always dominated the other two. He was king of Kerina Rut in all but title.

"Was?" she asked softly.

"I'm no fool. The days of the High Houses are behind us, or will be soon. Even if Kerina Rut is last to fall, fall it will. No tower can save us from that fate."

Did he somehow know of the tower Yi-Nereen had tried to build in Kerina Sol? Did he think she'd tried to imitate him? No. She wasn't like him.

He and the men before him had built the Tower of Arrested Stars as the centerpiece of their doomed dynasty—a monument to the power they'd grasped for even as time flowed through their fingers. Yi-Nereen wanted no dynasty. No power. Only to save as many people as she could.

"You discovered something, Nereena." Her father stared at her. "The secret of our bloodline. Yes, I know about Mount Vetelu. I know you met Zon-Ra."

Zon-Ra. She'd never heard the name before. But it could belong to only one man. Her great-uncle, who'd called himself Tibius Vann to conceal his identity as the twin brother of Yi-Nereen's grandfather, Shield Lord Zon-Lai.

It didn't matter how her father knew. Yi-Nereen had no secrets worth keeping from her father anymore. Everything was laid bare. She wanted to be free of him; he knew it. He would never let her go; she knew that, too.

Yi-Nereen returned Lai-Dan's stare. "The only secret he taught me was one I already knew. We can drain people of their mana. We can steal their Last Breath. *You* taught me that. But did you know, Father, that you don't have to kill them? You don't have to kiss them, either."

"Of course I knew." Irritation flashed across her father's face. "Better for them to die in service than to live Talentless and cost us all. You never had the stomach for sacrifice, my girl, but I was born to it. A lord must be ready to trade in lives."

"*I* never had the stomach for sacrifice?"

All those years on the Wall. Her body and mind ravaged by storms. Watching her mother suffer through miscarriage after miscarriage. Knowing her childbed and her deathbed would be one and the same.

Her father smiled thinly.

"Who did you think would bear the burdens you cast off so carelessly, Nereena? The Tower must have heirs. I wed both your sisters weeks ago so they wouldn't be tempted to follow in your cowardly footsteps. Let no man say I do not learn from my errors."

"No," Yi-Nereen said. "Tanai is only fifteen. What have you done?"

"Old enough for the Wall—old enough to do her duty. Besides, Lai-Ren will look after her. He will ensure she never falls prey to such wicked temptations as her eldest sister."

Yi-Nereen forgot how to breathe. In horror, through a mouthful of ashes, she said, "You wed my little sister to our uncle?"

"If you had never run away from your responsibilities, I would not have had to resort to such measures."

A scream welled inside Yi-Nereen; it brought her to her feet. Mana boiled in her veins. She burned the dregs of the mana in her blood and summoned a shield-blade, the sharpest she could. She would kill her father for this.

Her body wouldn't obey. She couldn't move, couldn't make a sound. Her eyes darted back and forth. Her body was enveloped in a skintight blue bubble that flowed over her shape like water.

It was a *shield*. Her father's shield.

"Settle down, Nereena."

The shield bent her legs, forced her back into her chair. Yi-Nereen stared at Lai-Dan in paralyzed terror. He smiled, his eyes glowing blue. His hands rested on the winged arms of his chair as he directed her with no more than a thought.

"I suspected you hadn't yet learned the *true* secret of our bloodline. How our Talent is heightened and evolved through sacrifice. Once you have consumed a metalcrafter, your shield can pierce flesh. A sparkrider's soul merged with yours will allow you to extend your shield beyond yourself. Bloom unlocks the ability to form precise shapes, as delicate and complex as you wish, the way a bloomweaver summons fruit to the vine."

Yi-Nereen's stomach churned. After she'd drunk the ambrosia

Flight of the Fallen

containing Faolin's power, she'd been able to separate her shield and float everyone in Mount Vetelu to safety as the ground collapsed beneath them. Then, after saving the metalcrafter at the spring, her shield had become a weapon. Toraka was a bloomweaver—and after Yi-Nereen had siphoned her, she'd been able to mold her shield into a lance.

Lai-Dan had known all these things already. For years. He'd hidden this power from her, from all her siblings. Why?

"My esteemed father discovered we could increase our power and form stronger shields, but he never made a study of his own Talent as I have. Your great-uncle, Zon-Ra, knew only the most rudimentary things about our abilities. Enough to crave your power, Nereena, which you alone possess among your siblings."

Part of Yi-Nereen clung to every word her father was saying. She had to understand this power before it ruined her. The rest of her was an unending shriek of horror and rage.

Her father's crimes were inhuman. Had it truly been necessary for him to siphon so many people to protect Kerina Rut, or had those lives merely served to fuel his experimentation?

She was horrified at herself, too, all over again, for even momentarily joining forces with Tibius Vann. Faolin had been right—Tibius and her father were just the same.

"I admit," Lai-Dan said, his voice soft as silk, "sometimes I craved that power for myself. What would happen if someone like me siphoned someone like you? My beautiful girl, so ignorant of her own potential."

Yi-Nereen had always assumed her brothers could siphon, too. If her father was telling the truth and Yi-Nereen was the only one of her siblings to have inherited his power, she could scarcely imagine his disappointment. A daughter, sole inheritor to his legacy. A useless girl who could be married only outside her House, unless her father found a way to bend the temple's marriage restrictions—as he must have, for her sisters.

Her father leaned toward her, across the table, and Yi-Nereen's skin crawled. Was this how she would die? Finally in Lai-Dan's clutches again, far from Kerina Rut and its laws and traditions. He could tear it from her, this power she'd never wanted in the first place, and he wouldn't stop once she was Talentless. He would stop only once she was dead.

The only thing worse than a daughter was a Talentless daughter.

Desperate, Yi-Nereen burned mana. She shaped her shield as close to her skin as she could, trying to force her way to freedom. But all she could manage was to move her lips and say, "If you kill me, Celwyn will never take you to the First City."

Lai-Dan laughed.

"If only you could see the visions I have had, Nereena. The Giver of Blessings *chose* us. Our family. The First City holds the secrets of divinity. Whoever claims them will become inheritor to Rasvel Himself. Can't you see, my girl, how everything else will cease to matter? Whether I siphon you now is irrelevant. I will ascend to godhood with or without you."

"You won't ever become a god," Yi-Nereen said. "Even if you save everyone—or destroy everything—you'll still be a man, Father. A man whose own children despise him."

Her heart pounded in terror. Her death felt close enough to touch. But more than anything, she wanted to wipe the smile from her father's face. A childish part of her was desperate for some sign that he cared enough for her to be hurt by her loathing. It was the only weapon she had—and if it was useless, it meant she'd never been anything to him besides a failed legacy.

Flight of the Fallen

Lai-Dan looked at her coldly, his smile never faltering.

"I think not," he said. "What is a father, but a god to his children?"

※

After everything that happened in Kerina Sol, Yi-Nereen had thought herself powerful, her shieldtalent unmatched. Now her mind was filled with the pressure of her father's shield, bending her into place, forcing her to submit. She'd been like wet clay in his hands.

Her body didn't feel like hers anymore. Not when Lai-Dan could take it from her whenever he wished.

"Reena?" Jin jumped to her feet. All Yi-Nereen could see of her was an indistinct figure in the darkness. Behind her were Celwyn and Eliesen, huddled together on the ground. "Thank the gods he didn't hurt you."

"He wants my Talent," Yi-Nereen whispered.

"Oh, fuck." Jin gripped Yi-Nereen's arms and her voice turned dusky and dangerous. "What did he do? *What did he do?*"

"Nothing yet. I don't think he'll try until we reach Avi'Kerina." Yi-Nereen felt a tear slip down her cheek; she hoped Jin couldn't see it in the dark. "If the stories about Avi'Kerina are true, if the gods really left the secrets of divinity there for mortals to find, I can't let him take their power. I have to kill him."

Jin pulled her into a crushing embrace, and only then did Yi-Nereen realize she was trembling.

"You can't kill your own father, Reena."

"I have to. I *have* to."

"No you don't. You're not alone. Do you think I came with you

285

to save the kerinas? I'm not that much of a hero. I came so I could keep *you* safe." Jin buried her face in Yi-Nereen's hair. "I know you think you have to do everything yourself. But you don't. I'm here."

I'm glad you're here, Jin, Yi-Nereen tried to say.

What came out instead was "I love you."

She'd written those words, but never in her life had she said them to anyone. They tasted sweeter than anything.

Jin froze. "You aren't going to die."

Yi-Nereen understood that in Jin's language, those words meant *I love you, too.*

There was more to talk about, but for now Yi-Nereen didn't want to say a thing. She just wanted to hold Jin under the faint glow of the wasteland moon and let the rest of the world fade away until the morning.

And then, before they reached the gates of Avi'Kerina, she would do what had to be done.

She would kill her father.

CHAPTER TWENTY-SEVEN

OUT OF THE FOG

Observation #478: Attended live dissection of a captive chandru at Academy. Observed multiple organs apparently used for water storage.

Conclusion: Of course saurians aren't plants. Orrin, you idiot. They're machines. —O

Third Age of Storms, 1st Summer, Day 87

The Barrens – No Fucking Clue

Jin woke up coughing, her nose and throat raw. The yellow fog had worsened overnight. She could hardly see through the thick haze to the other side of the campsite—but she could see everyone who mattered. Yi-Nereen, curled up next to her. Eliesen on Jin's other side. Both of them still asleep.

Celwyn had Eliesen's head in his lap, cradled on his folded jacket. He met Jin's quizzical stare calmly enough; his dark complexion made it hard to tell, but Jin thought he might be flushed. "She didn't sleep well. The pain."

Jin glanced around. She couldn't see any of Lai-Dan's knights, which meant they couldn't see her.

"We could make a run for it now. Use the fog to slip away."

Hana Lee

"They're guarding the bikes," Celwyn said. "We won't get far without those."

"We have to do *something*. Yi-Nereen's father will kill us as soon as Avi'Kerina's in sight. You do realize that? He isn't the type to hold up his end of a bargain."

Celwyn gave her a long, cool look. "Jin, you need to trust me."

"Why should I?" Jin simmered with frustration. "We don't know each other. Gods damn it, Celwyn. If you're planning something, just tell me so I can be ready."

Celwyn pursed his lips and said nothing.

Despite her fury, Jin understood. The moment Celwyn told her the way to Avi'Kerina, he'd be disposable to Lai-Dan. He was surely aware that neither Jin nor Yi-Nereen would put her life on the line for him, if it came down to it.

Kadrin would have, if he were here. But that was exactly why he wasn't here.

She couldn't let herself wonder what was happening back home. She had to trust that Kadrin was keeping his head down, staying out of trouble. Hopefully the situation had calmed with Yi-Nereen out of the city.

Jin's gaze fell on the princess, who was curled in the dust with her cheek pillowed on the back of her hand. Strands of black hair drooped over her twitching eyelids; Jin resisted the urge to tuck them back.

I love you, she'd said.

Jin hadn't said it back. She'd been struck by panic, and fear—fear that Yi-Nereen was only saying those words because she thought she was soon to die.

Cowardice. Utter cowardice. Jin loved Yi-Nereen and Kadrin to

Flight of the Fallen

the point of breathlessness. If Yi-Nereen *did* think she was soon to die, all the more reason for Jin to try honesty on for size, no matter whether Yi-Nereen was in her right mind.

The fog swirled to reveal two Knights of Rut, their faces hidden by bonehelms.

"Get up. All of you. The Shield Lord wishes to depart at once."

Yi-Nereen stirred. "Jin?"

"I'm here."

The rest of the words stuck in Jin's chest. And then Eliesen whimpered as Celwyn shifted her awake, and Jin lost her resolve.

The knights escorted the four of them to their bikes. Eliesen leaned on Celwyn, her face ashen. All around, Jin heard engines roaring to life and shouted orders as the expedition prepared to move. Obviously Lai-Dan's expedition was an organized affair, capable of mobilizing itself despite the conditions.

Jin straddled her magebike and leaned toward Celwyn to hiss, "Last chance. We can lose them in the fog."

Celwyn slid his pteropter bonehelm into place. "Too risky. *Trust me.*"

Jin didn't trust him. Not one whit. But she couldn't just take off on her own bike with Yi-Nereen, not if it meant leaving Eliesen behind. Fuck.

"Move to the front," a knight barked at Celwyn. "You're leading."

Celwyn gunned his bike toward the head of the formation. Jin moved to follow, but a gauntleted palm stopped her.

"You stay in the middle. Shield Lord's taking no chances with his daughter."

Now they were separated. She'd lost her chance. No choice but to hope Celwyn didn't betray her as easily as he'd betrayed Falka.

289

And maybe he wouldn't, with Amrys's voice in his head. If Amrys was half as loyal as her brother had been, and if she had any sway over Celwyn at all.

The expedition set off at a crawl. Jin had no memory of this road: a pitted highway that led west from the Mount Vetelu spring, deeper into the Barrens. The farther they went, the more thickly the fog coalesced. Jin had wrapped a scarf over her nose and mouth under her bonehelm and made Yi-Nereen do the same, but still she heard Yi-Nereen coughing behind her shoulder. The air grew hot and dry, like the inside of a kiln.

Hours passed. Then a distant shriek pierced the fog. Jin's blood chilled.

"That wasn't Screech," Yi-Nereen said.

She'd learned to recognize the pteropter's call as well as Jin. For some reason, Jin's heart warmed even as dread rose in her belly.

"Hopefully one of his friends," Jin muttered.

Lai-Dan's expedition was well organized, but it was also *large*. Noisy. Everything in the Barrens could probably hear them, knew exactly where they were.

Ahead, the column of bikes veered left. Off-road. Where was Celwyn leading them? Jin thought back to the tablet Toraka had shown her, but to her frustration, she couldn't remember if Avi'Kerina lay on a highway line or not.

Trust me, Celwyn had insisted. Did he plan to get them lost? That would certainly stop Lai-Dan from reaching Avi'Kerina, but it would also mean all their deaths.

Jin had no choice but to stay in formation and follow the bike ahead of her. The crumbled edge of the blacktop vanished into the fog behind her. Her bones rattled as small rocks and trenches passed under her wheels.

Flight of the Fallen

Gods, but it was difficult to steer the manacycle and match the speed of the knights before and behind her. Jin was lucky; the fog and her bonehelm had prevented anyone from noticing that her eyes didn't glow.

Another shriek. Right behind her. Chills skittered down her spine. That one had sounded human. Fucking saurians, playing tricks—

Something flew from the fog in front of her. Muscled limbs, a lashing tail, a single, slitted yellow eye. The creature sprang onto the knight in front of Jin and dragged him, screaming, from his bike. Then they were both gone.

"Oh, fuck!"

All hell broke loose.

The saurians had used the fog as cover to surround them. Cries of terror rang out all around Jin. She flashed back to the shrieks in the fog. Hunting calls. The saurians were hunting them.

Celwyn must have known from the first call. That's why he'd led them off-road. But why? Was he trying to escape the ambush, or lead the knights straight into it?

She'd never seen saurians like this before. Smaller than rovex, but similar in shape, stalking on two legs. Long, sinuous tails and wickedly sharp claws. Dull blue and auburn feathers. So *many* of them.

"Reena, hold on!"

Jin felt Yi-Nereen's answering clutch around her waist. She gunned the manacycle haphazardly through a chaotic melee of flailing knights and snarling saurians. The air was already thick with the stench of blood.

Yi-Nereen's fingers dug into Jin's ribs. "There!"

Jin saw the flash of metal and a bike toppled on the ground.

Celwyn stood over Eliesen's sprawled body, his blade whirling through the air as he fought off two saurians at once.

This was Jin's chance. If she could get Celwyn and Eliesen back on their bike, all four of them could flee while Lai-Dan's knights were busy dying.

Jin turned her bike in a tight loop and made straight for Celwyn. Before she could brake, Yi-Nereen leaped from the bike and landed crouched in the dirt. Her hair had come loose from her riding helm; it splayed around her, a swirl of black. She threw out her hands.

Bright blue shards of light shot toward the saurians menacing Celwyn. But they sizzled and vanished on contact with the saurians' hides.

"Lightning eaters!" Celwyn snapped, ducking under a set of scything claws.

But Yi-Nereen had used her shield, not sparks. Jin didn't have time to ponder her confusion. She dismounted her bike—and her foot caught under something hidden by the creeping fog.

She sprawled over the plate-clad corpse of a knight. The man's head had been torn from his body. Blood pooled in the dirt, dark and sticky.

His sword. Jin pried it from his still-warm hand.

"Jin!" Yi-Nereen screamed. "Where are you?"

Jin raised her head. Yi-Nereen had reached Celwyn; her shield flickered over the two of them and Eliesen, pulsing blue. The saurians clawed at the dome and howled. Jin's heart thundered in her chest.

Any moment, they'd see her. They'd come for her. She was defenseless, unshielded. Prey.

Maybe she could lead them away.

Flight of the Fallen

Jin threw a glance over her shoulder. The fog had swirled apart, and she saw—

Lai-Dan. He stood not ten paces away in his midnight-blue riding tunic, alone. He hadn't seen her. He was watching a saurian hunched over a corpse, its head ducked and jerking as it fed. Blue light pooled in Lai-Dan's hands, forming into the shape of a blade. He wasn't shielded.

Jin's blood sang in her ears. Her fingers curled around the unfamiliar weight of the sword in her hand.

I have to kill him.

No you don't.

Last night, Jin had lain awake in the darkness and thought about the first and only person she'd ever killed. Ziyal. Blood on her hands, warm and sticky. The wet gasps of a dying woman.

Jin hadn't meant to kill her. Could she take someone's life in cold blood?

It didn't matter. Her blood wasn't cold now. It surged through her, a hot and vicious tide, as she raised the dead knight's sword. One stroke and Yi-Nereen would never have to fear her father again. She'd be free.

Jin could be a killer for her.

"Jin!" Yi-Nereen screamed again. She'd seen her. "Come *here*!"

One more step. Sweat rolled down Jin's back as she raised the blade over her head. One more step and she'd be close enough to strike.

How hard would she have to swing, to end him in one stroke? She couldn't give him a chance to cast a shield. He had to die before he knew she was here.

This was a nightmare. But soon it would be over.

She felt a rush of air a moment before claws struck her from behind. Teeth like daggers bit deep into her leather jacket and hit flesh. Jin heard her bones splinter. The sword flew from her hand.

The force of the impact spun her around. The last thing Jin saw was Yi-Nereen running toward her, eyes blazing, hands outstretched. Like the goddess Makela. Her Herald.

Then the saurians dragged Jin into the fog.

PART FOUR

CHAPTER TWENTY-EIGHT

THE PRODIGAL SON

Observation #752: First- and third-form mana both suitable for
human consumption, while second form is not.
Conclusion: Third-form mana likely derived from first, not second.
A pyramid, not a line. —O

Third Age of Storms, 1st Summer, Day 87
Kerina Sol – Refugee Quarter

The city wasn't asleep. Beyond the Refugee Quarter, Kadrin heard a faint roar, like an oncoming storm—but the skies were clear. He counted on his fingers. Eleven days of mana rationing, and no word from the Council or the temple on when it might end. No surprise that people had begun to riot. Kadrin didn't know what it felt like to thirst for mana, but he understood suffering.

He should be out there, doing something. Not sitting in front of the physician's shack, twiddling his thumbs. He was helpless, torn between a city full of desperate people and a single man inside the building behind him who was going through the worst pain Kadrin could imagine.

The shack door creaked open and Sou-Zell walked out. He

moved unsteadily. Drunkenly. His head swiveled slowly until his gaze met Kadrin's: the blank, staring eyes of a ghost.

"It's over."

Kadrin stood. He had no idea what to say. Everything seemed inadequate, particularly in light of the fact that he was undoubtedly the last person Sou-Zell wanted to witness his grief.

I loathed you, he'd said.

Well. There was probably one thing that would make Sou-Zell feel better.

Kadrin spread his arms and braced himself. "Hit me." When Sou-Zell did nothing but stare at him, unblinking, Kadrin added, "I'm serious. As hard as you can. I'll even hit back if you'd like."

For a long moment, he thought Sou-Zell wouldn't take him up on it.

Then Sou-Zell lunged and grabbed Kadrin's shoulder. His other fist rose. Kadrin turned his cheek and shut his eyes.

The blow never came. Heart pounding, Kadrin opened his eyes to see Sou-Zell standing frozen, his fist still in the air, like he'd forgotten what he was doing. Sweat sheened his face; his eyes were wide and staring.

So much for *that*.

Kadrin grabbed Sou-Zell and pulled him into a hug.

He'd never in a thousand years pictured himself doing this. It had always seemed more likely that he'd end up with Sou-Zell's knife in his ribs. But in the end, it was a lot like hugging Jin. She and Sou-Zell were even about the same height. And both of them clearly hadn't been hugged enough in their lives.

There was a moment of stiff resistance. Then Sou-Zell collapsed like a house of cards, the fight gone out of him completely, without stabbing Kadrin even once.

Flight of the Fallen

Kadrin wasn't sure how long it was before Sou-Zell pulled away. Not more than a few seconds, certainly. He sat down heavily on the stoop outside the physician's shack; after a moment, Kadrin joined him.

The silence stretched. In the distance, the roar of the riots grew steadily louder. Sou-Zell didn't seem ready to talk, but he hadn't snarled at Kadrin to go away, either. Well, Kadrin could be patient. The city and Toraka needed him, yes—but once again, Sou-Zell needed him more.

Finally Sou-Zell spoke. "I made a mistake."

Kadrin swallowed, instantly tense. "Tell me about it."

"My brother," Sou-Zell said. "He refused to see her when I told him she was dying. I left him in a drug den to rot. I should have dragged him home. Not for his sake. For hers."

Ah. Kadrin had heard Sou-Zell's mother calling, over and over, for someone named Min-Chuul. He hadn't heard her say Sou-Zell's name once.

"That doesn't sound like it was your fault."

"Wrong." Sou-Zell didn't sound petulant, just tired. "He was there because I drove him there. I told him the only way he'd see the inside of our House again was if he became a better son. But it wasn't the lying or the stealing that made me turn him out—not even breaking our mother's heart. When I looked at him, all I saw was proof of our House's degeneracy. I couldn't stand the sight of him. A Talentless under my own roof."

Kadrin's stomach turned. For the first time in a long while, he felt a flicker of resentment toward Sou-Zell. Too little, too late. He swallowed it down.

"He didn't need to be a better son." Sou-Zell's voice was raw. "I needed to be a better brother. I never even tried."

Hana Lee

"Well," Kadrin said carefully, "he didn't ask to be born Talentless. It was wrong to treat him like that. But—"

"But nothing," Sou-Zell spat. He turned on Kadrin, eyes blazing. "He was right to hate me. I treated him every bit as cruelly as I've treated you. Why don't *you* hate me, princeling?" He inhaled sharply. "Or perhaps you do. You've done this—all of this—to destroy me. You stopped me from saving her. Were you trying to kill her?"

"Sou-Zell," Kadrin said. "I'm not that clever."

"Then *why?*"

"If you'd gone through with it, you would have hated yourself later. I didn't want that."

"Why *not?*"

"Because I think you're a good man. It's sad, actually. The harder you try not to be one, the more it shows."

Sou-Zell exhaled, long and slow. His knuckles were white in his lap.

"You're a fool. What about the High Priestess? Do you think she's a good woman, too, masquerading as a sadist?"

Kadrin shivered. The burns on his chest itched. "I don't think she's either of those things. But I know this: she's destroying Kerina Sol. She doesn't care about saving anyone, only for finding Yi-Nereen and punishing her. Even after Jin and the others come back, the Council won't listen if Edine's still in power."

Sou-Zell nodded slowly. "What will you do?"

What *could* Kadrin do? He was just one man. The Council had never taken him seriously. He couldn't enrapture and inspire people like Toraka could with a few elegant words. He was no genius, no Herald, no scarred survivor. He'd only ever siphoned his family's vaults to hand coin over to people who were smarter and more pow-

300

Flight of the Fallen

erful than he was. Yi-Nereen, Toraka, Jin, Orrin, even Sou-Zell . . . the list went on.

"I don't know," Kadrin said. "But there's only one place to start."

※

When it came down to it, Matrios was the Rain Lord, and Kadrin was nothing but his son.

The bare branches of the cherry trees bowed under an unseen wind as Kadrin strode down the avenue toward the House of Steel Heavens. Dawn would break soon, but he hoped it would remain dark a little longer—so his parents wouldn't see his bruises. Now wasn't the time to field reactions to news of his kidnapping and torture. If anyone asked where he'd been for two days, he could say he'd been helping in the Refugee Quarter.

He expected the House to still be asleep. But when he pushed open the carved wooden door to the foyer, he heard voices. His mother and father stood by the foot of the grand staircase, arguing in whispers.

Kadrin braced himself.

"I'm home."

His parents broke apart. "Kadrin!" his mother exclaimed. Kadrin submitted to her embrace—but like Sou-Zell, he was first to pull away. Gods, he desperately needed a bath. After days of captivity, he was sure he reeked.

"It's time you returned," Matrios said. He sounded exhausted. His hair was unkempt; there were hollows beneath his eyes.

Kadrin glanced at his mother, who looked similar. His gut twisted. It wasn't exhaustion; his parents were both suffering from mana thirst. As the city's ruling raincallers, their duties weren't optional. But he'd assumed neither of them would be subject to rationing.

His parents hadn't noticed his bruised face, and they didn't seem in a hurry to ask where he'd been. Kadrin felt a little deflated at that.

Your family neither knows nor cares about your whereabouts, Sou-Zell had said. Well. Apparently he'd been correct.

"The entire city is going mad," Kadrin's mother said. "High Priestess Edine is trying to restore order, but the refugees won't listen to reason. They're marching in the streets as we speak. Tethris has called an emergency Council meeting to order."

Matrios stared at Kadrin. "You must speak with the refugee leader, Toraka. Tell her to control her people. The mana restrictions can't be lifted until the temple finds a solution to the crisis. All this chaos will only bring the city to its knees. She must understand that."

Kadrin felt the floor falling away beneath him, tile by tile. "The temple isn't even looking for a solution, Father."

His mother sighed. "There are just too many people in the city. The spring can't support them all. But High Priestess Edine will find a way—"

"Stop saying her name," Kadrin snapped.

He could have slapped his mother and caused less of a stir. His parents both drew back with twin noises of shock. And to Kadrin's own surprise, his father looked away.

"Kadrin?" his mother asked. She'd finally noticed his face. "Did you get in a fight?"

Kadrin wasn't often angry. But he felt it now: heat creeping through his veins and up the back of his neck, boiling in his blood.

"Father. Did your dear friend the High Priestess happen to mention where I've been for the past two days?"

Flight of the Fallen

"Matrios, what's he talking about?"

The Rain Lord breathed deeply, nostrils flaring, and looked at Kadrin's mother. "She had questions for him." His voice was low, pacifying. "I was assured he wouldn't be harmed. He would be treated well, as my son. Edine gave me her word."

"Look at me, Father," Kadrin said.

He tore open his robe to reveal his chest, sticky with the salve the physician had given him but still covered in raw red marks. Ugly satisfaction filled him at the sight of his parents' expressions: his mother's horror, his father's grim understanding. For the first time in his life, it wasn't their approval he craved.

"You forgot something, Father. I'm not just your son. I'm your *Talentless* son. You made me think that if I just tried hard enough, I could fix that. Apparently the High Priestess didn't agree. She lied to you because she knew that in the end, you wouldn't care."

"Kadrin," his mother pleaded, "that isn't true—"

"Mother," Kadrin said, cutting her off. But his voice softened; he couldn't help it. He could see how much he was hurting her. "It was kind of you to hire Talentless servants after I was born. I'm sure you wanted to prove you don't see them as freaks—you'll even let them clean up after you. But the Talentless don't need your charity. They need an advocate on the Council. I noticed you never attend meetings, Mother. I suppose they're a distraction from your social life."

"How dare you speak to your mother that—"

"I really don't care," Kadrin said, breathing hard, "how either of you treat me anymore. I'll say this just once. *I* don't need you any longer—but the people of Kerina Sol do. Mother, you said there are too many people in the city. Well, I know an artificer who's working on a way to bottle mana, preserve it so it stays fresh outside a spring.

303

Let the refugees bottle as much as they need to cross the wastes, and they'll leave. Toraka will lead them to the First City. Jin and Reena should already be there by now."

His mother was staring at him, stricken, but the Rain Lord was already shaking his head. "No. It's an insane plan. The High Houses will never agree to take that much mana from the spring. It could destabilize it even further."

"You *are* a High House! Don't act like they wouldn't do it if you said it was a good idea. Convince them. If the High Priestess disagrees, overrule her. The temple gets a vote, but they don't get a veto."

"What about the rest of us, Kadrin?" his mother asked. "If the spring runs dry after the refugees leave, we'll die."

Kadrin crossed his arms. "Maybe you should consider going with them."

"Enough!" Kadrin's father struck the nearby banister with the flat of his palm. "I refuse to hear any more of this folly. The First City is a myth. I'm sorry your friends have risked their lives chasing after a fairy tale, Kadrin, but in all likelihood, they've gone to their deaths. I won't suggest to the Council that we follow them into the wastes to die."

This was pointless. Kadrin had known it would be, even before coming home. But still he had hoped. Hoped that for once in his life, his parents wouldn't disappoint him.

At some point he'd stopped being afraid of disappointing *them*.

"Eliesen went to the First City, too, you know," he said. "Did you notice *she* was gone?"

His parents exchanged thunderstruck looks. Clearly they hadn't noticed any such thing. It wasn't unusual for Eliesen to be out of the House several nights in a row; she liked to visit friends and rarely notified anyone of her comings and goings.

Flight of the Fallen

"You sent your sister on a dangerous journey," his mother sputtered, "and you didn't tell us?"

"This is beyond the pale," his father said.

Kadrin clenched his fists. "Maybe I would have had the chance to tell you if I wasn't getting *tortured*. Sorry about that. High Priestess Edine knew—because she burned me until I told her everything—so maybe you should—"

He stopped. Everything. He'd told Edine everything.

Including the names of everyone who had attended that secret meeting in the smithy, even the ones who hadn't gone on the expedition and weren't publicly associated with the conspiracy: Bloom Lord Feyrin, Renfir, and Jin's mother, Evemi.

Oh gods.

Maybe Edine hadn't taken note of the names amid the flood of useless information she'd pried from him. There was still a chance Jin's mother was safe. But she was Talentless, just like Kadrin. And Kadrin knew very well the methods High Priestess Edine used for extracting information from the Talentless.

He turned and made for the door.

"Kadrin," his father called after him. "We aren't finished with this conversation."

Kadrin stopped and turned around.

"Actually, we are. I'm done—with you, the House, and the Council. I'm not the Third Heir to the House of Steel Heavens anymore. As of today, I'm disinheriting myself."

He turned away from his parents and hurried away from them through the darkened corridors of the House, past sitting rooms and galleries and music rooms, until he'd left the luxurious royal quarters behind and entered the cramped hallways of the servant wing. For the first time in his life, he noticed how much empty space there was in the House he'd grown up in. How vast and beautiful and underutilized it was compared with the packed, stinking slums in the Refugee Quarter. He would miss it: his wardrobe full of fine clothes, his gilt-framed mirrors, his marble bathtub. He'd never known life without all these accoutrements.

Maybe he was too weak to survive without them.

He was almost to the kitchens. Jin's mother would be there, like she was every morning, baking bread and pastries before the sun rose so the whole House could enjoy them for breakfast. Kadrin had made a habit of visiting Evemi in the kitchens ever since she'd moved into the House. Sometimes Renfir was there, too, ostensibly going over the menu for the day in his function as the House's majordomo. Kadrin wasn't convinced tucking stray hairs back behind Evemi's ears was part of a majordomo's duties, but what did he know?

The wholesome aroma of baking bread wafted forth from the kitchen to greet him. Kadrin nearly collapsed in relief.

Jin's mother stood at a marble counter, sleeves rolled up to her elbows and forearms white with flour, massaging a sticky ball of dough.

"Kadrin! You're up early. Nothing's out of the oven yet, I'm afraid."

Kadrin couldn't find the words. He made his way around the counter and folded Evemi into a tight hug. His throat was burning; his eyes were wet. If *Evemi* had been strapped into that awful chair and tortured because Kadrin had given up her name . . .

"Kadrin, you're getting flour on your— Oh. Is that blood?" Evemi took him gently by the chin and turned his face this way and that, evidently no longer concerned about the flour on her hands. "What happened?"

Flight of the Fallen

"I'll explain later," Kadrin said. "I'm so sorry, but you and Renfir both need to leave the House. You aren't safe here. I can take you to some friends of mine, but we need to go right now."

He expected her to protest, ask questions. But he'd underestimated her—and forgotten that Evemi and Jin had been refugees once, too. Evemi nodded calmly, her jaw setting into a hard line. "I'll fetch Renfir and meet you in the outer courtyard."

Kadrin hugged her again. Then he hurried out of the kitchen and toward his own quarters.

There wasn't time to pack much, not with Evemi and Renfir waiting on him. He changed out of his filthy, bloodstained robe into a new set and stuffed a second change of clothes into a bag, followed by his quilted fencing jacket. He had a moment of regret for his sword; one of his kidnappers had kept it, probably to sell. At least he still had an ornate dagger in a case in his closet, crafted as a companion to the sword. Kadrin buckled the sheath onto his belt.

At the last moment, he dragged the box of Yi-Nereen's letters out from under his bed and emptied it into his bag. Foolish to bring the letters instead of more practical things, but he couldn't bear the thought of never reading them again.

Bag slung over his shoulder, Kadrin stepped out of his bedchamber—and froze.

His mother stood in the hallway, her hands clasped behind her back. For a moment neither of them spoke. Her dark eyes glittered in the lamplight as she looked Kadrin over.

"You can always come home," she said at last. "I'm so sorry, Kadrin—for everything. Can you forgive us? If not now, then someday?"

Kadrin couldn't forget watching Sou-Zell kneeling beside his dying mother, his eyes frozen in agony, the line of his shoulders stiff as starched cloth. He realized now that he had never seen the real Sou-Zell until that moment. He'd only seen a version of Sou-Zell carefully constructed to give his enemies no purchase. But with his mother, he was a raw nerve. And if Kadrin was honest with himself, he'd be no different when the end came for the woman standing in front of him now.

"I can forgive *you*, Mother. I just need time."

His mother closed her eyes for a moment. Then she revealed what she'd been holding behind her back, offering it to Kadrin: a small pouch on a string.

Kadrin took it from her. "What is this?"

"Seeds," she said. "From those flowers you grew two years ago. Take them with you, Kadrin, and find somewhere to plant them. That's always been your Talent—helping beautiful things bloom."

She'd been distraught those two years ago when Kadrin had shown her the flowers he'd grown from soil and water, immensely proud of the fragile blooms that had finally appeared on the stems. His father had called his efforts wasteful, but for reasons Kadrin still didn't understand, his mother couldn't bear the sight of the flowers. The knowledge that she'd kept these seeds long after the plants had crumbled to dust touched Kadrin to his core.

He wasn't sure he could ever bring himself to live under the same roof as either of his parents again. But Sou-Zell had given Kadrin a gift, even if he didn't know it, when he'd told Kadrin about his brother.

Some deeds couldn't be taken back. Some words couldn't be unsaid.

Flight of the Fallen

Kadrin fastened the pouch around his neck. "Farewell, Mother. I do love you."

She reached for him, the tips of her fingers brushing gently against his stubbled cheek.

"And I'll always love you."

CHAPTER TWENTY-NINE

END OF THE ROAD

Observation #753: Kadrin can keep a secret! The sly fox.
Never told me about all manner of things, from the Lost Highway
being more than a folktale to his pretty betrothed being a
heretical abomination.
Conclusion: Must stop underestimating the man. —O

Third Age of Storms, 1st Summer, Day 87
The Barrens – Somewhere West of Mount Vetelu

"Here," Celwyn said at last. "We can stop here and rest. Just for a minute."

Yi-Nereen fell to her hands and knees on the cracked asphalt and heaved for breath. Her lungs burned, choked with dust; her body shook like it was on the verge of falling apart.

This couldn't be real. She hadn't watched a pack of fanged saurians drag Jin into the fog.

Jin couldn't be gone.

The three of them—Celwyn, Eliesen, and Yi-Nereen—had fled on foot from the site of the massacre. Yi-Nereen didn't know how to work Jin's manacycle, and Eliesen had refused to let Celwyn abandon Yi-Nereen. In the chaos, they'd left all their supplies behind.

Flight of the Fallen

"It isn't far." Celwyn was gasping, too. Sweat dripped down his face in rivulets. He'd all but carried Eliesen to the highway. "Half a day's walk. We're almost there."

"We aren't going to Avi'Kerina," Yi-Nereen spat. "We need to look for Jin."

Celwyn's face darkened. "We can't go back. Saurians or knights—it's a death sentence either way."

There was a note of finality in his voice that brooked no argument. Yi-Nereen ignored it.

"She could have escaped from the saurians. If she did, she's lost in the fog, probably injured. You didn't tell any of us how to get to Avi'Kerina, so she can't meet us there. We have to find her. Eliesen—"

"She's unconscious," Celwyn said.

Yi-Nereen went cold. She hadn't noticed, but at some point during their desperate flight, Eliesen had gone from leaning on Celwyn's shoulder to cradled in his arms. One of her hands dangled limply; there was a sickly undertone to her brown skin.

"How? What happened?"

"She's running a fever. The wound must be infected."

Yi-Nereen's mind churned. All she could see was the saurians dragging Jin away, over and over. The sword flying from her hand. Her agonized scream as teeth sank into her flesh.

But if Eliesen's wound was infected, soon she wouldn't be able to walk or ride. She would certainly never make it back to Kerina Sol, even if they recovered the bikes. Her only chance was for them to forge onward to Avi'Kerina and hope that the secrets of divinity included a way to treat an infected wound. But that meant abandoning Jin. Who might be dead already.

Everything in Yi-Nereen screamed to go back for Jin no matter how hopeless it seemed. But the kerinas were counting on her to reach Avi'Kerina, the only place humanity could survive, safe from the city-killing storms. She knew what Jin would want her to do. What even Kadrin would want her to do.

Gods, how was she supposed to make this choice?

Celwyn's jaw was set. He held Eliesen as if she weighed nothing. "I'm taking her to Avi'Kerina. Come with us or go back. It's your decision, although obviously I'd prefer you came with us. We may need your shield."

He'd omitted the obvious: if Yi-Nereen went off on her own to find Jin and failed, she was a dead woman herself.

Yi-Nereen stared into the fog, her heart crumbling to pieces in her chest.

Please, Jin. Survive. Find us in Avi'Kerina.

She swallowed down a sob. "I'm coming with you."

The fog thinned as the day wore on. Yi-Nereen kept straining her ears for the sound of magebike engines on the road behind them, but she heard only Eliesen's fevered moans and Celwyn's panting as he carried her along the highway.

Had the saurians managed to kill all of her father's knights?

Gods, she hoped so. Without his knights, Lai-Dan wouldn't be able to follow her. He would die alone in the Barrens, just as he deserved.

The sun bore down, hotter as the fog thinned. Yi-Nereen had thought she knew what the wastes were like, but the Barrens were pure desolation. Everything washed out, the same shade of burnt red-orange, the air shimmering.

Flight of the Fallen

Yi-Nereen yearned for color. The sparkling blue fountains in the House of Steel Heavens. The beautiful gowns Kadrin had filled her wardrobe with: fabrics in every hue, silvery green to deep wine-purple. She longed for the cool wash of water down her scorched throat. As she staggered along, her mind wandered back to the gardens of her youth. Back to Kadrin: her first glimpse of the sun. And Jin, too, a version of her Yi-Nereen had never met, who smiled more easily and didn't have so many scars.

Their lips were moving. Yi-Nereen could almost hear them.

She could stare at them all day. The two people who mattered most to her in the world: brown-eyed, grinning Kadrin, and Jin with her deft hands and catlike step. Gods, if only they were here—or she were *there*. The world would be right if the three of them were together.

"Yi-Nereen. Stop. You're about to—"

Yi-Nereen slammed into something hard and fell backward, landing awkwardly on asphalt.

There was no garden. Only the hot orange sun and a heat shimmer in the air. Where Kadrin had stood a moment before, Celwyn was hunched with Eliesen draped over his shoulder, exhaustion etched into the lines on his face.

Yi-Nereen rubbed her aching head. Behind her, the cracked highway wound through a maze of stony ridges and out of sight. Ahead, it continued on to a flat plain until it disappeared into a distant bank of fog.

"What did I run into?"

"I tried to warn you," Celwyn said. "I kicked a rock and it bounced back. Look."

He toed his boot under a pebble and sent it flying. Yi-Nereen watched it soar through the air—until it hit something invisible with an audible *thump* and ricocheted back.

Yi-Nereen palmed her eyes, unsure if she'd just hallucinated. "What *is* that?"

"Avi'Kerina," Celwyn said. "At least, I hope it is. It's supposed to be right here."

Yi-Nereen climbed to her feet and took a step forward with her hand outstretched, feeling through the air. Her fingertips brushed against the impossible: a barrier, smooth and unyielding, exactly the same temperature as her skin. Thirst and headache forgotten, Yi-Nereen put both her hands on the barrier and felt along its length. How far did it go?

Thirty paces to the left of the highway, she gave up.

"It must go all the way around."

Celwyn looked thoughtful. "I used to wonder why Falka always had us take the underground highway to Mount Vetelu, instead of riding straight across the Barrens. I chalked it up to saurians, but Mount Vetelu is so close to the edge of the Barrens. It wouldn't be too risky to approach aboveground. It seemed particularly odd to me that no sparkriders ever stumbled across it or even saw it from a distance."

Yi-Nereen blinked. "You think Mount Vetelu had the same kind of barrier?"

The Knights of Rut had ridden right up to the ruins of the castle, but only after the storm had blasted the mountain to pieces. The barrier—if Mount Vetelu had had one—could have collapsed when the mountain did. If that had been the case, there was no way to prove it now.

"We have to find a way inside," she said. "Give me your sword."

She set the tip of Celwyn's blade against the barrier and pushed. It was like trying to cut through a stone wall.

Flight of the Fallen

Yi-Nereen pulled the sword away, held her breath, and swung.

Force exploded outward in a soundless pulse, whiting her vision. She was thrown backward, tumbling across the ground, arms scraped bloody against the asphalt.

Panting, Yi-Nereen sat up. Her body tingled with a dozen different complaints, but she hardly noticed. She concentrated, and from her hands grew a glowing blue spear, its tip narrowed to a point many times sharper than Celwyn's sword.

"You're getting better at that," Celwyn remarked.

He didn't question why she was able to perform feats of shield-casting he'd surely never seen before. Could he know something about her abilities? Amrys's consciousness merged with his gave him access to everything the wastelanders knew about Talent; Faolin had known things Yi-Nereen didn't, like Tibius Vann's ability to control saurians.

Well, if she wasn't able to breach Avi'Kerina, she and Celwyn would have plenty of time to talk as they starved to death.

She thrust her shield-lance at the barrier—delicately. Her caution paid off: the barrier answered her thrust with a pulse of its own, strong enough to send her skidding through the dirt. She kept on her feet this time.

Yi-Nereen's heart sank. "I don't think we can break through. It's Road Builder technology. I have no idea how it works."

They'd come all this way chasing a legend, and the legend was real. But even if they somehow returned to Kerina Sol, the Council would never accept stories of an invisible barrier as proof that the First City existed. They'd be right back where they started.

The gods wouldn't be so cruel as to let her walk up to the very gates of Avi'Kerina only to find it impenetrable. It was cruelty akin to giving Yi-Nereen the courage to tell Jin she loved her, just for saurians to drag her away before Yi-Nereen could hear those words in return.

Actually, the gods were *exactly* that cruel.

"Does Amrys know anything that could help?"

Celwyn's lips thinned. His eyes took on a new cast, almost frenzied. "We should never have come here. This place is cursed, it's where they'll return, we never should have—" He stopped, breathing raggedly, and sighed. "It seems not."

It can't end like this. Yi-Nereen racked her brain. She'd spent her childhood locked in a tower, passing the long days by studying every text she could get her hands on. She knew plenty of useless facts about kerina history and genealogy, but almost nothing about the Road Builders. There just wasn't much anyone knew about them. They'd built the highways; they'd left ruined temples and castles behind with strange technology like rising platforms and everlasting, self-lighting sconces . . .

Gods, it wasn't enough. A whole life wasted. Four lives.

Her thoughts turned to despair. Jin was gone. Eliesen surely had little time left. A deadly storm might have struck Kerina Sol already. It certainly *felt* like everything was lost. Unless . . .

"The only way to get to Mount Vetelu was underground," she whispered. "If there was a barrier, it didn't extend beneath the surface."

Celwyn kicked another rock into the barrier. "It's a good idea, but it would take days to tunnel under. Look at this ground. We don't have so much as a garden trowel."

"Maybe we don't need one."

Yi-Nereen's heart thrummed. She didn't dare imagine it would work, not yet. She burned mana once more, and with a thought she

Flight of the Fallen

transformed her shield into a broad, flat triangle—exactly like an oversized garden trowel.

Celwyn was right; she *was* getting better at this. But maintaining her shield in this shape was difficult; her temples and wrists ached, pulsing to the beat of her heart. She felt her mana reserve burning down with terrifying speed.

With a flick of her hand, she thrust the shield-trowel into the ground at the base of the barrier. Blinding pain shot through her skull as her power strained against the hard earth. But it wasn't like the barrier, didn't give back as good as it got. Her shield sank slowly into the earth with a quiet sizzle.

Yi-Nereen twisted, pushing with all her strength.

It was working. Through slitted eyes, she saw the earth giving way. Pebbles tumbled into the hole her power was burrowing under the barrier. Yi-Nereen gave another push, holding her breath until it felt like her lungs would explode.

She was through. The barrier *didn't* extend below the surface.

Glowing blue tendrils flowed from her extended hands into the dark, ragged opening. It wasn't large enough for a person to crawl through, not yet. But all she needed was time, and for her power not to run out before she finished her work.

Celwyn laid Eliesen down gently on the cracked asphalt and crouched beside the hole. "Keep going," he said.

Yi-Nereen's head was on fire. Her hands twitched madly. But she'd been training her whole life for this, to hold a shield even in bodily agony, to continue pouring forth her power until she had nothing left to give.

Even as her body screamed in torture, her mind exulted in the work. No wonder her father had grown addicted to siphoning people of lesser Talents, if exercising his newfound power felt like this.

317

Her shield could hardly be called a shield anymore. It was an extension of her will, a way to force herself upon the world around her and shape it to her desires.

Whatever she wanted, her power could make it so.

"That's it," Celwyn said from somewhere far away. "You can stop now. It's big enough."

Yi-Nereen let go of her power, gasping. The world dulled. When she could see clearly again, she saw Celwyn standing in the hole she'd dug. A wide swathe of earth burned away by her Talent.

She should have been able to see the opening on the other side where her tunnel reached the surface. But the highway leading into the plain beyond the barrier looked exactly the same as it had earlier. It was a mirage, a false image somehow projected by the barrier.

Celwyn climbed out of the hole. "Go on through. Then you can help me with Eliesen."

Yi-Nereen didn't need to be asked twice. She lowered herself into the hole and crawled underneath the barrier. The tunnel she'd dug was hardly smooth. Rocks scraped her sides and loose dirt sprinkled onto her back as she crawled. In short order, she emerged from the other side like a burrowing beetle.

There was the highway still, and the flat plain she'd seen before. But the plain wasn't empty. A city stood there, vast and glittering, like no city Yi-Nereen had seen before.

The kerinas were built from clay and stone, dull brown and coated in a perpetual layer of wasteland dust. The city Yi-Nereen was looking at now gleamed so brightly it hurt her eyes to look upon. Silver towers swept up to the heavens like slender arrows; delicate bridges connected the towers at various points along their height, turning the city from afar into a geometric cobweb of interwoven structures.

Flight of the Fallen

At the center of that cobweb hung an orb of burnished metal, perfectly smooth with no visible supports or openings. It was large enough to hold an entire kerina.

Tears sprang to Yi-Nereen's eyes. She'd expected a ruin, like the castle atop Mount Vetelu. But the city before her was breathtakingly, perfectly preserved. It was like time had stopped here. Like the gods themselves might still walk the streets and bridges of Avi'Kerina.

If the gods remained, what would she say to them?

The stories she'd been fed as a child had spoken of humanity's guilt. Of the sins that had made the gods turn away from them, of the purity that would one day beckon their return. A chance for forgiveness, but only for the chaste, the obedient, the pious.

Yi-Nereen knew she was none of these things. And she didn't know if she could bring herself to apologize for what she lacked. But if groveling before the gods was the only way to save her people, everyone she cared for . . .

She closed her eyes. What would Jin say?

Fuck them. Yi-Nereen could hear her so clearly, as if she were here. *We don't need them.*

"But you aren't here, Jin," Yi-Nereen whispered. "You promised you would be, and you aren't."

Whatever she faced in Avi'Kerina, she would face it alone.

CHAPTER THIRTY

LEAP OF FAITH

Observation #98: Hallucinations, euphoria, vomiting, panic,
and death all common reactions to ingesting wasteland flora.
Recreational drug potential?
Conclusion: If I cannot apprentice myself to an artificer,
perhaps I should become a chemist. —O

Third Age of Storms, 1st Summer, Day 87
The Barrens – No Fucking Clue

Pain was Jin's last memory, and the first sensation to return when she woke.

When the saurians had dragged her away, her world had turned to blood and screaming and yellow fog. Her murderous resolve had shattered into desperation to survive. She'd felt her flesh tearing— hot saurian breath on her face—the rocky ground shredding her exposed skin. She'd slashed blindly with her utility knife until it flew from her grip, kicked and clawed, but it was no use.

And in the moment of what must have been her death, she'd felt herself ripped from the saurians' claws and lifted into the air. Floating. Weightless.

Flight of the Fallen

As the wind dried the blood on her face, she'd closed her eyes and let it all go.

Kadrin. Yi-Nereen. Eomma. She'd never see them again.

She was going to join her father in that place where all sparkriders eventually went. Down the last highway, over the final horizon.

But now she was back. And so was the pain.

Her body twitched. A low groan left her lips. It was like waking up after flipping her bike. She hurt *everywhere*, but the brightest, most urgent fire was in her right arm.

Jin opened her eyes and blinked until she could focus.

Her arm was nearly flayed. The leather sleeve of her jacket had torn right along with the skin and flesh; it was such a mess she couldn't tell which of the hanging, bloody flaps were sleeve and which were hers.

Where was she? Cliffs loomed around her, lifeless and jagged against a forbidding gray sky. Milky white mist filled the chasms between the peaks. She was lying in a stone trough with a sheer drop on either side.

High enough that she wouldn't just shatter all her bones if she fell—she'd liquefy into soup.

Jin's mind froze over. She couldn't breathe. Gods, fuck, she *hated* heights.

This was like no place in the wastes she'd ever seen. Maybe she was dead after all. But if she was dead, surely she wouldn't still be bleeding.

Skreeeeeeee—

The mountains were screaming. No. It was just a familiar shriek echoing from cliff to cliff, doubling over on itself. Filling the emptiness.

Down from above swooped a huge, dark shape. Screech landed on the aerie, his massive wings almost buffeting Jin over the edge. His talons crunched against the stone, inches from her feet. Jin's paralysis broke. She curled into a ball, whimpering.

Rasvel help her. Screech had finally decided to make her a meal.

Something thumped onto the stone next to her head. A severed arm, clotted over at the stump. The limp hand was still clad in a fingerless leather glove.

Jin stared, stricken. It wasn't Celwyn's arm; the skin was too fair under all that blood. Yi-Nereen and Elie didn't wear gloves. It had to be a Knight of Rut.

She stole a glance upward. Screech leaned over her in unsettling silence, his head cocked. His bright eyes darted from the dismembered arm to Jin. Waiting.

Oh. It was for her.

It was supposed to be *food.*

Jin snapped. She grabbed the arm by its hand—disgust churned in her, hot and dark—and flung it over the cliff's edge.

"What the fuck? I'm not eating that!"

Screech warbled indignantly. Then he launched himself off the aerie and dove straight into the white fog between the peaks. Gone.

"Wait!" Jin scrambled toward the edge, her stomach lurching. "Come back!"

Her head spun anew at the sight of the drop. Gods, there was no way down. She'd die slowly up here, trapped and alone, or she'd die swiftly in the fall. Were either of those options better than being eaten alive by a pack of saurians? Maybe. Slightly.

Jin threw back her head and laughed. For weeks, she'd brought Screech food in the wastes. Now he was feeding her. Did he think she could just take off and find her own prey if she didn't like what he brought?

"Oh gods, help me."

She'd almost drifted back into unconsciousness when Screech returned. It had been hours. Her throat was bone-dry; she couldn't stop thinking about water. Gallons of it, sweet and cold, flowing through her veins instead of blood.

This time her only warning was a rush of wind. Screech dropped his offering right on top of her chest this time. Jin yelped, expecting another severed limb.

Well—it *was* an arm. A cactus arm. Bright blue-violet and covered in silver fuzz. Sticky juice leaked from the torn end; a spiral-shaped white flower bloomed from the other. It smelled faintly soapish.

"Ohh," Jin moaned.

Wasteland flora was all but guaranteed to fuck her up. Even if it sated her thirst and hunger cramps temporarily, she'd pay for it later. She was tempted to throw the thing off the cliff. But if she upset Screech a second time, maybe he wouldn't come back.

Or he'd come back with something worse than a severed arm. A whole corpse, maybe.

The pteropter watched her, his stare burrowing, talons scraping the stone.

Jin suckled gingerly at the cactus's leaking end. It didn't taste horrible. And she was *so* thirsty. Before she could summon back her sense, she was guzzling the sticky fluid, ignoring the tingle it left on her tongue and the roof of her mouth. The cactus flesh was soft and pink inside its hard, fuzzy rind. She ate that, too. If she'd already poisoned herself, she might as well die with her belly full.

"Thanks," Jin said. "That wasn't bad."

Screech opened his beak and hissed, raspy and discordant, "Don't mention it."

Jin clutched the rock beneath her. Her pulse fluttered in her chest. Suddenly she was sweating, cold and sticky. There went all the moisture she'd gotten from the cactus. What a waste.

"You don't look so good." Screech hopped along the edge of the aerie, his wings flared. Though Jin was sure the sky had been steel gray a moment before, sunlight streamed down and turned the colorful feathers on Screech's back into gems: red, blue, and green. "Is it the air up here? It's thinner than you're used to. No storms, though. You won't be struck by lightning again."

"Oh." Jin's voice was faint. "That's good."

"How's the arm?"

Jin looked at her forearm. The long gouges the saurians had left in her flesh weren't oozing anymore. They'd clotted a blue so dark it was almost black.

Blue? Her blood was red. Or it used to be.

"Doesn't hurt," Jin whispered. "Am I dying?"

"You're all dying," Screech said. "Why do you think I crashed into your bike that day, Jin? I had to get your attention."

"What for?"

Screech tucked all four of his wings tightly against his body and turned to face her. Framed by sunlight, standing upright, he looked odd, almost humanoid.

"You needed to know that you don't belong here. And I don't mean in these mountains. I mean *here*. In the world. You're a visitor.

The storms? That's the host telling you that you've overstayed your welcome. It's last call at the bar, but you aren't listening."

Screech's wings melted into his sides. His triangular beak liquefied and re-formed into a human face. Faolin's face. The boy spread his arms and smiled. Jewel-colored feathers swept up from his temples to form a high, proud crest.

"Hey, Jin. Good to see you."

Gods, that playful grin. Jin remembered the last time she'd seen him: huddled inside Yi-Nereen's shield as Jin raced away from them both. She'd abandoned him, and she'd failed in her promise to save his sister. No wonder he was back to haunt her now.

If this was Jin's divine punishment, it was far less than what she deserved.

"Faolin." Her voice broke. "I'm sorry."

The boy shrugged. "Don't apologize, Jin. Without me and Amrys around, my people are safer than they've been in a long time. Talent always causes trouble. The gods learned that too late. They broke the world they were trying to create and fought like children over how to put their toys back together. Now they're gone."

Jin flattened her palms against the stone beneath her. "Are the gods real? Are *you* real?"

Faolin glanced over his shoulder at the sky. "It's not a simple answer. You'll understand that soon. You'll have to. There isn't much time left."

"Because I'm going to die up here?"

Jin's head pounded. There was a warm, limp weight in her lap; she looked down and bile rose in her throat. The knight's severed arm lay across her legs, drained of blood. Tooth marks in the exposed bone. *Her* teeth.

She hurled it into the void. Again. Watched it fall into the mist.

"You'll live," Faolin said. "You're at the center of it all. It's why I found you in that storm. Why the pteropter crashed into your bike. Because you know how to keep your eyes on the road ahead, Jin. You don't look over your shoulder. You know what's waiting for you if you do."

"What in the hell does that mean?"

Faolin's voice lowered, becoming urgent. "You *have* to get to Avi'Kerina. No one is coming to get you out of this mess. You have to save yourself."

"I'm not going anywhere! I'm stuck here. I can't *fly*."

"Try," Faolin said. "Go on and try."

"Oh gods," Jin groaned. But she rolled onto her hands and knees and crawled to the edge of the aerie. Wind whistled through her hair. Her wounded arm itched. Feathers were growing from the gashes, long quills in every color. If she stripped off the rest of her skin, would there be feathers everywhere? Would she change?

Could she fly all the way to Avi'Kerina—and save everyone, not just herself?

"No," Faolin said. "You can't save everyone. But you already knew that, Jin."

He was dissolving in front of her. Turning into mist, little by little.

Jin reached for him, teetering at the edge of the drop.

"Faolin, don't go. Don't leave me—"

Jin opened her eyes with a gasp. Her body felt weak and feverish; the cactus's toxins were still coursing through her blood. Clouds

Flight of the Fallen

drifted across the sky above her. The air was cold—and strangely moist, like a raincaller was at work somewhere nearby.

She sat up. Color flashed on one of the nearby peaks, across the void. Screech was perched there among the rocks, still as a statue. Watching her. Waiting.

"Hey!" Jin shouted. Her voice echoed, fragmented. "You got me here. Now get me out. Take me to Avi'Kerina."

The pteropter didn't so much as twitch a feather. He looked small from this distance, just like he had the first day Jin had crashed into him on her bike.

I had to get your attention.

Just a hallucination. It hadn't been real. Of course Screech couldn't speak to her, and neither could Faolin—he was dead.

But she'd seen the mana saurian when no one else had. She'd dreamed of it almost every night for weeks. And Screech kept finding her, wherever she was. In the wastes. In the storm. In the fog. Anytime she was about to die.

She was going to die *here*.

"Only one way down," Jin breathed.

She rose to her hands and knees and crawled to the edge again. Her pulse thundered in her ears. Her mouth was bone-dry. Fear tied her guts into a hard knot.

The last time she'd fallen from a mountain, she'd known she was going to die—and she'd been wrong. How could she be certain of anything now? The wasteland was a strange place, alive with infinite possibilities. And out there somewhere were the people who needed her. The people she loved.

Jin had to come back for them. She had to *try*. Even if the fall was destined to shatter her, she still had to jump.

Just don't look, she told herself.

She turned her back on the drop. Summoned Kadrin's and Yi-Nereen's faces to her mind's eye, lingering over every detail. Felt love spreading through her, banishing her fear.

And fell.

CHAPTER THIRTY-ONE

SOMEWHERE ELSE

Observation #534: Talentless are immune to any Talent that directly affects the body or brain. Mindreading most well-known example. Hypothesis: Mindreading relies on blood mana. Impossible to prove.
—O

Third Age of Storms, 1st Summer, Day 87
Kerina Sol – Refugee Quarter

Once Kadrin was gone, Sou-Zell found he'd lost the will to move. He was sinking, little by little, into a void: a deep, infinite darkness. Falling out of time.

He had spent so many years trying to repair what couldn't be fixed. Nothing could fetch back the shades of his House from beyond death. No power stolen or bequeathed from the gods could restore his father to life, make his mother happy again, or transform Sou-Zell into the child he'd once been.

And everything he'd done in pursuit of those impossible goals had eaten him away until he was nothing. Less than nothing.

No House. No family. No fortune.

Just Sou-Zell. And who was he?

A man is the sum of two things, a knight called Ell-Tuin had told him once. *His deeds, and what he cares for. Nothing else matters.*

Sou-Zell cared for nothing anymore. So what of his deeds? He had helped steal power from the gods and placed it in the hands of a heretic. Falka. What would she do with the defuser Orrin had built? Surely she wouldn't simply destroy it.

Did Sou-Zell care about *that*?

Yes. He did care—if for no other reason than he needed *something* to care about. A way out of the void. A rope to climb.

Sou-Zell dragged himself back into the world. Physical sensation rushed back: an ache in his haunches from sitting for so long, a stiff twinge in his neck. Warm fetid air on his face. The roar of a nearby mob. Smoke.

Kerina Sol was more than restless tonight. It was livid.

Sou-Zell had heard stories of the riots that had consumed Kerina Tez in the weeks before it fell to the storms, sending refugees scurrying every which way across the wastes. When a city felt the specter of death approaching, people turned on one another. Fear turned to violence.

If Kerina Sol fell, Lai-Dan would reign supreme in this region of the wastes. Did Sou-Zell care about that?

Yes, he did. Very much, in fact.

Orrin's workshop still stood, though it looked dark and abandoned. Sou-Zell pushed open the door and called a spark to illuminate the interior. The restraining table stood in the center of the workshop, throwing an angular shadow against the wall. But the defuser itself was gone.

Flight of the Fallen

Sou-Zell stood in the doorway as the city roared behind him. Where would Falka and Orrin have taken the device? For what purpose?

He knew of only one person in Kerina Sol connected to Orrin besides Kadrin himself. Toraka, the refugee leader, who had led Sou-Zell to the artificer in the first place.

Wrapped in a hooded cloak, Sou-Zell slipped past rioters screaming abuse at outnumbered acolytes. He stepped over people who lay unmoving on the ground. He saw few guards, and none of the peacekeeping methods that metalcrafters were trained to undertake in times of unrest. No fences or cuffs or ground spikes. Once, he saw a squad of knights in armor marching toward a screaming crowd, lances raised. Sou-Zell moved on before the outcome made itself plain.

The Legion was meant to be turned outward at all times, a shield against outside threats. If they were deploying inside the Wall, the situation was dire. Was this the High Houses' doing, or the temple's?

The air was choked with smoke and dust. There must be fires raging out of control; Kerina Sol's raincallers would be busy tonight.

Finally Sou-Zell reached the squat building where Toraka held court. No guards, no line of petitioners. Had she already moved on? Sou-Zell descended the stairs to the basement.

Voices rose to meet him, all of them familiar.

"And what will you do once you control the chamber?" Orrin asked. Sou-Zell pictured the artificer running hands through their untidy black curls, pacing in agitation. "I didn't build this machine so the Guildery could replace the High Houses."

"I don't intend to seize control, Orrin. Merely to break the temple's hold on the Council so our voices can be heard. The High Houses must understand that Avi'Kerina is the home Rasvel intends for us. They *will* understand, without Edine's rhetoric clouding their judgment."

Toraka's voice, just as smooth and controlled as it was when Sou-Zell met her.

"To be perfectly honest," Orrin replied, "I don't care for any sort of religious rhetoric, including yours. We don't even know if Avi'Kerina exists, let alone if it can support life. Isn't this all premature?"

"If the next storm hits while we're waiting to find out, it won't matter." Falka, venomous as always. "Let's shortcut the endless debate. The spring here is running out of mana. Once word gets out that it can be preserved, the High Houses will start hoarding what they need. That's exactly what the fuckers do. We can't let that happen. So let's cut the head off the snake, shall we? If the lords and their families don't *need* mana, they can't take it from the mouths of people who do."

Sou-Zell pushed open the basement door. Orrin, Falka, and Toraka were gathered around a flickering oil lamp; they turned toward him. The defuser rested on the floor behind them.

"Sou-Zell," Falka said flatly.

Her gaze combed across him, and her mouth twisted. Sou-Zell saw understanding in her eyes. She knew his mother was dead, even though she hadn't stayed to witness it.

Had Lady Ren's life ever mattered to her? Or had this whole venture been her ploy to get back to doing what she did best: scheming against her betters?

"You're planning to use the defuser on the Council," Sou-Zell said. It wasn't a question. He'd overheard enough. "What exactly do you hope to accomplish by castrating the strongest Talented in the city? Are you trying to usher Kerina Sol into an early grave?"

Flight of the Fallen

"We're trying to save it," Falka said. "The High Houses are apparently content to watch their city rip itself apart so they don't have to admit we need to leave the wastes. But maybe they'll act to save their own skins."

"Leave the wastes?" Sou-Zell laughed harshly. "You're mad. There's nowhere to go."

"Tibius thought the same as you." Falka crossed her arms. "*There is no mythical Green Kingdom. It is the wastes that were once green but now lie in ashes.* But he was wrong, and so are you. Toraka. Why don't you tell Sou-Zell what you told me?"

Toraka gave Sou-Zell a long, considering look. "Let him see for himself."

So Falka had told the others of Sou-Zell's mindtalent. Perhaps he should return the favor and recite Falka's crimes. But—no. He hadn't come here to discredit Falka. He needed to understand what she meant to do.

"You'll let me read your thoughts?" Sou-Zell asked.

The memory of reading Guildmaster Xua's mind and the horrors within still burned fresh. Sou-Zell had no desire to see Kerina Lav fall twice over. And Toraka had doubtless received the same training as her fellow guildmaster in resisting his Talent. Not to mention she was Talentless now. Sou-Zell had no idea if it would work.

"Go ahead," Toraka said. "You have my invitation."

Sou-Zell bit the wall of his mouth. To abstain now would be cowardly.

He burned mana—

—and knelt on the damp earth, gently pushing a seed into the soil with his fingertips. *From the vault, carried by generations of wanderers until it was sealed away in the dark. I think it's called squash?* The air smelled of dung, but strangely it made him smile instead

Hana Lee

of wrinkling his nose. *Fertilizer. Not a pretty perfume, but the plants like it.*

Rows of earthen plots. A fruit tree, a spiny wasteland plant, the seed he'd just sown, and many more, each with a label stuck into the soil.

Lav peach (bloom). Kern fiber (wastes). Cucurbita pepo (vault).

A logbook lay on a bench nearby, its worn cover marked with grubby handprints. He picked it up, leafed through pages covered in loopy script. Almost time to start a new book.

Eomma, I've been calling you for dinner. A ponytailed girl with hands on her hips, standing in a doorway. *You never listen when you're with your plants.* Exasperation in her tone, but she couldn't hide her smile. *What are you up to now?*

I'm trying to hybridize sand cactus and Lav cucumber, but the cross-pollination onto the cactus won't take. It never works between wasteland plants and plants from the seed vault. I've tried hundreds of combinations and it never works.

The girl frowned. *Why are you always fiddling with those moldy vault seeds? Rasvel made us bloomweavers so we wouldn't have to mash flowers together and make plant babies.*

It's called pollination.

He found the last page in the logbook before the empty pages started. It wasn't covered in script like the others. Instead, a single phrase was circled in the center of the page.

Wasteland flora NOT genetic relative to vault seeds

The girl left, rolling her eyes, and he sank onto the bench next to the logbook. His thoughts buzzed against his temples like flies. He set his pencil to the page and wrote:

Bloomwoven plants mimic reproductive bodies but no pollination. Irrelevant to study

Flight of the Fallen

Vault seeds didn't come from wastes—so WHERE? How did we get them? Did we come from same place?

Somewhere else?

Chills raised the fine hair on his forearms. He put the pencil down and stared at the logbook, at what he'd written. Decades of study, of meticulous grafting and hand-pollination, failed hybridization after failed hybridization. Tolerant ridicule from the other bloomweavers, bemusement from the rest of the Guildery. They couldn't fathom why he did the experiments, and they would never believe the conclusion he'd drawn, no matter how much evidence he presented.

With a sigh, he ran a hand through his long hair—

—and rocked back into his own body with a gasp.

Toraka's eyes were wide. "Is that what it's like, having your mind read? I didn't expect to *feel* you doing it."

"No," Sou-Zell said, recovering quickly, though his hands still shook. Other mindreadings—like the one he'd performed on Guildmaster Xua—had been vivid, but none like this, none where he lived the memory as if it were his. A born Talentless had a mind closed to his abilities; it seemed a *made* Talentless had the doors to their soul thrown wide.

He'd always thought the reason he couldn't read Falka's mind, or Kadrin's, was because they didn't have souls. Talent was a person's soul. *So sing the priests.* But Toraka had lost hers, and it was like a veil between her soul and Sou-Zell's had dissolved away.

He couldn't think about the implications of that now. Or, perhaps, ever.

"Fascinating," Orrin muttered. "There is so very little we know about the mechanism of Talent, especially the lesser-known types."

Sou-Zell ignored the artificer. "Was that what you wanted to show me? I don't see how a memory of your daughter interrupting your gardening—however touching it may be for you to recall—explains why we need to leave the wastes."

"*Why* we need to leave is obvious. We'll die if we stay; our shield-casters are no match for the storms anymore. What I showed you was an answer to the question of where we can go."

Toraka withdrew a small paper packet from a pocket inside her robe and held it up to the light.

"Our ancestors carried seeds in packets just like these, hundreds of different varieties. Tibius Vann thought this land was once green, and that the Road Builders made it a wasteland. But if that were true, the plants that *do* grow in the wastes would have some genetic similarities to these seeds. You saw for yourself what it took me decades to prove: they don't come from the same place."

"And neither do we," Falka said.

Sou-Zell scoffed. "You're saying the Green Kingdom is real, and that it is humanity's birthplace."

Despite his mocking tone, he felt his stomach sink. Hadn't he been on the wrong side of a legend before? Not just once, but twice—assuming Yi-Nereen and Jin-Lu actually did find the First City.

"Not at all," Toraka said. "The Green Kingdom is a story. Allegory. But we must have come from somewhere, and it wasn't the wasteland. Rasvel is showing us the way to our home. He knows we cannot live in Avi'Kerina if we require mana, so he's draining our spring. It's a divine message."

"And that's where you've lost me." Orrin crossed their arms. "It's infinitely more likely that the Storm of Centuries cut off the supply somehow, clotted the vein. No deific interference required."

"Gods or no gods, who cares?" Falka stalked across the room

Flight of the Fallen

and jabbed her finger into Sou-Zell's chest. "This isn't your fight, Sou-Zell. This isn't even your city. Are you going to stop us?"

"Why is it *your* fight?" he countered.

Falka hadn't been there to watch his mother die. For all she'd claimed to feel affection toward Lady Ren, she'd lost all interest in her as soon as Sou-Zell decided not to prolong her suffering with the defuser.

At least, that was what he'd thought. Now, as he stared into her narrowed eyes, he began to wonder. His brother had also refused to watch their mother die, and as much as it irked Sou-Zell to admit, he knew it wasn't for lack of love.

"This is what I always wanted," Falka said. "It's what Tibius promised me—that we'd take out the High Houses and let the Talentless decide their fates. After that, I don't care. I'm not going to Avi'Kerina. I've roamed the wastes before; I can do it for the rest of my life."

Falka's confidence grated on him. Sou-Zell went for the weak spot. "What about Jin-Lu?"

Something bitter and twisted flashed across Falka's expression. "I think the odds of us getting back together dove below zero when I put a knife between her ribs. She's got a long life ahead of her. I'm not expecting to be part of it. Quit changing the subject, Sou-Zell. I've noticed you don't exactly have anyone left in your life, either. So I'll ask again. Are you going to stop us?"

Sou-Zell looked at the three of them: the artificer, lounging against a wall; the former guildmaster, watching him intently; the freckled woman he'd once longed to throttle with both hands. That familiar rage was gone now. He couldn't recall what it felt like to care so violently about anything.

He didn't share their cause, but he had no reason to oppose them.

Sou-Zell looked at Toraka. "Is your daughter still alive?"

Toraka smiled. "She is."

Sou-Zell nodded slowly, lost in a memory not his own. But maybe it was. Just as Guildmaster Xua's memories were now part of him, and Jin-Lu's, and Lai-Dan's, and everyone else whose mind he'd ever read.

In his mother's last hour, he'd even burned mana and lowered himself into the dying dregs of her mind. He'd wanted to know if she was in pain. If she was thinking of him. If she understood the choice he'd made: to let her die.

She'd been dreaming of herself as a young woman rocking an infant to sleep. Sou-Zell didn't know if the infant in the memory was himself or Min-Chuul. His mother's thoughts gave no indication, contained no names. Just love, deep and enduring as the mana veins that flowed under the earth, unceasing as both she and her son drifted into sleep. He'd felt the moment when her thoughts slowed and faded into the void, like her hand gently but inexorably pulling from his, retreating somewhere he couldn't follow.

His mother's body still rested in the hovel where he'd left it. That was one task left to him: laying her to rest in the spring.

"I won't stand in your way," Sou-Zell said. "Although I don't like your chances."

Falka didn't smile and her face didn't soften—not an inch. But she took a step back from Sou-Zell, giving him space.

"We'll worry about that," she said. "Now go on, you wretch. Find someone to care about."

CHAPTER THIRTY-TWO

AN ULTIMATUM

Observation #760: No physical sensation associated with
mindreading or way to detect when it's happening.
Yet, with training and discipline, possible to resist mindreading
if you know it's in progress.
To do: Obtain said training when schedule allows.
Discipline already in evidence. —O

Third Age of Storms, 1st Summer, Day 87
Kerina Sol – Jade District

Evemi and Renfir met Kadrin in the House's outer courtyard. Both of them were carrying packs and had changed clothes. It startled Kadrin to see Renfir out of his majordomo's uniform; when he was a boy, he'd made a bet with Eliesen that Renfir slept in it.

"Here." Evemi pushed half a loaf of bread into Kadrin's hands. "It's from yesterday, but you look hungry."

Gods, but he was. He hadn't had a proper meal in three days. Kadrin bit into the loaf; it was chewy, studded with golden raisins, and the best thing he'd ever tasted. For a moment he was too overwhelmed with gratitude to speak.

He could think of only one place to take Evemi and Renfir:

Toraka's safehouse beneath the ruined building in the Refugee Quarter. Hopefully Toraka was still there. Mouth full, Kadrin gestured for the two of them to follow.

They made it to the edge of Jade District without incident. The air was thick with smoke; Kadrin heard distant shouts and the tinkle of breaking glass. Sweat coated his hands. Once, he'd walked the streets of his own city without an ounce of fear—now he was nothing but fear sewn together into the shape of a man.

"Look! It's a raincaller."

Kadrin's head swiveled. Coming around the corner were a half-dozen men and women who looked nearly as wary and beaten down as he felt. They were all Lav-blood as far as he could tell, and had the lean, underfed look of refugees who'd spent weeks combing an abandoned district for food. They'd armed themselves with tools-turned-weapons: chisels, spades, hammers.

Kadrin glanced down at himself. In his haste, he'd changed into one of his finest sets of robes, resplendent in the colors of the House of Steel Heavens. Gold embroidery flowed in an intricate wave pattern along the rich blue satin of his sleeves. He couldn't look more like a scion of a High House if he tried.

"I'm not a raincaller," Kadrin called out. "I'm Talentless."

"Oh, sure," snorted a bearded man with a spade. "And I'm a guildmaster."

Kadrin's pulse thrummed. It was just his luck that every single one of the desperate faces eyeing his finery belonged to a Lav-blood refugee. Everyone in Kerina Sol knew about the Rain Lord's Talentless third heir, but none of these people had grown up in the city. And he couldn't prove he was Talentless any more than he could summon water from the sky.

Flight of the Fallen

He held up his hands in a pacifying gesture. "I'm not your enemy. Just let me pass."

"Is it true that the raincallers get all the mana they want?" a woman demanded. "We aren't even allowed to *bathe*."

"What does it matter?" someone else shot back. "Kerina Sol's going to burn. We need a raincaller if we're going to cross the wastes. Here's one, ripe for the picking. Grab him before he runs."

Kadrin's hand went to the hilt of his dagger. It was an automatic reaction, not calculated in the slightest. No one was taking him anywhere. Not again. *No one.*

"Wait," said a voice from behind him.

Evemi stepped forward. Kadrin snapped out of whatever heated trance he'd just gone into; he could take a beating, but he wouldn't stand here and let Jin's mother put herself in danger for him. Renfir's hand was clenched on Evemi's sleeve like he wanted to hold her back.

Evemi smiled, her hands spread wide. "He's telling the truth. He's Talentless. So am I. We have no quarrel with any of you."

"I know you," a girl who couldn't have been older than fourteen said to Evemi. "You gave us bread."

Most of the group relaxed visibly, though Kadrin's heart went on hammering in his chest. He fought for control over his breathing. But his body wouldn't obey him. There was a voice screaming in the back of his head; he couldn't understand what it was saying. He wanted to run and never stop running.

The bearded man slammed the butt of his spade into the ground, and Kadrin flinched. "This isn't a good time to wander the streets like a rich sot," the man spat. "There's to be a reckoning between your kind and ours. Go home, boy."

Kadrin swallowed, trying to find the wherewithal to speak. But Evemi spoke for him. "What kind of reckoning?"

"We're going to the Basilica. Toraka's put out word. Everyone willing and able's to head there and raise hell until the High Priestess shows her face."

"And what then?"

"Toraka didn't say. But mark my words, she'll be there."

Evemi nodded slowly, thoughtfully. Then she placed her hand over Renfir's and said, almost too quietly for Kadrin to catch, "You said you would follow me anywhere, love. Still true?"

Renfir flushed crimson, but his answer was swift. "Always."

Evemi smiled. "Then we'll come with you to the Basilica. The winds of change are blowing today; I can feel them. If that's where Toraka needs us, that's where we'll go."

"Hold on," Kadrin said sharply, finding his voice at last. "Edine is *looking* for you. Both of you. You can't just march up to her front door."

"I've always run away," Evemi said. "Not tonight. Come with us, Kadrin. Your people need their prince."

The knot in Kadrin's chest drew tighter. He pictured himself stepping into Temple Square, approaching the marble steps that led to the Basilica. To High Priestess Edine. His veins flowed with ice. Darkness ate at the edges of his vision. No, he couldn't go back. He couldn't.

"Kadrin?" Evemi asked.

Kadrin squeezed his eyes shut and fought desperately against the memory of that featureless stone room. But that only made it worse. Every particle of his being throbbed with the certainty that if he took a single step toward the Basilica, he'd die. He'd be killed and remade a hundred times under Edine's torturer's hands. Part of him was still there under the temple. Part of him had never left.

Over the sound of the blood rushing in his ears, he heard Evemi and Renfir talking to each other in low voices. Then a hand touched Kadrin's shoulder and Renfir said, "Let me take you home, Your Highness."

Kadrin wrenched free of his paralysis and took an unsteady step back. "No. No, I'm fine. I can't go with you. Not to the temple. There's somewhere else I need to be."

He was lying. Shame flowed through him, molten and sickening. But he couldn't take it back. He'd never felt so trapped before.

Evemi's brow furrowed. "We'll be all right, Kadrin. There's safety in numbers. Find us when you're finished, and take care of yourself. Do you hear me?"

Kadrin nodded wordlessly.

He watched Evemi and Renfir hurry after the departing refugees. Gods, if anything happened to them because he'd suddenly turned coward, he'd never be able to face Jin again. Whatever was wrong with him, Kadrin had to find a way to beat it into submission.

Fortunately, he knew someone who might be able to help.

No one answered Kadrin's knock at the physician's clinic, so he let himself in. A few of the candles set in alcoves along the wall still flickered, but most had guttered out. The one-room building was almost empty. Evidently the doctor had found somewhere else to move his patients who still drew breath—or perhaps they'd all been driven out by the riots.

But one person still lingered. Sou-Zell stood in silent vigil over a shrouded body lying in a cot beneath the only candles that were still lit. His back was to the door; he turned his head slightly as Kadrin stepped inside.

"Kadrin."

Kadrin's empty hands fell by his sides. It wasn't a pacifying gesture; he was suddenly too exhausted to do anything but stand there, framed by the open doorway.

"I didn't know where else to go."

That earned him a sneer, though it was a pale imitation of the far superior sneers he'd seen on Sou-Zell's face before. "So you came here? What were you hoping to find, princeling? I suppose it amuses you to pretend you belong in the slums with the rest of the Talentless."

It was almost a relief to hear the venom in Sou-Zell's voice. Kadrin had been too much of a coward to follow Evemi and Renfir, to protect them. He deserved this.

He wasn't in *real* danger, no matter what his body believed. His mother would take him back into the House in a heartbeat. She'd convince his father to overlook everything Kadrin had said. Kadrin's privations, brief as they were, could be over any moment he chose. He could crawl home and let Toraka fight for the Talentless in his stead.

"Go home," Sou-Zell said. Like he'd read Kadrin's mind.

"I left," Kadrin said, his voice low. "I told my father what I thought of him, and I told him I wasn't his son anymore."

He didn't know why he cared so much that Sou-Zell knew the truth. Kadrin hardly knew why he'd come here. He didn't want Sou-Zell's approval; the idea of ever getting it was laughable. His entire existence had earned Sou-Zell's ire from the day he was born.

Flight of the Fallen

"A prince no more, then." Sou-Zell scoffed. "You've given up the only advantage the gods saw fit to bequeath you. That does sound in character. Well, what's it to be now? No bride, no family, no power—you've done an astonishingly competent job of driving yourself to ruin."

"So have you."

Sou-Zell hissed. His eyes burned violet in the low light. "I am still *ten times* worthier than you are in the eyes of the gods, Talentless."

"And yet your tricks don't work on me. Funny, isn't it?"

Violet bled to orange, and sparks crackled around Sou-Zell's hands. "You burn as well as anyone else, I'm sure."

Kadrin crossed his arms, filled with a sick sense of satisfaction. "Oh, go ahead. Edine had the same idea, you know. I'm practically ruined goods."

Sou-Zell stared at him, the glow slowly fading from his eyes. His black hair had come undone from its usual bindings; it hung lank and dull around his face, matching the deep shadows under his eyes. He looked a thousand years old and too young at the same time. Kadrin thought again of Sou-Zell's mother and the only name she'd called out in her final moments.

"You should know something." Sou-Zell's voice was halting, uncertain. "Falka and Orrin brought the defuser to Toraka. They're laying a trap for the High Houses in the Council chambers. They'll give the royals an ultimatum: relinquish their Talent or die. How fortunate you've severed ties with your kin already. Several of them may not last the night."

Kadrin's blood ran cold. That night he'd gone to see Toraka in the shrine, before the expedition left, she'd said nothing of a plan like this. But she hadn't had a defuser in her hands then. And her people hadn't been rioting in the streets.

345

He couldn't let it happen. His father Devros and Satriu were headed to that Council meeting. They might already be in the Marble Palace.

The refugees! They must be part of the plan, too. Toraka had sent them to Temple Square to draw Edine out and . . . Oh. Of course. That would draw the guards, too.

In the chaos, Toraka would seize the chance to attack the Council.

I didn't think you were the type to play games like that.

Gods, Kadrin had been a fool. He'd trusted Toraka, even after he'd heard from her own lips the things she'd been willing to do back in Kerina Lav for the sake of a rivalry. Even now, Kadrin didn't know if what she was doing was wrong. But turning his back on his House didn't mean his kin weren't kin.

"I have to go there," Kadrin said, his mouth dry. "Are you coming?"

Sou-Zell blinked, clearly taken aback. "Why would I?"

Kadrin did *not* have time for this.

"You're the only friend I have who isn't out in the wastes or trying to kill my family right now. And I could really use some help."

"Friend?" Sou-Zell's eyes flashed. "I suspect you don't understand the meaning of the word."

Kadrin gave him one last long look. "No, I think I do."

He turned on his heel and left the room.

It didn't matter how many debts they'd repaid, or whether Kadrin believed Sou-Zell was a good man at heart; eventually Sou-Zell would have to decide that for himself. He could take Kadrin's hand and hoist himself back over the edge, or they could both fall into the abyss. Kadrin knew what *he* wanted, but he didn't know if . . .

He heard a low, breathless curse. And footsteps following in his wake.

CHAPTER THIRTY-THREE

THE FIRST CITY

Observation #762: Makela's so-called Herald can't be older than 25. Conclusion: Vaguely alarming to see that much power in the hands of someone so unformed. —O

Third Age of Storms, 1st Summer, Day 87
The Barrens – Avi'Kerina

With every step Yi-Nereen took, she expected Avi'Kerina to dissolve away, revealing itself as nothing more than a mirage. But instead, it grew more distinct—and more wondrous.

Even the arches lining the highway were a marvel, formed from impossibly delicate strands of metal twisted together into a thick, opalescent braid. Not a single speck of rust. The air was totally still. The barrier—it must have kept out the wind. No wind meant no constant scouring wasteland dust. No wonder the city was so well-preserved.

Yi-Nereen glanced over her shoulder. Celwyn was making slow progress, panting like a dog under the hot sun, weighed down by Eliesen's limp body.

Focus, Yi-Nereen told herself. She could study and speculate to her heart's desire later, after they found a way to help Eliesen. And after they found a way to stop her father from entering the city. And after they found Jin.

Avi'Kerina looked strangely naked, and it took Yi-Nereen a moment to realize why. There was no Wall. The highway terminated in a circular loop, branching into narrow paved walkways that snaked between towering buildings. In the center of the circle stood a massive obelisk covered in engravings.

"Road Builder script," Yi-Nereen said, gazing up at the obelisk. "I've seen it before, in a ruined temple."

"The Temple of Makela," Celwyn said, and Yi-Nereen remembered; he knew it as well as she did. His brow creased as he scanned the indecipherable lines. "It's a map. There. *Vida vilkam*. It means 'place of healing.'"

Yi-Nereen's blood chilled. "You can read it?"

Of course he could. Faolin had read the wall engravings in the Temple of Makela, and Amrys was his sister. Yi-Nereen felt a rush of envy. Gods, but she would give anything to understand the secrets of the Road Builders. To accomplish what no scholar in history ever had: deciphering every fragment of script they'd copied from every artifact discovered in the wastes.

What could they learn about the wasteland, about *themselves*, if they could understand the records of those who came before?

"Not everything," Celwyn said. "And knowing what the symbols mean doesn't mean I can translate it. But 'place of healing' is obvious enough. Let's go."

The city was silent around them, a sleeping giant. As they passed building after building, Yi-Nereen burned with longing to know what was inside each one. There were no windows. Had the Road Builders preferred artificial lights?

Thick metal cables hung suspended between the buildings,

Flight of the Fallen

above her head. Those were the impossibly slender "bridges" she'd spied from afar. What were *they* for?

From time to time, she caught glimpses of the immense burnished sphere that floated in the city's heart. Every sight plucked at the harp strings of Yi-Nereen's soul, tugging her toward the sphere. It was more than curiosity; it was compulsion.

But all of it had to wait.

The Road Builders had made this place in tribute to their deities, and if the legends were true, gods had once walked the same path Yi-Nereen's feet carried her down now. Perhaps they were still here, lurking at the heights of those glittering spires, watching Yi-Nereen and Celwyn trespass on hallowed ground.

But if this place had always been intended for the gods, why was there Road Builder script everywhere? Surely gods wouldn't need to read to navigate a city. And they wouldn't need a place of healing. Gods didn't get sick or injured.

Perhaps there were no secrets of divinity to be found in Avi'Kerina after all. Yi-Nereen should find that comforting. Even if her father reached this place, he wouldn't ascend to godhood as he hoped. But instead, she felt hollow.

She'd wanted to prove she was worthy of those secrets. She wouldn't take them by force like her father would, but still—she wanted them.

Was that truly so different?

Celwyn stopped in front of a tall, tapered building. "We're here."

No living green things grew in Avi'Kerina, but the "place of healing" was surrounded by flowers: metal sculptures painted in glittering shades of gold, copper, and vermilion. Yi-Nereen approached the building entrance: a rectangular outline of seams she assumed was a door.

349

"No handles," she said, putting her hand to the door. "How do we get— Oh!"

Her fingers sank straight through the metal. She felt her hand buzz—and the silver-gray door rippled, turning transparent. She could see straight through it, into a shadowy room.

"Fascinating," Celwyn said tersely. "All the way through, if you don't mind. Eliesen needs treatment *now*."

Yi-Nereen didn't need another reminder. She pushed through. For a moment her entire body buzzed unpleasantly. Then she was standing inside the shadowy room. A chest-high bar divided the room in half; two broad pillars stood on either side, stretching floor to ceiling. It was much colder in here. Had the barrier kept out the sunbaked air for all the centuries Avi'Kerina had lain abandoned?

It could take Yi-Nereen the rest of her life to work through every nook and cranny of this place, cataloging everything the Road Builders had left behind. She pictured a whole team of scholars working under her. It would be a thousand times more exhilarating than designing the tower in Kerina Sol.

This was her destiny. *This*.

But she couldn't lose track of why they were here.

"Look for anything that could be medicine." Celwyn had stepped through behind her without a moment's hesitation. "Or something to stitch a wound."

Though the room looked bare at first glance, Yi-Nereen quickly discovered it wasn't. The inside of the chest-high counter was hollow and lined with shelves. Shelves full of labeled boxes and containers.

"Celwyn, can you read these?"

Almost all of the boxes contained small colored capsules no bigger than Yi-Nereen's fingernail, but she finally found what she was

Flight of the Fallen

looking for. Needle, thread, and bandages. Celwyn picked up one of the boxes she'd discarded.

"This one has the symbol for fever. It might help."

"The Road Builders might not have been human," Yi-Nereen said. "What if their medicine hurts her?"

"If we don't try *something*," Celwyn said, his voice low and hard, "she'll die. The fever's gone too long. Now, if this is a place of healing, there must be better facilities here for treating wounds. Use that scholar's head of yours: How do we get to the upper floors?"

Yi-Nereen glanced at the floor-to-ceiling pillars. "I don't think those are for decoration."

She was right. When she placed her hand on one of the pillars, it rippled under her touch like the door had, and she stepped through. Inside the circular chamber was a sconce protruding from the wall. Yi-Nereen didn't have to tell Celwyn what to do; he touched the locus and blue sparks jumped across his knuckles.

The lift rose with shocking speed. Yi-Nereen's stomach swooped. On the floor at her feet, Eliesen stirred and groaned.

"I can— I can sense it," Celwyn said. "The entire building. This must be how Falka always knew where we were in Mount Vetelu."

"Does this mean the Road Builders were all sparktalented? Did Rasvel give them Talent, just like us, but only one?"

"Maybe it's the only one they needed." Celwyn smiled darkly. "Maybe it's got nothing to do with the gods at all."

The lift slowed to a stop. Yi-Nereen stepped through into darkness. No windows, she remembered. Celwyn snapped his fingers and a cluster of sparks lit the room.

It was filled with beds. Before Yi-Nereen noticed anything else, Eliesen made a strangled noise at her feet. She was shaking. Spasming violently, her neck and limbs rigid.

"Fuck," Celwyn said. "Help me, Yi-Nereen."

Yi-Nereen's heart pounded as she knelt to cushion Eliesen's head. The seizure was over in a few seconds, but Yi-Nereen's mind was filled with memories of the way Jin had looked as she lay dying beside the mana spring. Rasvel help her, Eliesen might die in front of her now.

She helped Celwyn carry Eliesen to a bed. Celwyn shook out one of the fever capsules and held Eliesen's mouth shut until she swallowed. "Gods, I hope that's enough," he said. "I have no idea what the correct dosage is. Now." His voice smoothed into something calm, almost detached. "Yi-Nereen. I need you to hold her down while I remove the bolt and stitch the wound closed. Do *not* let her move."

"I—" Yi-Nereen was sweating. She hadn't felt this powerless in a long time. "I don't know if I'm strong enough to—"

"Are you Makela's Herald, or aren't you?"

Another memory bloomed in Yi-Nereen's mind. Her father, shaping his shield to her body, holding her effortlessly in place. Her stomach roiled with nausea, but there was no other choice. She had to save Eliesen.

Yi-Nereen burned mana. Inch by glowing blue inch, she molded her power into a shimmering cradle for Eliesen's body, leaving her chest bare. She felt Eliesen's trembling muscles and sweat-slick skin as if with her own hands. Just as her father must have felt *her*. Gods. She *would* be sick after this.

To his credit, Celwyn worked quickly. He braced himself and yanked out the bolt in one swift stroke. Eliesen's scream cut Yi-Nereen like a knife, but Yi-Nereen screwed her eyes shut and held fast. She heard Eliesen's whimpers, felt her trembling.

"It's okay," Celwyn muttered, over and over, clearly oblivious

Flight of the Fallen

to the sound of his own voice. Yi-Nereen cracked her eyes open to peek and glimpsed his hands guiding the needle and thread through Eliesen's bloody, inflamed flesh in confident, practiced movements. He'd obviously done this before. Why would he . . . ?

The next thing Yi-Nereen saw was Celwyn's face, which was lined with exhaustion. She was on the floor. Her head pounded and her gut shivered.

"You passed out," Celwyn said. "I finished up without you."

Eliesen lay in bed, unmoving. The sheets were stained red, but Yi-Nereen could tell at once that she was better. That sickly tinge had left her flesh, though she was still pale. Her shoulder was wrapped in clean bandages.

"It's bad luck that we don't have Jin," Celwyn said. "A blood transfusion would work wonders, but neither of us are a match. Actually, I'm not sure Jin would be, either. She isn't the regular kind of Talentless."

Yi-Nereen looked at him. "Why would the kerinas exile a doctor?"

A muscle in Celwyn's jaw tensed.

"Funny story, that," he said softly. "A guildmaster of Kerina Lav exiled me for murdering his unborn heir. I did it at his wife's request, of course. She wouldn't have survived delivery."

"My mother died in childbed. Along with the baby." It was all Yi-Nereen could think to say.

"I wish I had been there to prevent it."

"My father wouldn't have exiled you. He would have killed you."

Yi-Nereen rose and walked in a daze to the far end of the room. As she drew near the wall, it shimmered and turned clear. *Oh.* The towers weren't windowless. They were built *entirely* of windows.

She could see the metallic orb at the city's heart, suspended in perfect stillness. And again the urge filled her to go there, to find a way inside. If there were any secrets of divinity to be found in Avi'Kerina, any gods who still remained to take the measure of her rotten soul, they were there. She knew it in her bones.

"Go," Celwyn said. "I need to stay with Eliesen, but we came here for a reason. Find a way to keep your father out of the city. Once that's done, we need to look for food and water. Not for us—for the kerinas."

Of course. They'd come here to find out if Avi'Kerina could support life. If it was their new home.

"I'll be back soon," Yi-Nereen said.

Celwyn gestured toward the column. "Get in. I'll send the lift down."

"No. Send me to the roof."

There was barely any wind atop the tower, despite the height. Yi-Nereen crouched at the edge of the roof and gazed down across Avi'Kerina. She tried to put names to what she felt. Curiosity. Desire. Ownership.

This place would be theirs. Hers.

Not Lai-Dan's.

Yi-Nereen burned mana. Her shield flickered into place, strong and cerulean blue. She raised herself slowly off the ground, veins buzzing with the effort. This was harder work than a stationary shield, but she'd grown stronger since that first experiment in the half-built tower. Much stronger.

Emptiness yawned below her feet as she sent her shield gliding toward the sphere. Flying. She was *flying*. A ledge jutted from the

Flight of the Fallen

sphere; Yi-Nereen landed with a metallic click as her heels met the surface. Now, up close, she saw the telltale outline of a hatch.

Heart thrumming wildly, she touched the sphere—and just as she'd hoped, it gave way.

※

At temple services, when the priests had placed the prayer veil over Yi-Nereen's head, she'd looked through the curtain of clinking beads and imagined seeing the world the way the gods did: broken into individual strands of a greater whole. The mortal and the divine had always existed side by side, parted by a veil.

Yi-Nereen crossed it and found herself in a garden.

She'd thought Faolin's canyon a living place. At the time, it was the most greenery she'd ever seen, lichen hanging from the canyon walls and soft grass blanketing the ground. It was nothing like the orchards in Kerina Rut, unending rows of brown-barked, leafless trees that groaned under the weight of their fruit, or even the nobility's carefully manicured gardens with their beds of bloomwoven flowers.

But it was stark and bare in comparison to *this*.

Trees, bushes, and shrubs in shades of verdure she'd never seen before surrounded her on all sides. The air was humid and smelled dark, rich, loamy. Yi-Nereen's feet sank into a thick layer of springy plant material.

Even the sky was green.

No. That wasn't the sky. She'd entered the sphere from the side, but through some godly trick, she was standing at its lowest point now. Above her the inside of the orb came curving around to its highest point. And it was all a garden, right side up and upside down, everywhere, filled with soft white light.

Gravity. A dusty scroll in the Tower archives had defined it as "the divine force that pulls all things earthward." What if here, in the sphere, earthward wasn't a single direction, but many?

Yi-Nereen had thought herself open-minded, a necessary trait for any scholar—but there were so many things she'd simply taken for granted. She knew nothing. Less than nothing.

She picked her way through the greenery, trying not to crush any plants. But soon she realized these plants weren't as fragile as bloom-woven flowers. They were like wasteland flora, tough and hardy, but lacking the usual spines and toxic spores. Somehow they'd survived here for the centuries the city had lain abandoned.

And more than just plants had survived.

Yi-Nereen shrieked as something large and white fluttered by her face. A flying insect with huge, rounded, paper-thin wings. More of them flitted between the flowering plants. She heard the hum of wasps, though she couldn't see them.

Vaguely, in the back of her mind, she remembered her mission. Keep Lai-Dan out of Avi'Kerina. Find a way for the kerinas to survive here.

But if the gods were anywhere in the world, they were here.

Yi-Nereen stepped out from a cluster of aromatic saplings and beheld the largest tree she'd ever seen. The roots wending in and out of the ground were so thick she'd barely be able to wrap her arms around them; the trunk was a living wall.

On the ceiling, high above and far away, she saw the outline of the metal hatch she'd stepped through. The tall plants that had surrounded her when she'd entered the sphere were mere branches in the goliath tree that stood before her now.

Up and down had simply changed places. It was impossible. And yet—her senses told her it was real.

Flight of the Fallen

Swallowing hard, she returned her attention to the tree. Nestled in its roots, looking wildly out of place, was a metal plinth with an angled top covered in a grid of carvings—more Road Builder script. Without Celwyn here, she couldn't read it.

A red light pulsed slowly, on and off, in one of the empty spaces of the grid.

The internal pull that had beckoned Yi-Nereen here rose suddenly to the surface, overwhelming her, closing her throat with its urgency. Before she knew what she was doing, she was standing in front of the pedestal, hand outstretched to that pulsing light.

She could almost hear a voice calling her name.

Yi-Nereen. My Herald. My daughter.

Yi-Nereen touched the light.

CHAPTER THIRTY-FOUR

COUP

Observation #759: If dealings with Kadrin have taught me anything, it's that one must never underestimate the power of an earnest fool. What is a wall, after all, but a door waiting to be made? —O

Third Age of Storms, 1st Summer, Day 87
Kerina Sol – Jade District

At first sight of the Marble Palace, Kadrin cursed and dragged Sou-Zell into an alley. "It's already started. Those are Toraka's people standing guard on the steps, not the city watch."

Sou-Zell removed Kadrin's hand from his arm like he was plucking off a bloodsucking insect. Some things hadn't changed. "Then we won't get in without a fight. Where's your weapon?"

"All I have is this." Kadrin unsheathed his dagger. It wasn't the weapon he would have chosen to lay siege to the Council chambers with; it was beautiful, but the blade was no longer than the span of his fingertips.

"You've outdone yourself," Sou-Zell said. "I didn't think anything could be worse than that theater prop of a sword you used to carry."

Kadrin flushed. "I don't see *your*—"

358

Flight of the Fallen

Wordlessly, Sou-Zell produced a long, gleaming stiletto from what must have been a hidden sheath in his knee-high riding boot.

"Ah," Kadrin said. He felt a faint tremble of nausea at the sight of the weapon; it looked like a *real* blade, unlike his dagger. "I don't want to hurt anyone unless we have to. I mean, they think they're doing the right thing. Maybe they *are*. I don't know. If I can talk to my father again, maybe he'll see . . ."

But Kadrin had tried that. He'd been trying to make his father see for his entire life. If Matrios hadn't *seen* with his Talentless son right in front of him, begging him to understand, he certainly wouldn't do it for a bunch of refugees.

He'd allowed the High Priestess to abduct and torture his son. Kadrin still couldn't quite believe it.

"We won't kill anyone." Sou-Zell sounded like he had a shard of glass stuck between his fingers. Kadrin realized with a jolt of shock that he was trying to sound *kind*. "I don't relish the thought of any more wasted lives."

"Any more?"

Sou-Zell's face darkened. "Kerina Rut. Two weeks ago. I watched the massacre."

Kadrin didn't understand at first. Then he put it together. A week ago, he'd watched Toraka pray over a bowl of memorial beads and give a bitter eulogy to a rival. Word took time to travel between kerinas, but the massacre Sou-Zell spoke of and the slaughter Toraka had mourned could only be one and the same.

"You *watched*?"

He didn't mean it to sound accusatory—like Sou-Zell was a villain, like he'd done nothing to help. Kadrin was simply horrified by the thought. Hundreds of people dead, and Sou-Zell had seen it happen.

But Sou-Zell reeled back as if Kadrin had slapped him. He looked sick, trembling in the torchlight, his sword hanging limply from his hand.

"No more," he said. "Let's get into that building."

Kadrin had a plan. It involved a window on the east side of the Council chambers, hidden behind a hedge. But as soon as he and Sou-Zell broke cover and made a dash for the hedge, Kadrin realized the error in his calculations: the hedge was bloomwoven, and over a week without a bloomweaver's attention had left it a shriveled, lifeless mass of twigs.

Shouts rang out. Kadrin glanced left and right to see men running at them from both directions.

Shit.

There wasn't time to convince anybody he was there on a mission of peace. For one thing, Sou-Zell's sword was drawn—and for another, Kadrin was still wearing his blasted raincaller robes.

Sou-Zell spun into action first. As the first of the refugees reached them, Sou-Zell sidestepped a swinging blow and sent the man sprawling to the cobblestones. Easy as breathing, like he'd known exactly where the man was going to swing. And he had. His eyes were glowing violet.

But that was one man. Kadrin realized swiftly that Sou-Zell's preferred tactics depended on their enemies being Talented—and most of them weren't.

As much as he loved to fence, Kadrin hated to fight. He'd only ever done it the one time. And he hadn't been fighting for himself, but to protect Jin, to distract her pursuers so she could rescue

Reena. Kadrin's mind and his conscience had been clear. But now—now he felt a tangled mass of anger and fear seething within him, shot through with flashes of Edine's face. He remembered the hurt.

Use that.

Kadrin grasped at anger and fear. Pulled them closer, like twin serpents. His heart thundered and his body hummed unpleasantly.

The men rushing toward him wanted to hurt him—just like the sparkrider who'd tortured him in the temple basement. What would Kadrin have done if he'd gotten free down there? If he'd had a blade in his hand?

The dagger he'd never used before felt light as silk. He spun, slashed. Launched himself past Sou-Zell and into the throng, shouting in a raw voice. Nothing could touch him. He was a storm incarnate, quick and furious.

"Kadrin. Kadrin!"

Kadrin crouched, panting. Men lay groaning on the cobblestones around him; the stench of copper thickened the air. Nearby, Sou-Zell flicked blood from his stiletto and stared at Kadrin with narrowed eyes, like he was seeing him for the first time.

I don't want to hurt anyone unless we have to.

Kadrin straightened.

"The window. Give me a boost."

He was numb. Shaking. Later, he'd think about this later. Right now he had to get to his family.

He stepped into Sou-Zell's waiting hands and pulled himself over the windowsill. They'd done this before, in a theater in a ruined castle while a rovex roared at their backs. It almost felt routine.

Kadrin dropped onto the floor on the other side. He was in an alcove on the uppermost tier of the Council chamber, which was thankfully empty; normally it would be occupied by serving staff, but he'd guessed correctly that an emergency meeting would be the exception. As long as he remained crouched, it would be easy to stay hidden from anyone below.

And here was the next flaw in his plan, though at least Kadrin had seen this one coming: the window was too high for him to pull Sou-Zell up behind him. Sou-Zell had to find another way in. Kadrin hoped he was doing exactly that right now.

For now, Kadrin was alone. And he'd walked in on a coup in progress.

Blue light blazed through the chamber, pulsating from a shieldcaster's dome that filled the central area at the bottom of the tiered seats. Inside the dome stood Shield Lord Tethris and most of the royals Kadrin recognized from Council meetings and a childhood of formal banquets, including Tethris's wife. Tethris's arms were raised; the corded muscles in her biceps strained visibly as she held the shield.

But not all the nobles had found refuge inside the shield. Several of them sat tied to chairs. Including Kadrin's father and Satriu.

Kadrin's pulse fluttered. He couldn't see Devros; he must be with the group inside the shield. Surrounding the shield were Toraka's conspirators. He spotted Falka's dirty-blond head of hair, striking amid a sea of dark heads. She stood beside the defuser Kadrin had glimpsed in Orrin's workshop.

And there was Orrin. Kadrin felt a deep surge of disappointment. He hadn't wanted to believe that Orrin was really part of this. He thought they were friends. But Kadrin himself might've been tied up here, had he not disinherited himself just that morning.

There was no time for lamentations. He had to come up with another plan, and quickly. Maybe he could sneak down to the lower tier, free his father and Satriu, and . . . and what?

Flight of the Fallen

They were raincallers. As far as Kadrin knew, no one had discovered a combat use for raincalling unless the enemy had great fear of wet shoes. And the conspirators were armed. Two freed men outside the dome would hardly turn the odds in the Council's favor.

And Kadrin wasn't on the Council's side anyway. Gods, he didn't know *whose* side he was on. Toraka and the conspirators had been driven to this out of desperation. By the looks of it, the Council was no more willing to listen than they ever had been. The High Priestess wasn't even in the building and her shadow still loomed over the scene. What could Kadrin do to stop this?

Down on the ground floor, Orrin turned. Their eyes met Kadrin's and they froze. So did Kadrin. Would Orrin raise the alarm?

Even from a distance, Kadrin saw Orrin's mouth thin. But they said nothing.

A chance. Orrin was giving him a chance. Kadrin had to do something with it. But what?

His frantic thoughts were drowned by the sudden, deafening peal of bells. Storm bells. So loud they had to be coming from the nearest stormwatch station on the Wall, no more than a hundred feet from the Marble Palace.

The Council chambers shook. Tethris's shield flickered; from his vantage point, Kadrin saw the nobles within turning to each other in panic. Outside the dome, Toraka's conspirators stared up at the ceiling.

"Well, well." Falka's drawl filled the chamber. Her back was turned to Kadrin, but he heard the smirk in her voice, the utter lack of fear. "This changes the situation, Shield Lord, wouldn't you say?"

Kadrin's blood chilled. Falka was right. With Tethris trapped along with the highest-ranking shieldcasters of her House, the Corps' chain of command was broken. The Wall would be thrown into chaos. They'd lost two shieldcasters in the last storm. How many would they lose this time?

"Guildmaster Toraka," Shield Lord Tethris said from inside the barrier. Her voice was strained. "You know what happens to this city if the dome falls. Your people are Sol-bloods now. Will you truly let their home be destroyed a second time?"

"Kerina Sol is not our home," Toraka said calmly. "The First City is our home. We must all make sacrifices to get there. If you make the right decision, Tethris, this will be the last storm our people endure. Give up your Talent. Set an example. Then you can lead the rest of the Corps against the storm. They need your guidance, not your power."

Kadrin's eyes flew to his father and Satriu. Had he arrived too late? Had they already been through the defuser? No—it wasn't possible. If the choice was the defuser or death, he knew what his father would choose.

Orrin was still watching him silently. It was time to speak.

"Shield Lord Tethris," Kadrin called out. Heads turned toward him. His stomach pitched like he'd jumped from a mountain peak. But he forced himself to breathe. "Toraka. Please listen to me. We can all survive this. No one has to give up their Talent unless they choose."

"Kadrin?" Satriu croaked. "Kadrin, get out of here. They'll kill you."

Well, at least someone cared. Kadrin resisted the urge to glance at his father again. He wasn't his father's heir any longer. Any words he spoke now were his own.

He tore the seed pouch from around his neck and held it aloft in shaking fingers.

"We can grow our food from seeds. We've done it before. If the bloomweavers don't need to work the orchards, they won't need as

Flight of the Fallen

much mana. The ones who are willing can give up their Talent, but no one needs to be forced. We *do* need our shieldcasters, but only until we can move everyone to the First City. And we don't need the Legion at all. Orrin finally cracked the sparkless bike."

"Who's Orrin?" asked a confused voice from inside the shield, and someone else bellowed, "Talentless don't get to make decisions for the rest of us."

"Why not?" Falka snarled, thumping her fist on the barrier. "The High fucking Houses have been deciding whether we live or die since the First Storm of Centuries."

Toraka shook her head slowly, her face shadowed. "Kadrin, it *is* possible to grow plants from seeds. But not in enough quantity to feed an entire city, and not quickly enough. We would starve waiting for the first crop to ripen."

Kadrin's heart beat faster. Maybe he'd missed the mark, but Toraka was listening. And so were the royals inside the dome, whether they wanted to or not.

"Well, what about the sparkriders? We're not at war. The Legion doesn't need to constantly patrol the wastes. Kerina Rut is the only city left to trade with. That means we hardly need couriers, either."

"Knight-Commander Ives isn't here," Tethris said, thin-lipped, her voice warped by the shield, "but I can't imagine he'll agree to defang the Legion because a Talentless suggested it."

"Why does it matter who suggested it?"

Kadrin gave Tethris a heated stare—and Edine's face flickered over hers. He fought to keep his composure.

"I'm long past believing that this Council practices what it preaches—shelter for the weak and liberty for all. But for Rasvel's sake, you're supposed to serve the people, and you refuse to consider even the tiniest sacrifice to protect everyone. You're cowards. Toraka isn't asking you to do anything she hasn't already done. Do you honestly believe being Talentless is a fate worse than death? *Do you?*"

In the silence, Falka said softly, "You know the answer."

Kadrin threw his arms wide. "Well, I'm alive. I'm Talentless. I never had a choice in the matter, but I don't feel sorry for myself. Don't you feel any shame? Any of you?"

The nobles inside the shield exchanged uneasy glances. Kadrin waited, sick with fury and trembling. He had spent his whole life trying to convince these people he was worthy of respect and attention. If they didn't listen to him now . . .

Well, he'd already disowned his family. He could disown his city, too. He'd leave them all to die in the storms.

You wouldn't do that, said a voice in his head. It sounded like Jin. *You could never do that.*

"I do," said another voice, loud and booming in the stillness.

Kadrin turned his head slowly, his throat thick with disbelief. It couldn't be . . . But it *was.* His father was the one who had spoken. Tied to a chair, Rain Lord Matrios still managed to project a commanding aura; everyone in the room immediately turned to look at him.

"I am ashamed of how little this Council has done to protect our people. Kerina Sol needs us more than ever before, and we've abandoned her, ceded responsibility to the temple. *I* believed High Priestess Edine would maintain order in the city. It's become clear she cares far more about hunting down Princess Yi-Nereen than handling our current crisis." Kadrin's father stared down each of the nobles inside the shield in turn. "I vote to institute the restrictions Kadrin has suggested, starting with an emergency decommissioning of the Legion. Knight-Commander Ives answers to the High Houses; he will submit to our authority in this matter."

Flight of the Fallen

"We are not in session," Tethris said, looking pale. "You cannot call a vote—"

"No, he can't," said Bloom Lord Feyrin. Kadrin hadn't noticed him before; now he saw him sitting inside the shield, flanked by his brothers. "However, since I am next in the rotation to preside over the chamber, I move to open a session and immediately call a vote on the aforementioned restrictions. I vote yes."

Gratitude flooded through Kadrin's chest. Sure, it would have been nice if the Bloom Lord had spoken up earlier, considering he'd been part of the so-called conspiracy from the start—but he was speaking up now that he wasn't the first Council member to do so. That was better than nothing.

Tethris set her jaw and said, "I vote no."

"Two for, one against," Feyrin said. "Stone and Metal have yet to cast their votes, and High Priestess Edine is absent."

Kadrin's stomach flipped. Two more votes and the fate of everyone in Kerina Sol would be decided. All he knew about Stone Lord Detram and Metal Lord Pavarta was that when it came to a vote, the Stone Lord always voted with—

"I vote no."

With Shield Lord Tethris. Kadrin sucked in a breath and, along with everyone else in the chamber, turned to look at the last person to vote.

Metal Lord Pavarta was inside the shield. She was the youngest of the Lords of the High Houses; her dark brown skin flushed burgundy under the weight of all those stares. But she raised her chin, and her voice carried clear through the shield's distortion.

"Princess Yi-Nereen saved my cousin's life after he fell into the spring. Yes, she took his Talent. But I'd rather have him alive and Talentless than the alternative."

She glanced at Kadrin, her lips curving into a smile.

"I vote yes."

Stunned silence fell over the chamber. The members of the Shield Lord's and Stone Lord's retinues wore stormy expressions, but none of them said a word. Finally Bloom Lord Feyrin said, astonishment leaking through his practiced nonchalance, "That's three for and two against. The proposal passes. Now, *I* don't plan to be the one who informs Knight-Commander Ives what we just voted for."

"What if it's not enough?" Tethris asked, her voice sharp as a blade. "Say everyone who chooses to sacrifice their Talent does so, and the restrictions remain in place for everyone else. What if the mana levels still keep dropping?"

"Then we'll be right back here," Kadrin's father said firmly, "but at least we'll have tried *something*."

Kadrin descended through the chamber until he stood before Toraka.

"Well?" he asked, a challenge in his voice. "Is that good enough?"

Toraka dipped her head. "A peaceful resolution," she said softly. "I didn't think it could be done. I had lost hope. I'm glad you didn't."

As soon as Tethris dropped her shield, she and the shieldcasters of her House hurriedly filed out of the Council chambers. Kadrin realized with a punch of surprise that the storm bells had stopped ringing. He wasn't sure when it had happened.

Movement by the entrance caught his eye. Sou-Zell.

"Where have you been?" Kadrin demanded, his voice sharp,

though his chest filled with warmth at the sight of him. He'd been worried.

Sou-Zell's mouth twitched. "Nearby. Did it work?"

"Did what work?"

"The *bells*, of course."

Kadrin shot Sou-Zell an incredulous stare. "That was— How did you—?"

Sou-Zell shrugged. "The stormwatch stations aren't guarded. I suspected they wouldn't be. Who would set off a false storm alarm?"

Kadrin opened his mouth to reply. But before he could, the bells began to ring. Again.

"On the other hand," Sou-Zell said, "those are real."

CHAPTER THIRTY-FIVE

LOOK TO THE SKIES

Observation #521: Perhaps the answer isn't a sparkless magebike.
Perhaps the answer isn't a bike at all. A pteropter can cross the
wastes in the span of a day.
Hypothesis: Rather than follow in the footsteps of the Road
Builders, we should look to the skies. —O

Third Age of Storms, 1st Summer, Day 87

The Barrens — No Fucking Clue

J in fell.

The wind gripped her like a savage thing, tangling her hair and wrenching at her limbs. She flailed, helpless. The mountain air was so thin that it rushed through her lungs like nothing. She caught glimpses of reflective rock, an impenetrable fog barrier, a sky splashed pink and orange with sunset.

At least she'd die with a view.

Then—

Whumph.

She hit a firm, bristling surface. Her body rolled, eager to return to falling to its death, but Jin snatched handfuls of warm feathers and clung for dear life.

Flight of the Fallen

Feathers. A massive body heaving beneath hers.

She was on Screech's back. And they were *both* still falling.

Jin screamed. The pteropter beat his wings furiously and screamed, too. The mountains rang with the music of their descent. Jin could do nothing but cling to Screech's back like a bug. And then slowly, surely, they leveled off—and began to rise.

Screech could *do* this. He was carrying her. Jin felt the inconceivable strength of his muscles moving within the titanic engine of his body. He'd been built for this.

They rose through the clouds, out of the dying sunlight's reach and into the dominion of night. Stars glowed crimson above. The air's chill touch brought goose bumps surging to Jin's skin. But she felt warm, blood rushing through her with every beat of her heart that marveled at being alive. Alive.

She'd jumped off a mountain and lived. Twice.

A hysterical, disbelieving laugh tore its way out of her. "God-*damn*."

She felt invincible. Unkillable. But then Screech tilted to the side to catch an air current and Jin shrieked and tightened her grip, reminded she was mortal.

If she fell, who knew if he'd catch her again?

"Who *are* you?" Jin asked. "Was any of it real? Can you understand me?"

One gleaming black eye rolled back to glare at her. A predator's glance, emotionally uninvolved, offering no answers.

All this time, he'd kept her alive. He'd saved her from a chandru herd, saved her from a storm, saved her from falling to her death. She'd always thought he was just an animal who was a little bit obsessed with her because she fed him. Animals understood *food*, not gratitude or debts owed. Except Screech.

Hana Lee

All she could think was: *It's all connected. The wasteland. The storms. The saurians. The cacti. Mana connects them all. It's in me, too. Talent or no Talent.*

Maybe she was still high on wasteland cactus.

"Hey." Jin cautiously loosed one hand from a tangle of feathers and patted Screech's shoulder. "Where are we going?"

He glided lower, toward the clouds that still glowed with the fading orange light of dusk. Down they soared, steeply enough to make Jin's stomach swoop. They passed through the clouds with a burst of cold damp that shocked her.

The mountains were gone. Below her stretched the wasteland. The roads gleamed silver, a great, sparse web of cracks in the desolation Jin called home. She imagined a courier's map spread over a table. She could trace all her usual routes, roads she'd traveled a hundred times before a kiss had stolen them all away. There was the familiar stretch of highway between Kerina Sol and Kerina Rut. Out in the west, the sun was sinking into the swampy fog of the Barrens.

What was *that*?

She'd never seen a storm from above before. But a storm was what it had to be: a mass of darkness and flickering light that raced across the wasteland toward Kerina Sol.

"Rasvel help us," Jin breathed. She'd hoped against hope that Kerina Sol would be spared another storm until the expedition to Avi'Kerina returned. Until they had a plan to save themselves. The first city-killer had been devastating enough—but now Kerina Sol was under martial law and running on rationed mana.

Kadrin and her mother were still there.

Jin yanked urgently at Screech's feathers. "Down there. We have to help."

372

Screech chirped. He cut a wide swathe through the air and angled himself to face the Barrens again.

You have to get to Avi'Kerina, Faolin said in Jin's memory.

Kadrin was in Kerina Sol, Yi-Nereen in Avi'Kerina. Gods, how Jin loved them both. She never should have walked away. If she'd fought her pride and broken heart in the garden that day, if she'd won, if she'd just *stayed*, they would have had so much more time.

But she couldn't dwell on the past now. They both needed her. So she wouldn't choose.

"All right." Jin took hold of Screech's feathers in both hands again. "But let's pick up Kadrin first."

Down they plunged, fast enough to convince Jin's brain that her body was dying. She would never get used to this. She clung to Screech's back like a burr, eyes streaming in the wind. Kerina Sol loomed below them—small at first and growing rapidly, until it was massive and *right there*.

Jin shouted at Screech to pull up, but he was already flaring his wings to slow their descent. Again, that gleaming black eye rolled back to give her a look that said, *Who's the one flying here?*

Jin had never seen Kerina Sol from above before. The streets and districts were almost unrecognizable. But Screech seemed to know where he was going; he glided toward the largest, flattest roof in the city. Jin only realized what building it belonged to when Screech's talons were inches away from the stone. The Marble Palace. The Council chambers were right below—

They landed hard. Jin's hands were already slick with sweat; she lost her grip and pitched forward over Screech's shoulder. She rolled across the roof and came to a panting stop with her face hanging over the edge. Oh, that was going to be a lot of bruises.

"We need to work on that."

Their arrival hadn't gone unnoticed. Jin heard shouts from below. She raised herself gingerly into a sitting position and sensed Screech behind her, looming over her like a gargoyle. The shouts became screams.

Jin pictured arrows whistling through the air toward Screech and her blood froze. She turned, hissing at Screech, "Get down—*hide*—"

Then she heard a familiar voice from below.

"Jin?" said Kadrin.

The moment Jin's feet touched the ground, she was folded into an embrace so tight she thought her bones might crack. Fire shot from her shoulder to her wrist; she yelped but didn't pull away. Her senses were overwhelmed by Kadrin. His warmth, his solidity, that indescribable floral scent she associated only with him.

"We've got to go," Jin muttered into his chest. She prickled with urgency, matched only by her unwillingness to bring this moment to an end. "The dome will close any minute, and we need to be in the sky before it does."

"In the sky? What do you—?"

"Reena and Elie need us. They're still in the Barrens."

That got Kadrin's attention. He let her go and held her at arm's length. Jin looked into his face—and immediately forgot anything else. She raised her hand. Her fingertips hovered over a swollen,

Flight of the Fallen

dark purple bruise around his eye. There were more bruises dotting both sides of his face; his stubble was tacky with dried blood.

"What happened? Who did this to you?"

Kadrin hesitated. His gaze darted from side to side. Jin looked past him and saw Sou-Zell standing just a few steps away, a familiar sneer on his waxen lips.

"You."

Fury boiled to steam in her veins. It didn't occur to her to wonder how the hell he'd gotten there when, as far as she knew, he was supposed to be in Kerina Rut. Jin tore herself away from Kadrin and took a single step toward Sou-Zell. Her hands were empty, but from the way his eyes widened, she might have been carrying a weapon.

"It wasn't—"

A harsh shriek drowned whatever Sou-Zell was going to say. Faster than Jin could react, a shadow unfurled from the sky and took Sou-Zell to the ground. A strong gust whooshed out from where it landed; Jin's hair blew back from her face. The crowd who'd gathered around the Marble Palace steps to watch her and Kadrin's reunion screamed and scattered.

Screech's beak snapped shut a hair's breadth from Sou-Zell's face. The pteropter was crouched over his supine form, talons fastened around his arms.

Jin stared. What on earth had Sou-Zell done to piss off her pteropter? Then she realized—he hadn't done anything. Screech was reacting to *her.* Jin had treated Sou-Zell like a threat, and Screech had pounced.

"It wasn't him!" Kadrin said. "Jin, please tell your saurian not to hurt him. It wasn't him. He saved me."

"He *what?*" Jin snapped her fingers. "Hey. Uh—down, boy?"

375

Screech turned his head and hissed. Pinned under the pteropter's talons, Sou-Zell remained perfectly still, though his face was white with fear.

"Would you look at that," drawled a familiar voice. "Someone found a way to shut the bastard up."

Falka loped down the marble steps, all tanned skin and sinew. Jin froze, and her hand went unconsciously to her rib cage. There was nothing there now, not even a scar. But Falka's mouth still twisted at the sight as if she'd been the one stabbed.

"Jin."

Falka stopped, less than a stride away, so close Jin could count the freckles on her face. She didn't need to count them. *Forty-three.* She could map them like the stars in the sky, constellations that had once pointed her way home. It hurt how so many things about Falka were the same, from the cleft in her chin to the swoop of her sandy hair over one green-flecked eye, and yet nothing was the same. Jin didn't know her anymore.

"Don't tell me," Falka said. "You rode here on a pteropter's back."

Jin could only nod, her mouth too dry to speak.

"Vann always said it was possible, if one of the wretched beasts ever grew big enough. He thought a sparkrider would be the one to do it. Since they can control saurians." The corner of Falka's mouth twitched. "And you did it without the spark. Of course you did."

"What's . . . ?" Jin swallowed, tried again. "What's that supposed to mean?"

"The princess might have taken your Talent," Falka said, "but she couldn't clip your wings. You'd be free, one way or another."

Something shone in her eyes as she looked at Jin. Envy? Bitter affection? Jin had never been able to read Falka's expressions, even when she'd slept beside her. There had always been a part of Falka

Flight of the Fallen

she couldn't touch, pacing a locked cell and snarling at whoever reached through the bars. Jin had lain awake for years after their parting, wondering if time would have softened Falka's rough edges if Jin had only brought her somewhere safe, like she'd promised so many times.

"City's going to shit," Jin said weakly. "Just like Tez. You can tell, can't you?"

Falka nodded. "Your prince patched the leak. But that High Priestess is the same breed as the fuckers who killed Tez. She won't take this lying down. Someone will have to deal with her."

Jin had a suspicion that she'd missed a lot of context. "When you say *deal with her*—"

A hand settled gently on Jin's uninjured shoulder. "I'm really sorry to interrupt," Kadrin said. "But you said something about my sister and Reena being in trouble, and us not having much time?"

"Right." Jin tore her eyes away from Falka. "Reena's father was waiting for us in the Barrens. We barely got away, and then we were separated. I think—I *hope* they made it to Avi'Kerina. But if Lai-Dan finds Reena again, he's going to kill her. Or she'll kill him. Either way, she needs us. And Eliesen is badly hurt."

"Hurt?" Kadrin went still. "Hurt how?"

"A crossbow bolt." There was no way to soften the blow; Jin felt a pang at the look on Kadrin's face. "I came because I can't do this alone. Reena's father won't be easy to kill. I think Screech can carry us both. Hey!" She clapped her hands, earning another glare from Screech. "Get off that lout. We don't have time for this."

To her great relief, Screech warbled testily and hopped off Sou-Zell. He flapped his way back up to the roof of the Council building, where he perched on the edge and glowered down at them all.

Sou-Zell got slowly to his feet. "The courier and her pet remain as charming as ever." Despite his snide tone, his hands were trembling.

Jin ignored him. "Where's my mother?"

"She's with Renfir," Kadrin said. "They went to Temple Square to join the other Talentless. There's— Well, things in the city have gone downhill since you left."

Jin cursed. "Damn it all, we just don't have time. Renfir is going to have to keep her safe for me, or I swear I'll punch him so hard all his pretty buttons fly off."

Kadrin turned to Sou-Zell. "I'd like to have a city to come back to once we save Reena and my sister. Can you—?"

Sou-Zell nodded. "I'll do what I can." He drew a long, elegant blade from a sheath in his boot and offered it, hilt first, to Kadrin. "If you're going to kill Lai-Dan, you'll need a lot more than this. But it's a start."

Jin looked between the two men, nonplussed. What in the name of the gods had happened here while she'd been gone? There was no time to ask. Just like there was no time to speak to Falka and untangle everything that had ever gone wrong between them. Jin would just have to stay alive and come back.

The clanging of the storm bells had reached a frantic pitch, which meant the storm would be on them in moments.

"Hurry, Kadrin."

They clambered back onto the roof of the Council chambers. Then Jin was confronted with a task she'd never attempted before: mounting Screech's back when he was stationary and she wasn't falling off a mountain.

Fortunately there was enough room for Kadrin to cling to the pteropter's back with her, his chest pressed against her back, heels jammed between Screech's two pairs of wings. Jin thought of the distance between sky and ground and choked down her fear. She didn't have time to be afraid.

"Just like a magebike," Kadrin said with a shaky laugh. "Right?"

"Right."

Jin didn't have to signal Screech to fly; the pteropter seemed to sense her intentions. He crouched and flung himself from the roof, all four wings flapping madly. Jin squeezed her eyes shut as her stomach threatened to eject itself from her throat. She heard Kadrin whooping in excitement.

When she finally worked up the courage to open her eyes, she saw Kerina Sol shrinking beneath them as they rose. Before them, a wall of darkness and howling wind rushed toward the city: the oncoming storm. Blue light flashed on the parapets. The shield climbed around them, shimmering and translucent. For a moment Jin thought they wouldn't make it, that they'd be trapped inside the dome.

Then a violent gust of wind from the approaching storm bore Screech aloft like a feather on a strong breeze, and they cleared the city an instant before the dome sealed beneath them.

"This is incredible," Kadrin breathed in her ear. Jin's entire body tingled, enveloped in his warmth, a barrier between her and the cool night air. It was almost enough to chase away her fear. Almost. "Are you okay? You're shaking."

"I hate heights," Jin said.

Kadrin laughed. "I think you're going to have to get used to it, saurian rider."

CHAPTER THIRTY-SIX

A SLEEPING GOD

Observation #771: The First City may well exist, but there's no evidence to suggest the gods ever did. It seems much more likely that whoever controls Avi'Kerina will become so powerful as to resemble a deity.
Hypothesis: This is exactly how the Road Builders went extinct. —O

Third Age of Storms, 1st Summer, Day 87
The Barrens – Avi'Kerina

The moment Yi-Nereen touched the pulsing red light on the metal plinth, the world shuddered. Outside, Avi'Kerina groaned in unknown torment, a trembling buzz like the earthquakes that sometimes shook the kerinas after a storm and leveled buildings.

Eliesen and Celwyn. They were in the towers.

She tried to turn, to run—but something held her in place. The roots of the tree were glowing: softly yellow at first, then with an incandescence so bright she had to close her eyes. Still, the light intensified. She couldn't move. It felt like her father's shield had when it molded itself to her shape and immobilized her.

Hear us.

Flight of the Fallen

The voice filled the sphere. Resonant, yet silent. Yi-Nereen could not say if it was male or female, young or old, or even if it was the voice of one or many.

We are the ones who inhabited this place. We speak to you now through an echo. Whether you are beast or spirit, hear us. This is our testament. This is what you who have come to this place must know.

We came to this world with the best of intentions. We wished to advance our species and make grand discoveries. We brought every tool required for success. Materials, instruments, chattel. For a time, there was progress.

Then there was war.

This place is a failure. The records will be closed. The specimens will be destroyed. What we leave behind is useless or abhorrent to us.

Hear us, and be warned. The air and soil of this place breed conflict. Conflict threatens society. Knowledge is not worth disorder. Prosperity over progress, unto eternity.

We will not return.

The voice faded from Yi-Nereen's awareness until she could hear only her ragged breathing and pounding heartbeat. The rumbling had stopped. She could move again.

She ran through the steaming garden, cutting her cheeks on thin twigs, the soles of her boots heavy with mud, until the ceiling of the sphere became the floor again and she found the hatch where she'd entered.

Had the gods spoken to her? Was that what they sounded like? What did they mean by *specimens*?

We will not return.

She couldn't begin to make sense of what she had heard. It was too much.

Yi-Nereen scrambled through the hatch and left the natal

warmth of the garden behind. Cool night air rushed into her lungs. She stood under the moon and stars and gazed over Avi'Kerina, expecting to see devastation. But everything looked as she had left it.

A strong breeze lifted her hair and made it dance around her face.

A breeze.

When she'd entered the sphere, the air had been utterly still. The invisible barrier around the city kept the winds at bay. But now there was a breeze, and that could mean only one thing.

When she'd touched the plinth, she'd lowered the barrier.

Now nothing would keep her father from entering Avi'Kerina.

Celwyn was pacing the tower roof when Yi-Nereen glided down to meet him and dismissed her shield.

"What happened? It felt like an earthquake." He eyed her, frowning. "You can *fly*?"

"The barrier's down," Yi-Nereen said, dodging the question. "Is Eliesen all right?"

"Still sleeping. The fever medicine seems to have worked." Celwyn chewed his lip. "What do you mean, the barrier's down? What happened?"

"I went into the sphere," Yi-Nereen said, and stopped. She was struck by the sudden, nauseating certainty that Celwyn wouldn't believe her. How could she explain what she'd just experienced? The change in gravity, the plants and insects alive after centuries, the glowing tree, and the voice she'd heard? *Gods, maybe none of it was real.* Maybe she was going mad. "Celwyn, I don't understand any-

Flight of the Fallen

thing about this place. I need more time. Time we don't have. My father is coming."

"I found something, too," Celwyn said. "But—"

His gaze sharpened, fixed on something over Yi-Nereen's shoulder. His hand crept to his sword. Yi-Nereen turned.

A huge, dark shape circled above Avi'Kerina, a shadow moving against the stars. Fear washed through Yi-Nereen like a cold tide; she was prey, helpless beneath a predator on the wing. Exposed. But then the massive saurian banked and angled directly toward the roof—and she realized she recognized it.

"Screech," Yi-Nereen gasped. Then she saw the two figures clinging to the saurian's back. "Jin? *Kadrin?*"

She would wake from this at any moment. It couldn't be real. She fell to her knees, and a sob of relief wrenched from her like an anguished scream. She didn't stop trembling when the saurian alighted on the roof's edge and Jin and Kadrin sank to the ground on either side of her. She couldn't stop until her face was pressed into the crook of Jin's neck and Kadrin's hands were stroking her back.

Part of her had been paralyzed ever since she'd seen Jin dragged away. She'd refused to accept the passage of time since that moment. Now it all came rushing in at once. This was real. Jin was alive.

"I knew you weren't dead," Yi-Nereen sobbed. "I'm sorry. I'm so sorry for leaving you."

"I'm hard to kill," Jin said with a choked laugh. "You did the right thing."

"Thank Rasvel you're all right." Kadrin's arms tightened around them both, protective and possessive in equal measure.

Yi-Nereen struggled to catch her breath. "My father will be here soon."

"He won't touch you," Jin growled. "We're with you."
"Seconded," Kadrin said. "Now where's my sister?"

The lift was cramped with all four of them stuffed inside, but Yi-Nereen hardly minded. Kadrin's arm was around her waist; she was holding Jin's hand. All the weeks she'd spent in Kerina Sol without doing this, exactly this, felt like the most egregious waste to her now. Her father could rain death on Avi'Kerina from above, and Yi-Nereen would still rather be nowhere else.

Steady blue light illuminated the room full of beds; Celwyn had activated the sconces lining the walls. Eliesen lay in bed, still unconscious, eyes moving restlessly beneath their lids. Kadrin traced the bandage over her shoulder with his fingertips.

"You did this?" he asked Celwyn. "Thank you."

"I have more supplies." Celwyn gave Jin an appraising look. "That arm could use stitches."

"We don't have time for that," Jin said.

Stitches? Yi-Nereen took in both Jin and Kadrin for the first time, and the warm thrill of reunion ebbed away. Jin's jacket was torn and her sleeve was a mess of clotted blood. Kadrin's face was bruised, his lip cut, and he held himself like there were more injuries under his clothes. Yi-Nereen knew where Jin's wound came from, but . . .

"Kadrin," she said. "What happened?"

Kadrin's smile faded. "Nothing."

Jin turned on him sharply, as if she'd just been reminded of something. "You said Sou-Zell saved you. Saved you from what?"

Sou-Zell? Clearly there was a lot Yi-Nereen needed catching up

Flight of the Fallen

on. But that could wait. Kadrin's shoulders were hunched forward. His gaze darted back and forth, avoiding resting on anyone's face. A cold numbness grew within Yi-Nereen as she watched him.

"The High Priestess had questions for me," he said, trying and failing to sound casual. "Since she couldn't read my mind, she wanted to make sure I wasn't lying to her. It was bad. But I'm all right now."

Jin kicked a bedpost. Not Eliesen's, but the one beside her. The ensuing strangled snarl that left her lips was like nothing Yi-Nereen had ever heard. "Fuck," Jin gasped, doubling over.

"*Jin,*" Kadrin said.

"I'll *kill* her."

Unlike Jin, Yi-Nereen didn't feel human enough to speak. Into her mind flashed images of High Priestess Edine in her pristine white robe, stained with Kadrin's blood. Was there a name for what she was feeling? She couldn't think of it. It was hotter than rage, this visceral desire to smudge out Edine's existence with the ball of her thumb like a blot of ink.

With the power of the gods, she could do it.

"I don't mean to interrupt." Celwyn's voice was far too calm to match how Yi-Nereen felt inside. "There's something all of you should see."

He touched a sconce on the wall, and an entire section of the wall flickered. Lines of Road Builder script flared across the wall as if penned by an invisible hand at lightning speed. Yi-Nereen took an involuntary step closer, entranced—not enough to forget her wrath, but enough to dull it momentarily. She was dimly aware of Kadrin and Jin behind her, crowding closer to the wall.

"How?"

"While you were exploring, I tried to decipher this. It's hard to explain." Celwyn turned to Jin. "You know what it's like to spark your bike, or to activate a locus? Like part of you is traveling *through* it, and you can feel everything inside?"

"Yeah," Jin said, biting her lip. "I remember."

"This locus is different, but the same. It's like there's a library inside, and I can feel my way around. But the library isn't real. It's just words and connections." The lines of script flickered and changed as Celwyn stared at the wall, hand still pressed to the sconce. "I found this. I think it's instructions. Instructions for how to activate the city."

"What does that mean?" Kadrin asked. "How do you activate a city?"

"Bring it all back to life. It's . . ." Celwyn sighed in frustration. "It's like it's asleep. The barrier was the only thing that remained awake until Yi-Nereen brought it down. If we activate the city, we can use everything without needing a spark. The lifts, the loci, and more. There's so much in here I don't understand, but I can tell it's useful."

What we leave behind is useless or abhorrent to us.

The words rang in Yi-Nereen's head like storm bells. If the gods had really left behind that message, what did it mean? What were the specimens they claimed to have destroyed?

Could the specimens be *people*?

She shook off her hesitation. There wasn't time. If the stories were true and the gods had abandoned this place, so much the better. Just because the gods had found all of this technology useless didn't mean it wasn't a priceless discovery for humanity.

"That's what we need to bring our people here," she said.

"Not just that. Whoever activates the city becomes its . . . guardian? Steward? I'm not sure of the translation. But the steward is

Flight of the Fallen

the only one who can control the citywide systems, like lowering and raising the barrier. There are other systems, too, but I haven't decoded them yet."

"But I lowered the barrier already, from inside the sphere."

"Oh." Celwyn frowned.

"Maybe it's something that can be done in emergencies," Jin said. "That's what happened. We were flying around the Barrens, lost as kittens, when suddenly the city appeared out of nowhere below us."

"But how do we activate the city?" Kadrin asked. "We'll need to do it quickly, before Reena's father gets here. We don't want *him* becoming the steward, or whatever it's called."

"I think we're out of time already," said a weak voice from behind them.

They all turned away from the wall. Eliesen was sitting up in bed, the blood-flecked sheets pooled around her waist as she stared out the window at the far end of the room.

Night had fallen over the city, the unrelenting glare of the sun having given way to cool darkness. The sky was bruise-purple; stars twinkled in the heavens. Something else glowed there, too: an electric-blue pinprick that grew larger the longer Yi-Nereen stared at it. She stood there, mesmerized, until with a sudden dreadful chill she realized exactly what it was.

"It's my father," she whispered.

PART FIVE

CHAPTER THIRTY-SEVEN

RACE AGAINST TIME

Observation #756: Kadrin described a ruined temple with lights
powered by the Spark, similar to my sparklamps, but more
advanced. Road Builder technology runs on electricity?
Hypothesis: Road Builders all sparktalented? —O

Third Age of Storms, 1st Summer, Day 87

The Barrens – Avi'Kerina

For a long moment, Kadrin could do nothing but stare at the bright blue star of Yi-Nereen's father sailing toward Avi'Kerina. Then he shook himself out of his trance and looked around, only to realize no one else had yet done the same. Yi-Nereen and Jin were frozen, eyes fixed on the window. Celwyn had his sword out; that seemed like a good start. Eliesen looked nauseated.

"We need a plan," Kadrin said. "Reena. Can we fight him?"

Yi-Nereen twitched and looked at him. "I couldn't even move," she said hoarsely. "He can immobilize you with his Talent. He's siphoned *far* more people than I have. Dozens, at least."

"I can distract him," Jin said. "On Screech. Celwyn can—"

Celwyn sheathed his sword with a decisive rasp. "If you were going to say *Celwyn can stab him*, I think not. Not while he's in the air. Realistically, the only two people who have a chance at going toe-to-toe with him are you and the princess."

Yi-Nereen cleared her throat. "If we fail—"

"We *won't*," Jin said, at the same time as Celwyn said, "We need a backup plan."

A familiar helplessness roiled inside Kadrin, threatening to paralyze him. He fingered the hilt of Sou-Zell's stiletto and forced himself to breathe. The cool, worn metal under his fingertips soothed him ever so slightly.

"Okay," he said. "Celwyn, you said whoever wakes the city becomes its steward. That needs to be one of us. We don't need to kill Lai-Dan; we just need to make sure he doesn't control the city."

"Won't he just kill us to take over control?" Eliesen asked, her voice weak but steady. Kadrin put his hand on top of hers. Gods, he was glad she was alive.

"Only if he knows that's an option," Celwyn said. "Besides, the steward gains access to everything the city can do. I haven't even scratched the surface of what that means. Weapons, probably. If the steward can figure it out quickly, Lai-Dan's abilities won't matter. We need to keep him distracted."

"Jin and Yi-Nereen are suited for that," Kadrin said, loathing the words as they left his mouth. It was the only option that made sense—but it put both of the women he loved in danger, and he would've swum through acid to find another way. Nonetheless, Jin and Yi-Nereen exchanged looks of resolve and reached for each other's hands at the same time. Kadrin swallowed back a lump in his throat.

"We'll keep him busy as long as it takes," Jin said. "How long *will* it take, exactly?"

Celwyn's fingers twitched on the locus, and the script covering

Flight of the Fallen

the wall vanished. In its place glowed a grid that Kadrin quickly recognized as a two-dimensional aerial map of Avi'Kerina. It helped that he'd seen it from above.

"There are loci here, here, and here." Orange dots glowed in the eastern, western, and northern quadrants of the city. "They all need to be activated manually. Then someone needs to enter the sphere and perform the final activation. It's not clear how."

"I think I know where it needs to be done," Yi-Nereen said. "There's a tree and a pedestal with—with a blinking light. It's how I brought down the barrier."

"We're fucked." Jin frowned at the wall. "Three loci only a sparkrider can activate, scattered across the city? It'll take Celwyn ages to get to all three."

Celwyn dragged a hand across his face. "No. They aren't like the rest of the loci. They can be activated without the spark. I don't know how. We'll find out when we get there."

"Time," Eliesen said, her eyes fixed on the window. "Running out of it."

Outside, the blue light had grown so large Kadrin could see a tiny dark silhouette in the center of it, like the shadow at the heart of a candle flame. Lai-Dan was almost upon the city.

"Jin takes Elie to the northern locus," Kadrin said, his heart hammering. "Celwyn makes a run west, and I head east. Reena keeps Lai-Dan busy until Jin can help. *Don't* take any unnecessary risks."

Yi-Nereen offered him a sickly smile. "Like trying to kill my father alone? Don't worry. With how powerful he's become, it'll take all my effort just to stay alive."

Don't think about that, Kadrin ordered himself.

"Once the loci are activated, whoever can get to the sphere

fastest wakes the city. Probably needs to be somebody airborne. Jin or Reena—if one of you gets an opening while you're distracting Lai-Dan, head for the sphere. Otherwise the rest of us will look for a way to get there."

Celwyn gestured toward one of the lifts. "This one goes to the roof. Kadrin and I head down in the other. The loci are at ground level. Outside, I think. Other than that, I have no idea what they look like."

Kadrin squeezed Eliesen's hand and let go. His sister gave him a flat stare. "Don't be a goddamn hero," she said. Then she climbed gingerly out of bed, leaning on Jin and Reena, and together the three women limped toward the lift headed to the roof. There wasn't time for more farewells; all Kadrin could do was lock eyes with Jin and Reena before the lift entrance shimmered and became opaque behind them.

Please, Rasvel. Let me see them again.

"Come on," Celwyn said, an edge to his voice. "Don't waste time."

They rode to the ground in strained silence. As soon as the chamber stopped moving, Kadrin left the building at a run, Celwyn close behind him. Above him he saw the dark shape of Screech on the wing, heading toward the northern quadrant of the city. Yi-Nereen's blue bubble floated almost serenely near the metal sphere, waiting.

Waiting for Lai-Dan to arrive and for all hell to break loose.

"Good luck," Kadrin said, clapping a hand on Celwyn's shoulder.

The other man didn't reply. There was something tense and purposeful to his posture, like he had a better idea of what they were about to face than Kadrin. And Kadrin wondered, briefly, what else he had seen in the Road Builder library. Surely there hadn't been time for him to tell them everything.

Flight of the Fallen

Fixing the glowing map in his head one more time, Kadrin sprinted eastward.

※

Yi-Nereen landed on the platform outside the sphere and dismissed her shield to save her mana stores. Her heart was beating quickly; she felt dizzy. She wasn't ready for this. But she had no choice.

Down from the sky like a shooting star came her father, leaving a trail of blue sparks glistening in the air. He slowed and stopped, suspended in the air before Yi-Nereen and the sphere. He smiled at her—that warm, affectionate smile he reserved for moments when Yi-Nereen was playing the role of a good daughter.

"You look well, Nereena. I feared for you after the attack, but when my knights couldn't find your body, I knew you and your friends must have escaped." Lai-Dan spread his arms wide. "The First City. Isn't it wonderful? It looks *exactly* how I thought it would."

Not for the first time, Yi-Nereen wondered if her father knew how absurd and self-congratulating he sounded. Like he was the first to know everything before it happened, as if he had personally made it so. She'd feared him for so long; she feared him still, but somehow she'd also grown *embarrassed* on his behalf.

Trying to engage him with conversation was a false hope. This could only end in violence. But every moment she kept him talking was another moment for Kadrin, Celwyn, and Eliesen to reach their loci.

"Where are your knights, Father?" she asked, summoning a lifetime of practice to hide the tremble in her voice. "Did you leave them behind?"

"Of course not." Lai-Dan placed a hand over his heart. "They are with me. From now on, forever."

Yi-Nereen had expected such an answer, but still a shiver ran through her body. Even her father wasn't powerful enough to have flown here from the site of the saurian attack, not without a massive infusion of power: the Last Breaths of his surviving knights. He still held most of that power within himself; she saw it in the pulse of his shield, a strength that showed no signs of waning.

She had only ever infused a single Last Breath: Faolin's. What was it like to drink so many, all at once? Only her father knew. It was a terrible, profane knowledge, and she would strike it from the world or die trying. But still, a part of her wanted to know.

What we leave behind is useless or abhorrent to us.

It was us, Yi-Nereen thought. People. Like her father, and like herself. The gods were long gone; they would never grant her redemption. Her salvation would come neither at their hands, nor at her father's. Only at her own.

"Nereena." Lai-Dan's voice sharpened. "I am no fool. You have always been the cleverest of my children, the most ambitious. The sand scorpion devours its parent once it hatches, and I know your sting, my dearest, so I can take no chances. The First City must be mine and mine alone. We cannot rule it together."

"I know, Father."

Yi-Nereen inched toward the edge of the platform, wind rustling through her hair and clothes, tension humming in every muscle. She had spent her whole life in high places, imagining what it would be like to fall. There were times when death had seemed like the only way out. Now she knew the only true escape was to live. Live free of Lai-Dan, of any man who wanted to become a god.

Flight of the Fallen

Death was still the solution. But it would be her father's death, not hers.

She saw her father's hand twitch, and she was ready. Before his shield could form to her shape and restrain her, she called hers forth as a protective dome. Lai-Dan's eyes narrowed. She felt him probing her barrier, testing his strength against hers, and she saw the fury flash across his face when he failed to overwhelm her instantly.

"Do not waste my time, Nereena. This can only end one way, and you know it."

He sent a barrage of slicing shield-blades flying toward her. A scream tore free of Yi-Nereen's lips. She felt the blades raking across her flesh; her shield guttered like a candle in the wind. She was already sweating, weak and trembling.

No. She had to be stronger than this. She had to keep Lai-Dan occupied long enough for her friends to seize Avi'Kerina. Cowering here under her shield wouldn't be enough. She had to defend herself *and* fight back. If her father could keep himself aloft and attack her at the same time, so could she.

She split her focus, shaping part of her shield into a lance while maintaining the bubble. A yelp escaped her lips as she dropped several inches in the air. It was like trying to hold on to a wet bar of soap and braid her hair with the same hand. Her pathetic attempt at a lance crumbled into glowing blue dust and disappeared.

Lai-Dan watched her with paternal disappointment. Yi-Nereen's blood boiled at the sight of that expression on his face. He hadn't earned the right to judge her; he had *never* treated her as a father should have.

The anger swelled inside her like a ripe fruit and burst. Her lance re-formed in an instant and shot across the air, shattering on contact with Lai-Dan's shield into a thousand glittering shards.

"You've always been a fast learner." Her father hadn't so much as flinched. "But cleverness cannot outpace strength. It's time you learned that."

More blades flew toward her, enough to shred her shield to pieces.

Yi-Nereen fled.

She shot across the sky with her father in pursuit, zigzagging to evade the glowing blue missiles he sent soaring after her. It wasn't a fair fight. But she didn't have to win. She just had to outlast him—his mana stores couldn't be endless, no matter how many knights he'd siphoned, and pressing the offensive like this would surely cost him.

All she had to do was survive.

Survive, like she'd done for twenty years under his roof. She could do this.

She had to.

Jin had no idea what the northern locus looked like or how she'd spot it from the air. A great glowing sign was probably too much to ask for.

She urged Screech to fly lower, weaving in between the metal towers. The pteropter was tiring noticeably. He'd flown Jin and Kadrin hundreds of miles in a single evening with hardly any rest. Now his muscles were quivering and he was slower to respond to Jin's commands, when he bothered to respond to them at all.

On the whole, Screech made his own choices and Jin was just along for the ride. As a pair, they needed a *lot* more practice flying together. If Lai-Dan took over Avi'Kerina and the kerinas fell, Jin supposed they'd have plenty of time to train; what else was there to do in the wastes, with no home to go back to? But anyway, that only mattered if they both survived tonight.

Clinging to Jin's back, Eliesen shouted, "There! That has to be it."

Below them, nestled between three towers, was a tiered pavilion carved into the ground. At its center was a black obelisk, almost invisible save for the moonlight that glinted off its reflective surface.

"Screech can't take off from the ground with a rider," Jin warned Eliesen. "I'm going to have to drop you. It's going to be rough."

"Thanks for the warning, darling," Eliesen said with a hysterical little laugh. "Do it."

"Down," Jin told Screech, pointing at the pavilion. *"Down."*

Apparently the pteropter was fed up with her. He folded his wings and careened like a dropped stone. Eliesen screamed, shrill in Jin's ear, and Jin let loose a string of curses. Her eyes watered in the wind.

At the last moment, Screech opened his wings and skimmed the top of the obelisk. Jin felt Eliesen's grip around her midsection loosen. As Screech beat his wings to regain altitude, Jin forced herself to look down, fully expecting to see Eliesen in a crumpled, broken heap on the ground.

Sitting on her rump, already small as Screech soared away, Eliesen waved. "I'm okay!" she called faintly.

Jin collapsed onto Screech's neck in relief.

"So much for being a fucking saurian rider. Let's go help Reena."

Kadrin stared at the glossy black surface of the obelisk. It was easily twice his height. *Think like a Road Builder*, he told himself. Which was completely useless, because the Road Builders had died out centuries before he was born, and all he knew about them was that they liked to build roads—and apparently, cities.

He placed a hand tentatively on the obelisk's side. Celwyn and Yi-Nereen had gotten a lot of mileage out of just *touching* Road Builder technology. But the obelisk didn't shimmer or light up or even burst into flames. The stone was cool under his palm.

Maybe Celwyn was wrong. Maybe you did have to be a sparkrider to activate these loci, just like all the others they'd encountered. If that was the case, they were screwed. But—Kadrin wrinkled his brow in thought—so was Lai-Dan.

Above him, two glowing blue spheres chased each other through the heavens, spitting shards of light at each other like sparks. Kadrin couldn't tell from the ground which was Yi-Nereen and which was her father. His pulse hadn't stopped racing in what felt like hours.

He didn't have time to stand here, wishing he'd struggled through more books on the Road Builders as a youth. He had to *do* something.

It's like it's asleep, Celwyn had said.

Kadrin didn't know anything about Road Builder cities. But he did have plenty of experience waking people up. Eliesen had an annoying habit of sleeping in past noon when they were supposed to go out together.

Hadn't Toraka used that word to describe what Celwyn had done to the tablet with the map? *Awaken?*

"Hey." He gave the obelisk a light slap. "Wake up. Rise and shine. Um . . . activate?"

Nothing. Desperation mounting, Kadrin slapped the stone again, hard enough to jar the bones in his hand.

"For Rasvel's sake, *wake the fuck up!*"

Flight of the Fallen

High on the obelisk, above his head, a pair of white lights appeared on its surface. Kadrin froze. He truly hadn't expected that to work. Even more oddly, the lights had a familiar shape to them: glowing white eyes. He'd seen those eyes before, in paintings and illustrated scrolls.

"Wake word: Rasvel, received," stated a calm, flat voice that seemed to originate from somewhere deep inside the obelisk. *"Initiating systems. Please be patient. Connecting to satellite network. Connection failed. Retrying . . . Please be patient. Connection failed. Retrying . . ."*

It was *talking.* The obelisk was talking to him. Had he done it? Or had he just gone quietly insane?

"Connection failed. Retrying . . . Connection succeeded."

CHAPTER THIRTY-EIGHT

THE CITY AWAKENS

Observation #671: May have been too hasty to declare saurians soulless. Rather dogmatic of me, wasn't it?
Future study: Define parameters for what a soul is before accusing anyone or anything of lacking one. —O

Third Age of Storms, 1st Summer, Day 87

The Barrens – Avi'Kerina

"*T*wo *access points are currently offline. Fail-safes are currently active. Warning. Sensors indicate wildlife activity inside city limits.*"

"Um," Kadrin said slowly, cautiously. "Are you activated?"

"*Yes,*" replied the obelisk. "*Access Point North is online.*"

He was standing in front of a talking obelisk in the city of the gods while Yi-Nereen battled her father in the sky above him. A screech rattled the towers and a dark shape blotted out the stars; Jin must have dropped off Eliesen and joined the fray.

Heaven help him, Kadrin had never felt so out of his element.

"*Two access points are currently offline. Fail-safes are currently active . . .*"

Celwyn and Eliesen hadn't activated their obelisks yet. Kadrin had stumbled across the wake word by pure chance; there was no guarantee the other two would. He had to go and help them.

Mentally orienting himself, Kadrin turned toward the northwest side of the pavilion—and froze. He wasn't alone.

The saurian stood on two legs, lean and corded with muscle. Its tail lashed slowly back and forth as it considered Kadrin, birdlike head cocked to one side. It resembled the rovex he'd faced with Sou-Zell on Mount Vetelu, only smaller and more svelte. For a single hopeful moment Kadrin wondered if it would speak to him, too.

"Sensors indicate wildlife activity inside city limits. Restoring power to the repulsion field is recommended."

The saurian stalked closer. Hooked claws gleamed on both of its forelimbs. Kadrin felt a droplet of cold sweat worming its way down the back of his collar. The worn hilt of Sou-Zell's stiletto utterly failed to provide him any comfort.

"Uh—any chance you can help me kill a saurian?"

"Opening emergency weapon cache."

The base of the obelisk opened along invisible hinges, and a drawer glided out. Holding his breath, Kadrin peered inside. Resting inside the metal drawer was the strangest object he'd ever seen in his life, including all the mysterious contraptions in Orrin's workshop. It looked like the bastard child of a crossbow and a fencing rapier, with neither string nor blade.

He reached in gingerly and picked it up, fitting his left hand to an obvious grip, running his right hand along the strangely shaped stock. It was heavier than a sword should be. Unwieldy. No sharp bits, either. A ranged weapon?

Kadrin turned his back on the obelisk. The saurian had prowled so close he could see its nostrils flaring in the moonlight. His hands tightened on the unfamiliar weapon. He might be about to die, but gods, tonight he'd seen wonders he'd never dreamed of before.

The saurian sprang.

Screech careened through the sky with Jin holding on for dear life. Once they'd cleared the pavilion and gained altitude, he'd seen Lai-Dan chasing Yi-Nereen across the city and his shrieking call had taken on a different pitch—something furious and territorial. Like he was pissed off that there was another predator hunting in his sky.

Below them, Lai-Dan broke off his pursuit, and his bubble went veering sideways. Screech pulled out of his dive and sailed past. For the briefest of instants, Jin locked eyes with Yi-Nereen's father through the glowing blue veil that separated them. She felt the searing heat of his hatred—or maybe it was her own.

Well, she had his attention now.

Blue light slashed toward Screech, and Jin flattened herself against his back with a curse. The pteropter shrieked, a sound of agony that rattled the heavens and left Jin's ears ringing.

Raising her head from his feathers, she saw that Lai-Dan's shield-blade had cut a deep gash across Screech's breastbone. Drops of blood pattered down from the sky like steaming rain. In a flash, Jin remembered the saurians who'd ambushed them in the Barrens; Yi-Nereen's blade had been useless against them. Was Screech different, or had Lai-Dan simply grown too powerful?

"Hey!" Jin screamed. "You motherfucker, why don't you—?"

Her voice dissolved into a yelp as Screech pitched to the left to avoid another slash of blue light. Jin locked her heels between

Flight of the Fallen

his wing joints and managed to stay seated—barely. Between his churning wings she saw Yi-Nereen hovering near a slim, needle-shaped tower. She shouted something, but Jin couldn't understand her across the distance and through her shield's distortion.

Then she saw a black mass sweep across the sky from the west, cloaking the stars. Pteropters.

In moments the flock was upon Avi'Kerina. The air became a ca-cophony of shrieks so deafening Jin almost let go of Screech's feathers to cover her ears. Screech flapped and spiraled through the sky, surrounded by a storm of swirling wings.

He'd called them somehow—or they'd responded to his shriek of pain.

Lai-Dan's blue bubble disappeared under a mass of small claw-ing, flapping bodies. Overwhelmed, but surely not for long.

Jin clung to Screech as he glided overhead. She pulled her-self forward, inch by inch, until she could see the wound on his breastbone.

"Land," she said in his ear. "He'll kill you. I mean it, you stupid little beast. Land!"

Screech clacked his beak testily. Blood flowed in an oozing stream down his feathered belly. He gave her another of those ob-stinate backward looks that Jin was beginning to interpret as *No, I don't think I will,* as if somehow he understood that the entire plan to keep Avi'Kerina from falling into Lai-Dan's hands hinged on him staying in the sky to play keep-away with Yi-Nereen.

Jin groaned in despair.

Below them, the ball of pteropters burst apart in a scorching wave of blue light. Lai-Dan surged out of the fray, untouched. Small bodies fell from the sky, striking towers, thumping off metal.

Jin remembered Screech the way he'd first appeared to her—a tiny, snapping creature with a broken wing, small enough to fit in her helm—and her chest seized and caught fire.

She wanted Lai-Dan dead. She *needed* it.

"Have it your way, then," she growled, wrapping her arms around Screech's neck. "Let's make the fucker dance."

Kadrin ran for all he was worth, the heavy Road Builder weapon cradled in his arm, boots pounding the pavement of Avi'Kerina. Behind him streamed a pack of fleet-footed saurians, howling for his blood.

He spotted the northern pavilion ahead, identical to the one where he'd found his obelisk: concentric rings separated by strips of darker stone, with a towering black obelisk in the middle. Eliesen's small figure crouched in front of the obelisk. No glowing lights—she hadn't activated it yet.

"Elie!" Kadrin shouted. "Run!"

He skidded to a stop, whirled around, fell to one knee, and braced the Road Builder weapon against his shoulder. It had taken him all of a few feverish, desperate seconds to figure out how it worked back at the eastern pavilion. As it turned out, unlike Orrin, the Road Builders had believed in simplicity of function.

The pack of saurians advanced on him in a ragged formation, eyes rolling in predatory hunger, foreclaws scything the air.

Kadrin pulled the trigger, and the weapon kicked back into his shoulder with a glorious roar and sprayed multicolored light in a wide arc.

The saurians let loose howling shrieks as the light seared through flesh and bone, filling the air with a horrid stench. One or two fell writhing to the ground. The rest retreated, snarling and nursing burns. Kadrin backed slowly away, weapon still held to his shoulder, until he was well into the pavilion. The saurians hissed at him but didn't pursue.

"What the fuck," said a voice from behind him, "was *that*."

Eliesen hadn't run. She was standing with her back to the obelisk, eyes wide and fixed on the weapon in Kadrin's hands.

Panting, covered in sweat, Kadrin grinned. "I have no idea, but I like it."

Eliesen blinked. Her lips pulled back into a feral smile.

"Can I have one?"

Down Screech plummeted, wings folded, claws raked forward. From the eastern half of the city hurtled Yi-Nereen, held aloft by her shield. They converged on Lai-Dan, who hung frozen in the air for a fraction of a second. Then he came to a decision—and shot away, leaving a trail of blue sparks in his wake.

"Yes," Jin whooped, momentarily forgetting her fear of heights as she pumped the air with her fist. "Run, you bastard!"

Screech angled his body and shot after Lai-Dan. Yi-Nereen crossed over them, so close Jin felt the sizzle of her shield an arm's length away, and in a flash she was perched at the top of a tower, shieldless, gripping a metal spire. From her outstretched fingers poured forth a barrage of blue shards. They streaked after Lai-Dan, and Screech bobbed and wove around them, braiding through the air, light and flesh.

Jin's heart was in her throat. They had Lai-Dan on the run. If he turned to attack Screech, Yi-Nereen's shards would catch his shield full-on. They were doing it, keeping him occupied—

Then Screech made a strangled sound, like an aborted shriek. His wings snapped open, all four of them. It was like hitting a brick wall midair.

Jin didn't have a chance to grab hold of anything; she simply flew forward, straight off his back, hundreds of feet above Avi'Kerina.

She saw flashes as she fell. Screech beating the air with his wings, twin orange lights burning deep in his black eyes. Where had she seen that before? Off to the side, a figure standing on the roof of a nearby tower. Not Yi-Nereen. A man with eyes glowing hot spark-orange, chanting with his hands raised as he held Screech suspended in the sky like a giant puppet.

Celwyn.

You absolute motherfucker, Jin wanted to say, but her lungs were empty.

For a breathless moment, Yi-Nereen watched Jin fall.

A voice whispered inside her. *Not again.*

She launched herself from the tower. Pure instinct and desperation summoned a wave of blue energy that propelled her forward and surged ahead. A faint shimmering bubble flickered around Jin's tiny figure as she fell, then disappeared.

Too far. She was too far away. Yi-Nereen's power wasn't strong enough to work over such a distance. *She* wasn't strong enough, hadn't siphoned enough—

"*No!*" she screamed, a raw sound that flayed open her throat, and

Flight of the Fallen

power bloomed inside her like a brutal flower opening to the sun. She felt the mana as it burned through her veins. The whole world came alive around her, a web of glistening threads, and she reached out along that network and gathered Jin into the palm of her invisible hand. Plucked her from the sky as she fell, like fruit from a tree. Her blood was on fire. She pulled Jin closer and the web bent around them into unnatural shapes.

It was *wrong*, she could feel it, but the world where she let Jin fall would have been even more wrong.

One more push, and—

They tumbled onto a roof together, high above the world but *safe*, a tangle of heaving chests and trembling limbs. Yi-Nereen reached out with a shaking hand to tuck Jin's hair behind her ear so she could see her face, to reassure herself Jin was alive—but Jin was struggling to her feet, yelling for her pteropter.

"Screech! Oh, that raider bastard, I'll *flay* him!"

"What?"

Yi-Nereen hadn't seen what happened, why Jin had fallen from Screech's back. Now she followed Jin's gaze to a rooftop several towers over.

Celwyn stood there, palm raised and eyes burning orange, and Jin's pteropter drifted toward him as if dazed. Yi-Nereen grabbed Jin's arm.

"He's using sparktalent to control him. It's what Tibius Vann did to the rovex."

"I don't give a fuck what he's doing, *why's he doing it?* He almost killed me!"

"That," Yi-Nereen said in a low voice, "is a very good question."

She burned mana to reach across the void toward Celwyn, to

crush him—only to stagger backward as pain ripped through her temples. Dry. She was dry. Whatever she'd done to catch Jin had taken everything she had.

Jin caught her as she slumped bonelessly onto the rooftop.

"Hey," she said, her voice husky with alarm, hair falling into her eyes as she leaned over Yi-Nereen. "Can you . . . is there anything you can take? From me?"

The question pricked Yi-Nereen like a thorn. For Rasvel's sake, she'd already stolen everything from Jin, and still Jin wanted to give her more. What was Yi-Nereen to deserve that kind of devotion? Nothing, no one. She loved Jin with all she had because she didn't know another way, not because she wanted anything in return.

She was about to say as much when a hand gripped Jin's shoulder and flung her aside.

Yi-Nereen's father loomed over her. Blood streamed from both nostrils and along the crease of his mouth; his skin was sickly gray. Clearly she wasn't the only one who'd overexerted herself. The chase had caught up to them both.

But Lai-Dan was still stronger than her. He always had been.

He wrapped his hands around her throat—like she was six years old and he'd caught her scribbling notes into the margins of her grandfather's biography again—and dragged her to her feet.

"Nereena," he breathed, his face inches from hers. "Flesh of my flesh. I made everything you are. And *I can take it back.*"

Yi-Nereen couldn't breathe. Couldn't cry out. Through the fog, she heard Jin scream her name. They'd changed places, but in the end it was the same. Love wouldn't save either of them.

Then her father descended on her, crushing and brutal, and in the agonizing rush of her soul leaving her body, she heard nothing more.

CHAPTER THIRTY-NINE

LAST BREATH

Observation #773: In light of observation #771, I'll need leverage on whoever does control Avi'Kerina. It won't be Kadrin, more's the pity. Someone close to Kadrin? Influence by proxy? Further study: Review Kadrin's family and friends. —O

Third Age of Storms, 1st Summer, Day 87
The Barrens – Avi'Kerina

"Rasvel," Kadrin said.

"Wake word: Rasvel, received. Initiating systems. Please be patient. Connecting to satellite network. Connection succeeded. All access points are currently online."

"What the fuck?" Eliesen whispered, her eyes wide and fixed on the obelisk.

Kadrin smiled. She was going to like what he said next.

"Give me a weapon."

"Opening emergency weapon cache."

The base of the obelisk slid open and Eliesen's jaw dropped.

Above them, intermittent flashes of blue lit up the sky and shrieks echoed through the heavens. Kadrin didn't bother looking anymore. His brain, which was normally engaged at all times in the task of finding fault with himself, had finally gone quiet and focused on a single task: finishing what he'd come here to do. Nothing else mattered.

"Fail-safes are currently active. Citywide connection pending removal of fail-safes from central hub access point. Would you like transport to the central hub?"

Kadrin raised an eyebrow. Was it really that easy? He glanced at the ground, wondering if a lift would appear beneath his feet.

"Yes, please."

"One moment."

The obelisk split open like a flower, unfurling into a reticulated spiral. A staircase assembling itself before Kadrin's eyes. It stretched upward, climbing impossibly high into the sky. Toward the metal sphere that hung motionless at the city's center.

"I'm sober, aren't I?" Eliesen whispered, cradling a second Road Builder weapon in her arms. "I don't feel sober."

Kadrin grabbed her hand. "Come on. Hurry."

"Where are Jin and Yi-Nereen? Did they make it to the sphere?"

"I don't know. Something's wrong."

The sky had gone quiet. Small pteropters still flitted back and forth between the towers, but Kadrin couldn't see Screech or Yi-Nereen's glowing bubble. Dread gripped him. He knew what the silence had to mean, but he couldn't—he couldn't let himself think. He had to keep going.

Nothing else mattered.

Eliesen's hand tightened on his. "Okay." The bandage on her shoulder was stained with fresh blood and her face was pale. "Let's go."

Together, they ran up the staircase.

Jin landed hard on her injured arm. She skidded toward the edge of the rooftop and caught herself against a raised rail. Pain blazed like fire along her forearm, but she barely noticed it. She was on her feet in moments, Yi-Nereen's name forming on her tongue, the genesis of a scream.

It was too late. Lai-Dan stood entwined with his daughter and around them glowed an impenetrable shield. Jin threw herself at it, alight with desperation. But it was hopeless. And it was Jin's fault. Yi-Nereen had spent her reserves and made herself vulnerable to save her.

"You should have let me fall!" Jin screamed, pounding her fists on the shield. Blood streamed fresh and hot from the reopened wound on her arm. *"Reena!"*

Lai-Dan wouldn't stop. And when he was done, when Yi-Nereen was dead, he'd come for Jin next. Tossing her from the top of this tower would be child's play, like flicking an insect from his robe. Then he'd go after Kadrin.

Jin spun around, searching the rooftops for Celwyn: the man who'd caused this, the man she'd kill if it was the last thing she did in this life.

He was nowhere to be seen. Neither was Screech.

Kadrin had listened to Yi-Nereen's description of what lay inside the sphere, but nothing could have truly prepared him for what it looked like. The air left his lungs as soon as he stepped inside.

The trees, the riotous flowers, the insects buzzing to and fro. The way the ground became the ceiling, like someone had taken the earth and folded it over on itself. The smell of life and decay all around.

"Which way?" Eliesen panted, clutching her shoulder. He heard pain in her voice, but he knew it wouldn't stop her. Kadrin might have spent years inuring himself to suffering, but Eliesen was stubborn enough to get there without practice.

Kadrin did a quick mental calculation based on where they'd entered the sphere and Yi-Nereen's described route to the plinth.

"This way," he said, less than half-sure.

But for once in his life, his intellect hadn't failed him. He and Eliesen burst out of the greenery into a clearing dominated by a massive tree. And there stood Celwyn, before a metal plinth nestled between the tree's roots.

His back was turned to Kadrin and Eliesen; he was staring down at an array of glowing lights.

"Celwyn?" Kadrin said. "How did you get here?"

At the sound of his voice, Celwyn stiffened. Slowly, he turned.

"I caught a ride." His voice was toneless. "The city only needs one steward, you know. Neither of you are needed here. You should go."

Kadrin frowned, baffled. "You just decided it should be you?" Suspicion wormed its way up his spine. "That wasn't the plan. Where are Reena and Jin?"

"Plans change," Celwyn said.

"What the fuck does that mean?" Eliesen demanded, shouldering her way past Kadrin. "If you wanted to be the steward, you should have— Oh." Eliesen blinked. "You're not Celwyn, are you?"

Kadrin wasn't following this conversation at all. His confusion only deepened as Celwyn's nostrils flared and he said, his voice harsh and clipped, "Clever, Eliesen. How did you know?"

Eliesen's jaw tightened. "Let's say we've gotten to know each other rather well over the past few days. I was thinking about asking you to my favorite tavern when we got back and seeing where the night took us. Besides, I can tell when someone's playing a part. I do it all the time."

"Eliesen," Kadrin said in a low voice, "I'm seriously lost."

"Remember, Celwyn isn't just Celwyn. He's sharing his body with one of the wastelanders Jin and Yi-Nereen met—or didn't meet, rather. Amrys, right? He told us they were symbiotic, but it looks like that was a load of saurian crap. I think they've been trading control back and forth and Celwyn just didn't know it."

Celwyn smiled thinly. "Close, but you're wrong. It was Celwyn's decision to cede control. It always is. This is the arrangement we found, and it works for us. It's not insanity or a constant battle of wits. And we even agree on most things: like the fact that Avi'Kerina is *dangerous*. And it must be destroyed."

From the moment of Yi-Nereen's birth, she'd been her father's possession: the unwilling heir to his legacy. A legacy he would never allow her to keep. Not *her*.

To him, she was nothing more than an empty womb.

She saw it all in fading starbursts of memory as her life slipped through her fingers. Eldest of three daughters, the first to taste her father's wrath when any of them made a mistake. His gaze lingering on her as she'd grown. The faces of the men and women she'd watched being led up the Tower steps to the chamber where her father waited to drain them. Her mother, still and lifeless on blood-stained sheets.

How many times had she tried to die on her own terms and escape him forever? He'd assigned her a bodyguard to keep Yi-Nereen safe from herself as much as anyone else. His way of saying *I control you, body and soul, from the day you were born until the day you die.*

But he hadn't counted on Teul-Kim's loyalty. His love for her, a devotion that had soon outstripped his fealty to the Shield Lord. It was Teul-Kim who had urged Yi-Nereen to escape. At the time she hadn't understood his love, hadn't understood how *anyone* could love someone like her. But he had, and he wasn't the last.

Yi-Nereen's body burned as her father's kiss tore the life from her. She couldn't fight him off. Didn't have the mana to burn for a shield.

All she had was what he'd given her: his cursed Talent, the ability to siphon.

Reversing the flow of mana between them was like reversing the direction of her blood as it moved through her veins. Impossible. Unthinkable. She had only moments before her life was snuffed out forever. But to live, she had to try.

And she *wanted* to live. For Kadrin, for Jin. For herself.

The sand scorpion devours its parent once it hatches.

It was a battle of wills. Her father's physical strength wouldn't help him here. Nor would his experience in siphoning. No—this was a simple matter of whose desire to survive was stronger. Who had more to live for.

She didn't need the gods for this.

Yi-Nereen fixed Kadrin's and Jin's faces in her mind, blazing stars in the darkness. Inch by inch, she clawed back the power as it flowed from her body. She sensed Lai-Dan's shock reverberating

Flight of the Fallen

along their connection. He had never imagined *she* could resist him. Never thought that by preying on her, he'd make himself vulnerable. And then—

—she was siphoning her father, drinking in his power in hungry gulps.

She was an endless well; she'd been starving all her life, and she'd never known it. Lai-Dan had deprived her of everything: safety, innocence, love. He'd created this void in her chest and now he would be the one to fill it.

She felt her father fighting back, struggling to reverse the flow as she'd done—but how could he? How could a man who knew nothing of sacrifice comprehend the bitterness of her hatred, and the strength it gave her?

Her father's power was sweeter than ambrosia, deeper than the fullest-bodied wine. All those souls, gathered together and aged for so many years. The deaths of a hundred innocents.

The more she drank, the more she understood.

Her father had never seen himself as a king, but as a shepherd ruling over a flock whose flesh would one day sustain him. A god. And in some ways, he was.

If she drank him whole, what did that make her?

She almost stopped. But no. *No.*

Her father had used this power to manipulate and subjugate, to hold himself over others, but she wasn't like him. This was not Tibius Vann all over again. She had a choice. To let this power fade away, to die with her father, or to make all those deaths mean something.

Reena, Jin was calling desperately somewhere distant. *Please.*

I'm coming back to you, Yi-Nereen thought fiercely.

And she wrenched away her father's Last Breath.

"Destroyed?" Kadrin repeated. "Why in Rasvel's name would you destroy it?"

A wild light danced in Celwyn's eyes. "You haven't seen what I've seen, Kadrin. The gods lived here, but not as gods do—as men do. Because they weren't gods. They were like us."

"Like us how?"

"They ate. They slept. They made war. Avi'Kerina may have been the First City, but it wasn't the last. There are more of them out there in the Barrens, concealed from the naked eye. And they contain weapons beyond our comprehension." Celwyn shuddered. "Can you imagine a city like this in the hands of every despot like the Shield Lord of Kerina Rut? The gods were right to abandon this place. To abandon *us*. If I destroy Avi'Kerina, no one will find the other cities. My people will be safe."

Kadrin couldn't help it; even though looking away from Celwyn was asking for trouble, he glanced at Elie and saw his disbelief reflected on her face. *More* cities?

Avi'Kerina was already legend made real, myth made material—and Kadrin knew he wasn't the only one who still had trouble believing it. But if Celwyn was telling the truth, Avi'Kerina wasn't the stuff of stories because gods had walked here. There hadn't been any gods to begin with. Just people.

And if there were no gods, then the fact that Kadrin was Talentless meant . . . Well, he still didn't know. But it had *changed* in ways he couldn't begin to process or contemplate right now, with Celwyn's hand hovering above the panel that would doom them all.

"Is that what you saw in the library? Why didn't you say anything?"

Flight of the Fallen

But Kadrin realized the answer even as he asked the question. Who would have believed Celwyn if he did tell them? Celwyn was the only true sparkrider, the only one who could access the library. And if he believed Avi'Kerina needed to be destroyed, then of course Lai-Dan had to be stopped. They'd all been on the same side until now.

Based on the horror in Eliesen's eyes, she'd come to the same conclusion. "Celwyn, you can't do this. We *need* Avi'Kerina. The people of the kerinas won't survive unless we can bring them here. The storms are out of control."

Celwyn sneered. "Your people. Not mine."

"What the fuck are you talking about?"

"This place is the cradle. Your people were created here: products of the gods' experiments. Chattel, saturated with the lifeblood of this planet to survive the storms and build their roads and shining cities. My people fled into the desert and remained pure. When the springs run dry and your people die, mine will survive."

"Celwyn," Eliesen said. "I don't care whose people are whose. *You* can stop this."

"Celwyn the Talentless exile? Celwyn the raider? Was he one of your people? He doesn't think so. All he wants is to atone for what he's done. The people he's killed. Myself among them." Celwyn smiled. "This is how he does it."

"Well," Eliesen snarled, "*I* won't let you do it."

Kadrin had never heard her sound so vicious. Eliesen was a prankster, his devil-may-care sister who could charm anyone into forgetting her many flaws. But in moments like these, he remembered that when Eliesen truly wanted something, she *always* got her way.

Slowly, Eliesen aimed her weapon at Celwyn.

419

"Move away from the . . . whatever it is. The thing with all the blinking lights. You don't want to see what this weapon does."

Hesitation flickered across Celwyn's face, but he set his jaw. "You won't use it."

Kadrin stiffened. "Celwyn, *don't*—"

Celwyn spun around and pressed one of the blinking lights on the plinth. The sphere shuddered. Kadrin raised his weapon, but he was slower than Eliesen, who screamed in wordless fury and fired.

Light poured from the barrel of her weapon. Celwyn fell to the ground, writhing and smoking. Kadrin couldn't tell if the hit had been fatal; Celwyn certainly wasn't dead yet, but the stench of charred flesh thickened the air.

"Self-destruction sequence initiated. The city will be destroyed in five minutes."

The calm voice issued from the pedestal and echoed around the inside of the sphere. Kadrin's stomach dropped.

"I should have been faster," Eliesen said, her face pale. "Kadrin . . ."

Gods, this couldn't be real. It couldn't end like this. Not when they were so close.

"Maybe it isn't too late." Kadrin stepped in front of the plinth and cleared his throat. "Um, hello. I'd like to cancel the self-destruction sequence. How do I do that, exactly?"

"The city's steward is authorized to cancel the sequence. Currently, there is no steward on file."

"I want to become steward of Avi'Kerina."

"Have you been examined by a trained physician and signed your waiver? If you would like to proceed, repeat the following code: Ascend."

"Don't be a fool," Celwyn gasped. He was curled up on the ground, clutching his chest. Blood seeped between his fingers.

Flight of the Fallen

"That system was meant for gods. You're only mortal. Your body won't survive it."

Kadrin stared hard at the plinth. He was sweating through his shirt, he had a vicious headache, and he didn't understand anything about this place or the technology they'd discovered. But in the end, it was all so horrendously simple.

"Even if I don't survive it," he said, "I'll live long enough to undo what you did, won't I? That's why you had to stop us."

"Kadrin." Eliesen's voice cut him like a dagger. She laid a hand on his arm and tugged his face until he looked her in the eye. "You don't get to do this." Her voice softened, became a plea. "I know you think you're only worth something if you're somebody else's sacrifice. You're wrong."

Kadrin fit a trembling hand to her cheek. "It's okay," he choked out. "Everything will be okay." He thought of his mother in the darkened hallway, holding out her bag of seeds, and his throat threatened to close. "Tell Mother I did forgive her. It didn't take long."

"I love you," Eliesen said. "You're the best person I know. I've always needed you—and so does everyone else. You show us how to be better."

She turned her face from him, a tear slipping from the corner of her eye, and Kadrin realized what she was about to do—a moment too late.

"Sorry, Kadrin. This one's mine. Ascend."

CHAPTER FORTY

THE STEWARD

Observation #685: Standing definition of a soul as linked to mana affinity is a theological argument. In other words, worthless. A sparkrider I interviewed made the claim that magebikes have souls. Conclusion: Likely worthless as well, but concept of a machine soul intrigues. —O

Third Age of Storms, 1st Summer, Day 87

The Barrens – Avi'Kerina

The moment the shield fell, Jin was there, ready to catch Yi-Nereen's lifeless body as she crumpled into her arms. Lai-Dan could kill her, but he couldn't stop her from holding his daughter one last time.

But it wasn't Yi-Nereen who fell. It was her father, limp as a broken doll. Jin froze as the Shield Lord of Kerina Rut collapsed onto the rooftop, his robes pooling around him. His eyes were open and glassy. Blood gleamed on his lips.

Yi-Nereen stood alone. Her head was bowed; her hair hung around her face like an inky veil. All Jin could see was her mouth, streaked with blood.

Was this real?

"Reena?" Jin whispered.

Slowly, Yi-Nereen raised her head. Jin's chest pulled tight. Yi-Nereen's eyes were pitch-black, irises and sclera both. As Jin stared at her, speechless, the black slowly bled away. Within moments, Yi-Nereen's eyes were ordinary again. But the chill that had pierced Jin's chest would take much longer to fade.

"I had to do it." Yi-Nereen's voice was small, broken. "Don't look at me like that, Jin. I *had* to kill him."

Jin blinked. "No, I—"

She wasn't horrified at Lai-Dan's death. Far from it. Gods, she couldn't be more pleased the bastard was dead. Words failed her. All she could do was reach for Yi-Nereen and draw her close, just as she'd planned—except Yi-Nereen was alive, warm in her arms, *alive*.

They sank to the rooftop together. Yi-Nereen trembled like her body was dissolving; Jin held her, stroking her hair. She pressed kiss after kiss to the crown of Yi-Nereen's head, delirious with relief.

A familiar shriek cut the air, and with a great gust of air Screech swooped down upon the rooftop. Jin hadn't cried while she was holding Reena, but now her eyes stung with tears.

"You damned little beast, where'd you go? You *dropped* me."

Screech chirped as if in apology and shuffled closer, dipping his head. The gash on his breastbone still bled slowly into his feathers. Jin reached out, one eye squeezed shut, and gingerly placed her palm on his beak. He closed both eyes and leaned into her touch.

"Look at us," Yi-Nereen said with a sobbing laugh. "A saurian tamer and a patricide."

Jin smiled. "Kadrin's a lucky man, isn't he?"

A moment ago Kadrin had been screaming. The garden drank the sound of his voice and turned it into silence, reflecting it back a thousandfold until he was crushed beneath its weight.

In the silence, a calm machine voice had uttered the words *Self-destruction sequence aborted.*

Now he sat with his legs folded beneath him, staring without seeing at a massive, knotted root snaking through the loam. The tranquil buzzing of insects and the hum of circulated air surrounded him.

There was a simple explanation for all that had happened.

He had never left that cold stone room beneath the temple. He was still there, strapped down and dreaming. His mind had spun a fantasy in which Sou-Zell—*Sou-Zell* of all people—came to his rescue and Jin flew down on a pteropter's back to take him to Avi'Kerina. Now the dream had become a nightmare.

But soon he would wake up. And when he did, he would welcome High Priestess Edine's renewed ministrations.

Kadrin shifted. *No*, cried out a voice in his mind. *Don't look.*

Too late. His gaze drifted to a spot just to the right of the massive tree root, where a body in a bloodstained tunic lay.

She'd said the code. *Ascend.* Then she'd taken a single, staggering step toward the plinth. Kadrin had wrapped his arms around her waist, pulling her back, but it didn't matter. She'd begun to scream. Pressed both her hands to her temples. Then she'd dropped to the ground, lifeless, leaking blood slowly from her nose and ears.

Then the silence had come. Celwyn was gone; Kadrin didn't know where. He must have crawled off into the greenery to die. Kadrin couldn't care less.

Move, Kadrin told himself. *You can't stay here.*

He willed his body forward until he was on his hands and knees beside her. His sister. Eliesen.

Her eyes were open, the exact shade of brown Kadrin saw every time he looked in a mirror.

I'm scared of what happens next. You should be, too.

He pulled her into his lap and smoothed the hair away from her forehead. Eliesen was always complaining about her hair. She couldn't wear any of the tiny hats that had been so fashionable in Kerina Sol a few years ago; her curls had too much volume. Even now, as Kadrin tried to tuck a coil behind her ear, it sprang back into place. Irrepressible. Just like Elie herself.

A strangled noise left him then, a choking gasp that didn't resemble speech. Kadrin hunched over until his forehead was touching Eliesen's. Until all he could see was an endless sea of brown.

She always had to have the last laugh. The last steamed bun from the platter. The last draft of plum wine from the carafe. The last word in any argument.

So he should have seen this coming. Should have known she'd swipe this from him, too.

He should have stopped her.

He didn't hear footsteps approaching through the underbrush. One moment there was no sound except his own harsh, ragged breathing; the next, there was Jin's voice calling out, "Reena, they're here. I found them. They're—"

A long, disbelieving pause. The crunch of bracken as Jin moved closer.

"They're— Kadrin? Oh. Please, no."

Jin fell to her knees beside Kadrin. Trembling, she reached out and tried to tuck that same curl behind Eliesen's ear—to no avail.

Then she made a sound Kadrin had never heard her make before: a sob that quickly dissolved into more. She kept one hand clenched over her mouth in a vain attempt to silence herself. Like her grief was a blade that would cut her to the bone if she let it fall.

Yi-Nereen appeared on Kadrin's other side, bringing with her the acrid stench of burned hair and ozone.

"What happened?"

"Celwyn." It was like someone else was talking, using Kadrin's lips and tongue. "No, Amrys. She tried to destroy Avi'Kerina so no one would be able to find the gods' other cities." Yi-Nereen and Jin glanced at each other, clearly lost, but Kadrin plowed on, unable to stop and explain. It didn't matter. None of it mattered. "Eliesen stepped in as steward to stop her. For a human, it was . . ."

Fatal. Whoever was saying these words using his mouth, they couldn't say that one. It would kill the dream and make this real. And Kadrin couldn't let it be real.

"Weird," said a different voice. *"Really, really weird. And it hurt. A lot, actually."*

Jin leaped to her feet with a curse. Yi-Nereen grabbed Kadrin's shoulder in alarm. All Kadrin could do was sit frozen in place and stare down at Eliesen's lifeless face. Because it was *her* voice, but her lips hadn't moved.

"It doesn't hurt anymore, though," his sister's voice continued. *"And can I just say—wow. This place is something else. It's going to take me a minute to get used to this."*

"Eliesen?" Jin demanded. "What the hell is going on?"

"I wish I could tell you. Honestly, I'm not sure. But first—can you feel this?"

For a long moment, nothing happened. Silence filled the garden again. Jin stood looking around, her hands curled into fists by her

Flight of the Fallen

sides; Yi-Nereen remained crouched beside Kadrin, her hand on his shoulder. None of them spoke.

Then Kadrin felt it: the icy sting of a droplet falling on the back of his hand from somewhere above. Another droplet landed on the bridge of Eliesen's nose, between her unseeing brown eyes. Then more came down, pattering all around him in the greenery, a soaking shower of cold rain. Water streamed down tree trunks, formed rivulets along the roots, and whispered through the leaves like a prayer.

"I feel it," Kadrin breathed. He gripped Eliesen's body tighter in his arms, shaking in disbelief even as hope roared to life inside him. "Is that . . . ?"

Jin burst into helpless laughter, not at all dissimilar to her raw sobs of a few moments before. "It's her."

"Sprinkler systems!" Eliesen crowed loudly enough to make the sphere tremble, her satisfaction unmistakable despite the mechanical quality of her voice. *"City of the gods? More like the city of me."*

Jin sank to her knees and buried her face in Kadrin's neck. Yi-Nereen encircled them both in her arms. And Kadrin closed his eyes and let himself *feel.*

He'd feared this moment—feared letting all the pain, grief, and terror catch up to him at last, afraid it would destroy him, and it very nearly did.

But he wasn't alone. He was drenched to the bone and trembling, but in Jin and Yi-Nereen's embrace, he felt everything but the cold.

CHAPTER FORTY-ONE

FALSE PROPHET

Observation #801: Previously hypothesized in observation #349 that science can be disguised as theology to better suit the masses. Good gods, I thought I was clever back then, but the High Priestess had me beaten by years. —O

Third Age of Storms, 1st Summer, Day 88
Kerina Sol – Temple Square

Screech's second landing in Kerina Sol was only slightly more graceful than the first. Jin slid off his back, her legs trembling from exhaustion. She patted his crest and received a weary chirrup in reply.

"You've earned a rest. And a *lot* of entrails. I won't forget."

Behind her, Yi-Nereen and Kadrin landed soundlessly on the cobblestones. Yi-Nereen dismissed the shield that had carried them from the Barrens, the glow fading from her eyes. After hours of flying, she'd hardly broken a sweat.

Jin shivered in unease, but reminded herself that Yi-Nereen's unsettling power was only temporary. She'd just drained Lai-Dan of his Last Breath. His strength and all the strength he'd stolen from

Flight of the Fallen

his knights flowed through Yi-Nereen's veins. It wouldn't last. She would soon be back to normal. At least, Jin hoped so.

And if she wasn't . . . well, they would cross that canyon when they came to it. Jin wouldn't let anyone call Yi-Nereen a monster for fighting to save herself, to save all of their people. And if Yi-Nereen herself forgot her own humanity, Jin would be there to remind her.

The hour was early and the city was quiet. Sparklamps glowed across the square, but Jin saw no one. She ached to cast herself down on a bunk and join the rest of Kerina Sol in sleep. But they still had work to do.

"Let's see if the Council is still in session," Kadrin said. "Otherwise we'll wake them up."

He was masking his exhaustion better than Jin. But she heard it in his voice, saw it in the slope of his shoulders. He'd been through so much in the past few days: torture at the High Priestess's hands, brokering a truce between the High Houses and the conspirators, trying to save Avi'Kerina from falling into a madman's grasp. Losing his sister, then seeing her return in a strange new form.

By comparison, Jin had gotten off easy. Sure, she'd been mauled by saurians, lost her bike, and nearly fallen to her death. But that was nothing new for her.

They were halfway up the steps to the Marble Palace when the double doors swung open. Out strode the tall, white-robed figure of the High Priestess, followed by a clanking contingent of metalcrafter guards and armored acolytes. They fanned out across the steps with the High Priestess at their center.

Hatred seared through Jin's chest and throat. Beside her, she heard Yi-Nereen hiss like a snake. On her other side, Kadrin froze into perfect stillness.

429

"So, you have returned." The High Priestess's voice was high but not shrill; it rang like a bell through the silent square. "Both of you: the heretic and the fallen prince. It's time to end this madness, Yi-Nereen. Turn yourself over, and I won't need to make an example of you."

Yi-Nereen said, her voice simmering with deadly calm, "You have twenty seconds to get out of my sight."

Her eyes glowed blue. A disc of azure light appeared and rotated slowly in front of her, casting reflections that slid across the marble steps like liquid shadows.

Jin's fists clenched. Perversely, she wanted nothing more than to see Edine diced into small pieces by Yi-Nereen's shield-blade. It was the least she deserved for what she'd done to Kadrin.

But if Yi-Nereen harmed her here, in front of her faithful, they'd have bigger problems than convincing the Council to prepare a city-wide evacuation to Avi'Kerina. They'd have holy war on their hands.

"The Talent Thief speaks with your wicked tongue," High Priestess Edine snapped. "What devilish powers she has bestowed upon you, I do not know. But I do not fear you. *I* am Rasvel's prophet. I will defend my people against your lies. I won't let you steal their souls, one by one, under the pretense of helping them find salvation. The First City is divine, ineffable, immortal. It is *not for us*."

Yi-Nereen's disc spun faster. "Ten seconds."

"Wait." Jin stepped forward. "Read my mind."

She felt Kadrin's and Yi-Nereen's stares on her back. Whispers broke out among the guards and acolytes at the top of the steps; the High Priestess's Talent clearly wasn't common knowledge, even among her own flock.

Edine gazed down at Jin, her lips pressed into a thin line, and said, "Who are you?"

Flight of the Fallen

"I used to be a courier," Jin said. "Then I shoveled shit for a while. I'm not anybody who matters. But you need to see what I've seen."

Kadrin touched Jin's arm, whispering "Don't do this," but Jin gently pushed him away. Her heart was racing; her skin crawled at the idea of opening her mind to Edine of all people. But she'd survived Sou-Zell's intrusions into her thoughts, hadn't she?

All the High Priestess would see was the truth. She'd see Avi'Kerina through Jin's eyes and be forced to understand that it was a real place with real Road Builder technology that they could use. And maybe Jin could show her more than that. Proof that Yi-Nereen wasn't a heretic or a Herald, but a princess in exile who'd done everything for her people.

"Jin," Yi-Nereen said in a low voice. "She's a fanatic. Like my father. She'll just twist whatever you show her to suit her own ends."

Jin took Yi-Nereen's hand in hers and squeezed it briefly. "I need to try."

She had to believe there weren't truly any lost causes. Not her—Talentless, useless Jin—and not the High Priestess. She'd done impossible things, *seen* impossible things, and Edine wouldn't be able to deny the truth if it were proved to her.

"Very well," the High Priestess said, the tiniest note of uncertainty chiseling away at her imperious calm. "Come closer, and we shall see."

Jin let go of Yi-Nereen's hand and ascended the steps until she stood just below the High Priestess. The woman towered over her like an alabaster statue. Up close, she was no less smooth and cold than she appeared from a distance. Jin, who had never believed that a person could speak for the gods or even been entirely convinced the gods were worth listening to, found she could hardly breathe.

She made herself fixate on a single stray wrinkle between Edine's eyebrows: proof that she was human, not divine.

Without warning, the High Priestess's eyes flared violet, and—

—Jin was soaring in the bitter cold, high above the Barrens, Kadrin's warmth nestled against her back. Below, a featureless plain suddenly flickered and gave way to the spires of a city. Air spilled from Screech's wings as he tilted downward. Jin's heart soared and her stomach plunged.

It was real. It was *real*, and Yi-Nereen must be there—

—lounging in a cushioned bower with candlelight playing over her lips and dancing in the dark of her eyes as she listened to Jin read aloud. She smiled, impossibly lovely, and Jin's heart shattered as if it were crystal dropped from a great height. Just like that.

She'd been falling for months, ever since the first letter, but this was the moment she realized: *Oh, shit.*

Her next thought was of Kadrin—

—laughing sheepishly as he swept the shards of a broken teacup into a cloth, despite Jin's protests that she should do it herself. *It's my fault. That'll teach me a lesson for getting too excited about damask.*

She watched a bright red drop bloom on the pad of his thumb, and something in her chest seized tight. Concern. Affection. A terrifying realization that she'd rather bleed herself than see him hurt.

Not again, she begged silently. *Please, Rasvel, not again.*

How foolish was she, to fall in love with two people who couldn't ever be hers? It was both—

—of them in the ruined castle above as she fell, plummeting into the belly of the storm, until she saw—

—rain falling in a garden inside a sphere as they held each other—

Flight of the Fallen

—in the dark, in her dreams, in an unlikely future—

The High Priestess staggered backward, a mortal woman, her face sheened with sweat. Jin sucked in a lungful of air. Her head was spinning like she'd held her breath for the past minute. For a few moments no one spoke.

Then Edine said in a halting voice, softly enough that no one but Jin would hear, "You tamed one of the great beasts? You rode on its back?"

Jin blinked. She hadn't expected the High Priestess to fixate on that detail.

"Well, yeah." She stuck a thumb over her shoulder, gesturing to where Screech stood like a massive silent sentinel in the middle of the town square.

From Edine's sharp intake of breath and the way her face paled, she hadn't noticed the pteropter before. Her gaze moved slowly back to Jin. A muscle in her jaw worked soundlessly.

"The beast led you there? To the First City—the home of the gods. But why *you*? I thought . . ."

Something was happening to the High Priestess. Jin saw it, sensed it: the single crack spreading into a spiderweb, like a mountain disintegrating in a storm. Jin held her breath. She watched Edine's eyes. *Believe me. Please believe me.*

"No," Edine said. "No, you cannot be His Herald. *I* am His prophet."

"His Herald? I'm not anyone's Herald. The city, you saw the city. That's real."

Edine shuddered. "If you set foot in the city of the gods, it was the blackest of heresies. I see now. The false prophet was never the princess. It was *you*."

433

Jin's gut twisted. She couldn't afford to lose her grip on Edine, not now, moments from the end. She needed this to be over. And the High Priestess, as much as Jin hated her, was the key to bringing it all to a close. If Jin could just get her to acquiesce . . .

"Please, just listen—"

Down the marble steps, out in the dark square, an orange light flickered to life. For a moment, Jin thought it was a sparklamp. Then she turned her head and saw a small figure standing a hundred paces off, limned by the sparks that crackled between their outstretched fingers. Who was that? Where had they come from? What were they—?

Kadrin shouted her name. He'd seen the figure, too. And Jin understood.

The world slowed. In her next breath, she saw the choice before her: to shove Edine out of harm's way, or to not move at all. Her muscles brimmed with energy; she wasn't frozen. She could save Edine. Perhaps she could save a city.

Jin didn't move.

Lightning struck Edine in the breast, and the smell of charred meat filled Jin's lungs. All the hair on her body stood on end. She watched Edine fall—and then she moved, to catch the High Priestess's body before it could hit the steps.

Shouts rang out around her. Temple guards streamed down the steps on either side of her. Someone else seized Edine's arm and tried to pull her from Jin's grasp. But Jin held her in a grip like iron, staring into her eyes.

"You'll never hurt them." The words welled up from somewhere deep within her. "Never again."

She didn't know if Edine was still alive to hear her. Jin collapsed on the steps and let two acolytes drag the High Priestess from her arms. She stayed there, dazed, until someone yanked her to her feet and marched her up the stairs into the Marble Palace. Behind her, Kadrin and Yi-Nereen were shouting. Screech shrieked, a sound to rattle the city.

All Jin could see was that dark figure down in the square, drenched in sparklight.

A tiny voice in her head asked, *Don't I know you?*

Jin wasn't in a cell for long. A few hours, maybe. Then two men dressed in the uniforms of the city guards—not temple acolytes, Jin noticed through her haze—moved her to a different room, where Jin found a soft bed and supper waiting for her. It was the first real food she'd had in a week; she devoured it.

She understood then that someone, somewhere, had decided she wasn't personally responsible for murdering the High Priestess. She also understood that the High Priestess was dead. If Edine were alive, Jin was pretty sure she would still be in the cell.

A page entered her room after supper to clear the plates and announce a visitor, followed shortly after by Jin's mother.

"Eomma," Jin said, weak with relief. She submitted to her mother's anguished ministrations over her injured arm for ten full minutes and listened to Eomma's recounting of the demonstration-turned-riot at the Basilica Sol during the storm.

That flushed smile on Eomma's face when she spoke of Renfir and the other rioters—Jin saw it, and satisfaction bloomed in her like the warm touch of sunlight. Her mother was happy. She'd found a home. Jin wouldn't have to worry about her anymore.

"Look who's become the dashing outlaw now," Jin teased, and reveled in Eomma's girlish laugh.

Then Eomma's smile faded. "The High Priestess is dead. You know that, don't you?"

"Yes." Jin hesitated. "Did they find . . . ?"

"Her killer?" Eomma gave Jin a look that said she knew exactly who Jin suspected of the crime. "No. The assassin was prepared. They had a magebike waiting in an alley near the square. The Wall guards weren't notified quickly enough to stop the assassin from fleeing the city."

"They don't know who it was?"

Eomma spread her hands. "Jin, dear, that's all I know. I've been waiting outside the palace all night for your release. The Council called another emergency session—Kadrin was kind enough to tell me that before he and Yi-Nereen had to rush away to attend."

"Oh." Jin had assumed Kadrin and Yi-Nereen were in cells, too. Thank the gods they were safe. "When is that? My release?"

"Sweetheart, it's now. You're free to go."

Free to go. Jin mulled over the words. Distantly, she knew she was still in shock; nothing had seemed quite real since she'd held Edine's lifeless body in her arms. But something about the phrase didn't feel right.

"I think I'll stay. Kadrin and Yi-Nereen will be finished with the Council eventually. I'd like to be here when they are." Jin tried for a smile. "Maybe they'll bring me more food."

No one brought more food. After half an hour, Jin wandered into the hallway and tried doors until she found what looked like a study. A bottle sat on a stone desk; Jin discovered, to her delight, that it contained the finest whiskey she'd ever tasted.

Back in the hallway, she heard voices echoing distantly from the direction of the Council chamber. Jin stuffed the whiskey down her shirt and hurried toward the sound.

When she rounded a corner, she saw Yi-Nereen at once. Beside her, to Jin's dismay, was Toraka. Jin took a cautious step toward the two women, her skin prickling with unease. But then Yi-Nereen turned her head and said "Jin" in a tone of such warmth that all of Jin's tension abruptly drained away.

"I'm here." Jin fell into Yi-Nereen's arms and closed her eyes. A moment later, she felt an even warmer, firmer body encircle them both. Kadrin's embrace was so tight it was almost painful. Fuck, he'd gotten strong.

Sandwiched between the two of them, Jin thought of the morning she'd woken in Kadrin's parlor to find Eliesen sitting at her bedside. She'd never see Eliesen again—not like that. A shard of glass worked its way between her ribs to join the thorns that had grown there since the day she left Falka behind in Kerina Tez.

For a long time, she'd thought that was all love was: little knives waiting to bite into her as soon as she let down her guard. Grief waiting to make a home in the wounds they left behind. A guarantee that for all the joy she felt, pain would follow.

From how tightly Kadrin and Yi-Nereen were holding her, Jin guessed they'd been afraid she wouldn't be here when the Council session ended.

It hadn't occurred to her even once to leave.

Later, when the three of them had bathed and were dressed in fresh new clothing and sitting in a wing of the official residence Toraka had been granted as the Guildery's representative on the Council, Jin brought out the whiskey. Kadrin took one sip, made a face, and gave her back his glass. Yi-Nereen smacked her lips so many times Jin thought she was dying—and kept drinking.

"That's foul," Kadrin said.

"I've never had alcohol before," Yi-Nereen mused. "Is it supposed to burn?"

Jin watched them both and thought, *I'll never get tired of this.* They'd been given a whole wing of rooms with bedchambers to spare, but she couldn't stomach the thought of letting either of them out of arm's reach. Apparently the two of them agreed. This was Jin's room, technically, but neither of them seemed in a hurry to leave.

"How did the Council meeting go?"

Yi-Nereen swallowed a gulp of whiskey. "It was three hours of damage control and pointing fingers. Once the High Priestess was declared dead, the rest of the priesthood insisted they couldn't make any decisions until they had time to appoint her successor. They wanted Toraka arrested—they're convinced one of her people was the assassin. They'll be questioning everyone in the Refugee Quarter in the coming days, I'm sure, but for now the Council refused to take anyone into custody without evidence. And after hearing what we had to say about Avi'Kerina, the High Houses were in no mood to wait for the priesthood to get their affairs in order. They've voted to send a larger expedition to the city to determine if we can all live there."

"Orrin's the happiest I've ever seen them." Kadrin scratched his head. "They weren't even upset when I told them you lost the manacycle in the Barrens. Somehow it feels like they've been planning this all along. But that's impossible, right?"

Jin shrugged. "Who knows? I've never trusted artificers. They're too clever."

Flight of the Fallen

"I'll reach out to the High Houses of Kerina Rut as well," Yi-Nereen said, "now that my father is out of the equation. My brothers aren't so different from him, unfortunately, but with any luck, they'll be too busy squabbling to cause problems."

"I told my family," Kadrin said. He let out a long exhale and stared at the ceiling, the muscles in his neck drawn and tight. "About Eliesen. My parents want to be part of the Council's first expedition, to see her again. Or at least speak with her."

Jin reached for his hand, at a loss for anything comforting to say. Kadrin gripped her hand and smiled at her, and Jin's heart cracked. What would it take for him to stop smiling? Whatever it was, she'd burn the world to prevent it from ever coming to pass.

Yi-Nereen wrapped her arm around Kadrin's waist, and in that moment Jin realized something.

All three of them were in a room together, and no one was about to die. No one had just discovered their Talent was missing. She wasn't keeping secrets from them anymore. The danger and deception had passed. Now they had a moment to breathe.

Jin's pulse quickened. The room she'd chosen for herself was the smallest of the bedchambers in this wing of Toraka's house. Just a divan and a bed, really. Kadrin and Yi-Nereen were sitting side by side on the divan; Jin was perched on the bed, less than an arm's length away. Close enough to reach out and touch both of them.

"Is the wedding back on?" she blurted out.

Kadrin stared at her. "What wedding?"

"*Our* wedding?" Yi-Nereen glanced at Kadrin. "Jin, everyone still believes I'm Makela's Herald. The only reason I was part of that Council meeting was because I happened to be standing next to Kadrin when they invited him inside. I might be the most hated person in Kerina Sol. The temple certainly won't be blessing my marriage to anyone."

Kadrin shrugged. "Well, no one cares who I marry. I'm just a Talentless ex-prince. Hey." His tone turned accusatory. "Jin. What you said earlier, outside the Council chambers? I want you to take it back."

"What did I say?"

"That you weren't anyone who mattered," Yi-Nereen said.

"It's just the truth." Jin shifted uneasily under the weight of both their stares. "In Avi'Kerina, I couldn't help you defeat your father. And, Kadrin, I couldn't save Eliesen. All I do is carry people around. That's all I've ever done."

Kadrin sighed. "That's a load of saurian shit."

"Agreed," said Yi-Nereen.

"Look," Kadrin said. "Jin, none of us are perfect. Gods know I spent years wishing I could do something useful, *be* something useful. I even tried to become Avi'Kerina's steward. But Elie wouldn't let me do it, because . . ." His hands twisted in his lap. "She saw something in me, something the world needed. And I see that in both of you. If it takes the rest of my life to convince you of that, so be it."

Yi-Nereen looked past Jin, at a blank patch on the wall. "I wanted to kill the High Priestess myself—I almost did. Now they'll need me to take everyone's Talent so they can live in Avi'Kerina. But all these people . . . I'm afraid of what taking their power will do to me. Everything my father was is part of me now. I see him in my future. I *am* him."

"You aren't," Jin said at the same moment Kadrin said, "Never going to happen."

Yi-Nereen took a shaky breath. "Suppose you *had* become the steward, Kadrin. Suppose I'd killed Edine. Then what would have become of our poor courier?"

Jin's gut clenched. "Let's not think about that."

"Then we all agree," Kadrin said. "No more unpleasant talk. We're together now. That's what matters."

"Yes," Yi-Nereen said softly. She gave Jin a long, soulful look. "We're together."

Jin gripped the edge of the mattress. Dizziness crept through her, a pleasant, heady feeling that threatened to bring her whole world crashing down in the next moment of sobriety. Nothing good could last. The better the night, the worse she'd feel in the morning.

That mantra had carried her through three years of loneliness. But that was all it was. Just words. She didn't even know if they were true anymore.

Yi-Nereen reached out to cup Jin's cheek gently in her palm, her lashes low over her brown eyes. "You'll always be my courier. I want you in my life, one way or another." Her gaze drifted sideways, to Kadrin's face. "Both of you. Whatever that looks like. If the temple doesn't approve, what do I care? I killed my father. Let them try to teach me the meaning of sin."

I'm not worth it, Jin almost said.

She believed it. It *felt* true to her. But here in this moment, for the first time, a splinter of doubt worked its way into her steel core. Maybe she could give Yi-Nereen and Kadrin the chance to prove her wrong.

She looked at Kadrin and said, "Convince me."

His grin was instantaneous and blinding.

"It'll take at least a night, to start."

Yi-Nereen's lips parted like she was about to speak; then her hand on Jin's cheek became a fist in her hair, and she was pressing her back into the bed with a kiss. Jin dissolved, sand in the face of a storm. The mattress creaked with Kadrin's weight as he joined them.

"If the gods really left us," he murmured in Jin's ear, "then nothing we did together would be a sin. Or everything would. I'm still not sure."

Jin broke away from Yi-Nereen's kiss, gasping, and replied, "Let's find out."

"Shh," Yi-Nereen admonished them. "No more talking."

Waking up in a sleepy tangle of limbs with Yi-Nereen's hair in her mouth and Kadrin's head pillowed on her stomach rated among the best experiences in Jin's life.

She hadn't the faintest idea what time it was. The curtains were thick as cowhide and the candles in the wall alcove had burned down to almost nothing. It could have been just before dawn, or the middle of the next day. Either way, Jin needed the latrine.

She eased her way out from underneath Yi-Nereen and Kadrin, moving with the utmost care not to wake either of them. Then she stood there in the flickering light of the dying candles and gazed down at them both, engraving the picture of them curled together on the bed into her memory.

It was agony to tear herself away, even though she'd be back in a minute.

The door to her chamber swung shut behind her as she padded into the corridor on bare feet. A shadow peeled away from the wall—and Sou-Zell stood before her, an indistinct silhouette in the gloom. She only recognized him from the faint odor that clung to his clothes. Smoke and leather: a sparkrider's perfume.

Flight of the Fallen

"Jin-Lu the saurian rider." His voice was low, cut through with quiet derision. "I hear congratulations are in order. You have everything you wanted . . . except your Talent."

Jin's ears warmed with familiar hatred. "What are you doing in Toraka's house?"

"I am here as a guest, obviously. Like you."

"If you think Yi-Nereen's going to change her mind and marry you because you decided to skulk around her quarters like a creepy jilted lover, you're mistaken." Jin felt her lips curl into a smirk. Gods, it felt good to boast. "Very sorely mistaken. She's moved on."

Sou-Zell was silent for a long moment. Then he asked, his voice changed in a way Jin couldn't pinpoint, "Do you love him?"

Jin blinked. "Who?"

Stupid question. There was only one *him* Sou-Zell could mean. Not that it made any fucking sense for him to ask. If only it weren't so dark and she could see his blasted face.

"If the High Priestess had survived the attempt on her life," Sou-Zell said, "would you have taken matters into your own hands? You must be aware that she tortured your beloved princeling. He was delirious and badly injured when I found him."

Jin's fists clenched. "Shame she died so quickly, if you ask me. But why does it matter?"

Did Sou-Zell know who had killed the High Priestess? Was this his way of threatening to go to the temple and expose Falka? Jin couldn't even be completely sure herself that it had been Falka . . . but she *was* sure. She knew it in her bones.

Sou-Zell's stillness offered her no clues. "Lai-Dan is dead, too. Isn't he?"

"Yes." Jin hesitated. It hadn't occurred to her until just now that killing the lord of a High House was definitely still a crime,

443

regardless of any extenuating factors, such as said lord being drunk on power and trying to gain total control over the kerinas. "It was me. I killed him."

Sou-Zell stared at her, obviously unconvinced. "How fortunate for you."

"What do you want, Sou-Zell?"

"Nothing," he said. "There is no one left in this world that I want dead."

Finally, Jin thought she could see where this was going.

"Sounds like you need to find something else to want. It's not normal to only have enemies, you know. Get a hobby. Find a job to do. Make some friends. Have a cup of tea, for Rasvel's sake."

"Don't condescend to me, Courier." But there was very little venom in Sou-Zell's voice, all things considering. "You've lost your Talent. Soon you'll ask everyone to give up theirs, too. So tell me, as someone who knows what it's like to lose your soul: How long will it take for you to lose that itch for the open road? When will you forget what it was like to be free?" Sou-Zell eyed her. "Perhaps you already have."

Free to go. Those words slithered through Jin's skull again. But she met Sou-Zell's gaze with an even stare of her own and said, "Those aren't real questions. You're just being rude."

Sou-Zell plowed on as if her reply hadn't mattered anyway. "In this world you're planning to build, where everyone is Talentless and equal in the city of the gods, what makes one man different from the next? If all life is interchangeable, what do any of us matter?"

Jin sighed.

"Two things you should know about me, Sou-Zell. I hate politics. And I hate philosophy." She narrowed her eyes at him. "But this isn't philosophy, is it?"

Flight of the Fallen

"Of course it is."

"No. It's not. It's simpler than that. You're asking what *you're* supposed to do without your Talent. What makes *you* different from anyone else. Whether *you* matter. Did I miss anything?"

Sou-Zell said nothing, which was answer enough.

"I have good news for you." Jin yawned. "I figure they'll need assholes in Avi'Kerina along with every other type of person. It's not going to be easy to move tens of thousands of people across the wastes and settle them into a new place. There'll be plenty of ways for you to make yourself useful, even if you can't read minds or light a mana-cig."

"It will never work," Sou-Zell said. "Our people haven't walked the wasteland in numbers like this since the First Age of Storms. Half of them will die during the crossing before they ever reach the Barrens. And that's a generous estimate."

"So stick around and help bring it under half. Being around Kadrin seems good for you, anyway." Jin squinted at him again. "Do *you* love him?"

Sou-Zell moved and Jin flinched away. He'd held a knife to her throat for less. But he just closed his hand around his own wrist, the movement quick and instinctive, as if he'd hardly realized he was doing it.

"Not like you do."

It was far from the denial she'd expected. Jin blinked, thrown off guard.

Without another word, Sou-Zell turned on his heel and swept down the corridor, leaving her alone in the dark.

CHAPTER FORTY-TWO

A NEW WORLD

Observation #802: With the Legion defanged, I've been commissioned to design an entire fleet based on my manacycle prototype. The blueprints are all in my head, of course. (Renzara's only useful lesson, incidentally—if you don't want your designs stolen, don't write them down! A shame the woman had the memory of a goldfish.) From disgraced former apprentice to Royal Artificer in less than five years. Conclusion: Not bad, Orrin. Not bad. —O

Third Age of Storms, 1st Summer, Day 91
The Wastes – North of Kerina Sol

With Kadrin and Yi-Nereen wholly absorbed in planning the Council's new expedition to Avi'Kerina, Jin took to the wastes. She had someone to find, and she didn't know how much time she had to do it. Maybe all the time in the world, or maybe she was already too late.

Three days into her search, something drew her north. An instinct. A memory. On Screech's back, high above the wasteland, she guided his tiny shadow along the road she'd once taken to Kerina

Flight of the Fallen

Sol as a girl-turned-refugee with her mother's arms tight around her waist.

It felt like cheating to fly back to Tez on a pteropter's back. The miles had seemed so insurmountable back then, with a shit bike and nothing waiting for them in Sol but the gilded promise of Rasvel's Sanctuary. Now Jin didn't have the spark or a bike between her legs. She had wings.

It wasn't better, just different. The same way *she* was different.

The great walls of Tez had fallen. Jin saw them from on high: heaps of stone, blocks scattered by the careless hand of a dozen storms. The shieldcasters of Tez had long since fled the kerina, and without their protection, the city barely resembled a city at all.

But it wasn't abandoned. Jin was surprised to see that, though she shouldn't have been. Tiny figures still walked and rode bikes among the bones of the fallen city, like ants from her vantage point. Survivors? Did they cower beneath rubble and somehow survive the continuing storms when they came? Was it here that Falka had recruited her raiders?

Parked on a high ridge west of the city was a single, lone bike. Gazing down upon it, Jin had no way of knowing who it belonged to. But she did know, the way she always knew.

She'd come to the right place.

Jin landed on the ridge and followed a set of tracks in the dust from the parked bike to a hammock slung between two cacti. She took care to walk silently. *Next time you sneak up on me, Jin, my dearest, I'll put your eye out. (Not if I kiss you first.) Oh, is that your game? A race between your lips and my knife?*

The figure in the hammock didn't stir as she drew near. Falka was sleeping with a red scarf over her eyes. The breeze tugged at strands of her dirty-blond hair. She was so still that she could have been dead.

"Hey, killer," Jin said.

Falka started awake with a curse. Jin tensed, waiting for a thrown knife or a bolt of lightning she wouldn't be able to redirect—but to her surprise, all Falka did was blink owlishly at her through the haze of dusk until her eyes narrowed in recognition.

"Oh," she said. "It's you. Figures."

"Why would you come back to Tez? Looking to start another revolution?"

Falka yawned. "This isn't Tez anymore. It's a carcass. I'm learning how to let those lie. Seems you could learn the same lesson."

"Only one of us is making new carcasses," Jin said as levelly as she could, "and it isn't me."

"Don't pretend you wept over the High Priestess of Sol," Falka said. "A quick end's the only way to deal with people like her. She would never have agreed to let your princess take away her gifts from Rasvel, or anyone else's. She didn't know how to adapt. How to say goodbye to the old world and live in the new one."

"You didn't give her a chance to try. You're lucky you didn't start a war and get everyone killed anyway."

Stay calm, Jin told herself. Always, Falka had known how to get under her skin. She had a way about her, as if she knew everything and Jin was only an ignorant child. Jin had been petty, too, sometimes. She'd done stupid things to remind Falka that between the two of them, Jin was the one who could ride a magebike. The one who was free.

"It was the right moment," Falka said. "Another breath, and she would have called holy retribution down on your head. Half of Kerina Sol was sick of the temple anyway—they just needed someone

Flight of the Fallen

to take the shot. But you wouldn't know, would you? You never could see the big picture."

Because you know how to keep your eyes on the road ahead, Jin. You don't look over your shoulder. You know what's waiting for you if you do.

"Maybe not," Jin replied through gritted teeth. "Maybe the High Priestess needed to die to clear the way. But you didn't just take her out of the picture. You took yourself out, too."

"That's fine." Falka waved her hand lazily, as if shooing a fly. "Go back to making your new world, Jin. You don't need me for that. I hope you didn't think I was coming to your First City."

Jin didn't move. "Why not? Are you scared to be Talentless again?"

Falka sprang out of the hammock with a hiss. She made the movement look graceful, somehow, which was a first for someone exiting a hammock in Jin's experience (and probably the history of the world). Her breath warmed the air in front of Jin's face as she said, "Don't fucking patronize me."

"I'm not," Jin said. Her voice trembled; her chest ached. She felt sixteen again. "I always said I'd take you someplace green, didn't I? Well, that place is real. It isn't paradise, but it's real. And I'm trying to keep my promise."

Falka shook her head slowly.

"The kid who made that promise is dead. I killed her. And I killed you, Jin." Her hand hovered over the place between Jin's ribs where the knife had gone in months ago. "Right here. Like this."

"They're letting murderers into the new world," Jin whispered. "I asked the gods, and no one said you weren't allowed. Come to Avi'Kerina with me. I'll take you there in secret, and by the time everyone else arrives, no one will suspect who you are or what you did."

449

Falka smiled crookedly. "No, I think I'll stay out here with the High Priestess and all the scavengers the world forgot. Get high on cactus juice and watch it all tumble down."

Why are you like this? Jin wanted to scream. But she knew.

She'd been Falka, once. Wounded. Stubborn. She'd turned her back on a dream and told herself it was too good for her. That if she stepped into that world, her very presence would blacken it.

"That's no life," Jin said. "You didn't escape Tez just to die here."

Falka stepped back, away from her. "Who says I'm going to die here?"

"A year." Jin did her best to sound nonchalant. It hadn't worked with Falka before, but that didn't mean she shouldn't try. They'd both grown. "I'll come back in a year to see if you're still kicking around. Be here, all right? Don't make me fly all over the wastes looking for you."

Falka squinted at her. For a moment, she looked lost. Uncertain.

"Learned my lesson about waiting for you a long time ago, Jin."

"Yeah. The wrong one." Jin looked her in the eyes. "I know you won't die between now and then. But I'm reminding you, just in case: don't die."

She looked over her shoulder once after walking back to the top of the ridge. Just a glance, enough to see Falka standing among the dark, bowed shapes of the cacti, still and alone. In the plain beyond her lay the heaped remains of Kerina Tez.

Falka just needed time, Jin thought. Hoped.

Time, and when the time came, a reminder that Jin hadn't given up on her.

Jin glided down amid the glistening spires of Avi'Kerina. The sun was just rising from a bed of mist; the sky was aglow. Screech alighted on a rooftop and held almost perfectly still while Jin slid down from his back.

"Good landing." She tossed him a strip of jerky, and he gulped it down almost faster than she could see.

She put her hand on his forewing and gazed out across the city. It reminded her of the wastes: desolate and beautiful, devoid of human life save for hers. Soon it would fill with chattering voices and the various odors and noises of civilization. It would be just like any kerina, except for the absence of one thing: a mana spring.

What would a world without Talent even look like?

Jin sighed. She couldn't picture it. But soon she wouldn't have to.

A delicate whirring sound caught her attention. Something small rose from the raised metal wall enclosing the rooftop and hovered in the air. Jin squinted at it. It looked like a large flying insect, but its wings flashed in the light of dawn like they were made of steel.

"Hey, Jin. Good to see you."

It was Eliesen's voice, tinny and metallic. It was coming from the bug. Jin stared.

"I'm still figuring out how the city works and what the steward can do. What do you think of this thing? I'm calling it a spy-fly."

Jin smiled. "Can you see me?"

"Yes."

"How about this?"

She made an obscene hand gesture, and warmth swept over her with the sound of Eliesen's laughter. The spy-fly buzzed through the air in lazy circles.

"Once everyone moves here, I'm going to have all the best gossip.

But first—you should know Celwyn is still alive. He's trapped in the Cradle."

"The Cradle?"

"The garden in the sphere. That's what it's called, according to the files. Phew. Jin, we have so much to talk about. But all that can wait. Celwyn stitched himself up and there's plenty of fruit to eat, so that's a problem you can deal with later. He'll keep."

"And so will Amrys," Jin said quietly.

Eliesen sighed, the sound as human as any Jin had ever heard her make.

"There's something funny about it all. I really did like him, Jin. I still do. But now there's two of them and none of me. Can't expect that to work out, can I?"

Jin swallowed down a lump in her throat and said, "This isn't the ending you deserved, Elie."

"It isn't an ending at all," Eliesen said. *"Can't lie—I'll miss my body and all the things it could do. But it's amazing in here, Jin. I know it doesn't make any sense, but for the first time in my life . . . I don't feel trapped."*

Jin thought of the way she'd always felt behind the walls of a kerina. That gnawing ache she'd inherited from her father: the need to be gone, away, free. Like somewhere out there, down the open road and beyond the horizon, was a place where she'd finally belong.

She'd never been able to picture that place. It wasn't a place at all—just a feeling, a longing. And after she'd woken up in the House of Steel Heavens without her Talent, she'd despaired of ever finding it.

Born to a broken world, her father used to say. They were some

Flight of the Fallen

of the first words Jin could remember. And if they were true, didn't that mean she was born broken, too?

"It does make sense," Jin said quietly.

The steel bug that was somehow Eliesen made a noisy loop around Screech's head and settled on Jin's shoulder. Screech croaked at it, obviously annoyed.

"*Celwyn said the gods abandoned this place,*" Eliesen said. "*Maybe our legends were true. Maybe we disappointed the gods so badly that they left us. Good riddance, I say. We get to make our own future now. We get to make beautiful things with our own two hands. You, Kadrin, Reena . . . even me. We'll make this place a home. Build on the bones of what came before and turn it into something magnificent enough to make the gods weep, if they ever come back to see it.*"

"Elie," Jin said, surprised. "That was almost poetry."

"*I have a sensitive side, too. I expect it'll get worse now that I have access to so many books. But what about you, Jin? I know the whole stoic-courier act isn't really an act for you, but still. I thought you'd have more to say. Savior of humanity and all.*"

Jin gazed out over the spires of the First City. She filled her lungs with a deep breath and felt the movement of Screech's breath and blood, too, the way she'd felt Yi-Nereen and Kadrin when they were all tangled together and moving as one. It was a new kind of feeling, yet older than time itself. She didn't have a word for it yet. Maybe she didn't need one.

The city and the road weren't so different in the end, all of it equal under the great canvas of blue sky. All broken, just as she was.

I followed the stars, Appa. And you were right. I did learn to fly.

"I don't know if we saved anyone," Jin said. "Long way to go before this place becomes home. But I think . . . I think I'm happy. It's been a while, but I'm getting to know what that feels like again."

"Well, good." The spy-fly shifted on Jin's shoulder. *"That'll have to do."*

Yes, Jin thought. It would.

ACKNOWLEDGMENTS

They weren't lying when they said the second novel is tougher than the first. Sophomore slump is real! But we got there.

You can open your copy of *Road to Ruin* and take a look at the acknowledgements in the back; I still have all of those people to thank for *Flight of the Fallen*. You can't have a second book in the series without the first. Here are some of them again, as well as some new names.

My agent, Paul Lucas, who's always in my corner (ride or die). My agent's assistants past and present, Eloy Bleifuss and Lansing Clark. The rest of the team at Janklow & Nesbit US.

My editor, Amara Hoshijo, whose keen understanding of my characters is an endless boon when I'm trying to fit the puzzle pieces together and write something that works. Jéla Lewter, assistant editor extraordinaire. My Saga publicist, Karintha Parker. Savannah Breckenridge and Camryn Johnson, Saga marketers. The rest of the amazing production team at Saga Press. And my cover artist, Raphael Lacoste!

All the fish in the cult. I can't say much more but you know who you are. You changed my life and showed me what it's like to be accepted for your whole, unapologetic self. I'll never look at gummy worms the same way. Remember: gay love can save the world.

The Bois (no connection to the show on Amazon Prime). I can't

Acknowledgments

overstate how grounding it is to have a solid community of real-life friends who show up for each other constantly, whether it's to grab dinner, play board games, help each other move, or go on wild international adventures together. Here's to our growing South Bay commune and all the Bois who've moved away but keep finding excuses to come back and visit.

My trusty local writer friends, who are always down to grab a coffee and commiserate: Victoria Shi, Julia Vee, and Kemi Ashing-Giwa. I'll be rooting for you guys forever.

My family and brothers, who are all getting older at roughly the same rate I am—how crazy is that? It's such a privilege (and a trial) to watch your younger siblings grow up.

My partner's family, a steadfast source of support no matter how hard times get. Thanks for all the dal dropped off at our front door and for letting me borrow a microphone when I need to record for a podcast.

Shalin, my partner of eleven years and companion in all things. Sorry it takes me fifty attempts to time the jump properly in a couch co-op game. Thanks for sticking with me anyway. And my cats, Saskia and Calcifer, who don't know or care that I'm a published author, as long as breakfast is on time.

Thank you to everyone who read *Road to Ruin* and stuck around for the sequel. It's been a wild ride.